COME FLY WITH ME

HELEN ROLFE

Boldwood

First published in Great Britain in 2024 by Boldwood Books Ltd.

Cover Design by Alexandra Allden

Cover Illustration: Shutterstock

Every effort has been made to obtain the necessary permissions with reference to copyright material, both illustrative and quoted. We apologise for any omissions in this respect and will be pleased to make the appropriate acknowledgements in any future edition.

A CIP catalogue record for this book is available from the British Library.

Paperback ISBN 978-1-83561-085-5

Large Print ISBN 978-1-83561-081-7

Hardback ISBN 978-1-83561-080-0

Ebook ISBN 978-1-83561-078-7

Kindle ISBN 978-1-83561-079-4

Audio CD ISBN 978-1-83561-086-2

MP3 CD ISBN 978-1-83561-083-1

Digital audio download ISBN 978-1-83561-077-0

Boldwood Books Ltd
23 Bowerdean Street
London SW6 3TN
www.boldwoodbooks.com

For my dad, Edward. Thank you for the unintentional provision of so much research when it comes to medical matters. We always laugh that life events weave their way into my books and this book is no exception. Your grit, your positivity and your sheer determination during such a tough time over the last few months is something to truly be admired. I hope I grow up to be just like you... love me x

CAST OF CHARACTERS

The Whistlestop River Air Ambulance Crew (The Skylarks)

Red team
Maya – pilot
Noah – critical care paramedic
Bess – critical care paramedic

Blue team
Vik – pilot
Kate – critical care paramedic
Brad – critical care paramedic

Other
Frank – engineer
Hudson – part-time patient and family liaison nurse
Paige – part-time patient and family liaison nurse
Nadia – operational support officer

The Whistlestop River Freewheelers

Rita
Dorothy
Alan
Mick

1

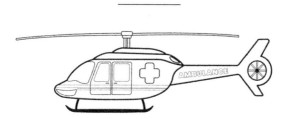

The Skylarks had been called to a road traffic accident. Maya was on shift with the red team. She grabbed her helmet and went out to the helipad to get the helicopter ready. It was all systems go and she usually had the crew up in the air within four or five minutes of the job coming in via the phones at the airbase.

Today was no different and as soon as the other crew members joined her with the extra gear they needed, they were off. As the pilot for The Skylarks, or by their official name, the Whistlestop River Air Ambulance, Maya's focus was on the flying, the transfer of a patient, the aircraft, keeping everyone safe. Her head couldn't be anywhere else, not on her personal problems, that was for sure.

The Whistlestop River Air Ambulance was afforded priority over other aircraft in the area by air traffic control, so the airspace was theirs on the route Maya would take to reach the patient. As she flew them to their destination, they discussed the job – the extent of the patient's injuries, possible treatments that might be necessary, landing sights to get Bess and Carl, the two critical care paramedics on board, as close to the patient as possible.

It was teamwork all the way. They approached the location indicated by not only the coordinates they had from dispatch but beaconed by the flashing lights of a road ambulance and police cars at the scene, first responder teams they were used to working with.

'Landing sites are few and far between, Maya.' Bess was in the seat in the cockpit next to Maya and along with Carl in the rear of the aircraft, both of them were scouting for somewhere to land safely using their iPads and by looking out the windows.

Maya deemed the field on their immediate right too small, the one next to that too hazardous because of the power lines.

'There's a field approximately forty-five degrees left from the farthest flashing blue lights,' Carl suggested.

'I don't see access in or out of it,' said Bess. 'Your best bet is the dual carriageway itself, Maya.'

They'd already been updated via radio that the police had cordoned off a big section of the road and Maya knew with no other option it was the safest and the most advantageous for her crew and for the patient to get the care they needed. The road ambulance paramedics would do as much as they could on scene but the critical care paramedics with the air ambulance could often do more. Then the decision would have to be made as to how best to get the patient to the further help they needed.

Adrenaline kicked in as she hovered above the strip she'd earmarked to land, Bess and Carl both checking the surrounding area to ensure safety for everyone involved.

It wasn't long before they touched down. Bess and Carl grabbed the gear and raced to attend to the patient. Maya stayed with the helicopter, ready to help them load the patient on if that was required. They had enough fuel, something she like other pilots was obsessed about, and she'd be ready to leave the moment her crew were back with her.

Maya loved her job. She'd dreamed of doing this since she was a kid. Being paid to soar high above the jaw-dropping landscapes of Dorset was a thrill in itself, never mind the privileged position of being a pilot with The Skylarks, whose name was displayed on the logo of their uniform along with the silhouetted wingspan of the bird in flight. Her job enabled her to be part of the team who could make a difference to people far and wide, and their loved ones; to give people the best chance of survival and recovery when they needed it the most. And in the world of employment, Maya knew it really didn't get much better than that.

As far as work went, Maya was sorted. It was her personal life that was causing her no end of issues: a father she felt had been against her almost from the start, an ex-husband who seemed to forget they were divorced, and a son with little to no bond with his dad, who would never be in line to win a father of the year award.

Her problems crept into her psyche briefly as she waited for her crew but she pushed them aside as soon as she heard over the radio that Bess and Carl's patient required airlifting. She spotted them hurrying towards her, aided by a police officer, carrying the scoop, a type of stretcher that separated into two, which enabled the crew to safely immobilise the patient and get them back to the aircraft.

Bess closed the rear door to the helicopter once the patient was secure and then climbed into the seat next to Maya, put on her helmet, and fastened her seatbelt. Up into the air they went with a forty-nine-year-old female driver of a vehicle who had lost control and crashed into the central reservation barrier on the dual carriageway. Given the location, the road ambulance would take almost four times as long as it would for Maya and the crew to fly the patient to the hospital and with head injuries that had the potential to be worse than first suspected, the crews on the ground had all agreed to err on the side of caution and transport via aircraft.

Landing on the hospital helipad was a breeze compared to the challenge of landing at the scene and once they safely touched down, the patient was handed over to the doctors and nurses.

Back on board the helicopter, Bess radioed the HEMS (Helicopter Emergency Medical Services team) desk to say the crew was clear and available. The crew secured the doors, put seatbelts on and Maya went through the familiar pre-flight checks.

'Clear left,' Bess, in the front left seat of the aircraft, confirmed through her headset, a vital piece of equipment for the team in order to communicate when they were up in the air given the noise of a helicopter. The headsets and microphones also provided radio contact with the HEMS desk, who had called through the initial job and continued to liaise with them en route.

'Clear right,' Maya confirmed into her own headset. 'And clear for take-off.'

She lifted the helicopter into the air and they were soon cruising at 1,000 ft above ground level on their way back to the Whistlestop River airbase, in the town of the same name. She steered the aircraft comfortably out of the way of hazards like trees, power lines and buildings – not that Dorset was well known for skyscrapers, only a handful of taller-than-usual structures.

Maya heard a whoop of joy over her headset from Carl in the back of the helicopter, followed by, 'Maya Anderson, that landing for the job was spectacular. You are one hell of a pilot!'

All of them were in good spirits knowing their patient was in good hands and the outcome likely to be a positive one. It wasn't always the case; sometimes they returned to base with heavy hearts and sadness that their best simply hadn't been good enough. And that feeling could swallow you whole if you let it.

'I hope that cheer has nothing to do with the fact that this is your last shift with us, Carl,' Maya laughed.

Bess groaned. 'Still can't believe he's deserting us.' In the absence of a co-pilot, Bess was also the technical crew member and her primary role was to assist Maya with aviation safety and navigations. All three of them were well versed at working together to ensure their own safety and that of anyone on the ground.

'Rest assured my cheer is only because of your skills as a pilot,' Carl assured Maya. 'Thanks to you, I've loved this job and I'm still in one piece.'

'I appreciate the vote of confidence,' she called out.

Bess finished off the snack bar she was eating. The crew often had to rush from one job to the next and eating when you could was often the way it went. 'Only an hour left on shift before you've got a few days off, Maya. Bet you're excited.'

Maya said nothing, which of course prompted Bess – who was a friend as well as a colleague – to ask whether everything was all right.

Maya knew she might as well admit the truth: that today, she'd started her shift with a funny feeling in the pit of her stomach. It wasn't because her sister Julie was getting married later today; she was excited for that. It was everything else. And some days, her messy life bothered her more than it did on others.

'I don't know what's going on with me; I woke up with a funny feeling this morning and I can't shake it.' She spoke loud enough for Bess to hear, Carl too if he wanted.

'As in you feel sick?' Bess probed.

'No, not sick or unwell. You know I'd never take chances as the pilot. It's more a feeling of... I don't know, anxiety, high alert.'

Carl piped up from the rear of the helicopter. 'Kind of the nature of the job, Maya.' Neither of them could see him, only hear him over the headsets. The back of the aircraft was separated from the front by a sheet of heavy-duty plastic required so that all the medical equipment in the rear didn't interfere with their night-vision goggles when they went out on a job in the darker hours.

'Unless she's planning on running off with the groom,' Bess

teased. She would know how excited Maya was about Julie's wedding; she'd been going on about it for long enough. But she also knew how Maya felt about seeing her father on any occasion, particularly one as big as this.

'Ha ha,' Maya replied. Bess always had the ability to make her feel better, even if all she'd done was share her concern.

Maya hadn't been able to arrange a stand-in for her shift today so had pre-warned her sister that she might be late to the wedding if she got a call. Julie being Julie had said no dramas, get there when you can. And much as it might appeal to conjure up an imaginary job so she could avoid her father for as long as possible, she didn't want to do that to her sister. They were as close as siblings could be, always had been.

'Ten minutes to go,' she said as they drew closer to the airbase. 'And yes, I suppose you're right, Carl. Nature of the job.' She liked him; she'd miss him when he left the crew to move up to the Lake District, where his wife had a new job as a teacher. He wasn't quite sure of his own career plans at this stage but he was ready for a change and Maya couldn't be happier for him.

'Maybe it's the looming birthday,' Bess suggested. 'Almost mid-forties, it's got to be scary.'

Maya laughed. 'Not at all. I'm embracing my age. And I'm turning forty-four so don't put me in the mid-forties bracket until I'm there, thank you very much.'

Bess still wanted to find out what was up. 'Are you worried about Isaac?' she asked Maya.

'No more than usual.' She mellowed at the thought of her son.

Isaac had chosen a university in Scotland and Maya did her best to believe it was because that was the place that offered the best course for him, that he wanted to see more of the UK, but part of her suspected it was to put some distance between himself and his dad. She'd been supportive when he told her, said that it was his decision and to have a wonderful time, but when other kids his age had chosen to go somewhere an hour or so from home or even stay living with their parents because of the cost of living, Scotland felt like a world away. Still, she'd put on a brave face and driven him up there last September, hugged him and told him to have the time of his life as well as working hard. And she'd left him with a heavy heart but also with the following summer to look forward to when he'd return home to Whistlestop River.

'Maybe the anxiety is because you miss him,' said Bess.

'All I know is it's a feeling that's new to me.' Maya was used to talking while she dealt with the array of gauges, dials, buttons, and screens in front of her and took charge of flight controls. 'I'm not a person who usually has much anxiety; I don't panic, I don't build things up in my head and catastrophise. If I did that, I'd never climb into this seat.'

Carl chimed in. 'Maya, it's my last day on the job with you and I want to make it back to base in one piece. So this feeling... please tell me it doesn't involve you losing control up here.'

'Course not. I'd never do that to you, Carl.'

'Yeah, right. Not sure I believe you. You're not planning a surprise mid-air drill, are you, as a send-off, and you're nervous about whether you can pull it off?'

As part of their ongoing and very regular training, they practised flight drills and Maya liked to do some of them up in the air – after all, that was where they were going to happen. She'd done one a few weeks ago and Carl hadn't enjoyed it at all, had said he was counting the days until he finished his time galivanting around the county in a helicopter.

'Carl, I'll miss the way you always say what's on your mind,' Maya said into her headset.

'I'll miss you girls too. You'd better hope my replacement is up to scratch.'

'You're a tough act to follow,' Bess declared.

Maya hadn't met the new critical care paramedic joining the red crew yet. All she knew was that Carl and Bess were the best people in the world to work with so whoever it was had high standards to live up to, both with their expertise and knowledge and in personality.

'See to it that it's another cracker of a landing back at base, would you, Maya?' Carl requested.

'Your wish is my command.' This was what she did best, after all. 'Relax, you two, no funny business with drills, and the helipad at the airbase is in the easy category, especially given the fine conditions.'

If it was windy, it made for some interesting landings no matter where you wanted to touch down but today couldn't be better with the sun shining, not much cloud in sight, bright blue skies – the sort of conditions that left Maya in no doubt that this really was the best job in the world.

'Cake back at the base,' Bess reminded them both: the send-off for Carl was to be short and sweet, as he preferred, but with his favourite cake – lemon drizzle – and a mug of tea.

The town of Whistlestop River came into view. Soon they'd be passing over its majestic, ribbon-like river veering to the right slightly as they continued on and prepared to land at the airbase on the outskirts of the town.

Maya might have a feeling of unease today but she never lost appreciation for the way she and the rest of the crew got to see views of the country and the county of Dorset not many others would ever get to witness.

A patchwork of fields spread out on the left, more on the right and from up here, Whistlestop River was like a make-believe town, toy-like in its dimensions. The river was at last in sight. They cruised well above the roofs of homes, above the local town hall, the handful of shops and businesses, the pub that backed onto the river and finally came in to touch down at the airfield.

When the doors were clear, the rotor blades slowed to a halt, Maya patted the door frame next to her twice. 'Thanks, Hilda, mission accomplished, again.'

As well as a make and model to identify the aircraft, this helicopter had a name – Hilda – an apt choice because the name Hilda meant 'Battle Woman' and although they weren't fighting in a war, it still felt appropriate with a battle to help patients survive and keep the crew safe. The name had been chosen in memory of one of the Whistlestop River Air Ambulance's first supporters, Hilda Browne, who passed away some five years ago. Hilda had been a dedicated volunteer with the charity-funded organisation and had been in charge of numerous fundraisers over the last twenty years. Her efforts had resulted in an upgrade to the aircraft and the name Hilda was now proudly displayed in white below the identifying wording, The Skylarks, as well as the air ambulance's logo on the helicopter's red and yellow body.

Inside the building at the airbase, located on a small airfield solely for their use, Maya put her helmet onto the shelf with the others. 'It's hotting up out there.' And in the aircraft. She pulled out her hair tie and let her chestnut-brown locks free, but only for a moment until she gathered her hair up again and deftly pulled it into a bun off her neck.

Bess shrugged off her bright-red jacket and restyled her hair too, favouring tying her tumble of curls up and well out of the way. 'You don't need to tell the pair of us who have been wearing this uniform.' She lifted her knee to indicate the hard-wearing, red trousers that matched the jackets with fluorescent strips.

'I'll consider myself lucky, shall I?' As the pilot, she wore a less bulky uniform apart from the heavy boots which were nobody's favourite come summer. Instead of bright-red trousers, she wore a black, all-in-one flight suit with four epaulettes on each shoulder to show captain status.

The shift ended with cake and Carl's farewell and Nadia, their operational support officer, in a panic that the blue team were one critical care paramedic short.

Maya gathered her things together and as she passed the desk out front in the reception area, Nadia was smiling. She'd found a last-minute fill-in quickly enough so neither Bess nor Carl would have to offer to do a double shift.

Maya smiled, waved goodbye and was about to head out when she spotted the familiar cocky swagger of the man heading for the entrance doors. And it was too late to hide and pretend she'd left already.

She cursed.

Bess came up behind her to pass a file to Nadia with one hand and shovel the remains of a slice of lemon drizzle cake into her mouth with the other. 'Your ex-husband won't take no for an answer.'

'No,' Maya sighed. She could feel a headache coming on from the frown that always seemed to appear whenever he showed up. 'I need to leave; I have a wedding to get to.'

And she was tired of having him ruin things time and time again.

'Saved by the bell,' Bess declared when the phones situated in various points throughout the airbase all rang out in unison, announcing a call. The pair of them had invented a similar sort of escape plan many a time when her ex thought it a good idea to show up at Maya's work just to remind her that he was still in her life. Maya shrugged in his direction, read his lips and the swear word, heard him yell, 'Seriously!' when she turned her back and she and Bess headed into one of the meeting rooms away from everyone else.

Conrad would assume she'd had to go out on the job and he'd leave.

And Maya only emerged from the meeting room and left the airbase once she knew he had.

Maya lived less than a ten-minute drive from the airbase. She got home, showered in record time, fixed her hair into an updo, did her make-up and very carefully pulled her bridesmaid dress on. After one last check in the hallway mirror, she slipped her Skechers onto her feet for driving in and hooked her strappy heels over her fingers. Her sister was getting married and, for now, her own stresses could be pushed into the compartment in her mind labelled, *Things to worry about another time.*

Or at least they were until she opened the front door and came face to face with Conrad, strutting up the path dressed in his leathers, motorbike parked out front at an angle.

Conrad stopped when he saw her. He whistled between his teeth, looking at her in a way she wished he wouldn't.

She gave him a ghost of a smile, adequate enough to keep the peace, a smile that wouldn't put him on the defensive. 'I can't stop,' she said as he came the rest of the way up the path.

But she wasn't quick enough. Before she could pre-empt it, he was up the steps and leaning against the door frame so she couldn't close it.

He took in her mocha silk bridesmaid dress, her rich chestnut hair pulled up at the back with ringlets tumbling to frame her face. 'You look hot. Damn hot.'

She shifted, he still hadn't taken his eyes off her and he was leaning in so close, she got a heady waft of the woody aftershave he'd worn their entire marriage, a smell she could pick up a mile off and would rather not. 'How's Whizzy?' If in doubt, talk about something other than herself, that was what Maya preferred to do.

In the divorce, their son Isaac might have been old enough to decide who he resided with when he wasn't at university but their cat, or rather her cat, Whizzy, had had no such luxury. Conrad had somehow got custody of Whizzy, the cat he hadn't even wanted, the cat Maya had rescued from down by the river. When an owner couldn't be traced, Maya had given the feline a new home. Maya was pretty sure in all the time Whizzy had lived with them, the cat had never dared to creep onto Conrad's lap, curl up and purr, never mind dribble when the affection was to her satisfaction. But Conrad had played the game well, told Maya the cat was settled in the house that had always been his since before they were married, and he'd insisted Maya's erratic hours meant Whizzy might be left wandering outside at all hours, onto the road that ran through the town which, while not busy, wasn't exactly brightly lit. Maya's focus had had to go on moving into her own cottage and leaving the marriage behind once and for all.

With a sigh, as though Maya's question was beyond irritating, Conrad told her, 'The cat is still alive, still Lady Muck around the house.'

Maya hated it when he called the cat Lady Muck. Whizzy was a cat, for heaven's sake. What did he expect, for the feline to don an apron and see to the washing up?

While his hackles were up, she told him, 'I've got a handyman coming to fit a cat flap next week. I can take her then.'

'Good for you. I hope you're not being ripped off.' His nostrils flared, the tension in his jaw showing.

'I trust the handyman; he's done a few jobs for me.' And before he could probe more because his mind would definitely be drawing its own conclusions, she added, 'He went to school with my uncle right here in Whistlestop River, so I'm not worried.' And that comment would give the man an age, an age that wouldn't have Conrad seething with jealousy. He had no claims on her in that respect but sometimes it was a case of saying what she needed to for a peaceful life. It had been the same in the latter years of their marriage, something she'd slowly realised was a red flag among several others.

'I'll let you know then,' she prompted, 'when I can collect Whizzy.' If he flat-out refused, there wouldn't be a lot she could do other than go and take the cat herself, which sometimes she was tempted to do.

'Fine,' he grumbled. 'We'll arrange a time for you to come over and get her. I'll need to be there.'

What, to say a tearful farewell? Maya doubted it. She suspected over the last few months, he'd got bored of having Whizzy, her demands for attention, having to feed her and generally have another being to think of other than himself. Maya's request right now had probably come at the perfect time for him.

'I really have to go, Conrad.'

'You don't have time for me?'

This again. Divorce seemed to come with its own set of rules for her ex-husband, its own set of expectations. She'd thought the decree absolute would've meant he finally got the message that she didn't want him butting in on her life, but it seemed not because he was forever showing up.

'It's Julie's wedding, I really do need to get a move on,' she persisted.

'Fine…' He stood away from the door so she could close it and lock up.

As she made her way down the path, she figured she might as well go all in and ask, 'Did you transfer the money to Isaac?'

Helmet over one arm, he grunted. 'He's getting through too much cash. Isn't this what the student loan is for?' His hair looked a bit greasy. He'd obviously used some product in it, though it was still schoolboy dark-brown and showed no signs of greying despite his fast approach to fifty-five. She wondered whether he'd been dyeing it perhaps, it wouldn't surprise her.

'We've been through this,' she said. 'Multiple times. The loan covers his accommodation but not much else. He still has to eat, buy books—'

'Go out on the lash with his mates.'

There was little point in contradicting him because he'd never back down on his opinions. 'I transferred some to him yesterday, but I need to know that he has enough for the rest of term.' Otherwise, she'd have to stop buying food herself and send the funds to her son instead.

'Fine, I'll do it. Don't go on about it.'

Isaac was past the age where Conrad had to provide child support so that had stopped but on only her wage, Maya knew it would be difficult to support their son through three years at university.

He huffed some more, took out his phone. 'I tell you what, I'll do it now.' Every time money was due, Conrad moaned, but after he'd said his piece, had a whinge, usually he transferred it right over.

Conrad had made a fuss when Isaac said he wanted to go to university. 'Waste of time and money,' he'd told his son when Isaac was part way through his A levels. He'd told Maya, 'The lad needs to learn hard graft; worked for me, didn't it?' Further education was something her ex-husband was very opinionated on. He didn't see the point. And when he found out Isaac was studying Philosophy and English, he claimed they were poncy subjects and a total waste of time. Luckily, Isaac hadn't been home to hear the declaration; he'd been out with his friends. Isaac and Conrad hadn't seen eye to eye for years and so Isaac had gone off to university without so much as a goodbye to his dad.

Maya wished Isaac was here now, that he was accompanying her to his auntie's wedding, but he was about to start his exams and with his university so far away, it was too difficult. He'd sent a gift, a card, called Julie too. He had a good heart, her son.

'You really do look beautiful,' Conrad told her yet again.

She opened up her car door. 'I have to—'

'I know, I know. You have a wedding to get to.' But he couldn't let it go. 'We once had a wedding in which we promised each other forever. Till death do us part.' His eyes only left hers to look down at her decolletage. 'We said those very words.'

'Please, Conrad. I want to move on with my life. And you should move on with yours.'

He reached out a hand and ran the back of his fingers down her cheek. 'Don't forget, Maya, I'm still around if you ever want to talk, if you ever need me. We're tied together for life with our son.' His hand left her face and instead grazed her bare shoulder and all the way down her arm. 'I miss you.'

Maya didn't look back when she climbed into her car and drove away, away from him. Because it wasn't only Isaac that kept this man in her life. It was also what he knew about her, things that nobody else did, and whenever he hinted that he was still around, that he was there for her, she knew what that meant. It meant that if she pushed him away too hard, he had all the power to let her past become public. And that had the potential to ruin everything for her.

* * *

Maya arrived at the church in the nick of time. The bride was waiting in the room at the side and the second Maya saw Julie, her breath caught in her throat. 'If Mum could see you now…'

Julie warned, 'Don't make me cry.' And, back in control, she clasped Maya's hands. 'I'm so pleased you made it on time.'

'Me too.' She squeezed her sister's hands, a promise that she was there for her on this, the most important day of her life.

Maya found a tissue and used the edge to carefully blot the very corners of Julie's eyes so her make-up wouldn't be ruined by any of her emotional tears. 'You ready?'

Julie beamed. 'I am. Can you believe it? I'm finally getting married.'

'You two are going to be so happy together.'

The door opened behind them and their dad, Nigel came in. As it should be, his focus was on Julie and only after he'd gushed at how beautiful she was, told her how her mother would be proud if she was here, did he turn to Maya.

'You made it,' he said as Julie's friend and second bridesmaid Niamh took the bride's attention by handing her her bouquet and fussing over her veil to make sure it fell across her shoulders just so.

'I did,' said Maya.

'More luck than judgement, am I right?'

'Dad, not today…'

And without even looking at him again, she picked up her own posy of flowers and joined Niamh before the bridal party made their way into the church, Julie on her father's arm, the two bridesmaids leading the way.

Maya nodded to Seth, the groom as she and Niamh reached the altar. He looked nervous, but he had nothing to worry about; her sister was as in love with him as he was with her. And when it was time for the bride's entrance, Maya couldn't take her eyes off her sister as she made her way down the aisle to the strains of 'Ave Maria'.

The ceremony began and Maya, despite her happiness for her sister, couldn't help the knot in her stomach that reminded her she'd once thought she had a happy ever after; she'd once stood up in front of family and friends and vowed to love a man for the rest of her life. Over time, however, since Isaac was born and their lives settled into the familiarity that came with a marriage, Conrad had soon forgotten that they were in a partnership, two equal parts to a whole.

Nigel approved of Seth, Julie's husband-to-be, but he'd never gelled with Conrad. It didn't help that Maya and Conrad had got together at a time when Maya and her father weren't even speaking, but it was more than that. Some thought of Conrad as a pillar of the community simply because he was a police detective and that position was one of authority. It commanded respect but he'd never earned Nigel's and he'd soon lost Maya's a few years into their marriage when she began to learn that behind the front was a bully, a man with an arrogance who always looked out for number one.

The photographs seemed to take forever after the ceremony but Julie enjoyed every second and the celebrations continued back at the Anderson family home, a vast and beautiful property in the Dorset countryside and the place where the girls felt closest to their late mother.

The food and drinks circulated at the informal reception the bride and groom had opted for with canapés rather than a sit-down meal. Julie and Seth had chosen not to have any speeches either, something Maya was grateful for so that she didn't have to endure her dad talking about their family as if they had no issues at all, as if everything in the Anderson clan was hunky dory without any stress whatsoever. Sometimes the Anderson family dynamics felt like a car crash, with her dad ushering people away, commanding *Nothing to see here.*

Finally came the part of the celebrations that saw Julie and Seth truly let go and relax – the dancing. The room known fondly as the games room in the house became party central. The space was vast, had originally been two rooms knocked into one and now had walnut floorboards, a pool table with the same wooden build, a bar. The oversized sofas in slate grey had been pushed from their position to against the walls to make way for the temporary dance floor and entertainment, the enormous rugs rolled up and put out of the way for the night, some of the breakable ornaments stowed elsewhere for safekeeping.

Maya accompanied Julie to the bathroom yet again – it wasn't easy to navigate going for a pee with an enormous dress on and required help every time. Everyone was in high spirits and the girls giggled on their way back from the bathroom when they found Rod, one of Seth's closest friends, going into a broom closet instead of the outside door so he could escape for a cigarette – the house was so big, it was easy to get lost in or take a wrong turn.

'Don't let Issy see you with that,' Maya scolded him. When he put a finger to his lips, she laughed and turned back the way she was going but her smile soon disappeared when her father came in the opposite direction. They'd exchanged few words so far today and she was happy to keep it that way.

Their dad was a striking man; with silver-fox hair, he was tall and commanded a presence, something that worked well in the world of law for him, but something she'd never found easy.

Julie gave their dad a hug and raced off to join her guests.

'You look beautiful, Maya.' He kissed her on each cheek. He'd never been one to let a façade slip, not when there were so many guests milling around.

'Thank you.' She could manage politeness. 'Julie and Seth are going to be so happy,' she said, steering the focus to safer ground.

'They are. And your mother would be so proud. Of both of you.'

Their mother would be, but what about him? She sometimes wondered how hard he had to work to maintain that tough shell or whether it came naturally to show little emotion, especially where his eldest daughter was concerned. She was tired of trying to work him out. She'd been trying to do that ever since her mother died.

'I'd better go and join Julie,' she said. 'She wants me to dance.'

'Of course. Off you go.' He nodded in her direction, much like she was a business colleague rather than his eldest daughter.

Maya danced with her sister, their family and friends, expending all her pent-up energy. Conrad had always detested this part of a wedding or any social gathering. He hated dancing and because he'd expected her to stay by his side, she'd rarely got to enjoy it either. But tonight, Maya couldn't get enough.

It was only when Seth came and claimed his bride for the interruption of a couple of slow dances to let people take a breath and enjoy more canapés that Maya stopped long enough for her troubles to come knocking in her mind yet again.

She plucked a glass of champagne from a passing tray and stood back to watch Julie and Seth, a couple who were in this together and who had each other's backs in a way she and Conrad never had. And despite their divorce being finalised just over six weeks ago, Maya felt like she couldn't move ten paces without turning round to find Conrad standing right there behind her. It was suffocating. And she'd had enough.

She needed Conrad to get the message once and for all that she and him were 100 per cent, totally over.

Except how she was going to do that, she had no idea.

3

Noah hadn't expected to start with the Whistlestop River Air Ambulance for another couple of days, but they were down one critical care paramedic on the blue team and so today he'd been thrown in at the deep end.

Perhaps he should be used to it. It seemed to be the way his life was panning out lately. One minute he had a live-in girlfriend, Tahlia; he resided in a swish high-rise in London; he spent his days carefree and enjoying life; and the next... well, everything had changed. His sister Cassie died, leaving him as the guardian of her then seven-month-old daughter Eva, and Eva's arrival in his life had started a cascade of other changes. He'd had to let go of his apartment when Tahlia left him because she couldn't handle the situation he had found himself in – or, in her words, 'been lumbered with'. They were words he wouldn't forgive or forget easily. Eva hadn't fitted in with Tahlia's picture of how her life would one day turn out and although some days he missed her being around, if that was her attitude, it had been better to split up now rather than further down the line.

The breakdown of his relationship meant that Noah was left

with crippling mortgage payments for one, childcare fees were much in the same price bracket as the cost of having his apartment, and his shift pattern was unforgiving when it came to personal commitments. Noah had had to find a solution, and fast, and so he'd left the familiarity of his previous air ambulance crew and moved from city to country, something he'd never thought was on the cards. Now, home took the form of a converted signal box cottage – thankfully mortgage free – surrounded by peace and tranquillity instead of bright lights and noise. And there wouldn't be a sexy woman waking him up in the night for the foreseeable future either. Instead, he'd likely be up at least once in the night or more likely a few times with Eva, who was taking as long as he was to get used to their new way of life.

He was used to responsibility at work but doing it at home too? That was in another league entirely.

And now, here he was out on a job already. Nothing like hitting the ground running.

'Welcome aboard, Noah,' the pilot Vik's voice came over the headset.

'Good to be here.' He was in good spirits, embracing the new adventure. At least that's what he kept telling himself. The alternative was to focus on the things he'd given up, what he'd lost, rather than his life as it was now and moving forwards.

Already, Noah knew being here in Whistlestop River was going to be different to what he was used to. He'd turned up at the airbase in the countryside surrounded by green fields, the fresh air of Dorset, and a heck of a lot of space. It was miles away from his usual work environment, both literally and metaphorically, landing on a helipad on top of a hospital in the country's capital. The views from the helicopter right now were spectacular, but of a different kind. Instead of seeing iconic, celebrated architecture and buildings of London – The Shard, The Gherkin, Tower Bridge, Big Ben, Buckingham Palace – this evening in the spring sunshine the view spread out below was of green fields and small clusters of houses.

Noah had embarked on his career as a paramedic in London some time ago, single with no real ties at the time, and he'd been on the lookout for new challenges. It hadn't been long before he yearned for more, before a desire to work with the crew of an air ambulance crept in. He'd wanted to learn something new, take himself to another level. Out on the road, he was growing increasingly frustrated at the limitations for paramedics. And so his passion had led him to get his master's in critical care and not long after he qualified, he'd applied for a job with a London-based air ambulance. He'd been offered the position, and he loved it from the start, with every day different and capable of bringing enormous challenges.

He hoped it would be the same here in Dorset and so far, so good; he was out on a call, in the helicopter with the rest of the crew. They weren't the crew he'd be with on a permanent basis but it was good to get a taster anyway and meet the other team as their paths would inevitably cross often enough, even if it was only at the changeover of shift.

Noah sat in the rear of the helicopter. The inside of the air ambulance was kitted out much like those he'd worked in before. It carried breathing apparatus, defibrillators, monitors, blood transfusion equipment and a comprehensive supply of medications. The floor was medical grade with rails to which they could fix equipment as needed; racks above allowed them to do the same.

As they made the journey, the crew talked over the headsets about the job. They didn't always have much detail to go on, that much was similar no matter which air ambulance you were with or which locations you covered, so their discussions went through possible scenarios, likely treatments, which other first responders would be at the scene before them or on their way.

Their discussions built up a picture so they could be prepared as much as possible when they landed. A thirty-two-year-old female had tripped and hit her head on a table, was semi-conscious at least at the time of the emergency call, there was no obvious bleeding and a road ambulance had been dispatched. The crew already knew the residence they were going to was quite a distance from a trauma centre and if the head injury was severe, the air ambulance making the transfer in a fraction of the time might well be the only way to give the patient a chance of survival and full recovery. It wasn't only about the time it took to get a patient to the hospital, though. Paramedics on the road ambulance attended many emergencies, saved countless lives. But critical care paramedics could administer higher-level medications, they had a higher portfolio of training and could do more procedures at the scene. Their attendance could result in a much better outcome for the patient. And part of what Noah loved about his job was that everyone who attended a job worked together as a big team, whether it was the air ambulance, the police, the fire brigade, the paramedics on a road ambulance, doctors or any other emergency crew.

Noah whistled at the sight of the sun beginning to set. Sunsets and sunrises looked great from ground level but from up here, they were utterly spectacular. He wasn't a country boy, never saw the attraction, but right now, up here, there was something to be said for vast expanses of land.

With a further six minutes to their destination, Noah was ready with the iPad so he could help out with landing spots. Both him and Kate, the critical care paramedic in the front of the aircraft next to the pilot, would help out where they could but it sounded as though the place they were going to had grounds big enough to land there so hopefully touching down would be straightforward. It wasn't guaranteed, of course – sometimes what seemed easy turned out to be more tricky when they arrived; that had happened plenty of times in London. Landing as close as possible to the scene of an incident was vital for an air ambulance and London's parks and green spaces were prime landing locations. Sometimes, however, particularly if it was a glorious summer's day or the school holidays, those parks were packed and the general public, no matter whether sirens were on and lights flashing as the air ambulance came in to try to land, didn't always have the common sense to clear the area.

The helicopter landed safely in the grounds of the house – the HEMS desk who'd called the job in with the team had been right; the gardens at this residence were big enough to allow for a helicopter landing. Or maybe a Boeing 747, Noah thought, because the grounds were massive, as was the house. It had him wondering who owned the place. Someone with a lot of money, he decided, as he climbed out of the aircraft and hefted a rucksack with medical equipment onto his back. The bag weighed in at twenty kilograms or thereabouts and the crew often had to carry these bags a long way as well as the blood bags and the drug bags. Sometimes their trek involved climbing over fences, through brambles, covering a decent distance to get to the scene in what felt like an assault course. Fitness in this job was paramount and despite the life changes Noah had had recently, as well as having turned forty-five, his exercise and strength training were something he'd refused to let go of.

A man who looked to be in his mid-sixties ran towards them on the lawn and led the way back to the house, past a tennis court on one side and a swimming pool on the other. The crew made their way up the sweeping outside steps to the patio of a mansion-like residence with its grand rear elevation featuring large doors and extensive glass. They were here for an emergency but Noah couldn't help taking in the grandeur of this place and knew Kate was doing the same.

Inside the house, they were led to a huge room filled with people. There was a cocktail-inspired island bar with people crowded around it, and the sound of ice cubes being dropped into a glass alerted Noah not everyone here was willing to stop what they were doing simply because someone needed medical attention.

As soon as he saw the patient, Noah realised what they'd walked in on wasn't a party but a wedding reception. And it was the bride who needed their help.

'Stand back, please.' Kate's voice rose, commanded her instructions.

Noah knelt down beside the bride, who was on her back, groaning, with a hand clasped to her head. Another woman was kneeling beside the patient in a stunning silk mocha-coloured dress, her hair semi-pinned up but now tumbling over her shoulders in enormous waves and settling over her chest. Kate clearly knew this woman because she'd put an arm around her briefly.

Noah focused. The woman holding the patient's hand was very much his type, the sort he might have met on a night out and would want to get to know. Except now he had other priorities when it came to the fairer sex in his life.

'Please stand back,' Noah repeated and while Kate talked to the patient, he stood, arms outstretched to push the onlookers back a few steps. Didn't they realise they made this job so much harder?

When he crouched down again and opened up the medical bag to get what he needed, Kate told him the patient's name was Julie.

'Hi, Julie. We've got you, don't worry.' His gaze fluttered to the other woman who still hadn't yet let go of Julie's hand until someone at her shoulder came to investigate.

The woman in the mocha dress stood up then and took over crowd control. Impressive. People took notice of her. And it let him and Kate get on with what they needed to do.

Kate and Noah tried to piece together what injuries Julie might have by talking to her. It wasn't always the injuries you could see or the pain the patient was focused on; there was always the chance of other issues and the crew needed to make sure they didn't miss anything. Talking to Julie like this would also help them observe her level of consciousness, whether she was confused or not.

Julie was talking a lot, she was coherent. She kept saying this was all an overreaction, that she really was fine and it was her own stupid fault she'd hurt herself. She'd got carried away, climbed onto a low table to dance pretending it was a stage and then she'd lost her footing, fallen and hit her head on another table before crashing to the ground.

Noah wrapped the blood pressure cuff around her arm and then put the pulse oximeter on the tip of her finger to check oxygen levels. Kate continued her assessment of the patient's torso. There were no signs of hip, leg or pelvic injuries.

Noah gently examined the egg-like lump that had appeared on Julie's right temple. 'You have a sizeable bump there.'

'I have ice.' The voice came from behind him and the beautiful woman in the mocha dress handed over a tea towel containing ice cubes.

'Thank you.' He held it gently against Julie's head. She winced but only briefly before he saw relief.

'What's your name?' Julie asked him.

The woman in the mocha dress warned, 'Julie...'

'What? I'm only being polite.' Julie gave him an approving look. 'You're way hotter than any doctor I've ever seen, except maybe the ones on *Grey's Anatomy* or *ER*. Some of those doctors are insanely hot.'

'Julie, you just got married,' the woman in the mocha dress said. The crowd had dispersed now and as she crouched down again, Noah did his best not to stare, not to take in the silky soft skin and the way her dress showed enough decolletage to be classy and sexy rather than tacky.

Kate, with a bit of a laugh at Noah being quizzed, asked Julie to let them ask the questions rather than the other way round.

'I'm sorry,' Julie groaned. 'You're trying to do your job.' But to Kate in a lower whisper, she added, 'Seriously, how do you concentrate working with him?'

'He's new,' Kate laughed. 'But I think I'll manage to control myself.' Although she was having a hard time not grinning from ear to ear at Noah's expense.

Julie was coherent, with injuries that appeared minor, and although Noah knew minor could mask bigger problems, he didn't think that was the case here. He wondered whether the caller had panicked and made the incident out to be worse than it was, which triggered the HEMS desk who triaged all emergency calls to deploy the air ambulance. And looking around at the crowd, he expected alcohol had been involved and fuelled the call.

He frowned, whether at himself or whoever had made the call, it was a toss-up. It was something he was trying to manage, not making snap judgements because of his own family history. He needed to get on top of it really so that he could do this job without bias, but sometimes his personal feelings crept right on in and did their best to interfere.

The woman in the mocha dress was still on the case if anyone tried to get closer to see the action. He almost smiled; she reminded him of a bouncer at a club anticipating trouble before it happened. Not a bad person to have here with them for backup, he supposed.

The chatter in the room had simmered a little at the presence of more medical people when the road ambulance crew arrived. The paramedics offered their assistance and the decision was made by both crews that this time round the patient didn't require transportation by air.

Kate put a hand on Julie's arm. 'I know it's your wedding day but you should go to the hospital in the road ambulance for a thorough check, make sure nothing has been missed.'

'I'm fine,' Julie insisted before recalling her name, date of birth, today's occasion, the name of the prime minister, although there'd been a few sniggers there because she didn't come up with it straight away. She assured both Kate and Noah that that was usual for her.

'I mean it,' Julie insisted. 'Ask me anything about *Love Island* and I'll tell you whatever you need to know.'

'Not a fan myself,' Noah smiled as he packed everything back into the kit bag.

The goddess in the mocha dress talked to Kate while Noah spoke with the road ambulance crew to hand over the patient.

Noah attracted the attention of another woman as he zipped up the last of the bags so they could head back to the helicopter. She was a friend of Julie's apparently; she wanted to know whether Julie would get to go on her honeymoon. He told her he wasn't sure but the signs were all good and he successfully managed to bat a couple of personal questions about himself away when she asked him if he was new to town and whether he was married.

Kate didn't miss a chance to tease him, even though they'd only met this evening. 'You're popular, although that woman might have left you in need of medical attention. I reckon you'd have passed out with the amount of perfume she has on. That or you'd have suffocated by cleavage.'

'I don't think I'll hang around to find out,' he grinned, hoping the red team were this friendly when he joined them officially.

'Oh, I don't know, look at that bar,' she said in a low whisper with a discreet glance that way. There appeared to be more variety here than in some of the London bars he'd been to. She gasped and nudged him, looking to the far corner of the room. 'There's even a roulette wheel, look! It's like small-scale Vegas in here.'

The words were out of his mouth before he had a chance to filter. 'Yeah, small-scale Vegas with too many rich people taking resources from someone who actually needs an air ambulance.' He cringed. He should've said it more quietly, kept his opinions to himself rather than letting his personal experiences creep back in again. It was damn hard to do, though.

'Not for us to decide.' Kate hoisted one of the bags onto her back. 'We get a job and we go.'

'She's right,' came a female voice from behind them. It was the woman in the mocha dress and she smiled at Kate then glared at him. 'It's not for you to say what jobs require your attention and which ones don't.'

Shit. He really had spoken too loudly.

'I apologise,' he said. He was riled because of personal history and he shouldn't hold the rich responsible for all of the world's evils. But still, he could lay some of it at their feet to make himself feel a little bit better when he needed to, couldn't he?

The woman hadn't finished.

'I wouldn't mind if I was a time waster; give me hell for that.' She had her hands on her hips now.

'Maya...' Kate began.

'You know me, Kate, I wouldn't do that.' Before Kate could say a word, the woman continued her rant. 'It was me who made the call; I thought it was worse than it actually was. I've seen enough and heard enough about head injuries to know they can be catastrophic.'

'You're a nurse?' he asked.

'Oh, this ought to be good,' Kate mumbled before she left him to sort this out for himself while she radioed in to let the HEMS desk know they were clear and available.

Maya leapt in with, 'I'm not a nurse, but—'

'I'm sorry I upset you,' he interrupted. He actually was. He had mouthed off and his words, his judgement really, had been more about him than anyone else. 'I hope Julie is home with you all soon.'

Her dark eyes and glossy hair drew him in all the more as they stood there facing off in the middle of the room until Kate prompted him to get a move on.

Noah followed Kate outside and down the steps to the grass level and the helicopter waiting on the lawn, which in size seemed more like a football pitch than one family's outdoor space.

Kate began to laugh as they walked, packs on their backs, back to the helicopter. 'I can't believe you've been here five minutes and already clashed with Maya.'

'How well do you know her?' he asked.

'Pretty well,' she yelled as the noise of the rotor blades grew louder as the aircraft started up, ready for their departure. 'Maya's the pilot on the red team,' she said with a wink before they stowed the kit bags and the drugs in the back of the aircraft.

'Shit. You're joking, right?'

She shook her head before she climbed into the front of the helicopter. 'Nope.'

Noah closed the rear sliding door and pulled on his headset. He'd been in town less than forty-eight hours, this was hardly the best start, was it?

They lifted into the air and the mansion became a much smaller version of itself below them. Once they were on their way back to base, he heard Kate pass on Maya's regards to Vik before she explained that Noah had met Maya too.

Of all the jobs to get as his first one with The Skylarks, why did it have to be here where he'd opened his big mouth and put his size tens right in it, offended someone he'd be working with closely very soon?

Sod's law, that was why.

And because for some reason, life just kept wanting to slap him in the face.

4

Noah was in the kitchen at the base making mugs of coffee all round. The caffeine was welcome at any time, especially the late evening and early hours of the morning shift that he was working now.

They'd not been out of the helicopter five minutes when Kate shared the story of his run-in with Maya with Rita, one of the Whistlestop River Freewheelers, the group of volunteers who offered a courier and transport service between medical establishments including hospitals, surgeries, ambulances, air ambulances and the community. Rita introduced herself as she handed over the fresh supplies of blood and plasma which had to be replaced every forty-eight hours. Keeping supplies on board was an absolute game changer for air ambulances because it meant that if a patient was bleeding at the scene, they didn't have to wait to get to hospital for lifesaving treatment.

'Lovely to meet you,' Noah told her as he took the cool box containing fresh supplies.

He'd already met Mick and Alan, two other members of the Whistlestop River Freewheelers who'd brought medical supplies for the crew to transport to a couple of the local hospitals and it felt good to get to know more and more people and feel a real part of things so quickly.

'I hope Maya takes it easy on me when I start with the red team,' Noah told Kate as they drank their coffees at the kitchen table. Maya might be the pilot rather than his boss but they still had to work together. Even more of a worry was that his life was literally in her hands and it would be reassuring to know she didn't harbour any ill feeling.

Kate took a sip from her mug and nodded her approval. 'Well, at least you'll be able to get her on side with a great cup of coffee.'

They took their drinks into the main office where calls came in, incidents were logged and paperwork updated, where the pilots could use technology to assess weather and conditions.

'Maya's great, you'll love her. But don't accuse her of being rich and entitled and taking valuable resources.'

'I messed up big time shooting my mouth off. But I didn't accuse her of anything. It wasn't her house.'

'No...' Kate paused before taking a sip of her drink. 'It's her father's.'

His face fell. 'Tell me you're joking.'

'Julie is her sister, you know that, right?'

'I missed that part.' He was a good critical care paramedic, he knew when to focus, and there wouldn't have been any need for anyone to update him as to the relationship between the women and if they had, he'd not taken it in.

They went through the notes on today. His interaction with Maya was still playing on his mind when they finished up the paperwork and returned their empty mugs to the kitchen. 'I only arrived in town very recently,' he told Kate as he washed up the crockery, 'I don't want to seem like a total arse to Maya or anyone else.'

'If it helps, you don't seem like an arse to me. Chin up, Maya's cool.' And off she went.

A woman poked her head around the doorway with a little knock on the door. 'I came to meet the new recruit.' She extended her hand. 'Delighted to have you joining the team. I'm Nadia, operational support officer. We spoke on the phone.'

He finished drying his hands on the towel before meeting her gesture. 'Good to meet you in person.'

Nadia recounted some of what her role involved even though he was familiar with the role given he'd been part of another crew. He guessed it was her way of fully introducing herself.

'Basically, I manage you all – keep the team in check.' She smiled. 'Any questions, fire them my way or to anyone else who's around. We're all very friendly at the airbase and in Whistlestop River.' She left the room with a call over her shoulder, 'Maya's a pussycat, by the way.'

He groaned as Kate came back along the corridor and past the kitchen, laughing, a sheaf of papers cradled in her arms. 'What can I say, Noah; word spreads fast around here,' she called as she walked, presumably to pass all the paperwork to Nadia.

'Careful or we'll know all your secrets,' said Kate when she came back to the kitchen.

'I hate to disappoint you but I don't have any; what you see is what you get.'

'Now why doesn't that surprise me? Come on, tell me more about yourself.' She peeled the skin from a banana and bit into it. 'You were thrown in at the deep end with us lot.'

But their chat was short-lived because the red telephone ringing announced another job. There were other phones dotted around the airbase so the crews never missed a call.

Noah went to get his jacket and collect his helmet. Kate retrieved the drug bags and followed swiftly. Vik had already noted the destination grids and gone out to the helicopter to start it up, having already assessed weather conditions and other essential flight information.

Once they were airborne, Kate ran through the details of where they were heading and what to expect on scene. They received a few more details from the HEMS desk and by now knew that it was a crash involving a single motorcycle and no other vehicle. The victim was a male in his fifties, the patient was unconscious and police were on scene. By the sounds of it, the motorcyclist had had a blowout and lost control, careering into the vacant layby at the side of the road. They had no details of injuries sustained but they would be able to land at one end of the layby itself, putting them nice and close to the patient. Noah and Kate had already talked about possible injuries en route – there could be a head injury, broken bones. A common injury for bikers was a damaged pelvis and even though not a drop of blood would be spilt, you could lose every single bit of blood in your body internally in your pelvis with so much space in there.

As they approached the grid reference, blue flashing lights were the beacon to help them land more easily and Vik skilfully set the aircraft down before Noah and Kate leapt into action. They were updated again on scene as they rushed to the patient with their kit bags.

But as they stopped by the patient, Noah heard Kate swear.

He set down his kit bag and unzipped it while Kate leaned in closer to the man, felt for a pulse in his neck. 'Conrad, can you hear me?'

Shit. She knew him.

Despite the personal connection, she was professional to a tee. 'Noah, we need to get the helmet off.'

Removing a rider's helmet at the scene of an accident was daunting. There was always the risk of doing more damage, but at the same time, they needed the helmet to come off so that they could assess injuries and the level of consciousness and more importantly to ensure the rider had a clear airway.

Once the helmet was removed, Noah checked it over. It could give them an idea of the kind of force that had been applied on the head and the neck as a result. 'The helmet is intact, a bit of a scrape and a dent.' The head could still rattle around inside a helmet in an accident like this, however, so it didn't mean the patient was out of the woods with regards to head injuries.

Between them, Noah and Kate followed procedures to get the patient stabilised. They got him on the scoop, spine immobilised, and fitted a c-collar as well as blocks on either side of his head. That's when he began to come around.

'Conrad, can you hear me?' Kate asked. 'Conrad?'

But he made no sense when he spoke, no indication he had any idea what was going on. His behaviour suggested a potential brain injury as he tried to move and push away their attempts to help him. Noah gave him pain relief, then checked his chest, the rest of his torso.

Because the helicopter was so close, Vik came to help them lift the scoop back to the aircraft where they got the patient onto the litter, the bed inside the helicopter that could slide out of the side door and then back in again.

Noah climbed in next to the patient. Kate called in their status to HEMS to update them on the situation and that they were leaving now to head to the nearest trauma centre.

It was only once they were up in the air that Noah spoke into his headset to finally ask Kate who the man was.

From her seat next to Vik, she told him, 'He's Maya's ex-husband.'

Noah looked at the guy next to him, the specks of blood on the side of his face from minor trauma to his jaw. When Tahlia left him,

Noah's emotions weren't extinguished just like that. He still cared for her, even though he'd been shocked at her inability to even try to factor in Eva.

Looking at Conrad, he wondered how Maya got on with this man? Did she feel the same as he did about his ex? That they may no longer be together, but he still cared?

And knowing loss so personally, so recently, he wouldn't wish the worry on anyone.

* * *

Maya let her silk bridesmaid dress slip down her body and pool onto the floor. She smiled. She rarely dressed up these days – she didn't have to go to many places that required formal attire. At the reception, her father had said how beautiful she looked, he'd commented on the fact that she'd made the wedding, which meant he'd expected her job to get in the way. The job he had never fully embraced. It wasn't that he'd ever said he disapproved of what she did for a living, but that was the problem. She didn't know what he honestly thought because they didn't communicate. They hadn't been able to in years. The last few references to her job had been over the last month as he used every possible opportunity to remind her that he thought she should be taking time off for her sister's wedding. He'd asked how she could risk being out on an emergency for strangers when she should be supporting her family? But that was the way it went. The crews she worked with always had personal stuff going on. And Julie got it; she'd always understood. Maybe because she'd always bothered to ask and listen.

Hair scooped out of the way and in a clip, Maya let the water in the shower wash away the parts of the wedding reception she wanted to forget – her dad, Julie's accident. The steam in the shower rose and enveloped her and deep breaths saw her sanity return. Julie was going to be fine; she'd had a message from Seth already to say his wife had been checked over at the hospital and they'd be off on honeymoon as planned, as Mr and Mrs.

Julie's accident could've been so much worse. She'd had a few drinks, she got carried away dancing on the table so she could see the crowds or the crowds could see her, Maya wasn't sure. Whatever way round it was, Julie had been having the time of her life. And then Maya had seen the accident play out in front of her. She'd heard the thump of her sister's head against the coffee table, heard a scream from the other bridesmaid, saw the panic on her father's face. And the next thing she knew, she'd made the call to the emergency services. Julie wasn't speaking, someone yelled that she wasn't breathing, Maya hadn't checked the facts, of course she hadn't, she'd made the call and the wheels were set in motion. The family property was a distance from a hospital, let alone a trauma centre, and if Julie's injuries had been worse, the air ambulance might well have been her only option of survival and whoever took her call would've known that and deployed the most appropriate emergency services.

The taps in the shower squeaked as Maya turned them both off. She'd made the call and she'd do it again. Never mind what that arsehole on the blue team, a guy she didn't even recognise, had implied. He must've been drafted in due to the staff shortage; it happened sometimes. All Maya hoped was that she wouldn't have to see his judgemental expression or hear his condescending voice ever again. He'd made her feel as though she'd done something wrong when she hadn't.

It was a little after midnight but Maya was buzzing too much to sleep, so, with hair wrapped in a towel and in her pyjamas, she found the cocoa from the cupboard and the milk from the fridge.

When her phone went, she groaned when she saw it was Kate's

number. Kate wouldn't be calling this late for a chat, which meant only one thing: they needed an emergency stand-in on shift.

'I've had a few drinks tonight,' she said the second she picked up the call. 'I'm sorry but you saw the wedding, Kate; the champagne was on tap.'

She'd expected a laugh in response, an assertion that it was fine, she'd try to get hold of someone else. But she didn't get that at all.

'Maya, I'm not calling about work. It's Conrad...'

5

Maya arrived at the hospital by taxi thirty minutes later, hair still damp, face dewy fresh with no make-up, in jeans and a sweatshirt hastily grabbed from the washing basket.

She went straight to the main reception. 'I'm here to see Conrad Miller.'

The nurse looked up from the form she was filling out. 'And you are?'

'I'm... his wife. Maya.' She'd add the Miller if she had to, to overcome the bureaucratic red tape and get the information she needed. She'd already reverted her surname back to Anderson, altered her next of kin on her medical records to be Julie rather than Conrad, but she felt pretty certain Conrad wouldn't have removed her contact details yet. Not only did he have no other family to speak of apart from her and their son Isaac, it was obvious he wanted to keep as closely connected to her as he could. Conrad had been unwilling to close the door on their relationship long before the divorce was finalised, even when they were living apart.

The nurse came around to her side of the desk. 'Please take a seat here in the waiting area and I'll find someone to come and let you know what's going on with your husband.'

That meant he was alive, right?

That had been her biggest fear on the journey here. She'd seen enough and heard enough to know that a person alive at the scene, someone taken to the hospital living and breathing, wasn't always out of danger. Internal injuries could creep up, even injuries they could see and deal with could be much worse than first expected. Kate hadn't told her much apart from the basics about the accident and that he was in this particular hospital and, to be honest, Maya might not have heard much of what she was saying anyway; her focus had been getting to the hospital as quickly as she could. It wasn't that she wanted Conrad to be a part of her life any more, but shouldn't he always be in Isaac's? Father and son didn't see eye to eye but that was a totally different thing to having your father die and never having the chance to salvage your relationship ever again. The irony of the situation wasn't lost on Maya given her relationship with her own father, but all she knew right now was that she wanted to give father and son the best chance of reconciling one day and having the sort of relationship she'd always longed for with her own dad.

It seemed to take forever before someone showed up, when in reality it was less than ten minutes going by the clock on the wall.

The nurse explained Conrad's injuries – a broken arm and two fingers on one hand, severe bruising down one side of his body, cuts to his jaw line that had required stitches, head trauma and a concussion. She ran through the tests that had been performed, the X-rays, the scans. Maya knew without being told that it was a blessing Conrad had always been so pedantic about wearing the full gear – the helmet, the leathers, the boots. Had he not been kitted out properly, it might well have been a different story.

'Your husband is in the high-dependency unit at the moment;

we're keeping a close eye on him given the head trauma.' She pushed her wire-framed glasses up her nose. 'I can take you to see him if you like.'

Maya followed the nurse along a corridor, into the lift, through the maze of the hospital until they reached the high-dependency unit. There was a bank of desks with computer monitors, a group of nurses talking in hushed voices, the bleep of machines, the smell that came with a hospital setting.

The nurse left her at Conrad's bedside.

It might seem strange to people that Maya didn't know many doctors and nurses when she worked for the Whistlestop River Air Ambulance but her part involved getting the patient from A to B and aside from meeting the odd emergency doctor or nurse who came out to the helipad when she landed the aircraft, she hadn't met many of them at all, even at this hospital where she'd come countless times before on duty. Right now, Maya was reminded of the reality of what she was a part of with her team at work.

Maya reached out to touch Conrad's hand, almost checking he was still there, still warm and alive. There was a cannula in place, he had electrodes on his chest, and machines beeped now and then, numbers flashing on and off. She knew enough to understand what they all were, that going by the numbers on the monitors, his condition was stable.

Conrad looked so different lying here in this bed – smaller somehow, unguarded. He murmured, perhaps aware of her presence.

Maya took in the bruising up his arm, creeping inside the hospital-issued gown, the injured arm and fingers on the opposite side to where she was sitting. She looked at his other hand, the finger she'd once slid a wedding band onto as she promised him forever.

She didn't stay long. He was helpless lying there, he wasn't badgering her, and yet she still didn't want to hang around. When the nurse came to do another round of checks, Maya picked up her bag to go.

'You're not driving, are you, love?' the nurse asked her as she made notes on her clipboard.

'No, I'm not driving. I'll call a taxi.'

She put a hand on Maya's shoulder. 'Come back and see him in the morning; get some sleep for now. He's in good hands.'

'Thank you.' The nurse mistook her worry as being for Conrad when really it was for Isaac. She'd have to call their son and let him know what had happened. She was finally registering that it wasn't always a given that the pair would get a second chance to reconcile.

She made her way back to reception and outside into the fresh air. Then she pulled her phone from her bag to call a taxi but heard a voice behind her before she could make the call.

Bess. Kate must have called her.

Bess, her colleague at work who had given her her spare room when she left Conrad the first time, and the second and again for the final time.

And here she was showing up for her again.

6

Noah lifted Eva out of her car seat in the supermarket car park and promptly put her back again. He needed the buggy first – he forgot every time – and assembling the thing one-handed was way too difficult.

He closed the back door and went to the boot but stopped and quickly backtracked – he hadn't fastened Eva into the seat given he'd only be a minute and it had taken a second to realise that now she could sit up on her own and bum shuffle around the floor at eleven months, she could very well propel herself out of the rear-facing car seat and hurt herself.

Were all new fathers like this? Did they learn as they went along, making mistakes and rectifying them just in time? Or did they have enough warning that a baby was coming that they could read up on parenthood and at least not be a total dipshit at the job like he was?

With Eva safely secure, he took the buggy from the boot and opened it up, almost trapping his hand the same way he'd done yesterday and the day before that. Sooner or later, he'd get the hang of it, surely, and when he did, it would feel like a slice of victory. He

clipped the relevant pieces into place so that it wouldn't concertina
when Eva was in it – that had happened to him before as well,
earning him a glare from a passer-by as though he'd done it on
purpose – and with the harness ensuring she was safe once again,
he felt as though he'd climbed a mountain, passed a test on *The
Krypton Factor*, all of the above.

'Come on, you, let's get me some dinner. You're on mush again
tonight, Eva, but I need something a bit more substantial than what
Geraldine has dreamed up for you.'

Geraldine was Noah's, or rather Eva's, nanny and a woman he'd
interviewed and locked in before he even arrived in Whistlestop
River. And so far she'd been an absolute godsend. She'd come to get
to know Eva before he was given a regular shift pattern which had
reassured him and given him the confidence he'd made the right
choice in hiring her. And that meant when he was rostered in last
minute to join the blue team last night, she was at his house fifteen
minutes before she needed to be and he left calm and sure that Eva
was in capable hands.

Geraldine was flexible with the hours she could work too which
meant she'd be able to accommodate his shift work with the air
ambulance and, although not yet a grandmother, a fact she'd told
Noah about ten minutes into the online interview, she'd rattled off
qualifications and experience including a degree in early childhood
studies. She'd told him that looking after Eva, especially overnight
when required, would be 'good practice for when I have my own
grandchildren'. She'd then leapt in to say that she'd already
brought up four children who were alive and thriving in case the
word 'practice' had sent Noah into a tailspin thinking she wouldn't
be up to the task. He'd loved her friendly demeanour, her down-to-
earth attitude, and he'd offered her the job over Zoom that evening
subject to references and official checks needed for this line of
work.

Beneath grey skies, the buggy rattled over the tarmac of the car park and the automatic door of the supermarket opened for him. At least it wasn't like the revolving door at the supermarket near his old apartment. He'd tried to go into that with the buggy and made the whole thing come to a standstill, the doors jerking forward only when he finally positioned himself and the buggy correctly, which was a feat of engineering. It had taken forever to get inside the building, he'd heard a good tut from the person in the section behind and he'd vowed never to tackle a revolving door again. It never ceased to amaze him how you used such things and went about your business without thinking about the difficulties for those in a different situation to yourself.

He positioned a basket on top of the hood of the stroller. It wasn't the most secure, but it would do for this supermarket dash. He'd slowly learned that despite a stroller making things difficult in some ways, they were good in others, with a nice little basket beneath to stash things once he'd paid for them, a resting place on top for a basket in the way he'd done now. It wasn't what they were designed for and if there were baby health and safety police anywhere around, he might well be reprimanded for the said basket now, but it worked.

The supermarket here in Whistlestop River wasn't huge. The size and relatively small selection of goods had him wondering whether this town was ever going to move with the times and intro-duce something more substantial because there were enough houses here that he wouldn't be the only one having to trek another five miles to reach the larger supermarket with more choice.

He picked up milk, yogurt, some chicken fillets and a marinade and as long as he kept the stroller moving along, Eva gurgled with contentment.

He stopped in the vegetable aisle, debated what to go for and ended up at the end of the cabinets, where he found a range of prepackaged stir fry components – noodles or rice, various vegetables, a selection of sauces. He only had to cook for himself because Geraldine had insisted she cook for Eva, even though it wasn't in the job description. She'd told Noah that Eva would be sleeping a lot when she was at his place and so she preferred to feel useful rather than sit around. She'd also deemed the pre-made jars of baby food rubbish – she'd spotted the few he had in the cupboard as backup even though Eva was moving on from that stage. And now he had to admit that whatever Geraldine had made, the day she first came to the house and used the limited fresh ingredients he had in the cupboard and fridge, smelt a damn sight better than anything that came out of one of those glass jars.

When Eva landed so suddenly in his life, Noah had figured she was a baby, she ate, made a mess, pooped and that was it, on repeat cycle, with a few tears in between. He hadn't been at all prepared for how stressful the eating stage could be. In the last couple of months, Eva had either kept her lips pursed tightly shut whenever the spoon came near or she'd worked herself into such a frenzy that he'd had to give up and give her a cracker to wave around and suck on. That was what he'd ended up doing the day they got to Whistlestop River when Eva refused pretty much everything, so much so that he thought he was going to have to take her to the doctor because something was clearly wrong. His last resort had been a hastily made piece of toast with jam – he wasn't even sure whether that was allowed for an eleven-month-old – which she'd wolfed down in seconds and tears had become smiles and giggles, and his stress had become a feeling of relief and joy.

'What do you think to a few beers for the fridge, Eva?' He took the basket from the top of the stroller as it got heavier, deeming it unsafe to hover above a baby's head and with one hand steered her chariot.

He wasn't very good at steering and almost collided with a

woman pushing another stroller, then an elderly gentleman who wasn't looking where he was going.

But it was the next aisle where he stopped short of ramming into the back of a woman's ankles and when he apologised for being a useless driver, he realised who it was as she turned round to face him.

'It's Maya, isn't it?' He went for polite seeing as he'd offended her the last time they met. 'I'm Noah. I was with the blue team attending the emergency for your sister last night.'

She looked different to the last time he'd seen her in a sexy, silky dress that clung to her every curve. Now she was in jeans and a sweatshirt with a little stain on its hem. Her hair was loose around her shoulders, not straight but with big beach waves. He didn't think he'd ever seen anyone look so beautiful.

'I recognise you.' Her mouth flatlined. She was cradling a loaf of bread in the crook of her arm, holding a jar of jam in her opposite hand.

'How's Julie?' he prompted as Maya registered Eva in the stroller. He thought it best to try to get on this woman's good side and show a bit of concern rather than address the comments he'd made last night.

She gave him a small smile, suggesting perhaps all was not lost thanks to his big mouth. 'She's fine, off on her honeymoon and posting photos with her good side until the bruise goes down.'

'Glad to hear it. Not about the bruise, the honeymoon.' He fluffed his words, unsure of the reaction he'd get given their last encounter. She looked tired and vulnerable, neither of which were words he would've associated her with when he saw her at the wedding. Last night, if someone had asked him to describe Maya, he would've said she was feisty, energetic, in charge.

'I'd better get going,' she said.

His voice stopped her. 'How about Conrad?'

Her brow furrowed with confusion and it took her a moment to grasp why he would be asking the question. 'I apologise, I'm not quite with it today. You would've been there at the scene with Kate.' She was all formalities, not much friendliness but that was his own stupid fault. He hoped this wouldn't cause issues at work. 'He's going to be okay.'

'That's a relief.' He wanted to probe for more details, ask whether there were any further injuries other than what they'd found on scene, but she didn't seem in the right frame of mind for any of that. Or maybe she was, just not with him.

Eva let out a howl that made them both jump, but it made Maya smile a little bit. It seemed she could be frosty with him but not an innocent little girl, and he kind of liked that about her already.

'I forgot to move,' he explained. 'She gets a bit antsy if we're still for too long.'

'She's cute,' said Maya.

'She can be. Listen, I'd—'

But she cut in. 'I need to get on, I've still got to hunt down peaches and cat food.'

'I think you're going to need a basket.'

She looked at what she was carrying. 'I always do this: come in here thinking I don't need one and end up with armfuls of groceries.' But the slight thawing didn't last long. 'Bye then.'

'I'll see you when you're back at work,' he said before she could walk away.

She stopped, seeming confused. 'Work? You weren't temporary for the shift?'

'I jumped in at the last minute with the blue team but I'm also here in town to start my new role as the critical care paramedic on the red team. To replace Carl.'

She frowned. 'Someone probably told me. I'd forgotten.'

Eva began shuffling about more in her buggy, a sure sign he'd stayed still far too long. 'No worries at all. I'd better get going with this one. I'll see you at the airbase when you're back.'

She said nothing, just went on her way.

'Women,' he muttered beneath his breath. Although perhaps she was thinking 'men' after his unwelcome comments at the wedding reception. He couldn't blame her, really.

'Do you think I've totally messed up my working life, Eva?' he asked, to no response.

He headed for the beer section. He wasn't a heavy drinker but when he got off shift and the house was quiet, Eva's bedtime routine depending, there was nothing nicer than a cold beer. Previously, he would've drunk it on the sofa with a view of the lights of London's surrounds but nowadays, he'd take it and sit on the back porch at the old signal box cottage looking out at Whistlestop River. Quiet, unassuming towns weren't his bag, but the ritual would be a respite and a way of keeping himself together when everything he knew so well had been blown apart.

Once he'd been through the checkout, he stashed all the shopping in the basket beneath the pram save the box of beers, which he cradled under one arm. But steering was nigh on impossible as he left the supermarket and he was halfway along the row of cars heading for his own when it began to slip.

'Here, let me help,' said the man coming towards him. He wasted no time taking the box so Noah could put both hands back on Eva's stroller.

Noah smiled. 'Frank. Good to see you again.' Frank was the engineer at the airbase and according to Nadia, he went above and beyond the call of duty and was at the airbase more hours than he really had to be, ensuring the helicopter was fit for purpose. 'And thank you.'

'No problem.' He crouched down and Eva warmed to him

instantly, reaching out for his moustache, which sat like a big, fluffy caterpillar across his top lip.

'Careful or she'll pull it really hard,' Noah advised as Eva tried to get a grip.

'Oh, she's fine, aren't you, little one?'

Noah chuckled. 'Don't say I didn't warn you.'

And because Frank was one of those guys you felt comfortable blabbing to and who seemed to have all the time in the world for people he liked, when he asked about Eva as they walked back to the car, with Frank still holding the box of beers, Noah found himself summarising his life story right there and then outside the town's supermarket.

7

'Good morning,' Bess trilled when Noah arrived at the airbase for his fifth shift with the red team. He hadn't had to face Maya yet (unless you counted the time at the supermarket) because she was still off work helping her ex-husband.

'You're very chirpy in the mornings,' he said. Bess's personality was a riot, much like her curls but from what he'd seen so far, Bess also had a heart of gold and a good rapport with everyone around her.

She pulled a face. 'Not a morning person?'

'I am usually.' He rubbed his face a few times with both hands. He was settling into a routine already. Geraldine and Eva were too, but it was still a big adjustment coming here. 'Eva kept me up all night.'

Bess tutted. 'At least you got some action.'

Frank was with them and probed at Bess's own private life. 'The last blind date didn't work out?'

She grumbled. 'No. The guy was terrible, ate with his mouth open for the entire date at a steak house and then sat with a tooth-pick getting the remains out of his teeth.' She shuddered. 'There are literally no decent men left, Frank. They broke the mould when they made you.'

Frank laughed. 'Ain't that the truth.'

But Bess zoned in on Noah again. 'I admire your honesty, by the way, although you might be erring on the side of TMI talking about a woman keeping you up all night.'

He and Frank exchanged a knowing grin. His shifts here so far had been unbelievably busy and he'd kept it professional as much as he could, wanting to get to know the people he worked with before he shared too much. He needed to suss out how things worked at Whistlestop River Air Ambulance compared to his previous job. He'd shied away from sharing his life story with anyone other than Frank, and Frank was the soul of discretion. What he'd also learned was that Bess had a penchant for finding out people's life stories; Frank had warned him to expect questions soon enough, but watching her itching to dig into his personal life was kind of amusing and kept both him and Frank entertained.

Bess was tapping her pencil against her fingers at the desk in the office. 'Eva... nice name... let me guess, legs as high as the Eiffel Tower, gorgeous curves in all the right places, a sensible job which means she's likely lying in your bed right now given it's a weekend.'

'You've got a weird way of describing people,' said Noah, enjoying this more than he should.

Frank butted in with a knowing wink in Noah's direction as he shrugged on his jacket. 'I've met her.'

Bess sat up straighter. 'You have?'

'She's cute,' said Frank, 'in a chubby, squidgy kind of way.'

'Frank!'

But Frank, amused at his own quick wit, waved and left them to it.

Bess poked her pencil into her pile of corkscrew curls. 'It's not like Frank to be disrespectful to the fairer sex.'

Noah couldn't resist carrying it on a bit longer. 'She's got these little rolls of fat on her arms too; it's a sign she's eating enough.' Bess's mouth fell open. 'Her legs, seeing as you mentioned those, are pretty short. She doesn't have a lot of hair and very few of her own teeth.'

At Bess's expression, he began to laugh. 'I'm messing with you. Eva isn't a girlfriend; she's an eleven-month-old baby.'

Now she was alert to forthcoming information. 'Wait... you have a baby?'

'Yeah, kind of.'

'You can't *kind of* have a baby.'

She was right. Either he had one or not. Either he was the parent or he wasn't.

This morning, after a disturbed night with Eva as well as heavy rain that lashed against the windows of the cottage, he'd driven to work and seen the brightest of rainbows in the sky. Before he thought about it, he was talking out loud, saying, 'Eva, look at that, all those colours.' And then he'd realised she wasn't in the car with him but back at the old signal box cottage with Geraldine. It was moments like that one that reminded him how Eva was now a major part of his life.

But Noah was really struggling because whilst at first he'd been committed to bringing up Eva, as the days went on, he became more and more unsure that he was even capable. He didn't feel cut out to be a parent, to be daddy to this incredible human being who deserved so much more than he had to give. Even today, when he'd left the house, he'd known Eva was way better off with Geraldine than with him. Geraldine made her laugh more, Geraldine knew what to do when she was upset and how to calm her down. Last night, Eva had been up three times, crying uncontrollably, and nothing he could do would make it stop. Geraldine had swooped into the house this morning with an air of Chanel No. 5 and a can-do attitude and scooped Eva up into her arms, settling her within seconds.

'She's teething,' Geraldine told him. 'Oh, you poor little thing,' she whispered into Eva's delicate blonde hair. 'Noah, do you have a teething ring?'

One look from Noah gave her the answer.

'Would you mind if I drove out to get one today?' she suggested, calm as you like. 'I have a car seat installed; we can check it now so you'll know it's safe.'

'I have to get to the airbase.' Yet he knew this was his responsibility. And only his. 'But let's go take a look, not that I'm an expert.'

With Eva in Geraldine's arms, they went out to her car and she showed him the seat facing backwards and secured properly, much the same as the seat he had in his own car.

'Anything that settles her down is fine by me,' he said as they went back into the house. 'And there's cash in the box on the kitchen counter.'

'Oh, we'll deal with money things later, won't we, young Eva?' Her voice had changed to the *universal baby tone* as Noah referred to it, the slightly high pitch that fell to a low pitch now and then as though the seesaw in volume was somehow all a part of the illusion for a child. It was a voice he hadn't quite brought himself to use yet. He was holding a part of himself back because he was scared, because he wasn't sure. He had no idea whether he could really do this and if it wasn't going to be a permanent arrangement for Eva then he needed to work out what was before their bond grew stronger and it left all of them open to intense pain and distress when it was broken.

At the airbase, Bess was still waiting to hear more about Eva, this baby he *kind* of had.

'Eva is my niece. And it's a long story...' he said.

Bess leaned forwards, her voice soft, understanding. 'I've got plenty of time; we're quiet.'

Noah heard the sound of paperwork being dumped in the tray beside him and Nadia, the one responsible, let out a sigh. 'Bess, you'll jinx us with comments like that and we're scheduled for a training session in half an hour.'

When Nadia left them to it, he shifted the focus to Maya and the fact he was still nervous about working with her. 'I saw her at the supermarket, you know.'

'When?' It was enough for Bess to latch onto a different direction for their conversation as she was obviously worried about her friend.

'Earlier in the week.'

'And how did she look to you?'

'I don't really know her well enough to comment but at the wedding, she was concerned about her sister yet in control, and when I saw her shopping, she seemed tired, worried.'

Bess's concern gave way to a tut and a sigh. 'That's because she's racing around after her *ex*-husband when she shouldn't be. I mean, I'm not a total bitch, I know he doesn't have any close relatives, but he's on the force, he knows people.'

'He's in the police?'

'He's a detective. Not here in Whistlestop River but in the next town and I heard enough of his colleagues turned up to see him in the hospital. You'd think it would take the burden off Maya, but she's not made it clear to the medical staff that they're no longer together. There's talk of discharging him but the doctors will only do so if there's someone at home with him.'

'Let me get this straight. He's her ex-husband and they no longer live together?'

'Correct. The divorce finalised nearly two months ago.' She opened her bottle of water. 'Conrad seems to have missed the memo about that, though. And now if the hospital assume they're together...' She shrugged. '...Maya will be saddled with the responsibility. For some reason, he clicks his fingers and she comes running when what she really needs to do is tell him to—'

The shrill alarm of the phone put a stop to the completion of Bess's sentence and everything else they were doing. Noah picked it up, the temporary pilot filling in for Maya went out to start the helicopter and it was action stations once again.

'Told you,' Nadia called to Bess as she and Noah picked up their helmets. 'Don't you ever say we're quiet again.'

'Sorry!' Bess hollered back before they went out to the waiting aircraft on the helipad.

It wasn't long before they were up in the air, their focus shifting from talk of anything else to the patient who needed them.

* * *

Maya parked up at the hospital. She could hear helicopter blades chopping through the air up above and when she peered out of her driver's side window, she saw the familiar red and yellow air ambulance she usually flew passing overhead, likely on the way to a job.

A week ago, life had seemed simple enough, with a son she adored, a job she loved and she was continuing to do her best to make it clear to Conrad that the both of them had to move on properly, separately. But then there was the accident and she felt as though she was back where she was before, putting his needs before any of her own. And he knew he held the trump card, that he could use what he knew to get his way. Already, she was tired of toing and froing at the hospital to visit. His work colleagues came and went, he had a bit of a chat and a laugh with them, but those visits were infrequent. Isaac had come down from Scotland the day after the accident and he'd been an incredible emotional support.

He'd stayed to see his dad for a couple of days but Maya suspected the main reason he'd come was for her because the pair had barely spoken and Isaac's relief when he got to go back to Scotland was obvious.

Maya grabbed the bag from the backseat. She'd found Conrad's other iPad for him so he could keep himself entertained since the one she'd brought was glitchy and giving him no end of bother. Keeping Conrad's spirits up was no walk in the park and she needed all the help she could get. It was an exhausting, constant rally managing his temperament from one minute to the next. When he'd first woken up, he was grateful to be alive, and when he realised he'd make a full recovery, he was full of gratitude until gratitude gave way to frustration. From that point, everything became something to complain about – the glitching iPad nearly took a journey across the room but Maya had rescued it at the last minute. His fingers were sore, couldn't they give him stronger painkillers? His arm itched and he had nothing to poke down the plaster to scratch it. He threatened to yank the plaster off if he didn't get something to ease the discomfort soon. He was being a complete arse by all accounts.

Maya smiled at one of the nurses coming off shift as she went inside the hospital. 'How is he today?'

'Your husband is in good spirits,' the redhead replied tactfully because so was she; she was heading home.

'I'm sorry if he's been difficult.'

'All in a day's work, love.' The nurse smiled and went on her way.

Maya still hadn't corrected anyone's referencing of Conrad as her husband or her as the wife. The only time their divorce was mentioned was when she'd seen Conrad's bag of personal effects with a little pot containing his wedding ring. The doctors and nurses would have had to remove the jewellery before he went for any x-rays or scans when he first came in. She'd asked him why he was still wearing it and he'd bitten her head off, saying their marriage had clearly meant more to him than it ever had to her. He admitted he wore it when he wasn't around her, took it off when he was so she wouldn't have a go at him.

Maya said hello to the nurses outside the ward but before she could get to Conrad's bedside, one of them called her back.

'We hear you fly the air ambulance,' she beamed at Maya.

Maya smiled. 'That's right, I'm with The Skylarks.'

All three nurses were suitably impressed. 'You do a wonderful job, all of you.'

'Right back at you,' said Maya.

'My son,' said one of the women, 'dreams of flying the air ambulance one day. Any tips?'

'Has he tried flying yet? Had lessons?' Maya adjusted the bag on her arm, glad of a delay to visit Conrad. He was always on at her to stay longer as it was and being there for the whole of visiting time was exhausting.

'He's seven.'

'Then tell him to keep on aiming high; he'll get there if he really wants it.'

Persistence was what it took; she should know. She'd known ever since she was a little girl that she wanted to fly helicopters. She'd saved her birthday and Christmas money every year in the gold pot of dreams moneybox her mother gave her. It was nowhere near enough but she added to it over the years with cash from weekend jobs, from part-time positions she grabbed hold of whenever they came her way. And once she finished school, she worked as a temp in offices around Dorset, she waited tables, she worked behind a bar, each job part of her pursuit to get the funds to one day fulfil her dream. It wasn't always easy to find work and for a while she hadn't had any, but she'd taken what she could when she could.

Maya was married by the time she had enough money to put herself through the rigorous training required to become a helicopter pilot. At first, Conrad had supported her, ever the husband wanting his wife to be happy, but it hadn't taken long for his distaste to show through. He'd thought she'd give up on the preposterous idea when she got pregnant, but she studied all the more, especially in the final few weeks of her pregnancy, when she wasn't able to work. Whenever she got the chance, she had those books open, her brain engaged. And after Isaac arrived, she slowed right down to take care of their son, but the career choice never went away, much to Conrad's chagrin.

Maya continued with her study and her training once Isaac was at nursery and then school and by the time he moved on to secondary education, Maya landed her first job as a helicopter pilot. Yet Conrad still talked about it like it was her hobby rather than a proper career. With his disapproval and her dad's disinterest, it had made Maya all the more determined to carry on flying helicopters but her end goal shifted because she didn't just want to be a helicopter pilot; she wanted to be a HEMS pilot for the air ambulance.

And she'd done it, in spite of them all. Isaac and Julie were endlessly proud and told her all the time but a tiny part of her would always be sad that Conrad hadn't and her dad would rather talk about anything other than his daughter and her job with the Whistlestop River Air Ambulance.

When Maya reached Conrad's bedside at the hospital, she sat down in relief. He was asleep.

But the relief was short-lived when she heard him murmur, 'What, no kiss?'

So only resting his eyes then. She put a smile on her face and ignored the question. 'Did I wake you?'

'I wasn't sleeping, too bloody noisy in here.' Another complaint.

'That's hospitals for you.' He was sulking like a kid, not something she'd ever been able to coax him out of. *How about being grateful for the doctors and nurses who've been caring for you?* she wanted to yell at him, but instead she asked, 'Are you in any pain?'

'It's not so bad,' he harrumphed. 'They've said I can probably go home tomorrow.'

'That's great news.' And it would cut out her having to come to the hospital, having to abide by visiting hours. His place was much closer to hers than here was. But it wasn't so great in that it would still require her to give him a lot of attention, make sure he was all right at home recovering.

A change of subject now was the only way to mask how she was feeling. 'The cat flap is in so I've taken Whizzy to mine.' She would add that the cat missed him, was devastated at moving house, but she'd be lying.

'Thanks.' He said it as if she was doing him a favour, which she probably was. He'd likely grown bored of using the cat as a pawn in his game and now he had her instead.

She pulled out his iPad from the bag. 'I brought this in for you; it's fully charged and should be a lot better than the other one.' She set it onto the cabinet beside his bed.

Maya had spent time looking after the cat at Conrad's before the cat flap was fitted at her place, which worked out well as she'd had to bring bits and pieces in to the hospital for him. During the time Maya had spent at the house that was once also her home, she'd realised how many reminders there were of her, as though she'd never really left. There were pictures of them together on his walls, on the mantelpiece, on the hallway table, a photo of both of them with Isaac on his first day at school, their wedding photograph – she'd put her own away in a box and shoved it into the storage cupboard, likely never to be looked at again.

She took out the carton of chocolate milk she'd picked up at the supermarket for him and poured it into the cup on his bedside table.

He picked up the drink. 'When I'm home, I'll enjoy this in a proper long glass. None of this plastic crap.'

She stayed for about an hour and when the aroma of dinner preceded the delivery of meals to the ward, she saw the chance to escape. 'I'll let you eat.' She braced herself for his reaction to what she said next. 'I can't come back again tonight. I'm on shift tomorrow so I'll have to go to bed early.'

'You're going back to work?'

'You seem surprised.'

'Well, yeah, you've been here, you've been good to me, but you must be tired.'

'I am but I've got to get back to it at some point. I need the money. And I'd only go if I knew I was safe, remember.' And it was a good reason not to come by again, give her a proper break from all of this.

'I'll miss the company later on.' He kept his voice low. 'I'm on the bloody geriatric ward, Maya.'

She sensed the other patients' lack of willingness to chat with Conrad was probably more down to their own individual health concerns than anything else. That or he'd really pissed them off when his colleagues stopped by and made so much noise they'd had a couple of warnings from the nursing staff.

'I'll be in again tomorrow after shift, so in plenty of time before you're discharged,' she assured him and then because the look he gave her expected it, leaned in to kiss him on the cheek.

He turned at the last minute and caught the edge of her lips, his good hand ran up the back of her neck to pull her in for a proper kiss and when she went to pull away, he held her there gently.

'I'm really sorry, Maya, about this, about everything. I wasn't a good husband to you. You deserve better.'

She said nothing. These were words she'd never expected. Usually, he used veiled threats, he never apologised or admitted fault.

'I don't deserve you, being here now,' he said.

All she could say before she left him to it was, 'I'll see you tomorrow.'

Because Maya could only agree with what he'd said. He didn't deserve her at all. Not then and not now. But she'd do this for Isaac, for the sake of father and son, and because if she didn't, she knew full well how hard he would make things for her.

8

'Come on, Eva...' Noah knew getting irate wasn't going to help matters but he was tired – new job, new town, surprise parenthood, all of it was taking its toll. All he wanted now was for Eva to eat the cauliflower cheese portion he'd heated up followed by the stewed apples and settle down for the night so he could do the same. He was on the early shift tomorrow and needed a decent sleep.

But it seemed like he was asking for a miracle for Eva to cooperate. He grunted in frustration, Eva let out an ear-piercing wail, went rigid in her highchair, bright red in the face with anger at him, her food, the world.

'I know how you feel, Eva!' he yelled before stomping over to the window.

He wasn't proud of himself for losing it. But some days were easier than others. Some days, he felt in control and on top of things, in a routine. On other days, like today, he didn't.

He pressed his forehead against the glass and closed his eyes.

Eva was still wailing and he turned to look at her. They were both as helpless here as each other. She wanted this less than him, he suspected. She'd lost her mum, she had a poor stand-in parent with him, and here he was being an absolute arse.

He went over to her, unclipped the highchair harness and scooped her up in his arms. 'I'm sorry, I'm really sorry.' Her wet cheek, stained with fat tears, pressed against his.

He went out into the kitchen, the cauliflower cheese abandoned, and took out the nice cold portion of stewed apples Geraldine had put in the fridge in a little plastic pot.

A bit calmer, he said, 'Why don't we try this one?' And instead of taking her back to the restrictions of her highchair, he collected a kiddie spoon from the drawer and went outside to the back porch. 'At least if you smack this away like you did the cauliflower cheese, we're outside so no clearing up involved.' The cauliflower cheese had gone all over the arm of the sofa when she'd unceremoniously hit out at the spoon he was holding because she wouldn't pick it up. Of course, the mixture had run down into the groove of the material too, which meant it would be harder to clean it all off.

Eva could lift up the spoon and feed herself but sometimes Noah had to take the lead and this was one of those times. He settled her on his lap and as the spoon went towards her lips, rather than her turning away or keeping them tightly shut, she opened wide and in went the stewed apples.

He'd never felt such relief, and at something so simple. 'You like this one? Thank goodness for that.' He got a second spoonful in before she could change her mind. Her forehead was sweaty, her hair stuck to her skin and her eyes were red from crying. Every now and then, she took in a ragged breath as she slowly calmed down.

As Noah fed Eva, he talked about the cottage that had once belonged to his grandparents, about Dorset, about the town of Whistlestop River. 'Your mum loved it here; even as a kid, she used to say she'd come back some day. Our parents were forever moving us around, but your mum said the countryside was the only place to bring up kids. Personally, I thought she was mad, I'm more of a city guy, but sitting out here, I'm inclined to admit she had a point.'

The sun had begun to set, the sky taking on a burnt-orange hue that fell across the river to give it a mystical sheen. The leaves on the trees beyond lost their colour with the fading light and silhouettes of branches danced across the water's surface. As Eva's body relaxed against his and she had more of the stewed apples, he looked down at her. 'I'm not very good at this parenting business, Eva. But for some reason, your mum, my sister, thought she was doing the right thing leaving you with me and I wanted this to work, I really did...'

His voice caught and he stopped talking. It didn't matter that Eva would have no idea what he was saying; he did, and he hated himself for it. He hated that he was a failure at the role he'd been given to do. He'd had no preparation, neither had Eva, and if it wasn't for Geraldine and having a job to escape to every day, he was pretty sure he would have totally lost it by now.

When Eva began to fuss again, not long after she finished her apples, he felt his tension rise. What if she was only a fidget away from a full-scale meltdown again? He wasn't sure he could handle much more. Not tonight.

He rocked her gently; that didn't work. He stood up and paced with her up and down the porch; that didn't work either. He sat down again and thought perhaps she wanted to look out to the river like he was rather than her view being of the side of the porch, but by now she was drooling and chewing on her fists.

Noah was close to calling Geraldine to ask what to do when he remembered his brilliant nanny had bought these funny rings she called teething rings and put them in the fridge. He'd seen Eva with one in her mouth before Geraldine left; he'd washed it when she dropped it and popped it back in the fridge before attempting the fiasco that was dinner.

He went into the kitchen and plucked the bright-orange ring

from the top shelf next to all the little portions of Eva's food in their tiny containers. As soon as he handed the ring over, Eva grasped it and put it straight in her mouth.

And she calmed down again.

Reprieve… for now.

'See what I mean by I'm not very good at this,' he said as darkness replaced any colour in the sky and the only light came from the wall lights out on the porch. 'Geraldine knew what to do when I didn't. She's the sort of parent you need, not me. Cassie was crazy to think this would work.'

They stayed out on the porch until Eva stopped sucking on the teething ring and her eyelids grew heavy. He'd learnt along the way that at this stage, it was a case of getting in there quick – when a baby was soothed and on the road to slumber, you didn't push it and make them overtired. He'd done that more than once and always paid the price.

Inside, he changed Eva's nappy with the lights in the smallest room of the cottage down low, he warmed her a bottle of formula and she drank every last drop, the latter part while she was almost asleep, before he settled her into her cot.

He tiptoed out of the room and pulled the door to behind him.

Another day, another bedtime, another tick on the survival spreadsheet for him.

With a cold beer, he went back to his position on the seat on the back porch. A night owl hooted from somewhere, a creature moved in the bushes beyond, creating a rustling of leaves. It was a far cry from the soundtrack of the city – sirens at night, voices outside at all hours, sounds he'd strangely got used to. Perhaps it would be the same here; perhaps he'd grow accustomed to the sounds of relative silence after a while.

Noah and Cassie's grandparents had lived in this signal box cottage after it was handed down to them by their grandmother's father, who worked with the railways. Noah and Cassie had come here a lot as kids, always enjoyed the adventure of being allowed to run along the path beside the river, fish using their colourful nets, even go out in a little rowing boat in the summer. The cottage had passed down to Noah and Cassie's parents but their father had always had a yearning to return to his native New Zealand and that was what they had done. They'd tried to persuade Noah and Cassie to go with them, told them tales of the wonderful life they could have, but by then Noah and Cassie had been settled here and stuck to holiday visits. Those had ended when both of their parents died within three years of each other. Their house in New Zealand had been sold to pay off the mortgage, while the signal box cottage had become Noah and Cassie's.

Noah and Cassie had agreed to rent the cottage out. He'd gone to London to join an air ambulance team; Cassie had taken a job as a legal secretary about an hour away. But she'd always said eventually she wanted to buy him out, live in the cottage herself. And he'd agreed; it would suit her down to the ground. Cassie's plans didn't change when she had Eva either. The flat she was in became even smaller, she said, she was more than ready for a big, big change and with the baby's father not in the picture – something Cassie rarely talked about, which had Noah wondering whether the guy was married or had something else to hide – she had nothing stopping her.

What stopped Cassie's lifelong dream and plan was the day she died. Eva was seven months old and Cassie was due to start back at work and utilise their creche. Cassie had always been a planner, she took things in her stride, and maternity leave and motherhood were no different. Eva was her world, and Cassie was Eva's. Cassie took her daughter away on a glamping weekend in Dorset where there were other parents and children and she'd planned a couple of hikes with Eva in the rigid baby carrier she wore on her back so well. It all sounded like a dream trip for them both before Cassie returned to work but it hadn't turned out that way. Cassie had left Eva with another mum and gone horse riding along the beach at sunset. It should've been a beautiful experience, but her horse had fallen, taking Cassie with him. The wait for medical help had been a lengthy one due to emergency services being deployed elsewhere. By the time help came, it was too late. And it was something that made Noah seethe if he thought about it too hard.

He would never forget that day. He'd never forget the call informing him of the accident, the doctor's voice as he gave him the shocking news, the journey from London to Dorset. He'd always remember Eva's cries mixed with his own as he walked the corridors of the hospital, leaving his sister behind for the very last time. He could still see his good mate Sid putting Eva into the car seat in the back of his own car and transporting them both back to his place, where they had enough baby paraphernalia to allow him to start learning this role of parenthood from scratch.

Eva had been safe in another woman's arms at the time of Cassie's accident; she was going to be fine. Except for having no mother, except that he'd become her parent in an instant. It was her and him against the world from now on. And he wasn't sure that was going to work.

Noah had known ever since Eva was born that he would be the guardian should anything happen to Cassie and he'd assured his sister he'd never have it any other way. The day she told him her wishes, she also informed Noah that in the event of her death, she wanted Eva brought up in Dorset. He'd wrapped her in a hug and said, 'You and your idyllic countryside life.' She'd shoved him, told him to take it seriously which he'd insisted he was but really, you never thought those wishes committed to paper would ever really surface, did you? He, like a lot of others, especially siblings who weren't that different in age, simply accepted the request and life carried on pretty much as normal.

When Noah lost Cassie, he hadn't immediately decided to head for Dorset. But his circumstances had made it the better option. And once he'd made the decision to relocate, the signal box cottage and life here became the link he saw to giving Cassie's daughter the future she deserved. Or at least that's what he'd thought before he realised what a crap parent he was.

Noah finished the last of his beer, but the peace was soon lost when he heard Eva crying. Again.

He let her go on for a couple of minutes but even he, with his lack of parental knowledge, knew that it was the sort of cry that was going to go on and on and on if he didn't do something.

He tried the other teething ring but this time, Eva wasn't having any of it. He tried putting on the mobile above her cot but that didn't work. She was kneeling now, her little fists at the bars of her cot as though she was a prisoner trying to escape the cell she was in.

'I know how you feel, Eva.' He moved to pick her up but then smelt the culprit. Most times when he changed the nappy pre-bottle, they were good, but given the aroma snaking its way around right now, it hadn't happened this time.

He lifted her out and put her onto the changing table mat. She thrashed from side to side, when he took off the nappy the contents would've had him stepping back in horror if he didn't know that you never ever left a baby unattended on a changing table. She twisted again and he tried to steady her, putting his hand in poo, which had him dry-heaving.

It took a good forty minutes to get that messy nappy off, clean her up, put another one on, sort himself out, get Eva calm again. And this time, after he settled her in her cot and pulled her door almost closed, he leant against the wall next to it. 'I'm sorry, Eva. I'm sorry, Cassie.'

This wasn't working. He couldn't do it. He was useless and Eva deserved a proper parent.

And the only option he could see was to find Eva's biological father. Married or not, as old as the hills or not, he didn't care. The guy had to be better than him, didn't he? It's what Cassie would've really wanted, wasn't it? For her daughter to be raised by a proper parent.

9

Maya had only been off work for a week but they were already into June and coming back today was like a breath of fresh air. A bit of normality. With her people again, doing what she loved. At least it was until she remembered the new recruit. They'd not got off to a very good start at her sister's wedding reception, but the encounter in the supermarket had been manageable and Maya hoped he was as professional as she was and moved on quickly. The job had to be their focus, nothing else.

Maya began her day the same way as she usually started a shift. She went to the desk she shared with Vik, or whoever was the pilot on the blue team, and checked the handover book, the log and whether any notices had been filed with an aviation authority regarding impending hazards or obstacles that might dictate the flight paths chosen today. There was only one, identifying a crane being used at a construction site twenty miles away, as well as an air show thirty miles in a different direction. The air show wouldn't be underway until well after her shift was over, but it was good to be aware in case her shift ended up being longer than it should be, something that happened with regularity depending on when the jobs came in and how long they took. She checked the weather conditions and then it was time to get Hilda ready.

The Whistlestop River Air Ambulance was operational for nineteen hours a day. Two shifts worked those nineteen hours with the time between 2 a.m. and 7 a.m. uncovered and the helicopter kept inside the hangar. Now it was time for Maya to use the tow cart to pull Hilda out and into position on the helipad before carrying out a thorough pre-flight check of the aircraft.

Training for the air ambulance crews was ongoing. There was always something to keep current with, and once Hilda was ready, it was into the briefing room for the organised session. Today, they focused on transfers and paediatrics, ran through various scenarios to work as a crew and decide what they would do in that situation. Nadia threw different things into the mix – inclement weather, a patient with co-morbidities, gave them locations they could see on the iPad which didn't have easy surrounds for landing the helicopter.

Maya surreptitiously watched the new recruit. She had to hand it to Noah, he seemed to know what he was doing on the job – he certainly had plenty of past experience – and neither of them had referenced their run-in at her father's house nor the supermarket. She liked that already about him, that he could leave what happened outside of the workplace behind. All he needed to do was watch what comments he made and not offend a patient or their family. But she supposed they'd all been there; she had. It was a definite learning curve. In the early days with the crew, she'd forgotten their patient's wife was with Bess and Carl as she rushed to help carry the scoop back to the helicopter. She'd made a remark that she was surprised the patient was still alive, something that really hadn't been necessary to say, but given the call and what they'd been warned to expect at the scene, she'd been shocked that it wasn't a fatality. The driver had crashed on the motorway, gone through the windscreen of the van he was driving. Maya had hated herself when she registered the patient's spouse that day. The woman seemed in such shock she hadn't heard. But Maya had never done it again.

They were only called out on one job during the morning shift – a twenty-minute flight took them to a girl who had fallen from a quad bike and had abdominal injuries and a compound fracture to her lower leg. The crew attended to her and airlifted her to the nearest trauma centre before returning to base. Patient and family liaison nurse Hudson had already been in touch with the family to talk about the girl's condition and his role from now would be to guide the patient and their loved ones as to what to expect during recovery and to provide a support base in the days ahead.

In the locker room at the end of the shift, Maya changed out of her flight suit and pulled on a pair of jeggings and a fresh T-shirt. When Noah came in, she gave an acknowledging nod in his direction. The locker room was unisex and they were all used to whipping clothes on and off before, during or after shift, but it was always a little strange when someone new worked with the crew.

Time to be polite, pretend they'd never ever had cross words. 'How are you settling in?' She turned in time to witness his T-shirt being discarded and the fresh one he'd grabbed from his own locker halfway down a muscular torso. You had to be fit in this job and he definitely lived up to that. Maya was glad Bess hadn't been here to catch her looking because she'd definitely have a smart remark or two to share right now.

'Put it this way, I'm glad it was a quiet shift; not sure I could've handled a busy one.'

'Happens sometimes, might be the total opposite next time.'

'I expect it might be.'

Bess poked her head around the door to the locker room.

'Who's up for the pub around 4 p.m.? I'm going, Nadia says she'll make it by six, Hudson is up for it.'

'Not for me,' Noah said, and Maya didn't miss a note of regret in his sigh. 'I've got to get home.'

'Babysitter issues?' Bess asked.

'Something like that.' Noah smiled at them both, picked up his things and said goodbye.

Bess came inside, scooped her riot of curls up into a ponytail and deftly tied it with the band that had been on her wrist. 'What's the story there?'

'How would I know?' Maya picked up her bag.

'You know he has a kid, right?'

'I know.'

'It's his niece, apparently.'

That had Maya's attention. But not for long – she had enough going on in her own life right now to worry about someone else's.

'Do you think he has a wife or a girlfriend?' Bess pondered out loud.

'I've no idea.'

Bess pulled a wrapped-up portion of flapjack from her bag. 'Doesn't it bug you?'

'He's only just joined us; maybe let him take a breath before you find out his life story.' But Bess was the most inquisitive person she knew; she'd want to know all of it, right now. 'You do like to get to know people, don't you?'

'Nothing wrong with that. I like openness, to know what's going on. I lay all my cards on the table. I know not everyone does…' She sighed. 'And that frustrates the hell out of me.'

'Don't I know it,' Maya laughed.

Bess let the subject of Noah and his personal life drop. 'So, pub for you?'

'Can't, it's Conrad's discharge today and I'm picking him up. What? Don't give me that look.'

'I'm not giving you any look.' To Maya's frown, she paused before she took another bite of her flapjack. 'All right, I am. I get that he has nobody else – although a force of police officers could offer up some options.' She held up her hand. 'I'm only saying, it's not like he'd be stranded.'

'The doctor doesn't want him home alone for the first few days; if he is, they'll keep him in. The sooner he's out, the sooner he'll recover and not need me around and I can get on with my own life.'

Bess fixed Maya with her stare. 'Do not tell me you're his nurse until he sees fit to dismiss you.'

Unfortunately, that was going to be the case. But Maya wanted to deflect away from it and so she said, 'You make him sound worse than he is.' Actually, Bess had him pretty much pegged, but Maya had to toe the line, at least for the time being.

'He likes to have you at his beck and call, that's all.'

'I will be at first but I won't do it for long. And I didn't visit him last night; I was firm about that.' She couldn't look like a complete pushover; Bess would never let her be that. She was a good friend. But she also knew Maya's feelings about Isaac and her desire to see him and his father at least try to work things out. 'He knows I have a life outside of what was once our marriage.'

'Does he, really?'

'Okay, so he's taking a while to accept it. But Bess, this is temporary.'

Bess chewed thoughtfully. 'You're too nice, that's your problem.' She had the last morsel of flapjack ready to pop into her mouth. 'Be careful, Maya. I can't help thinking he's playing you. He might not have planned this, but you have to admit it's kind of working out well for him. He never wanted to let you go.'

She looked at Bess as she picked up her bag and slung it over her shoulder. 'Try not to worry; I'm not getting sucked back in to being with him.'

Bess was right. Conrad hadn't ever wanted to let her go. But what Bess didn't know was that even if Maya wanted to, she couldn't simply walk away, not with the things he knew about her, things she never wanted to share.

As the girls left the locker room, they bumped into Frank. 'Maya, how are you doing?' His moustache covered his top lip and then some, and his skin was weathered with a tan that never faded from a life outdoors sailing boats before he'd become an engineer.

'Not too bad, thanks, Frank. And it's always good to be back at work doing what I love.'

He winked at her. 'That's our girl, isn't it, Bess?'

'Sure is,' Bess beamed. 'We missed her.'

'And how is Conrad?' Frank ventured. He knew the deal with him, the times Maya had tried to leave and never had, how much happier she was since the divorce was final, but the concern about her son and his father was never far from her mind.

'He's on the mend, discharged today so I'm sure it won't be long before he's back at work.'

'He was lucky.' Frank was here often enough to hear some of the horror stories. Sometimes the team came back in good spirits having safely got to a patient in time to not only save them but give them the best outcome. But other times, when the stories were grim, the outcomes not hopeful, Frank could see it on their faces, heard the hopelessness and regret in their voices. 'Well, send Conrad my regards for a speedy recovery.'

'Will do.' Maya knew what that meant too. It meant she should remember Frank to Conrad and that would serve as a reminder to him that Maya had plenty of people looking out for her should she need it. Over the years, Frank had been more of a father figure than her own could be. He was easy to talk to... he came here and did more hours than necessary and she knew why. He was lonely. His wife had passed away a decade ago and he'd drunk himself into oblivion until Bess, close to him also, had guided him to some counselling. Nowadays he rarely drank at all, he seemed content in his life and his work. Sometimes it made Maya sad, though, that perhaps he needed a little something more in his life other than work. Didn't they all?

* * *

There was a light shower as Maya drove to the hospital but by the time she arrived, it had finished and the puddles in the car park and on the pavements were already beginning to disappear.

When she reached the ward, the doctor was finishing up with Conrad and Conrad looked relieved to see her. Perhaps despite the hold he had over her, he had, even for a short moment, doubted she'd turn up. 'Here she is, Doc.'

'Hello, Maya. Good to see you again. He's all yours,' the doctor said before he went off to continue on with his rounds.

Conrad was already dressed and a bag of his belongings sat packed up on the chair beside the bed. 'I'm good to go.'

'That's great.' As she'd said to Bess, the sooner he got home and started proper recovery, the sooner Maya could begin to fade into the background as much as she could.

'Thanks again for doing this, Maya.'

Did she really have a choice? 'No worries.'

He lowered his voice. 'If you hadn't stepped up and said you'd help me, they'd have kept me in for longer. And I'll go insane if I have to spend another moment in here.'

Maya also knew that if he stayed much longer, he'd really piss someone off. Already he kept snapping at doctors and nurses, he'd moaned at the lack of privacy more times than she cared to remember, he'd abused the visiting rules and had too many rowdy people at his bedside. Some of the nurses were uncomfortable with his behaviour, although most were brilliant and took none of his shit, something Maya had quietly thanked them for whenever she left the ward after visiting.

'I need to get home for my sanity,' he grumbled. 'And you won't need to watch me like a baby; this is all so they let me out. Once I'm at home, I'll be fine.'

'I'll keep an eye on you, Conrad.' She knew he'd only said it to test whether she would hang around, to know whether he needed to deploy those threats he liked to issue whenever he felt she was pulling away that little bit too much.

'Why? I'm not going to be leaving the house for a while – not like I can go out on my bike, given it's a write-off.'

'I'll do it because the medical team advise it.' And because if she didn't, she'd soon know about it from him, despite the pretence otherwise, the claims that he hated being an imposition.

'I'll take the help today but perhaps I can have a word with one of the guys at work, see if they know someone who can come by every day for a while. I don't want my incapacity to fall to you; it's not your responsibility.'

He really was digging into his acting skills now. But she wasn't stupid. This was all part of his master plan, she knew; he was clever that way, pushing enough but not too much.

She might be kidding herself but her theory was that sooner or later, he would accept their marriage really was over and he'd grow tired of playing games. And if he didn't? Well, that meant that at some point she'd have to deal with him in another way.

She couldn't be frightened of him forever, worried about what he might say.

But right now, she didn't see a way out.

10

When it came to searching for Eva's biological father, Noah didn't have much to go on at all apart from the guy's name on Eva's birth certificate. But it was a start.

In the kitchen at the airbase, on a much-needed break after three jobs in quick succession, he made coffees for himself, Maya, Bess and Nadia and took his over to the table. He couldn't resist a bit more searching while he had a moment because over the last week, he'd come up with a big, fat nothing.

Paul Griffiths had been in Cassie's life so briefly that he and Noah had never met. Cassie and Paul had dated for only a couple of months before Eva was conceived and then during her pregnancy, the guy was offshore on an oil rig a lot, taking as much overtime as he could to supposedly put him in a good position to support his family. Noah, meanwhile, had a busy job of his own and saw his sister on snatched occasions. By the time Noah could take a few days off and meet Eva properly rather than the mad dash he'd made to the hospital to meet his niece for the first time, Paul had supposedly gone offshore to the rigs again for another stint as a mechanic.

Noah had known the first day he saw Eva in Cassie's arms that her daughter was his sister's whole world. She'd turned thirty-nine when she was pregnant and she'd told Noah that this was probably her one and only chance to have a baby.

Paul never did come back from offshore. There was no accident, no sudden tragedy. He simply disappeared from Cassie's life. There were tears from Cassie at first but not for long. Cassie had pragmatically carried on and Noah wasn't sure but he had wondered whether perhaps his sister was in fact glad at the turn of events. It frustrated him no end that now, he'd never be able to ask her why.

The only other information Noah had to go on about this guy Paul Griffiths was that he'd lived in the same town as Cassie, where they'd met at her local pub. He started a search on social media, thinking there had to be something there, but other than a few guys with the same name and getting his hopes up at the picture of an ocean next to one profile (which he thought might have implied the person worked out at sea, even on the rigs), he found nothing.

Bess came in to claim the coffee with one sugar and glanced over at Noah. 'You look like you've lost a tenner and found a quid.'

Noah frowned. 'I think the saying might be lost a shilling and found a penny... or is it lost a pound and found a penny?'

'Dunno,' Bess shrugged, 'but inflation changes things so I'm going with the tenner-quid version.' She peered over his shoulder and down at his phone screen. 'He looks beefy. Friend of yours?'

'Trying to find someone.' Noah closed the social media app. 'And that's not him.' Unless the father of his beautiful niece was young enough to be Cassie's son. The guy who'd got his hopes up was on a scuba-diving trip with sixth form according to the caption.

'Oh yeah, who?'

The thing about Bess was she liked to know what was what, but she was easily distracted when it came to the personal lives of the crew, so when Maya came in, she sighed. 'You and your stories,

Noah. One day, I'll find out all the details. Now, happy hour at the pub tomorrow, anyone?'

'Maybe,' he said, 'if I can get Geraldine over.'

'Do it,' she said, bossy as you like. He didn't miss Maya's grin at their colleague's persistence. And it was her turn next when Bess diverted her attention. 'Maya, what about you? Please don't say you can't; I've been trying to get you there for ages.'

When Maya smiled, she looked even more beautiful than when she was serious or concentrating on something. She was clever too; he liked listening to her talk about flight paths, technicalities with the helicopter. He had to wonder why with all her intellect, she was still giving that ex-husband of hers the time of day. He'd never met the man, not unless you included the night of his accident, but Noah had heard enough comments about Conrad here and there that he had a pretty good picture built up in his mind.

Maya picked up her own coffee and talk focused on happy hour, Bess trying to rally everyone to attend, but the phone let out its shrill ring to cut the conversation short and demand their attention.

Maya was first out of the door to get the helicopter ready. Noah and Bess abandoned their coffees in favour of grabbing the gear they needed for the job. The medical bags were stowed on the aircraft already but legally the drugs couldn't be left unattended so were kept at the airbase and retrieved each time they were needed. Blood was often left on the helicopter unless the temperatures were too hot or too cold. Today was the former, which meant Bess went to get those while Noah picked up the drugs.

Helmets on, Bess and Noah headed for the aircraft and inside of five minutes, they were soaring above the Dorset countryside. The crew batted back and forth in conversation about the job they were heading to. A horse rider had taken a fall when going over a jump at a local riding school and on approach to the scene, Noah thought about Cassie. He thought about her often but as soon as he'd heard the patient had had an accident involving a horse, it brought back the painful memories on a whole other level.

Putting his personal feelings aside, he spotted someone down below in a hi-vis jacket waving at them and pointed it out to Maya and Bess. Occasionally, people waved at the air ambulance regardless of whether they were in need of help, which wasn't particularly useful, but this time it was easy to suss out that this really was a wave meant for them to come in and land as close as they could to the patient.

'There are horses in the field on the right,' Bess advised from her position in the front.

From the rear of the aircraft, Noah could see three fields spread out to the left of the person in the hi-vis with easy access on one side. 'It's the best bet,' he said into his microphone. 'It's a bit of a walk for us but I don't see any other options.' And it looked like they could exit the field on foot, run down the laneway without having to climb any fences or cut back any bushes to do so.

The helicopter came in to land to Bess's call of, 'Clear on the left.'

'All clear on the right,' said Noah.

The crew touched down safely moments later.

'Thanks, Hilda,' said Maya, patting the inside of the aircraft the way she often did. It was another side to Maya, a softer side he quite liked. 'Good luck, you guys.'

Once Noah and Bess had the equipment bags on their backs and the bag containing the drugs, they trudged through the long grass to the other side and the lane.

A car pulled up with someone from the riding school and took them to the patient, saving them precious minutes as well as a long walk with a heavy load and Bess and Noah were at the patient's side in under two minutes.

Noah took the lead with this one. 'Hello there, can you tell me your name?' He was relieved their patient was conscious. The girl looked in her early twenties, slight and very scared.

'Clara,' she said quietly.

'Clara, I'm Noah, this is Bess, we're going to help you. But you need to lie still.' She was trying to move and it wouldn't help them or her if she did, given they didn't know the extent of her injuries.

'Milly,' she said all of a sudden, trying to move again. 'Milly... I have to collect Milly.'

The rider at his side told Noah that Milly was Clara's daughter and that she was at school. 'I'll call Clara's mum,' said the rider, 'let her know what's going on.' She crouched down to eye level with Clara. 'Don't you worry, your mum will collect Milly; she'll be safe.'

As tears welled in Clara's eyes, tears of relief and of pain, Noah thought again about Cassie and Eva, how lucky this girl Milly was that there was every chance of her mum making a good recovery judging by the injuries sustained. It would hopefully be a good outcome and he gulped at the reminder that his sister hadn't been so lucky.

The patient was given ketamine after paracetamol and morphine weren't strong enough to handle her pain while Noah and Bess stabilised Clara's leg.

Clara was soon on the scoop and they set off on the trek down the lane and into the field with the help of three other riders from the riding school. Maya ran over to them to take the drugs bag as soon as she spotted them and stowed it in the rear of the helicopter before the patient was transferred onto the litter from the scoop.

In the back of the helicopter, while he monitored the patient during transfer to the trauma centre, Noah reflected on the moment Clara had panicked about her daughter. Her daughter's welfare was her top priority, as it should be. And she was lucky; it sounded as though she had a grandparent to rely on. Noah didn't. He didn't have a partner either. There was nobody else aside from himself and Geraldine, who at the end of the day was an employee. What would happen to Eva if something happened to him? In all the commotion of the last few months, Cassie dying, him getting a daughter just like that, having to leave his job and his life and move down here, he hadn't thought about what would happen if he wasn't around.

And right now, it was a sobering, terrifying thought that if something happened to him then he'd let Eva down in the worst way possible. Because then she'd have nobody. Nobody at all. And his heart almost broke for the little girl.

* * *

Maya and Noah headed out of the airbase at the same time after their shift. The crew was in good spirits leaving for the day but not only that, they'd got their last patient the help they needed; it was a good outcome.

Noah slung his bag into the boot of his car.

'Here's trouble,' Maya grinned as a motorcyclist pulled in at the airbase. It was only when they took their helmet off that she knew which one of the Whistlestop River Freewheelers it was. 'Dorothy, hey there!' She waved over.

Dorothy ran a hand through grey, cropped hair a few times in quick succession to get it back to a style she'd be happy with and came over with more blood from the blood bank. 'You both finished for the day?'

'We are, blue team's turn now,' Maya smiled.

'Well done the both of you; go take a well-earned rest.' She smiled in Noah's direction; they'd met before.

Maya liked the way Noah smiled back at Dorothy, familiar with her already as though he'd worked here much longer than he actually had. Over time, their clash at her sister's wedding had been forgotten as they dug into their professional personas and did their jobs. But it wasn't only that: Maya was beginning to enjoy Noah's company. He seemed a genuinely nice guy and that wasn't always guaranteed; she should know, having picked Conrad only to find out he was nothing like she thought he was.

Dorothy headed inside the Whistlestop River airbase and Maya doubted Noah had missed the none-too-subtle wink in Maya's direction before she went.

'She seems a character,' said Noah. Perhaps he didn't want to think too much about what Dorothy's wink had meant either.

'Definitely. And she's lovely too. They're all remarkable people, don't you think? I mean, we get paid, but they do this out of the goodness of their hearts, covering miles and miles of the country day in, day out.' And now she was babbling to mask any discomfort that Dorothy might well have seen through her, the way she was looking at her colleague.

'Total heroes,' he agreed.

Maya liked where his heart was at. He must be a good dad. 'How's your little girl?'

'Eva's good,' he smiled. 'She slept through last night. That hasn't happened before now.'

'How old is she?'

'Almost twelve months.'

'She's very cute.'

'When she wants to be.'

When Maya's phone buzzed, she didn't check it. It would likely be Conrad asking where she was. 'I'll see you in a couple of days then,' she said to Noah. They were swapping to the late shift for a few days on the next rota.

'You're not coming to happy hour at the pub tomorrow night?'

'Oh... I...'

'Bess won't be happy if you're a no-show.'

Maya grinned. 'You do know that it'll be different from central London, don't you? You could probably get away with a lot more there than you ever will here. We're a decent sized town but just small enough that everyone knows everyone.'

'Noted.' His gaze held hers. 'So, you'll come?'

'I'll see.' And as she climbed into her car, she found herself wishing she could give him a definite *yes*.

11

Maya parked up outside Conrad's place, the house she'd once called home. She knocked twice but got no answer and eventually she let herself in. He was sitting in the lounge room.

'Didn't you hear me knocking?' she asked.

'I did... but I told you, you don't need to knock; you're here doing me a favour so let yourself in, treat it like your home.' He gave a wry smile. 'It was once upon a time.'

Whatever she said in reply would be wrong, so she simply closed the door behind her and went to put the kettle on. Anything to keep busy while she was here. Last night, she'd stopped by after shift and he'd tried to tell her the same thing about letting herself into the house. She'd taken the key to keep the peace but unless she thought there was something seriously wrong, she wouldn't be letting herself in in the future either. It would be too much like being married all over again and she wasn't going back there with him, not ever. Unfortunately, the term and official declaration of *divorce* didn't seem to hold the same meaning for Conrad as other people. Most would take it as a line drawn underneath a relationship but not him. He saw it as a line he could very much climb over whenever he wanted to.

'Milk is probably off,' he called out as she waited for the kettle to boil.

'Black tea it is then,' she said.

'Suits me,' he hollered.

It suited him but not her. She pulled out the milk from the fridge, sniffed it and there was no doubt it was well past its best-before date. She'd picked up a big bottle a few days ago, forgetting he didn't eat cereal or drink milk unless it was a splash in his coffee. She poured the remains down the sink.

'You not having one?' he asked when she took his drink into the lounge.

'No milk, remember.'

'I'm sure you could manage to take your tea black this once.'

'I can't stop, anyway, I need to go to the supermarket for you.' And she was almost glad at the lack of milk; it gave her an excuse not to loiter if she didn't have a cup of tea to finish.

He started his tea using his good arm to hold the cup and gave an almighty slurp because the tea was so hot. Oh, how she hated that sound.

'I'll go make a shopping list.' The less time she spent right next to him, the better.

She'd stayed two nights when Conrad initially came out of hospital. The doctors had advised he have someone with him for the first forty-eight hours after discharge and almost to the second she'd packed up her things and returned to her own place once the stint was over. Now it was only visiting and errands, bearable compared to being here all the time.

She quickly put together a list. She'd make batches of food, things that would last him a while and could easily be put, one-handed, into the microwave.

'What would I do without you?' he asked when she reappeared.

She hoped that at some point he'd actually find out, get on with his life like she was trying to do with hers.

He patted the sofa next to him. 'Sit with me for a minute.'

She sat down but only to put the list into her bag, which was on the coffee table.

'You on shift today?' he asked sleepily.

'Not for another couple of days but I've got lots to do at home; I want to do some painting near where the cat flap was fitted.'

'I knew it, the handyman messed it up, didn't he?'

'Not at all, the wall needed painting anyway and if I don't do it now, I'm not sure when I'll have a chance.' She had no intention of spending her days painting for a while, she was far too busy, but he didn't need to know that. She needed a few excuses to keep her out of this house as long as possible. 'And I have to do some batch cooking for you.'

'You could do that here.'

'Better at mine, I know what equipment I have, all the herbs and spices to use.'

His hand lifted momentarily and patted her knee. 'You're a great cook, Maya.'

'And you look tired.' She stood, moving away from his touch, and hooked her bag onto her shoulder. 'Go to bed, Conrad. Get a proper sleep.'

* * *

Once Maya had finished at the supermarket, an escape of sorts, she headed to the serenity of her own home. She made a beef stew, a chilli con carne and a chicken piccata all in the space of a few hours. She portioned all of it into small freezer bags, which was the easiest option given Conrad didn't have many plastic containers and she had nowhere near enough for this much food. The more she took around today, the fewer excuses he had to have her stop by with more rations of food.

It took Conrad a while again to come to the door when she arrived back at his place, but he looked brighter than before.

She headed straight for the kitchen with the box filled with food bags, jabbering on about what she'd made as if the faster she did it, the sooner she could be out of here.

'It all smells amazing,' he called after her from his place in the lounge.

She wondered whether he wanted something now and went through to ask him before she put all of the food into the freezer. That was when she spotted the box of beer in the lounge on the side table, the empty brown paper bags with the takeaway joint's logo on the front, suggesting his usual of burger and fries with a side of onion rings had likely been wolfed down prior to her return.

He followed the direction of her gaze. 'Jerry from work stopped by.'

She supposed it was a good thing that he had people other than her and it dawned then that the beer was likely why he looked more upbeat, alert.

'I'm missed at the station,' he went on. 'And before you assume the worst, I didn't have any of those beers. I can't with my medication, you know that.'

And she also knew what he was like. She could see at least three bottles standing empty near the box and she doubted his colleague had had all of them.

When he spotted her looking, he jumped in with further defence. 'You know Jerry, he likes a beer and a talk, so I cracked open a bottle.' He laughed. 'He didn't notice I wasn't even drinking it. I poured it down the sink when he wasn't looking.'

He was lying, of that she had no doubt, but instead of calling him on it, she said, 'It must've been good to catch up, have a bit of company. I'll go and put all the food in the freezer seeing as you've eaten something. It's labelled so take out whatever you need as you need it.'

He followed her this time. 'The doctor stopped by before Jerry turned up. Says another month off work ought to do it. He recommended light exercise and I have to go in for a check-up in a couple of weeks.' He tsked. 'He suggested when I go back to work, I might need to be on desk duty for a while. Can you imagine it? Me?'

'Not really.' Her smile was half-hearted at best.

'You know me so well.'

Unfortunately, she did.

Maya moved out of the conversation by heading for the discarded plates by the takeaway bags. Each of them had slops of ketchup on, one had a few discarded stubby fries.

'Here, let me take those,' he said.

'No, it's fi—'

He was having none of it, took the plates she'd piled one on top of the other. But his outing to the kitchen to dump them in the sink didn't go to plan when he stumbled into a wall and the plates went crashing to the floor.

He swore and Maya jumped. He swore again.

He froze in place, his good arm above him against the wall and she could see from his back that he was trying to take deep breaths and not lose it all together.

She picked up the plates, the food scraps and went to get a dustpan and brush. By the time she came back, he'd slumped onto the sofa and was rubbing his shoulder.

'Let me get you your painkillers.'

'I'm out,' he said. 'I forgot to ask you to get some more.'

'I'll go now.'

'No, it's fine, I'll manage.'

'You won't, you need them.'

'Then I'll come with you.'

'Conrad—'

'No, I'm coming, Maya. I'll go mental if I stay inside these walls any longer. Please, I won't even get out of the car; it's just a change of scene.'

She relented but only because the sooner they did this, the sooner she could bring him home and get going.

* * *

There was a parking spot right outside the pharmacy and Conrad waited in the car while Maya ran inside. And this time, she got him enough painkillers to last for a while.

'Maya,' a voice came from behind her as she let the door to the pharmacy fall closed after she came outside.

She turned to see Noah. 'Hey.'

'Hey, yourself.'

Maya looked at the little girl in the buggy. 'She's okay, isn't she?'

'What? Oh, yes, she's fine; I'm not going inside.' He indicated the pharmacy.

The sound of Conrad's window coming down on the car they were standing beside alerted her to the fact he wanted to be in on the exchange. She didn't even look at him but it was obvious Noah had registered his presence.

'I'm out for a sanity walk,' Noah continued when Maya's discomfort had her lost for words.

'I remember those when Isaac was little.' But she couldn't linger; already she knew this conversation would be dissected to the nth degree all the way back to Conrad's house. 'Well, it was good to see you.'

'See you at work,' he smiled.

Their exchange had been long enough that by the time Maya got in the car, Conrad's good fist was clenched on top of his knee, the vein in his temple pulsed and his lips stayed pursed shut but only until she pulled away from the kerb.

'Who was that?' he asked.

'I work with him.'

'Wasn't what I asked. Does pretty boy have a name?'

'Noah.'

'Noah... he building an ark or something?' He thought he was funny; Maya just hoped he'd let it go. But he didn't. 'He's interested in you.'

'Conrad—'

'I'm a bloke, I know the signs. Couldn't take his eyes off you.'

She gave way to her right and turned the corner. 'Neither could the baby but that doesn't mean she's interested in me, does it?'

He snorted. 'Watch yourself there, Maya.'

She knew that didn't mean he was worried about Noah treating her right if something were to happen between them. He meant watch what she did, or he'd make her life difficult in whatever way he saw fit.

She helped him back inside the house and dished out a couple of painkillers.

Conrad swore again after he swallowed the pills, his frustration showing through. 'I hate this, you know.'

Not as much as she did. But instead of labouring the point, she got herself back on course for what she needed from him. 'Did Isaac call today?' Their son had been good with contact since Conrad was discharged from the hospital. Maya had to wonder how much was for his dad and how much was as moral support for her.

'He called but he was on his way to another exam.' He said the word *exam* like Isaac was off to a pole-dancing class rather than studying to improve his future prospects. 'Good of him to care about his old man. Thought he might have hung around Whistlestop River a bit longer, though.'

'He came all this way from Scotland between exams, important exams,' Maya reminded him.

Conrad for once didn't leap in and accuse her of being on the defensive for her son. She watched as he laid his head back against the sofa as though his body was telling him he was doing too much too soon.

'Are you going to be okay on your own this evening?' *Please say yes.* Please say she didn't have to stay for too much longer.

'Watch a movie with me?'

'What?'

He had his eyes closed. There was no observing her closely like he usually did, the way he let others know he thought she belonged to him. 'You can choose what it is,' he said gently. 'I don't mind; I'd just appreciate the company.'

It was easier to do it than not. 'I'll stay another hour but then I have to get back to Whizzy.'

She picked up the remote control from the side table, ready to flip through Netflix and Prime and see what she could find. Anything to make the time pass as quickly as possible.

But she didn't absorb much of anything as Conrad began to fall asleep beside her. She wasn't thinking about a television show; her head was with the air ambulance's newest recruit, the kindness and excitement in his eyes earlier when they met in the street.

She was in trouble; a workplace romance had never been on her agenda. Especially with an ex-husband who refused to go away quietly.

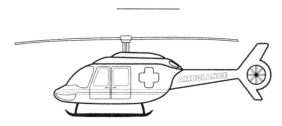

12

Noah had almost given happy hour at the pub a miss, he was so shattered, but after a whole day with Eva, he clung to the promise of some respite. And he already had Geraldine lined up to come over, he didn't want to mess her around.

Noah made his way from the signal box cottage to the Whistlestop River Inn. Steeped in history, with wonky walls, ancient beams and floorboards that creaked, the pub had a remarkably large beer garden out back overlooking the river itself. He'd come here once before since his arrival in town, but on his own, on an evening when he was much in need of a pint while Geraldine had her first shift with Eva, a short shift to test the waters for all of them.

The incredible sameness of days when looking after a baby was something that took a lot of getting used to and even though Noah and Eva had had a good day together without many meltdowns from either of them, his calmness had dissipated when he got a letter through the post and instead he felt tension, a sense of foreboding as to whether he was making the right choices in this situation.

Noah had started his search for Cassie's former partner Paul to no avail. Social media had drawn a blank and so had online forums for offshore workers with jobs on oil rigs. Nobody seemed to have heard of the guy. After Cassie died and Noah cleared out her flat, Cassie's former landlord had agreed to have the new tenant pass him any correspondence and he'd send it Noah's way should anything turn up. There would possibly be the odd person or business he hadn't yet informed of his sister's passing. Today, a brown envelope with Noah's handwriting – he'd left a few large, stamped, addressed envelopes with the former landlord to make it easier – arrived. He'd opened it to find a white envelope inside and that envelope had revealed a letter from none other than Eva's father. The letter, to Cassie, was brief and to the point. The man wanted contact. 'I'd like to see my child' were his exact words before requesting Cassie let him know when that could be arranged.

Noah had expected to feel elated when he found the man, positive that things would turn out fine. But he didn't. He was unsure, fearful, angry that the guy had run out on his sister and newborn baby. But you never knew what story people had until you asked it. There had to be a reason, didn't there? A reason other than Paul not wanting to be a father. Had he panicked at fatherhood? If he had, Noah understood it more now he'd had parenthood thrust upon him. And perhaps now, by Paul stepping up to the plate, it showed he wanted to be the best father possible for Eva.

As he pushed open the door to the ancient pub, Bess spotted him first.

'Noah, you're here!' Bess came over to him, bottle of beer held up high as she squeezed through the throng at the bar. 'Half an hour of happy hour left, get in there!' She gestured over to the bar.

Hudson, the patient and family liaison nurse, was getting a round in and kindly offered a drink to Noah, then, with a bottle of beer for himself and carrying a glass of wine for Nadia, he went to join the crowd. They were a great team, he'd settled in fast and tonight with beer, music and company, Noah should've felt on top of the world, especially given he'd found Eva's father. So why did he feel like he had a hole in the pit of his stomach?

The games of pool started, followed by darts, then more pool. They had small bets going, they had a laugh.

'How's that baby of yours?' Hudson, father of two, was on a rare night out but had already announced he was leaving by II p.m. or the missus would be sending out a search party.

'She's sleeping through the night a lot more,' Noah replied. 'Probably four nights out of seven.'

Noah had told people that Eva was his niece rather than his daughter, but it felt like some sort of betrayal when he did, like he was saying she wasn't his, implying she wasn't wanted. And it wasn't as simple as that. He never wanted anyone to think he was capable of cutting ties just like that.

Hudson rejoiced at his bullseye but was none too happy when Noah hit the triple twenty, the highest score on the board, to win the game.

'I'll stick to pool,' Hudson grumbled but his attention was grabbed by the latest arrival at the pub and he bellowed over to Maya to come join them.

Noah looked to where the pilot in his crew was making her way through the pub in jeans and a simple white shirt, and although she beamed a smile, there was a sadness, a weariness behind her eyes, the same look he'd seen in the supermarket the day after her sister's wedding. And after seeing that ex-husband of hers – he'd confirmed that was who it was with her in the car after talking about it with Bess when he got here – he could understand why her life might be hard right now. The way the guy had watched them, wound down his window so he could hear every word, it was creepy, possessive.

Bess gave Maya a hug and thrust a drink in her direction.

Noah put his pint glass on the windowsill in front of the stained-glass window so he could pick up the pool cue to start the game with Hudson. 'This can't be the original, can it?' he asked, pointing up at the coloured glass. The tiny windows in the master bedroom at his cottage were original and had much more wear and tear than this one.

'It's not,' Bess informed him. 'The original one was a beautiful colourful period piece but vandals broke it.'

'Charming,' he said.

'Yeah, that's one word for it,' Hudson remarked. 'I could think of a few others.'

While Hudson took his shot at the pool table, Noah watched Maya some more. He wished she didn't look so uncomfortable, like she wanted to walk away from the gathering at any moment. Perhaps whatever hold this ex-husband of hers had over her was taking its toll and she was tired of keeping up the pretence. She might even be embarrassed about the way her ex had behaved outside the pharmacy, looking at them like a disapproving parent when Maya was single and free to talk to whomever she pleased.

'An anonymous donation was received a few months after the window was smashed to cover the costs of a new one. Nobody ever found out who did that either,' Bess shrugged.

'Someone with a heart,' Hudson approved as Noah lined up his next shot. 'Hey, Maya, our man here would like to know how long it was before Isaac slept through the night.'

Noah stuffed up the shot and cursed. 'If you're referring to me, I didn't ask that.'

'No,' said Hudson, 'but always helpful to know.' He took his turn.

Maya smiled at Noah and told them both, 'He's eighteen. And I can't remember what I had for dinner last night, let alone remember those early days with a baby.'

Hudson nodded Noah and Bess's way. 'And she's responsible for getting you in the air and down to earth safely. Rather the both of you than me.'

While Noah circled the pool table, deciding on the best position for his shot, Bess and Maya sat on the stools behind them, out of the way enough for the cue not to be in their faces but not so far he couldn't hear what they were saying.

'What took you so long to get here?' Bess asked and Noah assumed Maya said nothing – he didn't hear anything – because Bess added, 'Don't tell me, Conrad again.'

'I had to lie to him to come out and not have to head over there again, Bess. I'm sneaking around trying to have my own life in the same way I did when we were married. I told him I'm meeting you for drinks; I didn't say anyone else would be here.'

'Do you remember the time he found out it was the whole team?' Bess asked.

'Which time? He did it more than once. He'd show up, Isaac in tow.'

'I seem to remember Conrad claiming he and Isaac were out for a father and son beer,' Hudson joined in, which told Noah that his suspicion was correct, the whole team knew what Conrad was like and Maya's feelings towards him.

Bess sniggered. 'Yep, forgetting Isaac wasn't even old enough to drink at that stage.'

Noah had to ask the girls to shift a bit to their right so he could take a shot. Hudson accused him of stalling and trying to out-psyche his far superior opponent.

Bess was still doling out advice behind him. 'I know you feel you owe it to Isaac to do everything you can to give him a relationship with his dad, but there are only two people who can do that and neither of those people are you.'

Maya recounted some story about Conrad dropping plates; Noah didn't quite catch it all as he continued with the game.

He moved out of Hudson's way so he could get in at the right angle and caught more of the girls' conversation.

'It happens with major concussions, Maya. I'll give him that,' said Bess.

'At least I've got custody of Whizzy now.'

Whizzy? Who was Whizzy?

Whoever Whizzy was, the girls clinked their glasses and smiled at each other.

It was only when Maya went off to the bathroom that Noah asked Bess what the deal was with their pilot and her ex-husband. He'd already mentioned bumping into her outside the pharmacy.

Bess's brows knitted together. 'Why do you want to know?'

She didn't miss a thing, but he wasn't about to share how he felt about Maya – that she was unexpected, that from the moment he'd met her he knew there was something special about her, even though they hadn't got off to the greatest start.

'What, so you can ask me about my private life, about Eva, but I can't ask any questions about anyone else without having a reason?'

Bess swigged her beer. 'Didn't say that, and how is Eva, by the way? I still know nothing about why you have your niece. I have my theories.' Probably the correct one given the softness in her voice now.

'Eva is good.' Perhaps if he wanted any information about Maya, it was time to be honest about himself. And with Paul in the picture, things might be about to change.

Bess sat forward, intrigued as he recalled the story about Cassie, and when he finished she got up, wrapped her arms around him and hugged him tight. 'I'm sorry, Noah, that's really awful. You must be heartbroken.'

'Taking each day as it comes. It's all I can do.' He picked up his beer before probing again about Conrad.

'Maya is helping him out by taking him readymade meals, being there on and off. Apparently he's not all that steady on his feet.'

'You don't believe it?'

'Not for me to decide.' She sipped from her bottle, disappointed to find it empty.

'So if he's her ex then why is she doing it for him?'

'Ties… with her son, I guess she feels she should. I don't know, I wouldn't if I was her, but if there's one thing I'll say about Maya, it's that she's strong-willed and it's difficult to change her mind about anything. She has a confidence in what she does. Good job, given she's a pilot.'

'Amen to that.'

After Maya returned, he watched as she and Bess took their turn at the dartboard for a game, which Maya won hands down to Bess's immediate demands for a rematch.

Bess won the next three games and Noah had to wonder whether it was because Maya kept checking her phone and tapping in replies. Perhaps to her son? He had no idea. Although she didn't look impressed by whoever it was, so it was more likely to be the ex.

Hudson waved his goodbyes to everyone, Nadia joined Noah in a game of pool and soon the gathering had whittled down to only the four of them.

Maya still seemed preoccupied by her phone.

'Everything all right?' Noah asked her when she slipped it into the rear pocket of her jeans yet again.

'Of course.' But even to his ears, not knowing her all that well, her claim sounded false. 'Actually, I'm going to follow Hudson's lead, get home.'

'I'll see you at shift tomorrow night then.'

Bess tried to persuade her it was too early to leave but had no luck and when Bess came over, shaking her head, he said, 'I wonder if her and her ex will ever really be over.'

'Dear God, let's hope so,' said Bess.

Noah made his excuses to leave too – he'd told Geraldine he'd be back at a reasonable hour, which to him meant this side of midnight at least.

He walked from the beer garden and along the track next to the water, keeping well away from the edge as if his actions might somehow transfer to Eva. Silly idea, but already he worried that when Eva was fully mobile and doing more than bum shuffling her way around the lounge, he'd have to be vigilant with their home backing onto the river.

Or would it even be a problem now he knew how to get in touch with Paul?

Eva had changed his life – well, Cassie had changed it by dying, but then Eva had come into his world like a paint bomb exploding and colouring everything in a totally different shade. Was he really going to hand it all over to Paul when his sister's wishes had been for him to look after Eva? And if he was able to ask her now, would she really tell him she didn't want Eva's dad in her daughter's life?

He passed the end of the alleyway that led from the river to the street not far past the pub and turned at the sound of rustling in the bushes, watched as a figure ran from this end of the alleyway to the other.

It was dark but Noah saw a definite flash of white beneath the streetlamp at the very end. It could be the person's shirtsleeve illuminated in the light, but Noah knew it wasn't. It was the white of an arm in a cast, the figure was male and definitely the right build to be who he suspected it was lurking out here.

Conrad. He'd put money on it. Keeping tabs on Maya.

13

The evening warmth as they tumbled into summer was pleasant and the walk home from the pub even better to clear her head. Maya let herself into her cottage and Whizzy trotted towards her.

She crouched down and scooped the cat up for a cuddle. 'It's nice to come home to you at long last.' She smiled at the rattling purr she was sure was far louder now the cat lived here rather than at Conrad's.

When her phone went again, she swore. Assuming it was Conrad, she snatched it from her pocket. He'd texted her five times at the pub. He hadn't called declaring an emergency so that was something because she might have felt obliged to go and check on him, but he'd even started the last two texts with their son's name as though she'd be more likely to click on the message when she saw Isaac's name. Which she had.

Her shoulders relaxed when she saw her son's name on the display now rather than her ex-husband's.

'Have you been out?' he asked her.

'I went to the pub.' The cat snuggled onto her lap when she sat on the sofa.

'Good for you. Me too.' He sounded relaxed, happy. And as a parent, that was all that you really wanted for your children.

'You're not out clubbing tonight?'

'Nah, can't face it, not when I still have one exam to go.'

She wished Conrad could process how hard their son was working, be proud rather than only seeing things his way. 'You're working hard, you deserve a nice, long summer away from study. I can't wait to see you. Do you have a date in mind yet?'

'Not yet, a few of us might do something here right after the exams.' He told her more about the idea that they would all go camping together, really kick back before they went their separate ways for the holidays. 'And I've been offered a part time job in my mate's parents' café.'

Her heart sank. 'Where?'

'Here in Scotland.'

She summoned some enthusiasm. She should be proud he was getting work even if it wasn't closer to this part of the country. 'That's great but where will you stay?'

'I can stay with the family. I'll get slightly less pay to allow for my board but it's still worth it.'

And it would avoid having to see his dad. Maya knew that was partly his reasoning, she didn't need to ask. 'Well I hope I get to see you at least for a short while.' Deflated, she tried to keep her emotions in check.

'I promise you will.'

He'd know she was disappointed but he shouldn't have to think about that; he was growing up, becoming more independent by the day. And she was delighted to see the wonderful young man he was turning into.

'I told my friends you were a pilot, by the way,' he said after she yawned and he matched it with a yawn of his own. 'They were impressed and asked me if we have our own helicopter.'

That made her laugh. 'Not quite.'

They talked a while longer – Isaac had called her on his way home and as he arrived at his student house, they finished up.

Maya knew how easy it would be to fall asleep here on the sofa but she forced herself to head on up to bed, the cat in her arms.

Conrad messaged her while she was cleaning her teeth asking whether she'd be able to stop by the pharmacy and pick up a prescription for him tomorrow. Why couldn't he have mentioned it when they went to the pharmacy earlier? She knew why... the more times he needed her, the better for him. And of course he apologised profusely for being a pain.

She texted back that she would collect it and said goodnight to put a full stop to their conversation. And then she put her phone on silent.

As she fell asleep, she thought about the pub this evening, about the friends she had in Whistlestop River, about Noah. She hadn't been interested in a relationship since the divorce but he ignited thoughts that maybe one day, she might be ready for one.

And for once, the feeling didn't fill her with absolute dread. But rather it was the promise of a new beginning.

* * *

The following morning, Maya stopped at the pharmacy, collected Conrad's medication and delivered it to his place. Again, he didn't answer the door and she was tempted to post everything through the letterbox but eventually, she let herself in and called out his name. No reply.

She found him still in bed and a lazy smile greeted her when she gingerly pushed open the bedroom door. He winced as he tried to lift himself up on the arm in plaster, perhaps not realising when he was half asleep that that was the one that was injured.

She held up the bag from the pharmacy. 'I can't stop for long; I can make you a cup of tea, though.'

'Coffee would be great.'

She backed out of the room, unkeen to see his bare chest as he sat up with the sheet fallen to his waist.

'Are you working today?' His voice followed her from the bedroom.

'Not today,' she hollered back.

The kettle hadn't even reached its peak when he appeared in the kitchen, tracksuit bottoms on, nothing covering his top half. 'What are you up to then if it's not work?'

That was code for asking whether Noah was a part of her plans. He'd have been stewing about the new man in town ever since he saw her talk to Noah outside the pharmacy.

'I'm going to Dad's,' she said before he could float any of his own theories. 'Julie's home from honeymoon today; I guess she wants to catch up.' Her sister was often trying to do this: get her and their dad in the same vicinity whether they liked it or not. Maya supposed she couldn't blame her for trying.

Conrad picked up the sugar jar from the back of the benchtop and set it next to the jar of coffee granules she'd already lined up next to the kettle and the mug. Nigel had never really liked Conrad and the feeling had always been mutual. Conrad tolerated Julie but had never been overly friendly to her. It was as though as soon as they were married, he regarded Maya as his and nobody else's.

Conrad went to use the bathroom and by the time he came back, Maya had set his mug of coffee on the table in the lounge. 'You look a lot steadier on your feet,' she commented.

'Getting there.' He rested his good hand on top of the shoulder of the injured arm and lowered himself down onto the sofa. 'I had a blinding headache last night, can't shake it.'

'You need to call the doctor.'

'I don't think it's anything to worry about. But that's why I was still in bed, couldn't face starting the day when I'd been up half the night. I was worried I might lose my balance too.'

She sat beside him. 'What sort of headache was it?'

'The painful kind.'

'You know what I mean. Was it one-sided, all over, dull ache or sharp pain?'

'Maya, I know you're looking out for me but no need to mother me. You're sounding like you used to with Isaac when he was little.' He softened. 'Remember when he was so tiny, I could rest him along my arm?'

He did this too. He changed the conversation and injected nostalgia as if it might make a difference to how she felt. Over time, she'd soon learned to recognise the segue.

'Call the doctor and at least mention it.'

'All right, but for now, could you grab me a couple of painkillers?'

After he took the painkillers with the glass of water she brought him, Maya left for her father's home, the house she'd grown up in. It wasn't all that far from Whistlestop River, a pleasant drive through the countryside along winding roads with fields on either side.

Today was the first time she'd seen her dad since the wedding reception and while she couldn't wait to see Julie, she'd prefer there to be a bigger lag until she had to see her father again.

She pulled up into the driveway, grand and sweeping like the rest of the grounds and the house. Growing up here had been a blast in so many ways and she'd been a happy kid right up until her mother Anya died. She was eleven when it happened; Julie was three, so too little to remember her the way Maya did.

After Anya died, the girls' grandparents had been there for the family and not long after the funeral service, they'd taken Maya and her sister back to their home in Cornwall, said it was for the best, that Nigel needed some time and space as well as help from the doctors. Maya, at eleven, didn't really know what that meant but later on she found out he'd suffered a depressive episode that had almost eaten him up whole. His strength and resilience had come into play and he got medical help and seven weeks after the girls had gone down to Cornwall, he turned up on their grandparents' doorstep.

Maya had answered the door that day and flung herself at his legs. He'd picked her up but the look on his face was one she'd never seen before. He was angry; he told Maya to take her sister and go outside in the garden to play. Her sister had been in their grandmother's arms and she reluctantly handed her over to Maya. Even from the end of the garden, Maya heard the yelling through the closed back door, it went on for ages, and her father, Maya and Julie left the house shortly afterwards, leaving behind two devastated grandparents who had lost their granddaughters as well as their daughter. Maya would never forget the look on their faces, her gramps with his arms around Granny's shoulders as though holding her in case she collapsed with the weight of it all. Maya, tears streaming down her cheeks, waved frantically from the back window of the car until they disappeared out of sight.

Maya parked and switched off her engine before looking upwards to the very top windows of the home. Her parents' bedroom. It didn't matter how many years went by, she could still recall the moment she was told her mum was dead, the way her dad had fallen to his knees in grief that Anya had gone.

Maya climbed out of the car and her shoes crunched on the gravel as she made her way from the driveway, around the back and across to the sweeping, concrete steps that led up to the house.

She'd love nothing more than to stay outside in the sunshine but she reluctantly trudged inside. Her dad was sitting in an armchair reading the newspaper and folded it shut when she arrived.

'Julie's not here yet.'

She checked her watch. Great, she'd have to make small talk, not an easy thing with her father. She couldn't even talk about work because he had never embraced her career choice. He'd implied for years that she should've found an office job, something reliable with normal hours.

The final time her dad had challenged her on her career, shortly after she started at the Whistlestop River Air Ambulance in a permanent role three years ago, he'd told her, 'In all these years, I thought you'd see sense.'

She'd bitten back, 'You mean you thought I'd see it your way. I don't want an office job. I never have done.'

'Ever since I let you go up in that blessed helicopter for your birthday when you were little, you wanted to fly the damn things for yourself.'

'And I'm good at it!' she'd roared.

'You could've had any job you wanted; you're a clever girl. I'm disappointed you never wanted to try anything else.'

And there it was. The way he felt. Disappointed.

With both of them clearly uncomfortable waiting for Julie to show up, Nigel asked after Isaac. It was a subject that always calmed things between them because as unsupportive as he'd been over her career along the way, he seemed to at least respect his grandson's choices. And Maya had made a point to not exclude her father from her son's life because she wanted Isaac to have as much family around him as possible. She knew what it was like to lose any one of them and it hurt, sometimes more than she could bear.

'He's doing well. He's worked hard, exams are over and he's taking some time out with his mates.'

'I expect he's looking forward to coming home.'

'He deserves the break. But he's got some work in a friend's parents' café before he heads back this way.'

'Well good for him.'

The stilted exchange was better than none at all and certainly better than conflict.

'I will look forward to catching up with him, give him a game of tennis when he's around,' said Nigel.

'He'd like that.'

Hands in his pockets as he grappled for more conversation, her father's relief matched hers when they both heard Julie come trotting up the back steps outside.

'I'm back!' She held out her arms first for Maya, who met her at the door in her excitement.

Maya hugged Julie tight. 'I missed you.' She could still remember hugs like this when her little sister came home from school, especially when Maya was in sixth form and Julie not even at high school. She pulled back. 'You look great! Happy and relaxed.'

'It was amazing,' she gushed. Unlike Maya, Julie's skin was fair and it looked like she'd done the right thing in the sun and stayed safe. Maya had seen the collection of sunhats her sister had packed in her suitcase too, heard her husband ask why she couldn't just bring her favourite, only to be told that certain outfits needed a different look. It had made her smile. The start of married life and all that it entailed.

Julie ran into her dad's arms next. She might be a married woman, but she was still his little girl. As Maya watched them smiling and talking, the light in both their eyes, she felt that familiar tug of sadness that somewhere along the way, she and her father had lost the ability to connect.

They migrated outside to the patio to make the most of the summer weather and beneath the shade of the wide umbrella, Julie told them all about the resort they'd honeymooned at, the sailing lessons, the chef who'd cooked the most delectable fish dishes every night of their stay. Julie and Seth had taken cooking lessons, learnt to make their own coconut curry, something Julie was most proud of and had the photos to prove it. She told them she'd make it again soon. They'd been scuba diving, snorkelling, seen the most beautiful marine life.

'And now I have to come back down to earth,' Julie admitted, taking the glass of lemonade with ice from her father. He handed the other one to Maya.

'When are you back to work?' Maya asked her sister.

'In a few days. But I'm down to three days a week to give me a chance to work on the house.'

'And to give you a chance to scope out starting a business from home?' Nigel probed.

Julie worked in accounts and had been part of a small team at a firm where she'd been since she left education. She enjoyed it, she had a head for figures, and she'd always said it would be a good job to do alongside parenthood. She was loyal to the firm she was with, but Maya knew she would leave the moment they started a family, at which point she'd have plans in place to continue accountancy in some capacity from home.

Maya listened to her sister and their dad talk about what Julie had planned – the website she'd need, how she'd build a client base from scratch. She was struck at how much her sister looked like their mother – the same colouring, the same high cheek bones. She knew it already, of course, but seeing Julie so happy, beaming, reminded Maya of how she liked to think of her mother, full of joy with a smile captured forever in so many photographs around the family home. Julie wouldn't remember the wrench it had been the day they left Cornwall, the shouting from their father, the tears from their grandparents. She'd been oblivious, safely ensconced in her bubble of three-year-old innocence.

The girls had seen their grandparents after that day but it had been the end to spending summers with them. There was no more going to the beach with their buckets and spades, no more sleeping in their mother's old bedroom and being able to feel her presence, no more Maya helping Granny make bread in her kitchen and talking about Anya while her little sister slept.

Instead of going to Cornwall, the girls' grandparents came here to the house. They were still Granny and Gramps, but it was never the same again and when they'd died within eleven months of each other less than two years later, it felt to Maya like losing her mother all over again.

14

Noah closed the rear door to the car and counted to ten. How could a twelve-month-old be so strong it had taken literal force to get her into the damn car seat? She'd screamed at the top of her lungs as if he'd put her in a straitjacket rather than a five-point harness.

After a few deep breaths, he got into the driver's seat and set off for home.

Earlier on, when he'd arrived home sooner than expected, he'd been full of confidence; he'd told Geraldine to finish early, that he had it all in hand. He'd given Eva her dinner, everything had been running smoothly until he realised he didn't have any dinner for himself. Without thinking too much about it, he'd bundled Eva into the car and headed for the supermarket for what was supposed to be a quick trip to collect enough groceries for a stir fry. Except it had turned out to be a trip from hell. He'd pushed it, decided to shop for enough food to get through the next week so he didn't have to come back and he'd taken Eva past the point of no return when nothing either of them did helped to soothe her. He should've settled her after dinner, let her have a play, given her a bottle and put her down for the night. He should've ordered himself a takeaway. Or, better still, he should've done the shopping before he went home and sent the nanny on her way.

Hindsight was a wonderful thing.

By the time he pulled onto the driveway at the signal box cottage, Eva had cried herself to sleep. Maybe she was pissed off at him for not giving her a birthday party. He'd considered it but with everything going on right now, all the uncertainty, he'd not done anything major. He, Eva and Geraldine had quietly celebrated with cake and gifts and Geraldine, being the surrogate grandparent that she was, had assured him it wouldn't scar Eva for life. He wondered, would he get the chance to make it up to Eva? Be the cool Uncle Noah who threw the best parties for her?

He thumped the steering wheel and then cringed in case he'd woken her up. A quick glance round told her he hadn't. 'I'm a shit dad,' he muttered, his face resting on his hands. 'You deserve better than me, Eva.'

He tried to transfer Eva from car seat to cot, which had never worked before. He'd been kidding himself it would this time to be honest and when she woke, he had to abandon her screaming in her cot while he got the groceries in.

He then spent a full hour trying to calm her down enough to have her bottle and hopefully go to sleep.

But that didn't happen either. She refused the milk, she wouldn't settle. He paced with her, he tried to set her on the floor to play with the funny set of pots and pans that emitted painfully repetitive tunes over and over again until he thought the only way to sanity was to remove the batteries. The only reason he hadn't was that he thought it might send Eva over the edge.

Finally she took the bottle, she seemed calm and content in his arms but the minute he tried to put her down for the night again, the crying started.

This was all his fault.

Noah had seen mothers around town with their iPhones tucked into their swish baby carriers lulling the babies to slumber with white noise and always thought they were only making things harder for themselves if the kid couldn't sleep without some kind of musical aid. But perhaps they were more savvy than he gave them credit for.

When Eva finally settled, Noah slumped down in the hallway outside her bedroom, exhausted.

He was failing at this. He was useless.

And that feeling was all he needed to propel him up and into the lounge where he grabbed Paul's letter and his phone.

Out on the back porch, he tapped out the phone number and Paul answered after only three rings.

The guy had no idea Cassie had died and after Noah delivered the terrible news, he seemed discombobulated and lost for words. In the end, he'd told Noah he'd have to call him back.

Noah stayed outside. He wondered whether Paul had wanted Cassie more than he wanted Eva. His letter had been written to Cassie requesting he see his daughter but maybe that was a cover story.

Paul did call back and this time was a lot calmer. He was sorry for Noah's loss and for Eva's and he wanted to come and meet Eva. Noah saw no point in asking the guy why he'd upped and left, at least not yet. Eva was the priority here, and Paul was keen. So they arranged a day and time when Paul would come over.

After the call, Noah grabbed a beer. He didn't dare go in to check on Eva but he listened at her bedroom door, closed his eyes and picked up on the gentle snuffly sounds of her breathing, indicating she was asleep.

Outside, he leaned on the porch railing, his bottle of beer in one hand. The gentle swish and swirl of the river's current beyond the back grass was a reminder, not that he needed one, of how much his life had changed. He missed his life in London but at the same time, he could see why Cassie had loved it here, why she wanted to settle here eventually. Whistlestop River had a peace he'd never find in the city, a peace he appreciated after having Eva sap him of every ounce of energy.

Finishing his beer, he slung the empty bottle into the recycling bin down below and locked the back door behind him. He stood at Eva's door and opened the gap slightly more until a strip of light fell across her cot. She was sleeping on her back, both arms thrown over her head. She was like a tiny angel, a miniature version of Cassie.

'You'll be better off without me, you know,' he admitted regretfully. 'I'm not cut out for this.'

He tiptoed away quietly, tears pricking his eyes. 'I'm sorry, Cassie, I'm sorry I'm not good enough.'

15

Maya was first out of the hangar, into the rain, across to the helicopter. It might well be July and summer, but low cloud was forecast and there was a chance they'd have to turn back if visibility was terrible. But the call had been made to at least try to attend the job via aircraft because their patient was in the depths of the countryside and had suffered a cardiac arrest. Speedy transport by air ambulance could mean the difference between life and death.

'We don't have much to go on,' said Noah from the rear of the helicopter once they were airborne. 'The caller only gave basic details when they called the emergency in. We know it's a male, in his twenties. CPR was performed and he hadn't re-arrested.'

The caller had given the location and hung up. More details would've been helpful but people didn't always think clearly in an emergency and if the caller had already performed CPR and needed to again, then they weren't going to hang around on the phone once they'd called for help.

The weather was atrocious. Maya always checked at start of shift for notifications of airspace hazards and throughout her working day, but along with flocks of birds and low-flying drones, bad weather came with no such warnings. The danger of flying too close to the cloud base was that clouds brought turbulence, which could cause structural damage to poor Hilda, not to mention making it a flight the crew would rather forget.

'Are we going to make it to our location?' Bess asked over her microphone.

'I'll do my best,' said Maya. A road ambulance would be on its way so if the air ambulance didn't get to the patient, they would instead, although with road closures near the location, it might take them a while to get through. That was exactly why Maya had said they should try to get to the job in Hilda. Sometimes they took the rapid response vehicle if flying conditions weren't on their side, but that option would've seen the crew encounter those same road closures.

The cloud level was manageable en route but visibility was nowhere near what Maya would like. Still, she'd trained for this, she'd flown in worse conditions. And the adrenaline pumping through her veins kept her going as well as her want to get to the patient and keep her entire crew safe. Luckily for her, both Bess and Noah had their heads screwed on, neither of them questioned her ability, neither of them panicked as wisps of cloud threatened to close in around them.

They were almost there.

Noah's voice came over the microphone next. 'I can see a hi-vis jacket on the ground, forty-five degrees west of our position.'

'I see it,' Maya confirmed. But she couldn't see anyone else with them and they weren't waving.

'I can't see anyone on the ground,' said Bess. 'Perhaps the patient is out of sight.'

'Thank goodness for hi-vis,' said Maya, 'or we'd have had no hope spotting anything down there.'

Noah suggested landing in the field adjacent to the person in hi-vis.

'Hang on,' Bess called over her microphone, 'there's an empty car park on our right with easy access, no hedges to contend with.'

Maya made the decision. 'I'll head for that.'

Maya would need all the help she could get from Bess and Noah landing today with the grey skies and the rain. There was also the chance that an empty space could quickly become occupied, thus endangering whoever was on the ground and whoever was in her helicopter.

'Clear to our left,' came Noah's voice as she approached the landing site.

The helicopter could withstand a beating from the weather but it didn't mean that you wouldn't feel those effects inside, with the wind moving them more than it ordinarily would as Maya finally landed on the tarmac.

With the rain lashing at every single piece of the helicopter, Bess and Noah grabbed the kit they needed. Maya wished them luck and stayed with the aircraft. They'd made it here in under eight minutes, she only hoped they were in time to save the patient.

Maya watched Bess and Noah battle the weather with their heavy backpacks. They left the car park and turned in the direction of the field.

Maya thought about Noah as she waited with Hilda. She now knew the circumstances surrounding his guardianship of Eva and it put him even higher in her estimation knowing what he'd given up, how he'd changed his life to look after his niece. She knew too that she thought about him a little too often, which might not be the best idea given they worked together. But she couldn't help it. Every time she looked into those eyes or heard the cadence of his voice, she knew it wasn't only platonic, at least from her side. And the thought both excited and terrified her at the same time.

She thought about the little girl descending into Noah's life. Parenthood was hard, let alone when it was sprung on you all of a sudden combined with the pain of loss. But she bet Noah was a good father, or father figure, or whatever he was to her at the moment. He was strong, capable and clearly kind to have taken on the responsibility. She'd heard the way he talked to patients in the back of the air ambulance too, seen the way he was with them when they were transferred from the scoop to the litter in the helicopter. Patients felt safe with him and Maya bet his little girl would feel the same way, even if she couldn't tell him.

When the HEMS desk radioed through an update, Maya's heart sank. Bess and Noah were going to be furious, much like she was, and sure enough when they reappeared their faces said it all.

They paced their way across the concrete with their heavy bags with no sign of the patient of course because it had all been a hoax.

Maya started up the rotor blades as they approached.

Bess climbed into the seat beside her. 'Can you believe it was some sicko's idea of a prank?'

'I heard over the radio,' said Maya, preparing for take-off. 'But there was a person in hi-vis; I don't understand.'

'Oh the hoax caller was clever. It was a bloody scarecrow.' Bess closed her eyes for a moment, a swear word leaving her lips. 'I suppose at least they called HEMS and gave them the tip off. Otherwise we'd have been searching for a long time, in case the scarecrow was a coincidence and there really was someone out there in need of our help.'

Noah swore into the microphone and had a mini rant until he pulled himself together because the cloud was still rolling in and they had to get back to base.

The mood was sombre on board, none of the usual chitchat.

Maya was fuming too, although she kept it in during the flight back to base. The hoax caller had wasted their time and, worse than that, they'd put the crew's lives at risk. Their lives were in danger every time they took to the skies. They did it for the good of everyone at ground level, put themselves in impossible situations, went out in all weathers even when it ramped up the danger level, and this was what people did for kicks?

Nadia was inside the hangar when they arrived back with long faces. 'What happened?' She wasn't always in the office to hear updates so right now, she'd be assuming they'd lost the patient; that was what usually brought the grim return, the lack of banter between the crew.

Maya put her helmet on the shelf and filled Nadia in while Bess and Noah put the gear away.

'Why do people do that?' Nadia moaned. 'I'll report it. We've very little to go on but it doesn't mean we ignore it.'

Nadia turned when they both heard Noah swear again as he went through to the kitchen.

'He's upset,' said Nadia.

'We all are,' Maya replied.

'He must have seen this before.'

Bess passed behind them. 'Doesn't make it any easier.' She added in her own swearwords for good measure. 'Whoever made that call had better wish I never find out who it was.'

'Go to the kitchen, have some of the chocolate cake I made for us all,' Nadia suggested. 'You need a bit of comfort.' She was good at watching out for her team at the airbase.

'I'll be in to join you soon,' Maya told Bess.

'And I'll go and report the absolute arsehole who did this to you guys today,' said Nadia. 'I know HEMS were the ones to advise you it was a hoax but it won't hurt to raise another complaint, will it?'

'I suppose not,' Maya agreed. 'Thank goodness we didn't get another job at the same time.'

'Well, quite,' said Nadia, hands on hips. 'Not only could this prank have wasted my team's time and compromised your safety going up in these conditions, it could've cost someone else their life.'

That was the reality of it. To whoever made the hoax call, it was a laugh, but in doing so, they could've killed someone.

The team occasionally got calls that weren't really essential, but those jobs were assigned because it was deemed necessary by dispatch, who didn't always have much to go on. And if it transpired the air ambulance wasn't needed, it was no big deal; sometimes it was impossible to know how serious a patient's condition was. But this was different. And Maya was reminded of how different it was when she went into the locker room and jumped when Noah slammed his locker door so hard, she was surprised the door survived.

'I know it's shit,' she said softly. 'But it happens. We all feel the same way.'

'Yeah.'

When he still said nothing, she added, 'There's chocolate cake in the kitchen. I'm going to make coffee. Can I get you a cup?'

He turned around as if he hadn't even been listening. 'I'm sorry, what?'

'Coffee. And cake.'

'And that makes it all better, does it?' His question hovered in the air until it fell to the floor as he slumped down on the bench next to the lockers, his hand back against the cold hard steel. 'Ignore me.'

She thought about it. She thought about walking away but instead went over and sat down beside him. 'I'm not sure about how things worked with your crew in London, but here in Whistlestop River, we're in this together. You're angry, so am I, so are Bess and Nadia. And I'm afraid here you have to talk about it.'

She waited for his reply.

'Why do people do it, Maya? Where's the thrill?'

Whoever had made that call had probably been watching from somewhere nearby to see their little joke played out when a helicopter landed and the critical care paramedics rushed over.

'I wish I'd stayed back to find the little sh—'

'I'm glad you didn't,' Maya interrupted. 'You might have got yourself in a lot of trouble.' He was fuming; she could see it in his eyes. But more than that, he looked devastated.

'There were no identifying marks or labels on the hi-vis either.' Noah's fists tensed against the tops of his knees. 'Fucking time wasters. I'd like to catch whoever did it and—'

'Do not finish that sentence. Whoever it was isn't worth you doing something terrible yourself, losing your job.'

He stood up, paced the locker room as though his anger had begun to simmer and then all of a sudden, it was on the boil again.

Maya decided to give him some space to process. 'I'll be in the kitchen cutting some cake, making the coffee. I know it won't fix things, but...'

'I'll give it a miss, thanks.'

'Well, you know where we are if you want to talk.'

Maya joined Bess in the kitchen and rustled up mugs of coffee. The sun streamed through the window as if the weather earlier had never happened at all. And as they ate their cake, drank their coffee, Maya thought about all the ways this job could get to you.

But she had to wonder whether there was more to it for Noah.

16

Geraldine saw to Eva while Noah got ready for Paul's visit. He wanted this to go well; he wasn't sure why he felt the need to impress, but he did. He wanted Paul to know that he was taking care of Eva – he might not be much good at it, but he'd kept his niece safe thus far. He wondered how Paul was feeling – nervous about meeting his daughter after all this time? Scared about coming face to face with Noah because of what he'd done to Cassie by walking out on her?

Noah opened up the packet of biscuits and put some on a plate as per Geraldine's suggestion when he was to host a guest. He'd never done this before. Usually, it was a few beers, perhaps wine, takeaway if ever he had guests back at his apartment in London.

'Tell me I'm doing the right thing, Geraldine.'

A kind smile formed. 'Only you can know that, Noah.' She had Eva in her arms, letting the little girl tug at her hair with fingers Noah was pretty sure were still sticky from her breakfast. 'Now let me get this one cleaned up so she can meet Paul.'

'Her dad,' said Noah, stopping her from walking away. 'And a much better one than I am.'

A weird look came over Geraldine's face, perhaps because she wasn't sure whether this was up for debate.

'I'm a terrible dad,' he went on, almost wanting her to agree so he'd know getting Paul to come here for Eva was what he should be doing.

'Noah, do you think I was born able to be a mother?'

'Er... yes. You're a natural.'

At that, she laughed. 'I'm nothing of the sort! With my first son, I gave him a bath at the hospital in one of those funny sinks with the slanted angle fit for purpose. He slipped off my arm and under the water. I felt terrible. He was this loud bundle of limbs, unpredictable, I had no idea what to do with him. I was a bit better with baby number two and by the time I had my fourth, I'd say that yes, I was a natural. It just took years of practice.'

She whisked Eva away to clean her up a bit.

Noah was nervous, which didn't happen very often. He'd been nervous before exams, nervous when he started his new job, but this was a whole different kind of nervous, accompanied by nausea in the pit of his stomach and clammy skin. He put it down to this being way bigger than any piece of paper he could put to his name or settling in with a new crowd.

He stared at his reflection in the mirror in the bathroom, at the lines on his face he forgot he had now he was in his mid-forties. Cassie hadn't been lucky enough to reach the forty milestone. She'd forever be thirty-nine, the blonde-haired, blue-eyed, beautiful girl full of smiles and laughter in the photograph he had pinned to his fridge and in the picture frame in Eva's bedroom.

When he emerged from the bathroom, Geraldine had changed Eva into a beautiful little polka-dot top with pale-green velvety trousers with flowers emblazoned on the pockets. He wondered if she shuffled around the floor long enough on her bottom whether the design would wear off.

Eva held her arms out for him when she spotted Noah and his breath caught in his throat. It was the first time that had happened.

Geraldine's voice was laced with emotion when she told him, 'She knows you.'

Eva settled in his arms, her body rested against his chest. He felt her little breaths against his chin, inhaled the scent of baby shampoo from hair that tickled the side of his face.

When he looked down, she was smiling up at him. She'd been doing that more lately when she wasn't grizzling about something and it would be easy not to notice it or think about it, especially when he was busy. But he was making an effort. Geraldine had told him the other day to appreciate the little things about Eva, not focus on the tiredness and the stress of it all, even if he wasn't going to be her father long term. And right now, as Eva reached up and ran her hand along his stubbly chin, giggling at the feel of it, he realised exactly what she meant.

Geraldine had been watching them without him even realising. She hovered. 'I don't want to interfere, Noah, you know that.'

'I also know that statements such as that one are usually accompanied by a *but*.'

'What I want to say is that you're doing all right, with Eva. It might not feel like it, but you are. You're learning, both of you.'

Noah suspected she would've said more but there was a knock at the door that sent his heart racing. Eva turned her head to the sound, and Geraldine said something about gathering up her things.

Noah answered the door, the plunging sensation in his guts increasing ten-fold as he came face to face with the man who'd abandoned his sister and her little girl.

* * *

Paul wasn't what Noah had expected. He'd pictured a rough and ready man, scruffily dressed, but here he was in a suit and tie, as though this might be the most important meeting of his life. Perhaps to him it was. And maybe that was a good sign?

'I'll leave you to it.' Geraldine pulled her bag onto her shoulder, a wary look in her eye. She smiled at Eva and planted a kiss on her forehead. 'Look forward to seeing you, little miss.' And then to Noah, 'Let me know if you need anything.'

'Thanks, appreciate it.' He closed the front door behind her and went into the lounge where Paul had already sat down.

'Can I get you a tea or coffee?' Noah offered. Eva's little arms were around his neck in a way that was comforting but made this so much harder. It was as if she was clinging onto him for safety and right now, it felt as though his heart would rip in two.

'I'll take a coffee.' Paul seemed shifty rather than nervous, or perhaps that was because Noah didn't know him well enough to tell the difference. 'Black, no sugar.'

Noah had expected him to ask to hold Eva, but he didn't. Was he wary of being too pushy given he walked out on Cassie and their daughter?

Cassie had never said much about the situation with Eva's father to Noah. She'd been upset at first, going it alone, but it was as though then she closed the doors around her little world of her and Eva and that was all that remained important to her. Noah had never pushed her for answers either because she blossomed as a single parent. Even on the days she said she was exhausted, she never stopped trying, never stopped smiling and taking in every little moment with Eva.

Noah delivered the cup of coffee to Paul. He'd made it one-handed, Eva well out of the way on his left hip, and carried the cup of hot liquid in his right hand, far away from her enough that if it spilt, it would only scald him.

'Help yourself.' Noah indicated the plate of colourful biscuits on the coffee table and sat on the sofa opposite the chair Paul had occupied.

'That your mum?' Paul asked.

'Excuse me?'

'The woman, earlier.'

The jerk must know that their mother had passed away. It wasn't something you forgot easily. Through gritted teeth, he said, 'That was the nanny. For Eva.' He added Eva's name because Paul hadn't reached for her or even indicated he wanted to yet.

But Noah shouldn't have wished for it because when Paul finished gobbling down a second biscuit, he stood and held out his arms. 'May I?'

'Sure.' He had to do it but transferring the little girl to Paul's arms went against all his natural instincts. It was harder than he'd ever imagined. What would it be like if this man took Eva for good?

Paul clearly had less experience with babies than Noah did. He was holding her but not engaging, he was tense, he was looking at her without much expression on his face at all. And Eva being Eva wasn't going to stand for that. She started to grizzle, moved about in his arms like she wanted to jump out of them.

'Maybe try sitting down with her,' Noah suggested. 'I'll get her a teething ring; she's having a tough time of it so that might help.' Really all he wanted to do right now was take her back and tell her that he was there, everything was going to be okay.

He went into the kitchen and pulled the ring out of the fridge and for a moment, he stood with it in his hand, looking at it, this thing that got in the way of his leftovers, one of the rings he'd knocked onto the floor countless times. And yet it would feel wrong to not have it here now.

Oh, Cassie, why did you have to go anywhere? You were born to be a mother. I'm not sure I'm doing anything right any more.

He pulled himself together, went back into the lounge and handed Eva the ring. She looked on the cusp of losing it and that was the last thing they needed right now. At least Paul had sat down and Eva shoved the ring in her mouth, her breath calming at the distraction from this stranger who'd picked her up.

'Did you have to come far?' Noah realised he hadn't even asked the guy where he was living. He could be in a squat for all Noah knew and he needed to be sure what future he was going to give Eva. It was all his responsibility now. And he wouldn't lie, it was overwhelming.

'Not really, I was already in Dorset.' He wasn't watching Eva. Every now and then, she looked at him, frowned and gnawed on her ring that little bit harder.

'So you live nearby?'

'Kind of.'

The guy was hard work. Noah pushed on. 'Are you still working offshore?'

His head snapped up. 'Not today.'

'But usually?' Noah had never been one to be thrown by a person's obvious deflection in a conversation and when it came to Eva's wellbeing, her safety, her future, he wasn't about to be steered away from the important facts. 'Aren't you some kind of mechanic?'

'Usually, yes.' He still didn't really look at Eva. Perhaps she reminded him too much of Cassie. 'Sorry, this is all a lot to take in.' His top lip was sweating; suddenly, he looked more uneasy.

Noah softened, but not too much. 'I'm sure it's all been a big shock for you.'

'Yes... I mean, I never knew about Cassie...'

'I had no way of contacting you.' And to be honest, an absent father hadn't been on his list of priorities when it came to saying goodbye to his sister either.

Eva had stopped fussing but when she dropped her teething

ring and Paul made no move to pick it up, it was Noah who grabbed it, rinsed it off in the kitchen and brought it back to her. By which time she was getting fractious again.

'I'm sorry, I'm new to fatherhood,' Paul apologised.

For once, Noah felt like the professional parent in comparison.

'So you're still working?' Noah asked.

'Yup.'

It was painful trying to get information out of this guy. He'd seen the green sports car out front and his first thought – other than that it must have cost a packet, so the man was obviously doing all right for himself – was that it was totally impractical for a baby seat. Was there even any room in the back where Eva would need to go?

Noah smiled back at Eva when she grinned at him, waving her teething ring in the air. 'When do you go back offshore?' he asked Paul, suspecting Eva's teeth weren't hurting at all but rather she was protesting at this man who had no clue about anyone her age.

'Dunno yet.'

'Tell me a bit about yourself and your family.' A bit of background would be good given he'd never heard much about the guy from Cassie. It might even put his mind at rest.

'Not much to say, really.' He handed Eva over as though she was a ball in a game and it was Noah's turn. And then he asked, 'How come Cassie gave her to you?'

'It was what my sister wanted.'

'So, the father has no rights?'

Now Noah found it hard to keep his cool. 'Hard to give him any when he buggered off.'

Paul looked about to argue back but reconsidered. 'I apologise. I've made some mistakes along the way.'

Noah took a moment to digest it. 'And Eva... was she a mistake?' With this little being in his arms, he felt protective.

'I didn't say that.'

'Good.' Noah paced across the room with Eva, more for himself than her. 'Didn't you feel guilty?'

Mouth full of digestive, Paul pulled a peculiar face, presumably to get the biscuit remnants out from his gums. 'About leaving the baby?'

'And Cassie.'

'Like I said, I had things going on. Life. I didn't plan to be a dad.'

'But you're stepping up now?' It was a question rather than a statement.

He brushed crumbs from his shirt, showing no regard that they were going all over the furniture. 'I'd like to get to know my daughter.'

'You're welcome to come back again tomorrow perhaps, see her again, maybe in the morning when she's less tired? I should put her down for a nap soon.' He had no intention of doing that. All he wanted was to watch her play in the corner on the mat with the sensory pads, the little mirror, watch her bum shuffle her way over to the coffee table and grizzle when she couldn't get under or over it. He'd lost count of how many times he'd had to rescue her from that situation. He found it frustrating usually but right now, he wanted to see it happen so he could help her and embrace her world of discovery.

'Can't do tomorrow, but the day after is fine by me.'

'Day after then, mid-morning suits us. She won't be napping then and I won't be at work.'

Paul took a couple more biscuits from the plate. 'Didn't have lunch today,' he said, as if that excused the apparent greed.

If he was more pleasant, if the bond between father and daughter was obvious, Noah would've offered to make him a sandwich, or another coffee. But right now, he couldn't wait to get this guy out of his house.

'I'll be back on Wednesday.' Two days away.

Paul had the biscuits in one hand, his keys in the other. 'And Noah, this shouldn't come as a surprise, but I'll be going after custody of Eva.'

He left, out of the front door Noah held open for him without a single word and pushed closed with more of a bang than he'd intended.

He stood in the hallway, Eva in his arms, shellshocked. A week ago, he would've been thrilled to have a way out of being landed with a baby all of a sudden, elated he'd found Eva's dad. But now, the thought of this man being the one to raise Eva filled him with dread.

What the hell had he done?

17

At the Whistlestop River Air Ambulance base, the entire crew mucked in with cleaning Hilda between jobs. Today was a full clean and Hilda needed it. Maya took charge of cleaning the helicopter's exterior with the special shampoo and although she didn't always admit it, she quite enjoyed the polishing stage that followed, when Hilda began to take on a high sheen and show herself off.

As a little girl, Maya had been interested in aviation but her fascination soon turned to helicopters after she saw one land so close, she could feel the wind from the blades on her face. There'd been an accident near her primary school that day and the field was cleared to allow an air ambulance to land. Maya could remember watching from the open classroom window when her attention should've been on her spellings. She'd been in awe of the shiny red helicopter against the rich green of the grass, the pilot standing guard with his aircraft. She'd leaned out of the window, and the pilot had waved. Maya would never forget that moment, and even when the teacher ushered her away and closed the window as the crew brought a patient to the helicopter on a stretcher, Maya still sneaked a look from her place at her desk. She watched the aircraft take off, amazed that there wasn't a runway and that it lifted into the air as if by magic.

Maya must have gone on and on about helicopters after that day because her birthday gift was a Meccano helicopter and the year after that, she got a model helicopter her dad helped her put together and paint in intricate detail. The year she turned ten, her dad had said that because she was in double figures, it meant a big birthday treat for her and that treat was a helicopter ride over the countryside that cemented her fascination and passion for aviation.

Sometimes she wondered how her dad had gone from embracing her hobby and her desire to fly to not wanting to hear anything about it.

Maya finished off buffing Hilda's front windscreen and climbed down off the stepladder she'd had to use to reach the very top. She breathed in the fresh air outside, smiling at the beauty of the great outdoors. She loved the fact that it was still summer and when this shift came to an end and the other crew took over, there'd be hours of daylight still left before the sun even dared to drop in the sky.

Bess had headed inside after cleaning some of the interior and Noah was finishing up with the mopping of the helicopter's floor using Stumpy, the name they'd given to the mop with the handle hacked off as it was too tall for the aircraft's interior.

'Hilda scrubs up pretty well,' he beamed as he climbed out onto the tarmac and stood next to Maya.

'She does. Great job all round.'

He might have smiled, but ever since the day of the hoax call, a light in his eyes had dulled, he didn't have the same joviality or upbeat approach. Not that it had affected his work. They'd been out on four calls today, one of their busiest shifts in a while, with no fatalities which was always a win. But while Noah had been professional and focused during the job and joined in the chatter on the way back with her and Bess in the helicopter, Maya had noticed as he was cleaning that the chatter stopped, he went into his own head whenever he could, there was no joking about or teasing and laughing the way the crew usually did, which was probably why Bess had got her part finished and headed inside already.

Noah picked up the bucket of water, took it over to the grass area and tipped it out before coming back to retrieve the mop.

'Is everything okay with you?' Maya had picked up her cleaning gear and they were heading towards the hangar. She didn't need to put Hilda away today; she'd stay on the helipad for the blue team who would finish their shift at around 2 a.m. and put the helicopter to bed for the night.

'All good,' he assured her with another smile she sensed took some effort.

They put the cleaning equipment away and as Noah headed for the locker room, Maya washed out the rags and cloths. It was as she was hanging the last one up to dry that she picked up on a heated conversation coming from reception.

She went to find out what was going on and found Officer Ryan Tucker talking to Nadia, Noah on the periphery, asking questions. Ryan was a former colleague of Conrad's before Conrad took a detective position and transferred to another station in the next town.

Maya acknowledged Ryan's presence with a smile and a nod. He did the same in return but was soon back to business. He directed his address to Maya and Noah, although Maya sensed Noah had already heard the spiel.

'As I've explained to Nadia, the likelihood of us finding the culprit for the prank call is very low. I appreciate how frustrating this is for you. It is for us too, but we don't have anything to go on unfortunately.'

Noah wasn't happy. 'So they get away with it?'

'Like I said, nothing more we can do at this stage.' Officer Tucker was pragmatic in his approach. 'If we find anything, we will let you know. Probably kids.'

Maya held the door open for him. 'Thanks, Ryan.'

'No worries. Good to see you, Maya, and please do send my regards to Conrad.'

'Of course.' And it was no surprise that Officer Tucker and probably the rest of the force assumed she was seeing Conrad on a regular basis. She wondered whether he'd told anyone about the divorce at all.

Before their shift came to an end, the crew got one more job ten minutes away but they returned in good spirits after a positive outcome for their young patient. Bess and Noah completed the patient report forms and updated the database. Maya had her own paperwork to do as she was responsible for keeping the technical log up to date with maintenance requests – none today – details of each flight and fuel calculations.

After shift, Maya went to get her things from her locker. She'd expected Noah to have left as she'd been waylaid chatting with Vik, the other pilot, as she handed over. But he was still in the locker room, as though this might be the best place for peace and quiet, even though it rarely was with the comings and goings of the team, the shrill alerts of the multiple phones when a job came in at the airbase.

She undid her locker and retrieved her bag. She couldn't wait to get home and take a shower. Hilda was cleaner than she was right now.

Noah opened his own locker now he was no longer alone and got his things out before closing the steel door once again.

Maya couldn't leave it. 'Noah, I know I don't know you all that well but if you need to talk...'

He turned to face her, his expression one she couldn't read.

'I mean it. We're working together every shift and if there's something bothering you, it might help to get it out in the open.' She sensed he wasn't one to usually do that. 'It might not, but the offer is there...' Maybe it was best if he didn't let her in, if they didn't get too close given she was starting to feel more than friendship towards him. She'd known it all the more the day Conrad had watched them outside the pharmacy. If it was totally platonic on her part, she would've dismissed Conrad's comments and not thought about it since. But the fact was, she'd thought about Noah a lot more than she should have.

His voice stopped her as she turned to leave. 'I can't stand it, you know.'

She turned back. 'Can't stand what?'

'Not knowing who made that prank call.' He slumped down on the bench near the row of lockers. 'It's eating me up.'

She went over and sat down next to him, detecting a faint smell of the aftershave he usually brought with him at the start of shift. She was pretty sure any scent from her shampoo or shower gel hand long gone by now and it made her want to hold her arms down in case she smelt bad.

'It's horrible, it makes us all angry,' she said. 'But we can't control the stupidity of some people. It'll drive us insane if we try.'

He leaned forwards, forearms resting along his thighs. 'Eva isn't actually my daughter.'

'I know, she's your niece.'

He looked sideways at her briefly, eyes watery, forearms still laid against his thighs, palms pressed together. 'Did Bess tell you anything else?'

'She didn't.'

He took a deep breath. 'I have Eva because my sister Cassie

died.' He leaned back, shook his head as though he couldn't really believe it.

'I'm so sorry, Noah.' Her heart sank in sympathy at what this man had been through. She couldn't imagine his pain – if she were to lose Julie, it would crush her. 'When did it happen?'

He looked at her briefly but then up at the strip light on the ceiling. 'Five months ago.'

'Noah, that's barely any time at all.'

'Some days, I wake up from a dream that she's coming over to see Eva. Then I remember...' His voice caught. 'Cassie was a great mum. Eva was her whole world.'

'May I ask what happened?'

He explained the weekend away, the horse falling, Cassie's catastrophic injuries.

'I'm not sure how you move on from that.' She wanted to reach out and hug him, try to make him feel at least a little bit better if only for a moment. 'She must've loved you to want Eva to grow up with you.'

'We got on well as far as siblings go. But when I agreed to her wishes, I never thought...'

'Nobody ever does.'

'When my sister had the accident that day, emergency services were called but it was hard to get to the location by road ambulance and it took forever. An air ambulance would've been her best chance, but the air ambulance had already been dispatched on another call and by the time it was re-routed, it was too late.'

'Oh, Noah...'

'That's not the worst of it.' And now, piecing it together, she knew what was coming even before he said, 'The call the crew were on when Cassie was lying there with life-threatening injuries was a prank call. Made by some rich kid for his kicks, an entitled teenager

who thought the world revolved around him and stuff the consequences. He was sorry, of course he was, but that wasn't going to
bring Cassie back. Nothing was.'

She finally got it, why he was so angry about the hoax they'd
been victim to.

'That's also why I said what I did when we first met,' he
told her.

She thought back to the words that scored her conscience that
night at her father's house, his reaction, her defensiveness.

'Before Cassie died, I would've attended the job at your family
home, I would've seen that our attention wasn't needed, no big
deal.'

'I get it, Noah. You don't need to explain.'

'Doesn't make it right.'

'No, but it lets me understand you.' It felt like an intimate thing
to say and she wondered whether he was thinking the same thing.
She'd never got involved with anyone in the workplace. She'd been
with Conrad for so long and after that, she hadn't been interested in
anything other than forging her own path away from her ex-
husband and making sure Isaac was happy.

'Why can't I get my shit together, Maya?' The way he added her
name to the end of his question indicated he saw her as a friend
and for that she was grateful.

'It's only been five months. You'll never get over losing your
sister. But with time, the grief can get a little bit easier to manage
day by day.'

'You sound like you're talking from experience.'

'My mum died when I was eleven. And it took years to process
it. I'm in my forties now and on some days, I'm still not sure I've
fully come to terms with it.'

'What happened to her?'

'She fell at home, hit her head and we all thought she was fine.

It was days later that she collapsed and died from a brain bleed nobody knew she had.'

'And that's why you were so quick to call when your sister was hurt.' He shook his head, berating himself some more about his reaction and words that night at her father's house.

'I panicked, I made the call. You'd think I'd be more used to dealing with an emergency given the job I do. I think I'll always wonder whether I could've done something different with Mum. Dad probably wonders it too. She had some dizziness after the fall, some confusion but she claimed it was tiredness. She mentioned a headache on and off, but knowing Mum, the pain was worse than she made out, the frequency more than she admitted. She never liked to make a fuss. She was always so strong.'

'Like someone else I can think of,' he said softly. His words and his tone gave her the same fluttery feeling in her tummy she got when he looked at her for longer than necessary. 'Don't you talk to your dad about it now?'

'No. Dad and I don't have much of a relationship these days. And we don't see eye to eye about a lot of things. Especially when it comes to my job.'

'I'd have thought he was proud of you.'

'He never wants to know about it, and that's been the case the whole time I've been flying helicopters.'

'I'm sorry, Maya. That must be tough.'

'Sometimes it really is.' It was as though he saw parts of her she didn't always reveal.

'How is your sister now?'

She smiled. 'Disgustingly happy with her new husband.'

Noah laughed despite the melancholy, despite the topics of conversation. 'Good for her.' He looked at his watch. 'I should get going. My nanny needs her break given she's coming back this evening. I think she feels sorry for me – she told me to head out for a run after work, grab some time for myself, so right now, at the end of shift, I mustn't dilly-dally – her words, not mine.'

Maya picked up her bag. 'I mustn't dilly-dally either,' she teased.

'Exciting plans this evening?'

'Not particularly. I said I'd drop in on Conrad, see how he's doing.'

They left the locker room together and Noah asked, 'How's his recovery?'

'Frustratingly slow.' For him and for her.

Maya waved to Nadia, who was deep in conversation with pilot Vik. She thanked Noah for holding the front door to the airbase building open for her to go out first.

'So he's not up and about at all yet?'

'He can walk okay but he says he's unsteady on his feet,' she said, noticing Noah had a weird look on his face. 'That's normal after his injuries, isn't it? You'd know more than me.'

He pointed a remote to his car and it bleeped. 'It can be. But every case is different.'

'Well, hopefully he'll be up and about before too long.'

'I hope so too.' There was a hesitancy before he added, 'Does he have friends who can pitch in so it doesn't all fall on your shoulders?'

It felt nice to have someone thinking of her, especially him. 'Not really, but it's fine.' It wasn't but she didn't really want to air all her grievances. By the sounds of it, Noah had enough of his own.

'You guys are divorced, right?'

'Yes, although he tends to forget.'

'Doesn't that bug you?' When he clocked her surprise at the question, he apologised. 'I shouldn't ask; we barely know one another.'

And yet she felt closer to him than any man in a long time. 'I think we know more about each other than we did earlier,' she smiled.

'Well, that's true. And about Cassie... thanks for listening.'

'Any time.'

And the thought of *any time* with Noah had her smiling right up until she remembered she was still at Conrad's beck and call. She crossed her fingers that there would be an end to it soon.

18

Noah only realised he was whistling when a woman turned in the pharmacy to glare at him over the shelf of painkillers.

'Oops,' he whispered to Eva, who was reasonably content in the buggy. If he wasn't moving, he found it best to at least keep talking to her so she didn't protest at being pinned into a contraption when she wanted to shuffle around on the floor and explore her environment. 'Maybe she's not well, hence the pharmacy visit and the mood,' he floated to the twelve-month-old.

He wasn't even sure why he was whistling anyway. Perhaps he was trying to pretend that everything was going to be okay and subconsciously wanted Eva to pick up on that vibe rather than any other. He hadn't slept very well thinking about Paul's impending visit and Eva's future – even the run after work and a visit to the pub with Bess and Frank for a few games of pool hadn't been the tonic he needed.

When it was his turn in the queue, he smiled at the pharmacist and requested Bonjela, Calpol and some eye drops. 'The eye drops are for me,' he clarified. 'Too many late nights.'

The pharmacist bagged everything up and he embraced the

benefits of the buggy by shoving it into the basket beneath along with the dozen eggs, a loaf of bread and the bottle of milk he'd bought.

Someone held the door open for him and he passed through, thanking them before he even clocked that it was Maya and he instantly felt a weight lift. He'd noticed it at home too; even when it felt as though everything was against him, when the sexy pilot at work flitted into his mind, it had the power to put him in an entirely new headspace.

'We keep meeting here,' he grinned.

'Seems that way.' She matched his smile and for that, he was pleased.

'What brings you here again so soon?' He stood out of the way of a customer coming out behind him.

'Picking up another prescription,' she answered.

Eva wasn't at all impressed with the hold-up and she screeched, making both of them start.

Noah crouched down and put his hand on Eva's knee. It was a good distraction from the realisation that the last time he'd seen Maya, they'd had a candid conversation and he'd shared a lot more personal details than he probably should have when he was this new in town. 'What have we said about screeching, Eva?'

Eva responded to his question with another screech.

He stood up again. 'She'll rupture my ear drums at this rate.'

Maya laughed. 'She's discovering her sounds, her voice. Isaac was the same.' She crouched down to meet Eva properly and when she said hello, Eva grinned and reached out to her.

'Your son is at university, isn't he?'

'That's right. In Scotland.' She was still paying Eva all the attention she wanted and instead of screeches, they got giggles. 'Hopefully no longer discovering his sounds or at least I hope he's not.'

'He might do if he's at the pub,' Noah laughed.

Maya handed Eva back the toy duck she'd dropped out of the side of the buggy, although Eva's response was to drop it again.

Noah picked up the toy this time. 'Her new game.'

'She seems to love it,' Maya approved.

Noah felt suddenly nervous in her presence. He wanted to keep her here, talk some more. 'It's nice to have a couple of days off work, isn't it?' Not the most imaginative of things to say but it would do. Because she still looked happy enough to be here talking to him and at least this time, they weren't being watched by an ex-husband who really needed the term *divorce* explaining to him.

'I love my job but yes, so good to have a rest.' She pointed into the pharmacy. 'I'd better get inside before it closes.'

'Closes? It's not even 5 p.m. yet.'

Maya kept her voice to a whisper. 'We're not quite up to the standards of the London pharmacies here in Whistlestop River. The pharmacy closes at 4 p.m. Tuesdays and Thursdays.'

'I'll try to remember to schedule being unwell,' he joked.

'You'll get used to it. There's a bigger pharmacy in the next town that's open twenty-four hours so most people can get something there if they have to.'

Whistlestop River kept taking him by surprise and by far the biggest surprise, and a pleasant one at that, was Maya. Strong, capable, beautiful Maya. He bet Conrad was kicking himself that he hadn't been able to hold onto her. Noah hadn't yet mentioned that he was pretty sure he'd seen Conrad that night near the pub. He almost had when she said she was heading over to see him, but he'd held back, wondering whether it would be better to mind his own business. He was too new to town, to Maya's life, and the last thing he wanted was to make her feel uncomfortable.

Maya waved to Eva to say goodbye as she stepped inside the pharmacy, but Eva was back to screeching as Maya moved out of the way of a woman who was coming the other way.

'Hello, Mrs Simms.' Maya held the door a bit wider to allow her to pass.

The woman grunted and Maya rolled her eyes.

'Not a kid person?' Noah wondered as they watched Mrs Simms head across the road.

'She has two grown-up kids of her own.' She shrugged. 'She means well but she's not been happy since they both left Whistlestop River so soon after one another. No idea what went on there.'

'You know a lot about the town.'

'Lived here a long time.'

'Then you need to teach me about the locals – who shouldn't be on the receiving end of Eva's squeals and who might laugh it off.' He attempted humour but his words brought back the reality that Eva might well not be with him if Paul got his way. Noah had done a one-eighty on the idea ever since meeting Paul; giving Eva to him was impossible to imagine. But her needs came first, he had to remember that. And perhaps being with her biological father was the right thing to do, no matter Noah's opinions on the guy.

'You'll get to know everyone gradually, I'm sure.'

'How about tonight?' he asked before she could get away. With Maya, he felt as though he needed to take a chance, go for it before he lost his nerve. 'You could tell me about the locals over a beer.'

'I'm not sure I can face the pub this evening.'

'Neither can I.' He indicated Eva. 'I was thinking my place.' A risky move when they worked together but he couldn't help himself. He was so attracted to her. His former girlfriend Tahlia had been beautiful and career-minded too, but she'd also had an edge he hadn't really thought about until he met Maya. Maya had the same level of confidence as Tahlia but also a softness she hid until you got to know her better.

'Your place?'

'I have to put Eva down around 7 p.m. but I have a lovely porch overlooking the river. You might enjoy the peace and quiet. Nobody would see us from the street, nobody would discover where you'd sneaked off to.' So if her ex-husband decided to go on the prowl and find out what she was up to, he'd have a hard time coming down the side of the house. Noah doubted the guy would have any idea where he lived either, although he wouldn't put it past him to use the police computer to his own advantage if he got any hint that Maya might have a social life aside from attending to his needs.

'Actually, that sounds like a really lovely idea.'

He'd assumed she'd turn him down, thought he'd hear some excuse about Conrad. His words spilled out of him after he shared his address. 'I'll be home all evening, any time after 7 p.m.'

'I'll see you then.' And with a smile for him and a wave for Eva, the door to the pharmacy closed behind her.

Eva tested out her screech all the way down the street to the car park and this time, Noah was so happy Maya had said yes that he almost joined in.

19

Maya hammered on the front door for the third time when Conrad didn't answer. She knew he'd want her to use her key – 'treat this place as your own' he'd say for the umpteenth time – but today, she couldn't because she was carrying a rather heavy container with a casserole as well as a bag of fresh fruit and his medicines, which she'd picked up for him yet again. He was giving her the run around with so many trips to the pharmacy but the fact that she'd bumped into Noah again when she was there had made it easier to bear. It was tempting to tell Conrad she'd seen Noah just like the last time because watching him mentally kick himself for sending her in the first place would be fun.

When Conrad finally opened the door, she warned, 'Do not tell me I should've used my key, kind of got my hands full.' And the July temperatures meant she was also hot and bothered, not a good combination when she needed to find the patience for this man.

'Wasn't going to say a word.' He closed the door behind her and followed her into the kitchen. 'Something smells good.'

'Did you get a visit from the doctor?' She couldn't help snapping; she was hot and pissed off at him for the latest game he'd introduced with their son.

'No need to take that tone, Maya.'

Oh, there was every need. Coming here interfered with any down time she might have in her own busy life. She was well and truly over it, especially given what he was up to with regards to Isaac. And now she had an alternative option, a beer on a porch overlooking the river with Noah, an escape from all of this, spending time with her ex-husband was even less appealing. To others, including Bess, she looked crazy running after her Conrad like this, but she wondered how many of them would do the same thing in her shoes. She suspected most of them would do anything to keep the piece of their life they were most ashamed of buried deep.

Isaac had called her on her way here. She'd answered on hands-free in the car with the usual excitement she felt when her son phoned but when he told her what Conrad had been up to, she passed from a state of excitement to one of frustration.

Conrad had called Isaac earlier today, probably when she was running around after him, and told Isaac that he wanted Christmas with his son this year. Not just Christmas but New Year as well. And he wanted to do it in Ireland at some fancy hotel. Sometimes she wished divorce came with a forcefield around her and Isaac that Conrad had no means of penetrating, but unfortunately real life wasn't like that.

'He can't make me go, can he?' Isaac had moaned on the phone, tired after working all day in his friend's parents' café. 'I don't want to travel to Ireland on my Christmas break, Mum.'

'Nobody can make you do anything, Isaac.' She flicked her indicator off angrily when it failed to do the job itself after she turned at a roundabout.

'It'll make things hard for you if I say no.'

And then it dawned. 'So I take it from that you mean he's not including me in this invite for the festive season.'

Isaac swore, which he rarely did when she was within earshot. 'He said you'd be welcome to come along.'

'I'll be working over Christmas so I won't be able to go away anywhere; I'll need to be in Whistlestop River. He knows that. I've already told him.' But she hadn't realised why he'd been so interested when he asked her a couple of weeks ago. She did now.

'I want to be home, Mum.'

'I know you do.' Her heart went out to him. He'd want to come back to Whistlestop River, catch up with friends, have a proper break. 'Do you want me to talk to him?'

With a sigh, Isaac said he could fight his own battles. He could but Conrad liked to fight dirty and that was what she was worried about.

'You never know,' she said, upbeat, 'it might be fun in Ireland. Knowing your dad, it will be a nice hotel, maybe with a golf course.' She injected a bit of enthusiasm she hardly felt.

'I don't like golf. I like tennis. And it'll be winter, Mum.'

She wished she could take away all of his angst. 'Isaac, I really wish—'

'Do not say you wish we could get on. We don't hate each other, Mum, but Dad only thinks of himself and I can't see that changing any time soon.'

And neither could she. It hurt all the more because of her emotional distance from her own father, but she'd never thought her dad only considered himself. He thought deeply about others, he put them first, which made it harder to grasp why he seemed so against Maya's life choices. Whatever was going on between her and her dad seemed to run a lot deeper than Isaac's problems with Conrad. Conrad wasn't a complex character; he was shifty and prone to moods but he wasn't hard to work out. Isaac had got it pretty much spot on when he claimed Conrad thought only about himself. Even what he'd done for Maya all those years ago when she'd left her family home at such a tender age, what she'd seen as an action to rescue her and help her had really, all along, been for his own benefit. It had taken years, however, for her to see it that way.

Maya suspected there wouldn't be anything she could do to convince Conrad not to enforce this trip. And she knew if Isaac turned him down, he'd put pressure on Maya instead and she'd have no choice but to do her very best to persuade their son to change his mind. If she didn't then Conrad would remind her gently of how difficult he could make her life if things didn't go his way.

In Conrad's kitchen now she found three old plastic containers from the back of a cupboard and spooned the casserole into separate portions. 'This will keep you going a few days. I'll pop them all into the freezer.'

She felt him watching her as she divided up the casserole that he liked, but didn't love. It was somewhat childish to have made it for him knowing that, but it was something Maya could do to keep her sanity and feel that in some situations maybe she got a turn to have the upper hand.

'Are you going to tell me what's bugging you?' he asked. 'There's obviously a reason for the casserole and the attitude. I'm sorry I'm such a burden.'

'Stop being dramatic. I said I'd cook for you for a while seeing as you can't manage it. And I made the casserole for myself as well; I've left half of it at home.' She hadn't, but he'd never know that.

'There's something going on,' he huffed. 'We were married long enough that—'

'You know exactly what's going on.' She didn't need to hear

about their marriage, whatever spin he was going to put on things with examples of how they knew each other.

'I don't or I wouldn't ask, would I?'

'Microwave the casserole portions for about three or four minutes, maybe five from frozen,' she instructed. 'Stir after to avoid the hotspots or you'll burn your mouth.' With any luck.

She put the last of the containers into the freezer. He'd hate using the microwave and it gave her another little flicker of gratification. He'd always sneered at reheated leftovers unless they were done in the oven, said they didn't taste right.

'Oh, you'd love it if I burnt myself, wouldn't you?'

She rounded on him. 'You know what I would love? If you could actually have an adult relationship with your own son!'

'Ah, so that's what this mood is about.' He seemed smug he'd caused it.

'What's wrong with you?'

'With me?' He jabbed his healthy thumb towards his chest. 'I want to spend time with him.'

'On your terms. In Ireland. At Christmas.'

'What's so wrong with Ireland, for fuck's sake?' He shoved back a chair from the kitchen table but then fell against the table to steady himself.

She helped him into the chair.

'Head rush,' he claimed. 'Catches me out sometimes.'

'Are you still getting the headaches?' It didn't matter how much she didn't like the man; she didn't wish him harm and headaches following the type of accident he'd had might be a real cause for concern.

'I've got the hospital appointment coming up, remember.'

'I remember.' She couldn't forget, she had it marked on her wall calendar because it would be her who was taking him.

Sometimes she wondered if she'd ever get the distance she

needed to start her own life properly without his hold over her. Her mistake had been to trust him in the first place, to let herself be taken in by him, but at the time, she hadn't had much choice and she'd been grappling for help from someone, anyone. At first, he was kind to her; she felt special and seen. But over the years, that had changed and cracks soon began to show. They'd been subtle at first, little digs her way, especially his doubt about her career path, his certainty that she'd stay home with her child and forget about the silly idea of flying helicopters for a living.

'You women might think you're equals,' he'd said to her when she started her pilot training. She'd been saving it to be a surprise, worked until she had enough money to start, thought it would show she wasn't assuming he'd pay for her now they were married. 'But you're not. The fact is there are some jobs men are better at doing. Take my job, for example. Some of the female officers can't handle the more boisterous prisoners, the rougher arrests; that puts them in danger and it's a risky game.'

Part of Maya had tried to see it as Conrad being respectful of women and not wanting them to come to any harm, but she knew she was scrabbling for hope that her husband hadn't just hinted that female officers were inferior, hinted that her wanting to become a pilot was ridiculous, a word he'd actually used to describe her career choice as time wore on. Her job as a pilot came under the same title of *jobs unsuitable for women*.

After diminishing her career aspirations, then had come his affairs, his carelessness exposing him each time. Their marriage had been like a domino rally and once that first domino fell, the rest just kept getting knocked over until they were left with a mess she had to walk away from.

She took a deep breath and sat next to him at the table. He looked fine now he was seated. 'Think about it, Conrad, about

Ireland, I mean. A trip like that should bring two people together, not drive a bigger wedge.'

'Is Isaac really so hellbent he doesn't want to do it that he asked his mummy to intervene?'

The comment rankled but she bit the corner of her mouth to stop herself rising to the bait.

'I've booked accommodation in a castle,' Conrad went on. 'And there's a golf course. Talk about being bloody ungrateful.'

'It's not that he's ungrateful; it's because of the way things are between you both.' *And for the last time, Isaac doesn't like golf!* She'd told Conrad enough times but as usual he hadn't absorbed the fact, just kept thinking about himself.

'Yeah, well, the way I see it, you'll have him with you this summer, when he finally gets his backside home, so why can't I have him over the winter?'

She ignored the dig about Isaac working up in Scotland, annoyed he didn't see their son for the amazing, independent young man that he was. 'He's not a toy you shunt back and forth. Do you actually want him in your life? Because the way you're going, you're going to lose him.'

He sucked in breath between his teeth. 'Now, now, Maya, that sounds a bit like a threat to me.'

'It's not a threat.' But she had to get through to him. 'You're pushing him away. And a blood tie doesn't mean a guarantee he'll always be around, not when the emotions aren't there.'

His good arm shot out and grabbed hold of hers. 'Do not come between me and my boy.'

She yanked her arm away. 'I'm doing everything I can to make sure you have a relationship with him!'

'You make it sound as if it wasn't for you, we'd have no bond at all,' he harrumphed but he soon turned serious. 'Oh, that is what you mean. Well, can't change your opinion, I've learnt that along the way. He's my son and I say we're doing Christmas and New Year in Ireland. Either you like it and come with us, or you stay here. Up to you.'

'Have you ever thought that maybe he will have had a whole term at university and doesn't want to be traipsing miles even if it is to a fancy castle?'

She picked up her things.

'What you mean is he wants to come home to his mummy so she can coddle him.' His words dripped with disdain. 'I get it, you're number one. Usually. But Maya, this year it's me; I'm going to be number one.'

She wasn't going to say another word. She'd tried.

'You'd better make him see sense or you know what'll happen!' he yelled as she walked out of the kitchen, out of the front door and left him behind.

Didn't she deserve the chance to be happy?

She knew she did. But she had no idea how to achieve that with Conrad always waiting in the wings.

20

'Do you think we can call this evening a date?' Noah asked Eva after he'd given her a bottle and she sat on his lap in the rocking chair beside her cot. He still didn't think he was much good at this parenting lark, but she was definitely calmer the last few days. Maybe her gums weren't quite as sore now another couple of teeth were poking through. Or maybe it was because Paul hadn't shown his face again... yet. He'd cancelled their arranged meeting and rescheduled for a few days' time and Noah hadn't exactly been sorry to put it on hold. It gave him a chance to think about things. Not that he'd come to any conclusions or found any answers.

With Eva on his hip, he stood up and pulled the curtains closed. 'Not going to answer me?'

She belched in response and then smiled up at him. He couldn't deny every time she gave him that look, it felt special and it made him feel that if she wasn't in his life, he would lose more and more pieces of Cassie. It made him treasure the time with her all the more and perhaps his patience as a result contributed to her being that bit more settled.

Eva hiccupped and Noah plucked a story book from the shelf

beside her bed. The house was liveable for now, but this room was the most comfortable and homely. Eva came with a lot of paraphernalia and it was the room he'd made the most effort in – he'd put stencils on the walls, there was the rocking chair that Cassie had picked out and all of the other baby bits and pieces including the colourful mobile, the soft toys, the changing table and brightly coloured, wipeable mat, and a nice, sturdy bookcase filled with the books Cassie had bought for her daughter.

He read the title out loud. '*Goodnight Moon.*' Eva promptly took the book from his hands and grasped it in her own. 'Oh, you're reading tonight, are you?'

When he laughed as he watched Eva, it made him realise he hadn't been doing a whole lot of that lately. He was usually on tenterhooks waiting to mess something up. But perhaps that was parenthood all over, even temporary parenthood, if that's what this turned out to be.

The thought left him more unsettled than he would've liked.

Custody. When Paul had said the word the other day, he'd been within his rights. It didn't matter what Noah felt about the guy, did it? The man was Eva's father and it was a good sign if he was determined to be in her life, wasn't it?

Noah suspected he might feel better about it all if Paul had even tried to bond with Eva when he was here, but he hadn't.

He started to read *Goodnight Moon* when Eva finally relinquished the book.

As he read, Eva's little hands reached out to touch the brightly coloured pages, Noah paused at the end of each one to let her savour the vivid colours, the joy of story time when she wasn't yet able to read for herself. Their parents had been big on story time, and judging by the amount of books Cassie had bought for Eva, despite her being nowhere near ready for most of them, so was Cassie.

It was Eva who closed the book and he turned it over, read it again, by which time her eyelids were growing heavy, she wasn't as interested in the pages this time.

He stood with her in his arms, he dimmed the lights until they were almost as low as they could go and corrected the curtains so that the sunlight could no longer filter in via the gap he'd left.

He took Eva over to her cot, ready to lower her in but he felt her breath against his cheek and he froze on the spot.

'Dadda,' she said again. All he could do was stare at her.

'Dadda…' She said it a third time, almost as if she was convincing him he wasn't hearing things.

Noah had had surprises over the years, he'd had special moments like when he passed his driving test when he was sure he'd failed, or on his twenty-first when an old friend from way back had come over from Cyprus to help celebrate, or the day he'd joined the air ambulance crew in London and couldn't believe how lucky he was to have such a job. But none of those moments had made him feel the way he did right now.

He cleared his throat after planting a kiss on Eva's forehead. 'No, I'm Noah,' he said, for the sake of full disclosure.

But his words were ignored. 'Dadda, dadda, dadda…' She was trying it on for size with a big smile for good measure.

And all at once he wished Cassie were here, that his sister could've seen this. 'Oh, Eva…' He pressed a kiss to her forehead. He couldn't lower her into the cot. He didn't want to let her go.

He didn't move from her room until the doorbell chimed.

He had learned along the way, from experience and Geraldine's advice, that when a baby was tired and they were set for bed, you shouldn't ignore it. No riling them up or keeping them awake for your convenience; get them down and it would be easier in the long run. Knowing Maya, she'd understand his delay in getting to the door so he lowered Eva into her cot the way he usually did at bedtime, he stroked her head and said goodnight in his soft voice and then he switched off the light, leaving only the soft glow of the night light on top of the chest of drawers before he tiptoed out.

'I've come at a bad time, haven't I?' was the first thing Maya said when he opened the door.

He whispered, 'No, you're here at the time we agreed, but I was ten minutes late putting Eva down.' He beckoned her inside. 'Don't worry, we won't have to whisper all night.'

'You're quite the expert by the sounds of it.' She matched his volume.

'Why don't we head out to the back porch with a beer each?' He led her into the kitchen, grabbed two beers and headed outside.

'I'm tempted to look in every time I go past her room,' he admitted when they were settled on the bench. To get to the back door it meant going past Eva's bedroom, but it was handy where it was positioned because it meant he'd always be able to hear her if she needed him. There was a baby monitor Cassie had bought, somewhere, he just hadn't found it yet and with the cottage so small, it hadn't really been a problem so far.

'I was the same when Isaac was little,' said Maya. 'I'd sneak in and watch him sleep; it was mesmerising.'

'I've done it too, then with a little snuffle from Eva I freeze in full-on panic that her eyes will ping open and all that hard work to settle her will be out of the window.'

'I remember that feeling all too well.' She looked out at the river, back at the house. 'It's a beautiful evening.'

'It's been a lovely summer,' he agreed.

'Are you managing to get organised here?'

'I'd call it organised chaos right now. And if I didn't have Geraldine helping me out the way she does, it'd be a whole lot worse. She insists on cooking for Eva and sometimes she tidies the house, which I told her not to, and now I've reached the point where I tidy up before she arrives so I don't have to feel guilty all day that she might be back here doing it.'

'She probably does it because she'd be at a loose end when Eva sleeps.'

'She said the same.'

Their eyes met briefly until Maya looked away and took a sip of her own beer.

'Would you ever live anywhere else but here?' he asked.

She shook her head. 'Not now. I love it. It's beautiful, it's peaceful, it's home. Do you think it might feel that way for you too some day?'

'Only time will tell, I suppose.' And he couldn't help wondering whether she might have a lot to do with his feelings about the town too.

Noah had sailed through most of his life facing challenges as they came, moving forwards in his career exactly the way he wanted. And then his life changed in an instant. But, he had to keep reminding himself, so had Eva's. That's what had kept him going on the days when he felt sorry for himself, when he felt selfish for being pissed off at how this had altered things for him.

Noah had had a good life in London, a routine of sorts, even though it had no permanency, not until he'd been appointed Eva's legal guardian after Cassie died. Even living with Tahlia hadn't been considered with regards to the long term. She'd moved in, she helped with the mortgage, it had all just worked itself out. Perhaps that had been his mistake; he should've questioned what they both really wanted, then he might have realised how different they were.

He and Maya got talking about The Skylarks, both the red team and the blue team, about Frank the engineer and how long he'd been there, about the Whistlestop River Freewheelers and their camaraderie between themselves and everyone else. It had been the same with his previous air ambulance crew; you had to work as a team or the job would be a bust. But what Whistlestop River and the air ambulance had over the team he'd left was a sense of belonging to the place as well as to the job. Perhaps that was to be expected in a smaller town compared to the big city.

'What made you want to become a pilot with the air ambulance?' Noah asked when he'd finished recapping on his career journey in response to Maya's similar question.

'I was fascinated by aviation as a kid.' Her whole face lit up with passion. 'I funded my training when I was able and studied really hard, did the hours on the ground, the time in the air. I started as a helicopter pilot for a sightseeing company in and around Dorset. Then I worked for a charter company flying businesspeople all over the place. But I'd always been in awe of what the air ambulance did, since I was a little girl and saw an emergency evacuation after a helicopter landed on the school field.'

'Wow, that'll do it.'

When she laughed, the sound was welcome in his world that felt as though these days, it was one stress added on top of another. 'I love my job, most days. The losses are hard, the bad outcomes.'

It didn't matter that she was the pilot and not attending to the patient directly the way he was; she felt the pain as much as the critical care paramedics on board. They were a team.

They looked out at the river, the evening stretching out ahead of them. Noah's hand shot up to swat at a mosquito.

'Perils of living near the river,' she laughed.

'Yeah, didn't really have this problem in my place in London.' The mosquito left him alone for now. 'How's your son getting on at university?' He was enjoying her company, more relaxed than he'd been in a while, and he wanted to know more about her.

'Really well.' She filled him in on Isaac's study path, his passions, but as she finished, the frown she sometimes showed was back.

'You miss him,' said Noah.

'Yeah, of course.'

'But that's not what's troubling you.'

Her fingers pulled at the label on the beer bottle. 'I've a few things on my mind, that's all.' She tilted her head back to get the rest of the beer and when he offered her a second, she accepted.

He grabbed another two beers from the fridge, peeked in on Eva, who was fast asleep, and returned to the back porch.

'It's my ex,' she confessed before taking a sip of her beer.

He should've known.

When she finished telling him all about Conrad's plan to have Christmas and New Year in Ireland with Isaac, he asked, 'And are you invited?'

'I am, but I'm not going. I can't for one thing, with work, but I wouldn't want to either. It's a way for Conrad to be in control, for him to get me to do what he wants and probably another attempt at making me see that I can't live without him.' She said the last part of the sentence louder and more dramatically. And then clasped a hand over her mouth. 'Sorry...' she cringed.

Noah shook his head. 'The smoke alarm went off when I burnt toast a couple of days ago and Eva didn't stir; I doubt you'll have woken her. Getting her to sleep can be a challenge but once she's asleep, she won't wake unless she wants to and that's usually in the middle of the night.'

He missed her smile when it faded again. 'I know this is going to sound crazy...'

'Try me.'

'Sometimes I ask myself whether Conrad had that accident so he could get me to play nursemaid and be around him more. Ridiculous, I know.'

'It's not ridiculous...' He wiped the condensation his hand had gathered from the bottle onto the leg of his jeans. 'I'm not sure how to say this...'

'I find it's easiest to blurt these things out.'

'I think I saw him.' He spoke up before he could chicken out. 'Remember happy hour at the pub that night?'

'Conrad wasn't there.'

'Not inside, no. But when I was walking back here along the path beside the river, I'm almost positive I saw him running down the alleyway.'

She didn't say anything straight away.

'You're sure it was him?' she said eventually.

'Not totally sure, but I saw the cast on the man's arm.'

'Right...' She took a couple of sips of beer in quick succession before adding, 'You know, I shouldn't be surprised.'

'You're not angry?'

Her sigh was one of defeat; if it was him and he'd been waiting on someone hand and foot, he'd be cursing out loud and heading straight round there to demand answers.

'You must think I'm crazy to put up with all his shit,' she said.

Totally, which told him the man was manipulating her in a way she couldn't escape from, like the cruelty of holding onto the leg of a dragonfly and watching its body wriggle around and try to get out of your grasp, except that it never quite could.

But he didn't want to make her feel worse. 'Not at all.'

'I've been wondering if he'd been putting it on a bit, you know.' Shaking her head, she added, 'At least now I won't feel guilty when I pretend I've been called into work and make him get a taxi to his hospital appointment.' She grinned. 'I'll enjoy that.'

'Are you going to confront him?'

'At the moment, I try to keep things calm.' She filled him in a bit on the relationship between Conrad and Isaac. 'I don't have the best of relationships with my own father for reasons I won't go into and I don't want the same for Isaac.'

But he had a feeling it was a whole lot more than that.

She leaned back, closed her eyes. 'My place is great but this house, Noah, is something to treasure.' Her eyes opened again. 'Did you know this was once the original signal box for the railway line that ran through the town?'

'It's been passed down through my family, a little slice of Whistlestop River history right here.'

'Is that so?'

He nodded. 'We actually came here a lot as kids, Cassie and me. I remember my grandad making kites with us. Cassie and I would run along the path next to the river when it wasn't even windy, wondering why we couldn't launch them into the air.'

'That would've been heartbreaking for a kid.'

'I do seem to remember it wasn't only Cassie who looked like she might cry.' He began to laugh. 'And I can't believe I admitted that.'

'You must have loads of great memories with Cassie.'

'I do.' And he could probably spend a whole week talking about them and still not be able to share them all.

'I didn't know your sister but if she could see you right now, the way you've changed your life to bring up Eva, I think she'd be really proud.'

'I hope so. That or she'd tell me, "Noah, you're totally messing this up."'

'Siblings always have a way of telling it like it is.'

'I don't know what she'd think of my latest move.'

'And what's that?'

'I'm not sure I'm the right person to be doing this and so I took steps to find Eva's birth father.'

If she was shocked, she hid it well. 'And how did that go?'

'Crap at first. But then he tried to get in touch with Cassie. He wrote a letter which came to me, I called him and he's been here to the house to meet Eva.' When she stayed silent, he wondered what she was thinking. 'It's not that I want rid of Eva; I love her. But I'm her uncle, you know. Isn't it better for her to be with her actual dad?'

'Maybe... although that depends on why he wasn't in her life in the first place.'

'He left my sister and pretty much disappeared.'

'So reliability isn't his strong point.'

'Maybe... although that depends on why he left.'

She smiled at his repetition of her own words. 'I suppose. And if he's her dad, he deserves a look in at least.'

'I sense you want to say something else,' he said, turning his body to face hers on the bench. He knew she was holding back.

'Call it experience, but just because this guy is the biological father, it doesn't mean to say he'll be the best parent.'

'But isn't it his legal right?'

She shrugged. 'I don't know the ins and outs of custody. Cassie entrusted Eva to you. I don't know what to advise apart from not to do anything rash.'

Both of them heard a grizzling coming from inside and Noah held his breath that it would stop, releasing it when the sound passed.

'I won't hand her over easily, you know.'

'I know.'

For months, he'd thought that that was exactly what he'd do with a kiss goodbye and a 'see you later' from Uncle Noah, but now, with Eva a part of his life and his home, he already knew it wasn't going to work like that. 'She called me dadda earlier.'

'Noah...' She put a hand against her chest. 'That's really beautiful.'

He took a glug of beer and after he swallowed said, 'Except that I'm not her dad.'

'To her, you very much are.'

They finished their beers and when it was time for Maya to go, Noah wished he could walk her home. 'I have Eva so I can't see you home safely,' he said. He'd love nothing more than to accompany her through Whistlestop River, along the main street, past the shops closed for the night and the pub with its beer garden likely filled with revellers making the most of the long summer nights.

'It's fine, I'm happy to walk on my own and I can handle myself, remember.'

He saw her to the door and wondered whether she was thinking the same as he was, that it had been a great evening, good company, and he wished it could end with a goodnight kiss.

But instead, he watched from the front gate as she walked to the end of the street and turned at the corner, giving him a little wave as she did so.

Maya could definitely handle herself, although not when it came to an overly attentive ex-husband, it seemed. He hoped for her sake she'd find a way of getting him to leave her alone, let her move on in her own way. Clearly a divorce wasn't enough for the man to keep his distance.

21

With weather conditions making it unsuitable to take the helicopter up, the crew had been out in the rapid response vehicle this morning on three jobs and by the time Bess and Noah got back to the airbase, they were both keeping everything crossed that that would be it. They'd stayed out in the field after the first call, not knowing where they'd go to next, but with a couple of hours left on shift and the cloud lifting, Maya had sent a message to them on the road – any other calls would be responded to in the helicopter – and so they headed back to base.

Luckily for them, the remainder of their shift wasn't too demanding and it gave them a chance to give the rapid response vehicle a decent clean. It was seriously muddy and Bess explained their last job that had seen them trek into a farmer's field to get to a patient who had had hay bales topple over onto him. He'd been trapped beneath. Noah and Bess had been there to help with more adequate pain relief using the stronger drugs; Noah had gone with him in the ambulance to the nearest hospital with Bess following on to pick him up.

Maya flicked water from the sponge she'd used on the vehicle's windscreen in Bess's direction when Bess moaned that she was too hot as she finished scraping off the last of the water from the glass with the squeegee.

Bess gave a squeal. 'I shouldn't yelp. That was nice! But roll on autumn; far too warm to be working in this weather.'

'What are you on about, girl?' Noah, who was using a chamois leather for the roof to buff it to a shine, called across the vehicle's rooftop, 'Make the most of it, won't be long before we're all moaning at how cold we are.'

'Definitely don't wish summer away,' said Maya.

Bess emptied the dirty water from the bucket onto the grass beyond the parking bays. 'I bet you can't wait to see Isaac when he eventually gets here.'

Maya smiled. 'I really can't. It's a shame he'll be home for such a short period before his second year at university starts, but I'm pleased he's got work; it's good for him.'

'Has he talked his dad out of the Ireland idea yet?'

She'd told Bess all about it and Noah knew after the other night, but it still felt weird answering the question in front of both of them. 'What do you think?'

'That Conrad is one stubborn man.' Bess threw the pieces of heavy-duty wiping paper they'd used to clean the rapid response vehicle's hubcaps into a rubbish bag. 'Why can't Conrad do something closer to here? Isaac will get to see you too then, catch up with his friends, everyone is a winner.'

'But then Conrad wouldn't get one up on anyone else, would he?'

When Noah stayed behind to vacuum the interior of the vehicle, Maya and Bess loaded up buckets, cloths and as much else as they could take in their arms and went back inside the hangar. Maya dried the bucket with wiping paper before setting it onto its rightful shelf.

'Why do you let him do it, Maya?' Bess asked. 'Not just the games he plays when it comes to Isaac but everything else: the running around you do for him when he's supposedly still suffering so badly, he can't manage on his own.'

'I don't *let* him,' said Maya. But at Bess's look, she admitted, 'All right, maybe I do. I need to start being firmer, I know that.' She stopped what she was doing and took out her phone from her back pocket. 'Talking of which...' She held up a finger, meaning Bess should wait to see what she was up to.

Maya called Conrad. She told him she was stuck at work doing a double shift and he'd have to get a taxi to the hospital for his appointment.

'It can't be helped, I'm afraid,' she said in her most regretful voice. 'You could reschedule but I don't think that's a good idea; you know what it's like trying to get an appointment.'

He grumbled but relented and when she hung up, she and Bess were smiling.

'Well, it's a start.' Bess put her arm around Maya. 'You need to do that more.'

Maya had deliberately left it until the last minute to tell Conrad she wasn't taking him to the hospital. He was messing her around and right now, it felt good to do the same back to him. The small victory gave her a modicum of satisfaction.

But Bess wouldn't let it go as they went into the bathrooms and washed their hands. 'This needs to stop; he can't keep you in his life like this when you're divorced.'

Maya shook her hands over the sink before grabbing a paper towel. She could feel the usual exhaustion creeping up on her at having to try to explain away why she appeased her ex-husband.

'I don't want to give up on them,' she told Bess. 'Conrad and Isaac.'

Bess pulled a paper towel from the dispenser to use on her own hands. 'You wouldn't be you if you didn't want the best for your son. But are you absolutely sure having Conrad in his life is going to be the best thing for Isaac when already they can't see eye to eye? I mean, I get that you wouldn't want them estranged, but they're not; they still have contact. Why can't Isaac tell Conrad to bloody well bugger off with this Ireland idea, tell him it's somewhere closer to here or nowhere at all?'

If only it were that simple.

Bess moved the conversation on now she'd said her piece about Conrad. 'So... you and Noah,' she began.

Maya turned to head for the locker room to get a change of T-shirt. 'We are colleagues.'

Bess closed in behind her. 'You walking away from me tells me very much that you're more than that.'

Maya knew better than to flat-out deny it. Bess had been shooting her looks for days now and Maya knew she wasn't that great at hiding her feelings. She admitted, 'We've been getting on well.'

'I knew it.'

Maya undid her locker and took out a fresh T-shirt. 'He's so unlike Conrad, in every way.'

A slow smile crept onto Bess's face. 'You really like him. Anyone could see you were attracted to him, but I didn't know your feelings were that strong.'

'They're not... or at least they can't be.'

'You mean because you're colleagues?' She dismissed the worry with a swish of her hand. 'You two are professional; you'd make it work.'

'It's not just the job. He's complicated, I'm complicated; it's a recipe for disaster.'

'Or...' Bess grinned. 'It's a recipe with a lot of heat and spice. My favourite kind.'

And with her laughter ringing around the air ambulance base, Maya began to think about her own future and whether Conrad would ever leave it. But more importantly, could Noah be a part of it?

* * *

Noah admired their handiwork with the rapid response vehicle. It had been a busy shift but one he'd desperately needed to stop him thinking about Paul's impending visit. His mind kept conjuring up his sister and the look he imagined would pass across her face if she was here to see him so much as considering handing over her daughter to that man.

Nadia arrived shortly after Noah headed back inside the airbase and into the kitchen. She was carrying a platter on one forearm in the way a waiter would bring the food to your table in a restaurant. 'I come bearing gifts!'

'I should think so too,' Maya joked as she came from the office into the kitchen. 'While you've been off living it up, Bess and Noah have been out on a job, we've cleaned the rapid response vehicle, I've been doing paperwork, and the admin is piling up.'

'I'll get to it, don't you worry.' She set the platter down. 'I was at my friend's daughter's christening, where I laid it on thick, saying my poor crew, they barely get to eat on some days, they're so busy flying or driving around the county saving lives. And so, ta-da!' She gestured to the platter once again.

Bess must have sniffed the sandwiches out from the back room and joined them.

But Nadia didn't let anyone at the food until she'd asked whether the posters for the upcoming open day had been done.

'Remind me of the date,' said Noah. 'I'll put it in my diary.'

'Oh, there'll be little chance of forgetting,' said Bess, 'and Nadia, the posters are done. Vik and I did them last week, loads of colour, you'll be impressed. And the flyers are ready for distribution.'

Noah felt bad he hadn't helped with any of it yet. 'I can distribute those if you like.'

'You're on,' said Bess. 'I'll give them to you next, it's less than a month away, so if you could get them out to local businesses and homes pronto. There's a few thousand of them.' When his face fell, she laughed. 'Don't worry, each of us will take a bundle and Nadia usually has a plan of the streets we each need to deliver to.'

'The plan is ready,' said Nadia. 'I'll send the email out to you all soon so you don't duplicate deliveries.'

'Sorted,' said Bess, one eye on the food.

Noah asked Bess about the open days, wondered whether it would be similar to those he'd been involved in before.

It sounded like it would be. As with his previous team and others in the country, this air ambulance received no direct government funding towards running costs and they relied on charity donations, wills and grants. The good thing about that was that they got to spend money on what they wanted, upgrade equipment as needed and put patient care first without a whole load of red tape. But it also meant that fundraising, including open days, was a vital part of what they did. On open days, the team here at Whistlestop River would open their hangar doors to welcome in the public. There wouldn't be an entrance fee, but donations would be encouraged.

'Folks around here are very generous,' Bess smiled. 'We're very lucky in that respect.'

The open day would be a good opportunity to generate donations as they shared what they did with demonstrations of life-saving treatment, question and answer sessions with the crews, kit demonstrations and real-life stories from some of the members of the public whose lives they'd saved along the way.

'Those are my favourite,' said Maya. 'It's lovely to have people come here not only to thank us but to know the difference we all made.' She and Bess talked about Patrick, the amateur cyclist who came off his bike almost a year ago and was miraculously back to riding again. 'He's coming to the open day to give a speech about his journey since the accident.'

Noah could listen to Maya talk for hours, watch her, absorb her company. She was the other thing he had on his mind right now, when Paul wasn't getting centre stage in his head. He really liked her, he couldn't deny it, but as much as his life was complicated, he wondered, was hers actually far worse?

Noah squeezed in next to Maya as Nadia pulled the cling film off the platter of food. 'It must've been a fancy christening. I don't know what half that stuff is.'

Maya picked up something in an oval shape covered in bread-crumbs. She bit into it without delay.

'What is it?' he asked.

She shrugged as if to say she had no idea.

'She'll put anything in her mouth,' Bess joked and immediately got a rebuke from Nadia, who told her to keep it clean.

Noah had taken a while to get the lie of the land here at the Whistlestop River Air Ambulance headquarters. Maya was strong-willed, the quieter of the bunch but absolutely no pushover, Bess was loud and confident and always up for a joke but damn good at her job and someone he'd want at his side on every shift. Nadia was the mother hen of the team, organising them all, which he supposed came as part of her job description, but it filtered into things like bringing them food or yesterday when they'd used the rapid response vehicle she'd made both him and Bess a little packed lunch. They'd joked about it and said they were like her children, except they were all roughly the same age. Nadia, Maya, Bess and himself were all in their forties, so perhaps that helped with the bonding and camaraderie. Mind you, there were no limits as to how friendly the likes of Frank and all of the Whistlestop River Freewheelers were either so that blew his own theory right out of the window.

Right now, Noah didn't care about anything other than how hungry he was and how good this mini quiche-like morsel that he'd shoved into his mouth tasted.

'Do you even know what it is?' Maya threw his own question back at him.

'Quiche,' he said through a mouthful. 'I think.'

'Yes, but what quiche exactly?'

'The quiche kind.' He popped another identical one into his mouth.

When Maya's phone went, she took it out, looked at the display and promptly shoved it back in her pocket. It rang three or four more times, while the whole crew enjoyed more food and by the time it rang again over an hour later, she finally excused herself to take the call and Noah didn't see her until almost the end of their shift.

'Come grab a slice of cake,' Noah urged Dorothy, who came into the airbase to drop off more blood supplies after they called the request in earlier. 'No quiche left, we ate all of that, but it's almost home time for me so I'm sneaking in a slice first. It's chocolate with a thick addition of buttercream icing.'

Dorothy wasn't going to argue. 'Better get it while there's some left with Bess around. That one likes her chocolate.'

'Heard that!' Bess's voice hollered from reception.

Maya finally came into the kitchen, uninterested in the offer of cake and Noah discreetly asked her whether everything was okay.

'Not really, but thanks for asking.'

'You know where I am if you want to talk.'

'The beers and conversation the other night were exactly what I needed.' She smiled. 'Isaac called me when I was walking home from yours. He seemed to like hearing that I had a life outside of work. And outside of Conrad's.'

'Glad to have been of help. Come over again. Any time.'

'Thanks.' Her eyes held his. 'How's Eva?'

'She's good. Paul is coming over tomorrow.'

'And how do you feel about that?'

He took a deep breath, searching for the answer, but it didn't help. 'I've no idea.'

'Take your time; it's a huge thing you're dealing with.'

'As are you.' He wasn't about to let her give him sympathy when she was very much in need of some too. 'I mean it when I say that beers are always up for grabs. At my place, because of Eva, but it's better than nothing.'

'It's way better than nothing, Noah.' She cleared her throat when Bess came over with Dorothy extolling the virtues of the cake.

When the others moved away again, Noah took a chance. 'How about tonight for those beers?'

'I can't.' She seemed regretful which was something. 'Rain check?'

'Are you going to Conrad's?' He watched her shoulders slump. 'I apologise, it's none of my business.'

'We're friends, I appreciate your concern.'

Her response was way too formal and she'd lumped him in the friend zone, not a place he particularly wanted to be. He wanted so much more.

'I'm going to see my sister,' she said brightly, before adding with slightly less enthusiasm, 'Then it'll be on to Conrad's quickly.'

'Right.' Well, at least it wasn't an entire evening with Conrad then.

'Go on, say it.'

He shook his head. 'It's easy to have an opinion, not so easy to be the person in turmoil; I should know given my situation.'

'You must wonder what the hell I'm doing still going to see him given the divorce, his pretence at how bad he really is.'

'Kind of.'

'I ask myself that same question every single time I go over there.' But checking herself, she added, 'I need to make sure he and Isaac have a chance, you know?'

He kept his gaze on hers. 'That's what you told me. I'm not sure I believe it, though.' He added gently, 'There's more to the story, isn't there?'

She didn't say a word, but he picked up on the almost imperceptible nod and it left him wondering what the hell this man had on her that meant she couldn't shake him off?

22

In the supermarket on his way home from shift, Noah put three different kinds of biscuits into his basket and grabbed more coffee in case he ran out. He picked up a cake, for goodness' sake – he didn't buy cake! He ate it, but he never bought it. He'd be purchasing those funny doily things his gran had used if he wasn't careful, laying everything out with impeccable presentation. He was doing it again, overthinking tomorrow's impending events, wanting to make a good impression. And for what? For a guy he didn't like?

It was all in Eva's best interests, he told himself, as he threw a packet of pre-sliced vegetables plus a packet of chicken and a stir fry sauce into his basket, an easy dinner to concoct in a wok for one this evening.

As he swiped the barcode of the carrot cake box, it made him think of eating the leftover cake earlier, the way he and Maya had laughed over the excessively thick chocolate icing that Bess had managed to get on her chin and that Dorothy had told them would add at least ten pounds to her hips before she accepted a second chunk from Nadia and gleefully ate it. It was nice to see

Maya relax and laugh. She probably wouldn't be doing much of that this evening when she had to go and see that ex-husband of hers.

At home, he unpacked the groceries and thanked Geraldine the way he always did when it was time for her to leave.

'I enjoy looking after Eva,' she smiled. 'It's like having babies of my own all over again, except without the full responsibility. It's true what they say, you know…' She handed Eva to him when the little girl reached for Noah as soon as he balled up the reusable shopping bag and stuffed it into its place in the back of a cupboard.

'And what's that?'

'That being a grandparent is the best thing in the world. It's the chance to do it all over again.' She caught herself. 'Oh, no, silly me, I know Eva isn't my grandchild. It's just, well, I imagine that this is what it feels like when—'

He reached out and put an arm around her shoulders. 'Stop apologising. You're the closest thing this little one has to a grand-parent and I'm pretty happy about that.'

She waved a hand in front of her face. 'Oh, now you're getting me all emotional.'

'Dadda…' said Eva.

Geraldine's face registered the word. 'Did she…?'

'She did. I'm still trying to get used to it.'

'Oh, Noah…'

'And it was her first word. Unless you know otherwise.'

She shook her head. 'No, the honour is all yours. You got to hear her first word and it was a good one.' She nudged him. 'How do you feel?'

'Yeah, it's pretty special.' But his emotions began to bubble up. 'I wish Cassie was here. It should've been mumma, not dadda.' He gulped; he'd been too honest.

Geraldine put a hand on his arm. 'I know you wish things were different. But you're doing your best. I'm sure Cassie would've been proud of how you're taking care of Eva for her.'

Noah bathed in the compliment but only for a millisecond because they both knew what tomorrow was: a second chance for Eva's biological father to get to know her. Noah briefly hoped the guy wouldn't show, problem solved. Last night, he'd had a dream that Paul had disappeared all over again, the way he'd done to Cassie, and Noah had taken Eva to school on her first day, walked her down the aisle when she got married.

'I'll leave you to it,' said Geraldine, insightful to his emotions, knowing he'd likely need a bit of time to gather himself. She'd done it before, walked away when he had so much going on in his head, he needed a moment. He bet she was an amazing mother with her children, both when they were little and now they were adults.

But before she gathered her things, he couldn't resist asking, 'You don't like him, do you?' Her opinion mattered to him.

She zipped up her bag after taking out a set of keys. 'That's not for me to decide.'

'Your opinion is all I'm asking; we're all entitled to one of those.'

She didn't hesitate for long and set down her bag again. 'There's something shifty about him. He wouldn't look me straight in the eye.'

'Maybe he's shy,' Noah teased.

'Men like that aren't shy; they're brash, full of themselves. And I'm afraid I don't think he can be trusted. Watch yourself, Noah.' She gave Eva a little hug goodbye while she was still in Noah's arms. 'And watch this one.'

'I will, don't you worry.'

'Trust your gut instinct. It's important when you're a parent.'

Her words stayed with him after she left and while he made his dinner as Eva played on her play mat, making a heck of a noise whacking a xylophone with a stick that had a big rubber ball on the end. This sort of noise had become the soundtrack of his life.

What if he was about to lose another piece of himself?

* * *

Paul arrived the next day without much fanfare at all. He seemed neither excited nor nervous; he simply turned up and came over the threshold, hands in his trouser pockets, something stuck in his teeth given the way he kept sucking at them as though trying to get it out without using his fingers. Noah supposed he should be grateful for that.

Noah offered Paul a coffee in an attempt to shake off his dislike of the man, for Eva's sake, but when he spotted Paul's obscene, bright-green, expensive car parked outside as if to announce his presence, Noah's resentment and aversion towards the man came back.

'I won't bother today.' Paul's brash response reminded Noah of Geraldine's parting words about gut instinct. 'Can't stop.'

The guy didn't ask to hold Eva and he showed little interest in her this time and Noah's feelings took a downturn from 'dislike' towards 'despise and mistrust'. Something about the way he even stood here, cocky, hands in pockets as though he was sure all of this would work out for his benefit, made Noah increasingly uneasy.

'What do you mean you can't stop?' Noah asked. 'I thought you wanted to see Eva again.'

'I do. And I have. She's right there.'

Yep, in *his* arms!

'I've come to tell you that I intend to fight for custody.'

'You told me that the last time.' Was he going to serve papers? Already?

'Unless...' Paul walked back through the house from the kitchen as if he owned the place and Noah had no choice but to follow after him. 'Unless we can come to an alternative arrangement.' The guy had the audacity to sit in the armchair devoid of any of Eva's toys, manspreading his thighs, sitting there as if this was his throne and he was about to lay down the law of the land.

'Arrangement? You mean like visitation?' Maybe this guy didn't want full-time fatherhood and it gave Noah an immense sense of relief.

'No, not like visitation. I mean an arrangement.' He slapped his hands onto his knees. 'Look, I can see you and Eve have a bond—'

'It's Ev-*a*,' Noah corrected, emphasis on the 'a'.

'You have a bond, you're good with her.' Was he waiting for a thank you? 'We could take this to court and I'm sure as the biological father, I'd stand a good chance of winning—'

Noah interrupted again. 'Not necessarily. You buggered off and I became the legal guardian.' He was done with being polite.

'There were extenuating circumstances.'

'Like what? Come on, explain.' He shifted Eva, who had no interest in this stranger, to his other hip. At twelve months, she wasn't overly heavy but she was when held for a long time and right now, he didn't want to put her down on her play mat with her toys because he wanted to guard her with everything he had. He had no idea where this conversation was going but he sensed it wasn't anywhere good.

And when Paul spoke again, told Noah what he had in mind, Noah felt like a bull let out of the bucking chute and he was more than ready to hurl this cowboy off his back.

'Get out! Get out now!' His roar made Eva whimper.

'You might want to think about that,' Paul said calmly. This guy had some balls. His feet were rooted to the spot.

'I don't. Get out!'

Eva started to cry more, the ferocity in Noah's voice enough to knock her off centre. He wished she was in her cot so he could physically take this guy by the scruff of his neck and send him packing.

Paul walked slowly towards the door, smug as anything, and turned back only once. 'I'll be in touch. But don't even think of telling anyone about this little conversation because I'll deny it and then you'll look even worse in the eyes of the law when I go for custody and turn it around and say you offered me money to take Eve.'

It's Ev-a, you moron! he wanted to yell.

'Get the hell out,' he said in a lower voice, not keen to upset Eva more than she already was.

With a smirk that Noah longed to smack right off his face, Paul left the old signal box cottage.

And Noah clung to Eva tighter than ever.

He never wanted to let her go.

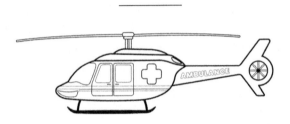

23

Maya loved Julie's new home. It might not be finished yet, but it was filled with her sister's characteristic warmth and welcome already. She and Seth had bought a spacious, detached, characterful property in an idyllic setting a little outside of Whistlestop River. It had far-reaching country views and a big list of things that had to be done. The home was thatched but not grade listed, which meant they could do whatever they liked to it for their renovations and it had a generous back garden with plenty of space for a growing family.

'So what's next on the renovation agenda?' Maya asked as they sat on the deck chairs in the kitchen with a cup of tea each. The deck chairs were in lieu of proper furniture, which Julie refused to buy until they'd done the kitchen and right now, she and Seth couldn't agree on the colour scheme so were putting up with barely any bench space and the tatty floor and doing the dining room while they came to a decision.

'I'd love to say kitchen...' Julie set her cup of tea on the floor while she re-tied her ponytail. With old jeans and a worn, flannel, gingham shirt, she looked like a glamorous renovator.

'But...'

'Well, as you know, neither of us can see the other's point of view.' She said it with a smile. Had this been Conrad and Maya, the same sentence would've been laced with frustration, Maya knowing that he wouldn't be the one to budge. 'I want to knock the wall through to make it a little more open plan. Seth would rather have the kitchen separate, says it's in keeping with the house and tradition. But at least we've agreed on midnight-blue units for the kitchen and a butler's sink.'

'Well, that's a start.' Maya blew across the top of her tea. 'What about worktops?'

'Wooden but as to which wood...'

'You two will get there in the end. And I'm enjoying seeing it in progress.'

From her position on the deckchair, Julie reached into the nearest cupboard and when she looked like she might fall out of the chair at any second, she pulled her body back upright with the prize: a packet of chocolate hobnobs in her hand.

Maya readily took two and they settled back to talk more about the house, the other plans Julie and Seth had, what they wanted to do with the garden.

Julie caught a crumb from her biscuit with her hand before it dropped to her lap. 'From the minute I stepped through the gate... or rather lifted the disintegrating wood out of the way to get to the path, I knew this was the place I wanted to bring up my family.'

'Mum would've loved to see you here, settling down.'

'I like to think she would have too.'

The way Julie looked reminded Maya so much of their mother, it almost hurt. Julie didn't really remember their mother, who died when she was only three years old, but she and Maya talked about her often. They didn't shy away from the pain of losing her; they faced it together. Sometimes it made them melancholy but not always, not today.

'Has Dad been over since you did the stairs?' Maya asked. The stairs had rotted in a few places and so the entire staircase had been replaced in a beautiful natural oak with turned newel posts and spindles.

'He has, he approves. And he's been helping me a bit in the garden too.'

Maya almost spat out her tea. 'Dad... *our* dad... got his hands dirty?' She took another hobnob from the packet standing upright between them. 'He hates gardening, that's why he employs someone else to do his own.'

'Let's face it, Maya, his place is huge; no way could he take care of it all even if he wanted to.'

'Good point. But still, I never expected gardening. What did he do? Mow the lawn?'

'Oh, I had him on more heavy-duty stuff than that. He cut back all the hedges and overgrown shrubbery, he pulled out weeds, cleared debris behind the shed. We can see a rockery now at the foot of the garden, which I thought we'd get rid of but Dad had some good ideas of what to plant.' She sipped her tea. 'He was talking about your garden while he was here.'

'Mine?'

'He was saying you could do a lot with small gardens now. He had images on his iPad; he's been looking into it. And I can't help wondering whether that's because he wants a way to connect to you.'

'But he's never asked me about my garden.'

'Maybe he doesn't know how.'

Maya didn't know what to make of it; it felt surreal to have him interested in anything she did.

Julie went on. 'Dad overheard us talking out on the patio one day – remember when we sat out back at Dad's with hot chocolates on that really cold afternoon the week before my wedding?'

Maya remembered. Julie had been looking after her elderly neighbour Barbara's dog Rufus so he could get some exercise. The dog was a bit too lively for Barbara but when Julie headed to the family home, he was also too lively to be inside their father's house and so they took him out back and let him run around the garden. The sisters had nursed hot chocolates and snuggled under a blanket each for warmth as they chatted.

That day, they had talked about the house Julie and Seth had bought and about Maya's cottage of modest size with a small back garden that was low maintenance, largely because she didn't bother with it rather than it having been designed that way. Maya had admitted she'd love to be able to sit outside properly rather than dragging out a plastic chair every time. They discussed what it would be like if she added a small seating area, or if she added a gazebo at the back, they talked about the types of flowers they could put in tubs to add colour depending on seasons.

'I still haven't done anything with it,' Maya admitted. 'The old vegetable patch is still there, still growing weeds. I haven't yet found the time or energy to do anything.'

'Well, Dad heard us that day and when he came to see the stairs, he asked if you'd planned anything for your garden yet. I told him you never seemed to have the time with your job.' She locked eyes with her sister. 'He said the air ambulance was lucky to have you.'

Maya set down her mug with the dregs of tea inside. 'He never said that. You must have misheard.'

'This is why I didn't say anything before now. I didn't mishear, Maya; why do you automatically assume the worst with him?'

'I do not.'

'Do too,' she retorted.

'He's always hated what I do.'

'I don't think he hates it. He might have wanted different for you and who knows why, as neither of you talk to each other. But after I fell and hit my head at the wedding and the air ambulance crew came out, I think he started to see it all a bit differently. It was like it wasn't real before, but seeing the helicopter land in the back garden, everyone rush inside to help, maybe he began to see the reality.'

When Maya said nothing, Julie started to get annoyed. Maya could tell it was happening because her posture changed; she was no longer leaning back in her chair but sitting ramrod straight.

'You have a different dad to the one I know,' said Maya.

'Don't be ridiculous.'

'Julie, it's not ridiculous. And we've been through this, many a time.'

'I think he actually wants to start making amends with whatever it is that makes you two clash. Can't you meet him halfway?' Julie always saw the best in people; she was good at it.

'Let's see how it goes,' Maya answered noncommittally.

Julie snatched the packet of hobnobs up plus the mugs and went over to dump them in the old aluminium sink that had a single piece of worn benchtop next to it. 'It will *always* be different if you don't let him try to be the dad he really is.'

Maya saw the hurt in her sister's eyes. 'I've been waiting for him to approve of me and my life choices for years, Julie. I got tired waiting.'

'Do you know that when Dad was talking about your garden, he thought he might send some of his gardening team round to you, give you some ideas and quotes? I told him not to, that you'd appreciate him more than a bunch of strangers. But now I wonder whether you would or whether you'd close the door in his face.'

'You make me sound so callous.'

'Well, he didn't say he would, but I think he might want to and is worried he won't get very far.' She pulled her sister into a hug. 'I don't think you're callous, I think you're strong and wonderful, and so is Dad. But try? Not because I'm asking you but for you and for him. If you put as much effort into your relationship with Dad as you do trying to get Conrad and Isaac on track...'

Maya relented. 'Next time I see Dad, I'll make an effort.'

'Which will only be when I orchestrate it.'

Maya grinned. 'I knew you kept throwing us together on purpose.'

'And yet you still show up.'

'Of course I do.' She hugged Julie back. 'Now show me around the house again; let's park the subject of Dad and me for now. I've taken what you've said on board. I promise.'

'Do you really promise?'

'Yes. Now I want to see more, including the drawings for the loft conversion.'

'Okay, I'll let it go for now but only because I can't wait to show you the plans.'

'Lead the way.'

Maya arrived at Conrad's with so many containers of pre-cooked food ready for his freezer that he could have a dinner party for ten, three times over. He'd transferred her money for the shopping and as it was way too much for what she needed, she'd gone for it, batch cooking for hours so that she could cut down on these visits. The freezer was almost at bursting point and even he couldn't argue that his one-armed abilities would hamper his nutrition now.

'I can't tell you how much I appreciate this, Maya.'

Well, he could. But that didn't mean she hadn't had enough. She was over it. She didn't want thanks. She didn't want gratitude. She wanted her freedom back. And she'd heard a whispering from someone else at the air ambulance base that Conrad, or someone who looked very much like Conrad, had been spotted out again after dark nipping in to pick up a box of beer from the supermarket.

'I'm going to have to shoot off, I'm afraid.' She put on enough regret to be believable but not so much he'd take it as sarcasm. It was a fine line, especially when she was annoyed at him for the pretence.

'You all right?' he asked, holding the shoulder of his bad arm with his good one to make sure she didn't forget his injuries.

'I am, work has been really busy lately. Same shifts as usual but we've had a lot of callouts each time. It doesn't always work like that but recently...'

'How's Noah?'

'Noah is good. So is Bess. So is Nadia.' She refused to take the bait.

She picked up the empty cardboard box she'd used to transport the containers and held it against her body so she wouldn't have to face the lingering hug he liked to give if her guard was down. She spotted some files on the sofa. 'Are you working?'

He shrugged. 'I asked work to send me something. I want to keep my mind active, you know. And they're always happy to offload paperwork.'

She headed for the front door rather than questioning him further. The day Conrad volunteered for paperwork would be the day she'd look up and see pigs flying between the clouds. He was a man who wanted to be involved with cases, out investigating; he didn't want to sit there shuffling papers.

'You working tonight?' he asked before she reached the front door.

'No, I'd be useless to anyone this evening. I'm going to take a bath, have an early night.'

She was straight out of the door and to her car, she had the engine on within thirty seconds and she pulled away from the kerb in less than another ten.

Maya's home was small but the bathroom was fitted perfectly with a slipper tub with Victorian-style taps, a sink, toilet and shower and a window low enough that when she lifted up the blind, she could see out to her back garden. It would be nice when she got around to sprucing it up a bit, but for now she closed the blind so she didn't have to think about it or Julie's claims that her dad wanted to help.

She started the bath running, added some bubble bath and when her landline rang, she ran into the bedroom to grab it because she knew it would be Conrad. It wasn't that she wanted to speak to him but she wanted him to know she was here. He had a habit of doing this, calling her on the landline and pretending he'd hit the wrong button in his contacts rather than calling her mobile number. It was his way of checking she was where she claimed to be and right now, she'd rather pander to his need than have him repetitively calling her.

She took the phone into the bathroom. The water thundered from the taps, the bubbles rising. 'Conrad, I'm about to step into the tub.'

'Sorry, it was a butt dial,' he laughed.

Did he seriously expect her to believe that?

'Well, an accidental dial at any rate,' he corrected.

She leaned over and the taps squeaked as she turned them off. Whizzy padded into the bathroom to keep her company.

'I'll let you go,' he said when she didn't engage in more conversation.

'Yep, don't want the water to get cold.'

She must have been tetchier than she realised because his amused tone altered. 'No need to snap.'

'It's been a long day.' She didn't point out that as well as work, she had the emotional turmoil of Isaac and Conrad churning over in her head constantly, not to mention being a meals-on-wheels service for a lying ex-husband. 'I want to climb into a warm bath and then go to bed.'

'There was a time when you did that here.'

'Conrad, we are divorced. Doesn't that mean anything to you?' She calmed herself by fussing over Whizzy.

'Marriage did.'

'I have to go.'

'Have you thought any more about Ireland?'

'Seriously, you want to talk about this now? No, I haven't thought about it.'

She couldn't see it but no doubt there'd be an amused sneer on his face right now as he said, 'Maya, don't push it, babe.'

'Please don't call me babe.' She hadn't liked it when they were married and she sure as hell didn't like it now. 'I'm going now, Conrad.'

'Suit yourself.' And so that he had an upper hand of sorts, it was him who put the phone down on her.

Maya sank into the tub, Whizzy leapt up on the small faded-blue cabinet with drawers beneath that she'd painted and put at one end and curled up into a ball, happy to be near her for the company.

Maya didn't have the long bath she'd wanted, not that Conrad bothered her again. But after ten minutes, she couldn't relax and so she climbed out, dried off, pulled on her jeans again and hoped that Noah's offer of a beer was an open invitation for tonight too.

24

Noah had had an impromptu visit from Paul again this morning but when he saw the car pull up, he'd purposely run with Eva to the back of the house and closed the kitchen door, where he'd stayed until the knocking ceased and he was sure Paul had gone. He knew he'd have to face the guy sooner or later but he was still fuming at his audacity, asking for money, proving that he had zero interest in Eva. What sort of man could do that? He had no idea but he did know if Paul was to come here before he'd had a chance to calm down some more, Noah might well kill him with his bare hands.

It was the height of summer, which meant the days went on forever, sunlight lasted and lasted, but still Noah had the curtains in the house closed at the front. Nobody could get around the back, not without scaling fences and bushes, so at least that was something. Eva had refused to go down for her nap today and so every time she picked up one of her toys, he cringed at its volume in case Paul came to the door and he would know they were inside.

Before he became Eva's guardian, Noah would have assumed that babies who skipped a daytime sleep would sleep for much longer at night. But it didn't work that way. She was grouchy and his attempt to put her down early had met with screams and the kind of sobbing you couldn't ignore unless you were prepared to have your heart totally broken.

He was pacing in the lounge, shushing Eva, the little girl in his arms with barely open eyes by now. She was fighting the sleep, or she was so overtired her body wouldn't let her settle. And whatever he tried didn't work. He attempted to sing a lullaby – that went about as well as if he'd blasted out Metallica on the stereo. He tried to give her a teething ring – she slung that across the room with a deft flick of her wrist and it crashed into a glass he'd left on the mantelpiece, sending it toppling to the floor with an almighty smash. It was as if the universe knew this was a trying time for Noah, more so than usual, and it wanted to make him doubly pay for even wishing this guy Paul into their lives.

Noah had to leave Eva to scream in her cot while he cleaned up the glass and made sure every last speck of it was gone from the rug and it had been torture listening to her cry for him, but he had no choice.

Her tear-stained face when he finally went to get her rested against his cheek but she began to settle in his arms as he paced in the lounge, jostling her up and down a little by bending his knees as he walked.

A knock at the door sent him hot-footing it out to the kitchen at the back.

'Shit.' He'd have thought he'd hear the roar of that obnoxious engine on Paul's car which had one of those annoying exhausts boy racers thought were a status symbol, the sort of exhaust that pissed off everyone within a mile's radius apart from the car's occupant, who was convinced it gave him bigger balls than anything else.

The knocks kept coming. Did this guy ever give up? He'd said he'd be in touch, but Noah hadn't expected him to be this persistent, showing up twice in one day.

With Eva quiet apart from the odd whimper, he tiptoed out of the kitchen and hovered at the door to the lounge, which he'd left open this time. And then he heard a voice coming through the letterbox. And it wasn't Paul's.

He went into the hallway and opened up the door. 'Maya.'

Her face registered his exhaustion.

'Oh, God, I shouldn't have come. You've got your hands full—'

He reached out with one arm before she could turn and leave and he tugged her gently to come inside. 'I have but I don't mind you being here. I could use the company.'

She closed the door behind her and followed him into the lounge. 'Are you sure?'

'Absolutely.' And right now, he really needed a friend.

She took one look at him and then at Eva and held out her arms. 'Give her to me for a bit; sometimes a change is good. If you're tense, she'll pick up on it.'

He expected Eva to make a fuss as he handed her over, but she didn't; she nuzzled her head against Maya's neck as if she knew her.

'It's been a day,' he told Maya, but the way she looked at him had him adding, 'Who am I kidding? It's been months of total chaos and not knowing what the hell I'm doing.'

'I know the feeling.' Maya seemed content holding Eva. Perhaps she needed the cuddle too.

'How long can you stay?'

'A while,' she smiled.

'Then we're going to need coffee, hot chocolate or a beer.'

'Hot chocolate, please,' she said softly, the little girl still in her arms, lulled into what looked very much like a wind-down routine. Maya had the magic touch.

While he made the hot chocolates, Maya went into the lounge. From where he was, he heard the soft strains of Maya singing a lullaby and by the time he went through with the two mugs, Eva had fallen asleep.

Noah led the way to Eva's bedroom, which was already dimly lit, and Maya lowered her inside the cot before he pulled up the rail as quietly as possible.

They tiptoed away, collected the hot chocolates from the lounge and headed out back. He excused himself straight away though and went back to put the chain on the front door, have a peep through the curtains to be sure there was no sign of Paul.

When he joined Maya again on the back porch, he talked as though everything was fine. 'I didn't expect to see you this evening.'

'It was spur of the moment. One minute, I was exhausted and pissed off with Conrad, then I was in the bath trying to relax, then I was dressed and coming here.'

He knew he shouldn't be thinking it when he had so much other stuff on his mind, but he liked the connection between her in the bath and then coming to see him.

'What's he done this time?' It was easier to focus on someone else's problems than delve into his own, at least for tonight.

'Nothing different to usual.' She sounded weary and he wondered how long this guy had been a pain for her; had it been their whole marriage? 'It's wearing me down, that's all.'

Noah took a sip of hot chocolate, in far more need of this than a beer. Having Eva had been a massive change in the obvious ways – moving here to Whistlestop River, exchanging a bachelor pad for a cottage, having responsibility. But being a parent to his niece had subtly softened his edges too – he made sure he got as much sleep as he could so that he was alert and available for Eva, he spent more time at home between shifts, and now he chose hot chocolate rather than alcohol.

There was a gentle breeze out here on the back porch and it was still light but cool, so at least he wouldn't have to worry about Eva waking because she was too hot.

Maya's fingers threaded through the handle of her mug. 'How did it go with Eva's biological father?' One look told her all she needed to know. 'That bad?'

He ran a free hand across the back of his neck. 'He floated the idea that instead of him going for custody, we come to some sort of arrangement.'

She sat forwards. 'That could be a really good thing. Visitation rights. Then you'll keep Eva in your life, you both get to see her, she'll have two father figures.'

'Yeah, don't get too excited. That wasn't exactly what he meant.' Tension built inside him again. 'By *arrangement,* Paul meant that I pay him a sum of money – twenty thousand – and he'll drop his case for child custody. He'll disappear again, so he says.'

Maya's reaction was almost the same as his had been when Paul suggested it – at least in terms of shock. She probably didn't have the same urge to punch the guy in the face, though.

'He wants you to pay him to keep Eva in your life? What a lowlife, and that's way too polite for him. Who does that?'

The biggest dickhead to walk the earth?

'Not anyone nice or a person with morals. I could've strangled him when he said it. It's lucky for him I was holding Eva.'

'Surely you say no and when he tries to get custody, you let your lawyer know what he suggested. That shows exactly what type of man he is: not the sort you want parenting a young child, no matter the blood ties.'

'Nice in theory,' Noah sighed. 'But he says if I say anything, he'll switch it around and tell everyone that it was me who offered him money to take Eva. After all, I've given up a lot to be here. My girl-friend left me, I gave up my apartment, my job in London, the life I once had. And I'm afraid that with him being the father, and with that accusation, he'll be believed and he'll get Eva.'

Maya set down her mug. 'I didn't realise you were in a relationship.'

'I was, but it's fine, honestly. Eva coming into my life so suddenly taught me about the woman I was with. I have no regrets that we ended, none at all.' He was sure about that, especially since meeting Maya.

She waited a beat. 'Can I ask you something? And when I say this, I really don't mean to offend.'

'Go on.'

'Do you want to be a full-time dad to Eva? Permanently?'

He hesitated before answering. 'If you'd asked me that question when I first came here, I would've said no, that I was doing it out of duty to Cassie, and that I thought her biological father would be the better parent.'

'And now?'

'Now I know what Paul is like, I know without a doubt I don't want him anywhere near Eva. And it isn't only that. With every day that passes, I love Eva that little bit more and I'm beginning to realise how hard it'll be to imagine her not in my life on a full-time basis.'

He finished his hot chocolate and set the empty mug down on the ground. 'I haven't told you what else I found.'

And as the sun showed signs of getting ready to give up for the day, Noah told her what had happened after Paul left earlier today.

Noah had given Eva lunch and for once, she ate it quite happily. It was a small victory that made him feel like he was getting somewhere with this parenting lark, which only served to remind him that it might well not be forever, and he was all over the place with how to feel about that.

Noah smiled at Eva as she finished up the last of the stewed lamb and carrots. He'd served it in the little plastic bowl and spoon he'd picked up from the supermarket when Eva started on solids because he hadn't had the time or energy to go through all of Cassie's things to find the little set his sister had bought for her daughter. He'd felt bad not finding it, but he'd been focused on survival. Today, however, he felt he was doing a disservice to his sister's memory. She'd shown him the set when Eva was only two months old, every day getting closer to when she'd be able to use it herself. Cassie couldn't wait to see it. And then she'd been gone before Eva had a chance to reach that particular milestone.

And it was that memory that had led him to search for the set. He'd shoved a whole load of boxes way up high in the wardrobe in Eva's room when he moved into the old signal box cottage with every intention of going through them at some point. And that point hadn't arrived until now.

'Where is it?' he sighed. Eva had shuffled over to the baby gym she didn't use now unless it was to tug at its parts and see what moved, what made a noise, what didn't do much at all.

He climbed onto a chair and pulled out a box he'd pushed onto the uppermost shelf. He rifled through it to find the tiny sleepsuits Eva had worn when she first came home from the hospital. It was hard to believe she'd ever been that small. He put the box down by the door. Those would go to a charity shop for someone else to use now she'd grown out of them. He pulled out another plastic bag filled with muslin squares and wraps that would be too small for Eva, followed by a much bigger box. That one was filled with Cassie's stuff, however, not Eva's. He put it on the floor out of the way so he could yank out the bag from the very back which almost tumbled down on top of him.

Settled on the floor, with Eva amusing herself with the wooden shape sorter he'd bought her for her first birthday, Noah opened up the bag. First, he took out the monitor and set it to one side; maybe he'd use it at some point, could be handy. And then he pulled out the set: the cream plate and bowl made of the type of thick plastic necessary for babies and toddlers so it would survive being dropped, thrown, bashed against things. 'Bingo.'

He handed the plate to Eva and she grabbed it like it was a new toy. He jerked back when she waved it in the air and almost collided with his lip.

He pointed to the picture on the base of the plate. A giraffe. 'Can you say giraffe, Eva?' he asked. 'Gi-raffe... gi-raffe.' When she didn't respond with anything other than a grin, he shrugged. 'It's a hard word.'

The set also had a knife and a fork, but he wasn't about to hand those over, and the plate had lost its allure already because she'd let it fall from her grasp. Instead, she'd shuffled over to the big teddy bear on the bottom shelf of the bookcase and pulled it out before pushing her face into its fur.

With Eva content, he took the opportunity to go through the box of Cassie's things. It would be a start to getting this place straight, although right now he couldn't get his head around the long term, what it meant now that Paul was in the picture.

He hadn't predicted what an emotional slap in the face it would be opening up the box. He would've thought seeing his sister's photo pinned to his fridge or in the frame in Eva's bedroom every day would be what brought on a tidal wave of grief each time, but this was worse. These were her things, her personal things. He took out a little recipe book bursting with Post-its and all held together with a band; there was the little Victorian teddy bear she'd got from their parents on her eighteenth birthday; the leather purse she'd used for years, old and worn and touched by his sister a thousand times over.

He didn't want to cry. Not with Eva watching him now.

He picked up the Victorian teddy bear, checked it for any

choking hazards – another habit he'd got into pretty quickly – and handed it to her. 'This was your mum's. I think she'd really like you to have it.'

Eva took it with glee and it made Noah laugh out loud, particularly when she squished it into her face the same way as she'd done with the other one. Maybe that was her way of introducing herself to teddy bears, he had no idea. What he did know was that her dribble had now been transferred to this toy but he also knew without a doubt that if Cassie were here, the look on her daughter's face would mean the world. Because it did for him.

Noah had packed up Cassie's flat in a daze shortly after the funeral. It was horrible; the clothes had been the worst thing because it made her feel so alive in his mind's eye, but a mate from work had helped him and between them, they'd dealt with it all reasonably quickly. The clothes went to the charity shop at the end of the road, the place Cassie often shopped herself. They'd thrown a lot of stuff away – pens and stationery that wouldn't be used, the food from the cupboards – and those funny fruit teas she always drank were taken away by his work colleague.

Noah had kept some things for Eva – Cassie's china trinket box with roses on its lid, the vintage jewellery box with a velvet interior, Cassie's favourite blanket in duck-egg blue, jewellery including his sister's favourite white-gold, aquamarine pendant she wore when she went out somewhere posh. She said it made her feel glamorous, even though it wasn't expensive.

He'd also kept all the documents from Cassie's bureau drawers, knowing he'd have to sort through those. And here they were. Piles and piles of them.

Eva, to her credit, played contentedly while he sorted through bills, making an enormous pile ready to shred. And she was still happy enough when Noah pulled out a small folder containing letters.

He recognised Cassie's handwriting on the letters and when he pulled out one after the other, he realised these were the letters Cassie had sent to their mum before their mum passed away. They'd both enjoyed corresponding that way; it hadn't mattered that a text message or phone call was easier. They'd both argued that there was nothing like old-fashioned pen to paper and so they'd kept up the habit. Letters had gone back and forth for years. He remembered now that when their mother died, Cassie wanted to take all her letters back to put with those from their mum, for her own memories. And here they all were.

Noah opened up another one and between laughs and emotional tugs, he read correspondence about the time Cassie had gone to Glastonbury and was the only one of her friends who had worn wellies for the mud; he read about Cassie's first day at her job and how nervous she was; he read the letter from his mum that talked about her frustration when she sprained her ankle and couldn't do her garden for over a week; the letter in which his mum shared a new recipe for an apple and cinnamon loaf.

Noah should've done this sooner. It made him feel closer to Cassie, closer to their mum. It was oddly cathartic.

At the bottom of the box was a photo album and he flipped through it after he'd passed the bigger teddy bear to Eva when she got fed up with the Victorian one and didn't seem willing to bum shuffle her way over to get the other.

In the album were pictures of him and Cassie, the night they'd gone to a dress-up party in bubble wrap – he couldn't remember who had the crazy idea, but he'd fashioned a bubble wrap hat and tie and Cassie had a skirt somehow coloured in bright pink. There were photographs of Cassie's holiday to Greece with friends. She looked so happy, so full of life. There was one of her and her best friend Justine, their cheeks pressed together as they smiled into the camera lens, their grins demonstrative of the strong bond they'd always had. Justine had been devasted at the funeral, barely able to deliver her eulogy, and she'd come to talk to Noah at the wake, something he appreciated given her own grief was so raw.

As he put the album back and lifted the box into his arms to put it away again, he remembered what Justine had said to him that day: 'You'll be a far better father to Eva. She's lucky to have you; it's what Cassie wanted.'

At the time, he'd not really registered the exact phrasing, or perhaps he had but his own interpretation was that his sister had wanted him to be Eva's guardian should anything happen to her and he'd be a good enough choice. He hadn't thought anything other than that. But now, as those words came back to him, he wondered whether Justine might know more about Paul than he did, whether Cassie had been more honest with her best friend than her brother.

As Noah tried to get Eva down for her daytime nap, the thought continued to niggle at him.

And it was still playing on his mind when he gave up on the nap and instead took Eva into the lounge where she had plenty more toys. Except she wasn't having any of it. The only thing she wanted was to sit on his lap and so eventually he relented and ended up watching a football game, partly relieved she was staring at all the colours, partly feeling like a terrible parent for resorting to the television option.

But his interest wasn't on the game; it was on Justine and what she'd said. And with Eva in his arms when she grew bored of the game on television, he picked up his phone. He'd been emailing Justine on and off with the odd photograph of Eva and a short update on how they both were. They'd both wanted that, Eva a part of Cassie they could both share. He and Justine had planned the funeral together, being the two people who knew Cassie the best. Justine had been a godsend, grieving but doing her best to share with Noah as much as she knew about her best friend and the tastes that saw a funeral where mourners were not allowed to wear black, a wake that had lively music in the background, no sandwiches but savouries including quiche, samosas and wraps as well as three types of cake. All Cassie's favourite foods.

He jostled Eva to keep her calm as he made the call.

He hadn't been sure what Justine was going to tell him, whether she'd tell him anything much at all, but as she talked, he felt his body sag back against the sofa with the weight of responsibility for Eva's lifelong happiness now resting entirely on his shoulders. Because now he'd spoken to Justine, Paul wasn't someone he wanted within a hundred yards of his sister's daughter.

Which meant he had a fight on his hands.

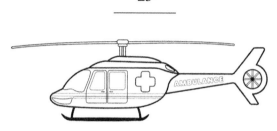

25

Maya wasn't used to men showing their vulnerability, never mind their emotions. Isaac did, but he was her child. Her dad rarely did, Conrad certainly hadn't and watching Noah now felt discombobulating, as though she was an intruder and she should be walking away out of respect.

And yet she couldn't. And it appeared he didn't want her to either.

She'd shown up here at Noah's place tonight for her own benefit but the moment he'd opened the door, she'd known something was wrong. She never could've predicted quite how much turmoil he was in until they came out here to the back porch and he told her everything.

'Cassie never told me any of it,' he said. 'I don't understand why she wouldn't confide in me.'

'I do.' She thought how best to word this. 'I'm really close to my sister but I didn't tell her what was going on with Conrad for some time. I didn't want her to shoulder my burden.'

A barely-there dimple appeared in one cheek as he smiled

across at her ever so slightly. 'I suspect it was less about Cassie thinking she'd burden me, and more that she knew I'd go after the guy and have a word in his ear if I knew too much about him.'

'He didn't hit her, did he?' She braced herself for the acknowledgement but thankfully it never came.

'No, nothing like that. If he had...'

'I bet she looked out for you too.'

'She did.' He disappeared into his memories. 'She made me talk when I really didn't want to, more than once. She was all about sharing feelings. It used to do my head in a bit. But I admit sometimes talking helped.'

He turned to face the river again. 'Justine said that Cassie never trusted Paul. Even at the start, she thought he might be hiding something. He worked offshore on the rigs a lot so they saw one another sporadically and it sounds as though Cassie struggled to get a handle on the sort of man Paul was. Then she'd hear things from bar staff at the pub they went to, murmurs from a couple of her friends that they were sure they'd seen him out and about when he was supposed to be away. When he was offshore, he wouldn't call my sister often, said he couldn't because lack of mobile coverage or some such bullshit. And when she'd ask him where he was, he'd give her a country; it was up to her whether to believe him, she knew that.'

'And she didn't?'

'According to Justine, sometimes she did. Other times not so much. She wanted to end things – he started gambling, putting bets on for this, that and the other. Even with what little she saw of him, he was a different man to the one she'd met and begun dating. There was no trust there at all. Justine said that when Cassie found out she was pregnant, my sister toyed with the idea of not telling Paul about the baby but Cassie wasn't a liar. She told him. Justine said he seemed over the moon, showered Cassie with attention, and my sister, always one to give people a second chance, began to think perhaps she'd misjudged him.

'She didn't tell me any of this. I thought she was with a guy she liked, so when she announced she was pregnant, I was happy for her. I saw the way her face lit up when she said it; I knew how much she wanted a baby. Sometimes I wondered whether she'd got pregnant on purpose, but I mean, what did it matter? She was happy. Paul was still working offshore – said he'd do more hours to make more money ready for when the baby arrived. She barely saw him until he came home right before Eva was born.'

Maya waited patiently every time Noah's voice caught. This had to be hard. She could tell how much he missed his sister, this latest development doing nothing to help him through his grief.

'Justine told me that Paul showed up at the hospital but he was disinterested in Eva. Justine could barely tolerate being in his orbit. He made her uncomfortable, the way he looked at her as though he might well set his sights on her next. When Eva was a week old, Paul and Cassie registered the birth. Then Paul buggered off.'

'Offshore?'

'Justine says Cassie assumed so but really she had no idea where he'd gone. He didn't use the work excuse this time, but he was certainly uncontactable. He didn't answer his phone, he never called her. That was it. He just left. It was then Cassie realised he'd taken her iPad along with all the cash from her money saving jar, which she rarely checked. It likely wasn't much but that wasn't the point. Justine also said she was at Cassie's house one day when a guy showed up looking for Paul. By the looks and sounds of things, it was obvious he was high and looking for his supplier and they deduced it was likely Paul going by what the man said.'

Noah's jaw tensed. 'And now I've brought Paul back into Eva's life. I'll never forgive myself for that.'

'You weren't to know. You were trying to do the right thing by responding to his letter.'

'I realise now that Paul is exactly the man I thought he was when he first turned up at my house – not to be trusted, a liar, a man out for himself and himself only.'

She couldn't imagine what it must be like for him and she didn't miss the tension when Eva's snuffly noises turned into bigger ones that couldn't be ignored.

'How about I go?' Maya suggested. 'You sit here, I won't be long, I hope.'

The little girl was surprisingly calm at seeing a stranger and she stopped crying the moment Maya held her in her arms.

Holding her reminded Maya so much of Isaac. She'd longed to have another baby, maybe even two more, but she'd known early on that Conrad wasn't the man she'd thought he was when she got married and bringing another child or children into that wasn't what she wanted. It wouldn't have been fair on them.

After a few minutes, she settled Eva back down in the cot. 'I think your mummy and I might have had something in common when it came to choosing men. We went for the wrong ones.' She stroked her head. 'They're not all like that, though. Noah isn't, he's kind and wonderful and you're lucky to have him in your life.'

She quietly pulled the side of the cot back up, knowing this could go one of two ways. Either Eva would fall to sleep again after some comfort or she'd scream bloody murder when Maya left the room.

She tiptoed along the corridor and out onto the back porch. Thankfully, Eva had gone for the former. So far, at least.

Noah had got two beers from the fridge. She hoped he hadn't heard what she said to Eva. 'Onto the hard stuff, eh?'

'I've not opened yours, wasn't sure whether you'd want it.'

'I couldn't possibly let you drink alone.' She thanked him when he removed the top and handed her the bottle. If he'd heard her, he wasn't letting on.

'You know what you could use,' she said as they sat there, the darkness surrounding them now. 'A porch swing, rather than a bench.'

'A swing?' She didn't look at him but she'd come to know when he considered something carefully, he adopted a frown that creased his forehead in a way that suggested he was a man who thought deeply about things that mattered. 'That might work.'

'Could be good for Eva when she won't settle. And for you to kick back after a hard day.'

'You sound as though you have porch swing experience.'

'Hardly, my house isn't big enough for a porch, let along something swinging on it, but I've seen it in the movies and always wanted one.'

He nodded but after a beat, his frown was back. 'What am I supposed to do, Maya?'

'The man is a turd.'

'Definitely a turd,' Noah chuckled. 'I mean, who does that, walks away from a baby and doesn't look back? And when they do, they want paying to stay away or they'll go for custody. It's all wrong and disturbing on so many levels.'

'How did Cassie pick up the pieces when he left her and Eva?'

His beer sloshed in the bottle when he brought it down from his lips. 'She had me and Justine; we were both there for her. Cassie cried a lot in the weeks after the birth. She never explained why and I never pushed her, I assumed a lot was down to baby blues. But she did confide in Justine and I was happy with that. Justine got her to the doctor a couple of times. And then, a few weeks after it seemed that she was going to be messed up forever, it was like a little ray of sunshine came out. She became the Cassie I'd always known, the one who took charge of her own life and who got things done. She became a single parent and somehow managed to blossom doing it.

'The stronger Cassie got, the more she started to see her situation differently. Justine told me that rather than worrying about the lack of paternal support, Cassie started to feel relief that Paul wasn't around. She no longer had to worry about the sort of father Paul would be because he was out of their lives. She loved Eva with her whole heart. She swore Justine to secrecy, said she didn't need me hunting Paul down – which I would've done, for the record – and so life continued until...' His voice broke off and emotion caught in the back of his throat.

Maya couldn't imagine the devastation at losing a sibling. If it were Julie, she knew she'd fall apart at the seams.

'What's your next step?' She was distracted by the warmth of his citrusy aftershave or shower gel carried on the night breeze. 'I know you said you've got no idea what to do, but you might have to start thinking of a plan. Have you thought about contacting a lawyer?'

'I haven't got the kind of money a lawyer will charge if this fight is a long one. Bringing up a kid doesn't come cheap. And then there's Paul's threat that he could very well turn around and say I asked for money to take Eva. Nothing was written down between us; it's my word against his.' He put his face in his hands. 'I could lose contact with Eva for good and I couldn't bear it if that happened.'

She waited for him to gather himself. He might show hurt and vulnerability, but Noah was strong too and she imagined he wouldn't want her to see him completely undone.

'I can't let that man have Eva, Maya. I can't. I love her. My sister was glad he was out of their lives, so how can I let him back in?'

'He will have rights as the biological father.'

'I know and I can't stand that that part is out of my control. Legally, he has rights but knowing what he was like, how Cassie felt, and that he was prepared to take money to stay out of Eva's life, how can I stand back and let it happen?'

'When is he coming back?'

'I don't know; he shows up when he feels like it.' He ran his fingers around the mouth of his bottle, deep in thought.

'You should get some sleep. We're on early shift tomorrow.'

'You're right, I should.' He followed after her as she led the way back through the house. 'Thanks for working your magic with Eva.'

'It was my pleasure.' She stopped at the door. The last time they got this close was in the helicopter the other day when she'd helped move the patient from the scoop onto the litter inside and she'd fallen against his hard chest. He'd caught her arms and helped her upright and she'd turned away before he'd seen the effect he'd had on her. 'I should go.'

'Work is a good distraction for me these days, you know,' he admitted.

'Yeah?' The tension between them crackled and she wanted nothing more than to stay a while longer.

'It takes my head to a whole different place.'

'It always did that for me too.'

When he leaned past to take the chain off the door, he was so close, she only had to turn her head slightly and she'd be able to kiss him. But it wasn't the right time. Not now, not when both of them had so much going on. Would it ever be?

Before she left, Maya reached for his hand and held it briefly. 'You're more than a stand-in with Eva, you know, Noah. So much more.' And when she saw him distracted, his gaze perusing the street, left, right, then back again now they were on the front step, she asked, 'Do you think he'll come back tonight?'

'I hope not.'

She wanted to tell him that everything would be better in the morning.

But she knew it wouldn't be.

26

Maya flew the crew to the next job. The helicopter was capable of reaching over 170 miles per hour but with all the equipment they carried on board, it was difficult to achieve that speed. They could fly a lot higher too but that was no good for scoping out landing sights which they would be doing shortly as they made their way to a patient who'd fallen off a ladder at his home in the countryside.

'Good for fuel?' Bess checked. They'd gone to this job from their previous one and so far, the rain had held back despite the bruised clouds lurking.

'All good for fuel,' Maya confirmed. Pilots were obsessed with fuel, which was calculated according to the weight you were carrying on board as well as other factors including outside temperature and air density. Every ninety days, the crew underwent a review ensuring they were all current with the technical aspects of aviation for the air ambulance and part of the tests involved getting weighed, which in winter included all the cold weather gear which made a significant difference. At the last weigh-in, Maya and Bess had joked that they were carrying a bit of extra Easter weight given the number of eggs that had been given to the crews by the general public to show their appreciation and support. Those chocolate eggs had kept them going for almost a month at the airbase.

Dorset was laid out below them, beautiful despite the murky weather, a low-lying valley giving way to their destination. Bess and Noah were on the lookout for a suitable landing spot because the man's home was in a cluster of houses in a village and there were scant options for setting the helicopter down too close.

'There's a school,' Bess began before immediately backtracking. 'Nope, the playground is far too small and doesn't seem as though they have a field.' She was using the iPad which would let her assess size and looking down at the landscape to draw her own conclusions. 'What's that over there to our left?'

Noah's voice came over the headset. 'Looks like the cricket pitch I mentioned earlier.' Maya knew he'd be zooming in on his own iPad. 'As long as they aren't playing a game or practising, we should be good.'

Maya directed the helicopter that way, keeping the aircraft as steady as she could in the wind which seemed to be picking up. The rain had started, big, fat droplets hitting the windscreen. She only hoped it wouldn't get any heavier. 'I've got a visual of the pitch. Looks empty.'

'All clear from what I can see,' Bess confirmed.

'All clear for me,' said Noah.

The pitch unfortunately wasn't that close to the actual job address but it was as good as they were going to get in a village with so many houses and not a lot of open spaces. Even the roads were the sort of country roads with sharp turns and blind bends that rendered them impossible to land on.

Maya's wish for the rain to hold back wasn't granted and already the skies had decided to unleash their fury, with rain coming down harder, and the wind doing its best to jostle the helicopter. But

Maya had done this plenty of times before. She'd flown in worse conditions.

Bess and Noah grabbed their gear as a man waving his arms came running towards them. The man stayed a distance back as the helicopter blades slowed, but only just. As soon as Noah and Bess went over to him, he led the way. Hopefully, he had a car and they'd get to the patient quicker.

Sometimes Maya hated waiting by when her crew had such a tough job. Going a distance to a patient was always hard and then there was the trek back to the helicopter. It was her job to be ready and waiting. Often, while she was on standby, passers-by would come over, ask what she was doing – it was a good chance to promote the Whistlestop River Air Ambulance. Mostly it was kids who wanted to approach but adults were interested too, although today the weather was so awful, she doubted anyone in their right mind would be outside unless they had to be.

As soon as Maya got word over the radio that Bess and Noah were coming back with the patient, she prepared the helicopter and from there, they transported the man to the closest major trauma centre. The patient had a blow to the head from his fall off a ladder cleaning out guttering – a job he'd apparently started before the weather turned from the dry morning they'd had earlier, and a job which, according to his wife, he'd refused to stop doing because of a little rain.

Once the patient – who was mostly concerned about his wife and how she'd manage without him, as she was housebound – was handed over to the staff at the hospital, it was back to base. First up was to talk with patient and family liaison nurse Hudson who would be able to alert the appropriate support services and ensure that the patient's wife was all right, which would in turn allay the patient's fears. Over time, Hudson and Paige, who both worked part time for the air ambulance, had built and enhanced relationships with hospitals to provide the much-needed support for patients and their families.

As Maya finished her paperwork, Frank cornered her on her way to the kitchen and asked whether she had any idea what was up with Noah. 'He's none too chirpy,' said Frank, his top lip and moustache clinging onto a bit of froth from his coffee.

Maya pointed it out and he wiped it off with a smile.

'He has a few things on his mind,' she said, 'but he's okay.' It wasn't for her to elaborate.

In the kitchen, she found Noah looking out of the window as he finished a cup of tea. He didn't turn round so she prompted him with a 'Hey.'

He came out of his trance. 'Hey. Good job today, nasty weather for that call.'

Bess came in and grabbed a cold can of Fanta from the fridge.

'You and Bess are the heroes,' said Maya, 'it was a long way for you to have to take the kit, but you got to our patient in good time and Hudson spoke with the hospital; he'll likely only be in for twenty-four hours and then back to his wife. She's got help in the meantime.'

'That's good,' said Bess.

Noah rinsed his cup and set it into the dishwasher. 'He was worrying in the helicopter on the way to the hospital, not about himself, only her.'

'That's sweet.' Bess had a thirsty gulp from her can. 'And Maya, it's not just me and Noah, we're all heroes and don't you forget it.' With a smile, she left them to it.

Noah sounded like himself when he called after her, 'You'll be my hero if you do the paperwork.'

'Can't hear you,' came Bess's voice, fading as she walked away.

When it was just the two of them again, Maya couldn't ignore the conversation they'd had last night. 'Did you get any sleep?'

'Some. Eva must've known I had things on my mind. She slept through.'

'Bless her.'

His smile disappeared and he turned to look out of the window again.

'I'll leave you to it. Half an hour till end of shift. Bess and Frank are up for a late lunch, or you could call it early dinner, at the pub if you can make it. Eva would be quite welcome in there; they have highchairs.'

'Appreciate the invite. But I've got a few things to do.'

'Noah...'

He ignored the concern in her voice. 'Actually, while you're here, do you know much about how overtime works? Is it best to ask Nadia?'

'There isn't usually a lot of overtime unless one of the blue team is out sick. And even then, it's a stressful job; are you sure that with a baby you could even do more hours without pushing yourself to the limit?'

'I've got to raise some serious cash and fast. I don't have a choice.'

Maya left him to it and after shift she decided to give the pub a miss.

There was somewhere else she needed to be. And this time, it wasn't Conrad's. He still had the cast on his arm but this morning, he'd left a message to say that his dizzy spells had passed, he was steadier on his feet, he was going to go out for a short walk. Maya had almost laughed. He'd been going stir-crazy stuck inside, more like it, so had decided to be honest and admit he was on the road to recovery.

Now it was time to swallow her pride, push aside any of their grievances, and go to see another man in her life. She needed help and she was about to request it from the one person she'd vowed never to ask.

* * *

'I wasn't expecting you.' Her dad looked past Maya, who had come in the back way, having parked by the garages. He was most likely looking for Julie because that was usually the only reason for Maya to come here.

'It's just me today, Dad.'

'Oh. Well, would you like a coffee or a tea?'

'No, thanks.'

He seemed disappointed not to have something to occupy his hands. 'How's Isaac?'

If in doubt, talk about Isaac.

'He's good, looking forward to being home soon.'

'I shall look forward to seeing him.'

Maya knew she had to come out with it; it was too awkward standing here knowing what she needed to say, her dad waiting for her to reveal why she'd turned up.

'I need some help,' she blurted out. 'It's not for me, actually; it's for a friend.'

She told him the basics: that Noah had guardianship but the biological father was going to go for custody. She didn't get a chance to add in anything about the blackmail before her father's defences came up and rendered her silent.

'So you want me to give legal advice to this Noah, for free.' Nigel folded his arms in front of him and moved backwards to the island in the centre of the kitchen, leaning against it, his legs crossed at the ankles.

'I know it's a big ask—'

'And this is so he can stop a biological father going for custody.'

'There's a bit more to it than that.' She felt like a little kid caught doing something wrong; she could barely meet his gaze, uncomfortable at being here and having to ask him for a favour. Maya had always been determined and part of that determination had been to maintain independence, which meant not turning to her dad for money or favours. After she left the family home and their relationship became even more strained, she didn't want to have to rely on him for anything; she wanted to make it on her own. She'd put herself through flight training, she'd parented Isaac, she'd built herself a different home when her marriage ended.

Nigel shifted edgily, crossing his feet the opposite way round. His arms were still tightly folded across his chest. 'Don't you think biological fathers have rights?'

Her gaze snapped up. The morality of this thing was what he was questioning? She'd expected him to say something along the lines of he couldn't give much more than basic advice for free, that he was too busy with his paying clients, she hadn't expected an argument so directly related to the case itself.

'Dad, there's stuff you don't know—'

But he cut her off. 'Biological fathers have rights.' He turned and faced the island bench, his back to his daughter.

And all Maya wanted to do was get out of there. Julie might want her to try but the effort had to come from both sides. And right now, he wasn't even willing to hear her out.

'Forget I asked,' was all she said before she fled.

She wished she'd never even bothered.

27

Noah had to find a way to pay for legal advice because he knew deep down that the problem of Paul wasn't going to disappear without a fight.

He put his name down for extra shifts should they arise, but Nadia said much the same as Maya, that there wouldn't be many and, even if there were, he wouldn't want to wear himself out completely. And he could see why when, after three days straight of shifts that were busier than ever, he was exhausted. The saving grace was Geraldine looking after Eva so well that Eva was settled enough to sleep through the night a few times in a row.

Eva was down for an afternoon nap and Noah lay on the sofa, scrolling through job adverts online to see whether there was some kind of job he could do on the side on his days off. A shelf stacker position was available, as was a cleaner at a fitness centre in the next town, but the jobs were unsurprisingly fixed hours and days. And that was no good to him. And neither was the hourly rate, which wouldn't even cover Geraldine's fees.

When he heard the familiar throaty sound of Paul's car, much like the noise of a horror film you grappled to switch off as soon as it started, he leapt up. The curtains were closed despite the sunshine battling to filter in.

He sat frozen in position, not daring to move an inch.

After the thunk of the car door, followed by a short pause, as expected, his visitor hammered on the door, with every thump threatening to wake Eva up at any second.

His grating tone came through the letterbox. 'I know you're in there. Answer the damn door.'

Good, he was pissed off. Well, that made two of them.

But he couldn't ignore him forever. And to save the neighbours complaining at the racket and Eva being woken, Noah emerged into the hallway and reluctantly wrenched open the door.

'Given any thought to my proposal?' No preamble accompanied his pathetic demands.

Noah did, however, note somewhat smugly that Paul stepped back down the few steps that led up to the door to put a distance between them. The man did confrontation, he was a bully, but he was a coward too. Noah knew he could flatten him if he really wanted to.

'I need more time,' Noah told him.

'Sorry, no can do.'

'I don't have the sort of cash you're asking for lying around.' If the guy wanted the money that bad, he'd wait.

'Do I need to call my lawyer and set the wheels in motion?'

'I'll get it,' Noah snapped. 'But I need another couple of weeks.'

'No chance!' Paul yelled, as if Noah was the unreasonable one. He turned to go.

'One week,' said Noah in a bid to stop him calling his lawyer as soon as he was in his car.

Paul stopped, protected from Noah around the other side of the revolting green vehicle. 'One week. And that's your limit. I'll let you know a date and time. Be ready.'

Noah closed the door, leaned his head against the glass. 'Cassie...' he said out loud. 'Cassie, I'm sorry.'

It was only Eva's stirring that stopped him from sinking to his knees with the hopelessness of it all.

* * *

Noah overcooked the first lot of cauliflower cheese for Eva by leaving it too long in the microwave. It was so dried up, he had to throw it. He knocked her sippy cup off the highchair table soon after he'd made another portion and because he mustn't have put the lid on properly, it broke off, sending water showering everywhere.

He finished clearing everything up, fed her and changed her nappy when there was another knock at the door.

Surely Paul wasn't back already. But just in case, Noah grabbed his phone and set it to record the conversation. He was likely to be on guard for that, but you never knew, maybe he'd slip up and Noah could use the information to get rid of him rather than giving in to his demands.

But with Eva in his arms, he peeked through the gap he made in the curtains to find there was no sign of a green car.

He opened the door to find the lesser of two evils – Maya's ex-husband.

'What can I do for you?' Noah pulled Eva's hand away from his lips. She seemed to want to push her fingers into his mouth right now.

'I think it's best I say what I need to say inside.'

'Is this official business?'

He seemed to take pleasure in the fact that Noah clearly knew what he did for a living. 'I don't think you want to do this on the doorstep. And you're going to want to hear what I have to say so...'

He gestured for Noah to step aside using the brown folder he was holding.

Arrogant tosser.

Reluctantly, Noah tilted his head, indicating Conrad could come in. 'I hope it won't take too long; this one needs a nap.' The guy, already heading along the hallway towards the lounge, would have no idea that was a bare-faced lie and it would be another good five hours before Eva went down again.

Conrad gave the lounge a cursory glance as if trying to size it up in seconds before he turned back to face Noah. His tanned forearm burst out from the pushed-up shirt sleeve, his other still sporting a cast. He had a cocky air about him that had Noah wondering how Maya had ever got mixed up with him in the first place. Maybe she wondered that as well.

'I'll get straight to the point,' said Conrad. 'Why are you sniffing around Maya?'

'Really, that's what you're here about? Your ex-wife.'

Conrad's top lip curled into a sneer. 'I'm looking out for her, always will, remember that.'

'I'm sure she can look after herself. Now, if there's nothing else—'

'What are you doing associating with Russel? Or it could be Dale, maybe Richard?'

'I've got no idea what you're talking about.' Noah's language would be way stronger had Eva not been in his care. She kept him on the straight and narrow as far as his vocabulary was concerned. He'd had a dream the other night that he was fighting for custody in court and claiming to be the better parent. Eva had been sitting in her pram beside him and yelled the F word at the top of her voice in front of the judge, who'd quickly ruled in Paul's favour. Noah had woken up in a cold sweat from that one.

'The green car,' Conrad grunted, 'it doesn't exactly blend in.

Fucking idiot.' He glanced at Eva. 'Apologies. I should mind my language in front of a little one.'

'Would appreciate it.' Noah still had no idea what was going on here. 'You mention a green car, so I assume you're talking about Paul, right?'

'So that's the name he's going by these days, is it?'

'Look, I've got to get this one down,' he reiterated, even though Eva now looked as though she had enough energy to dance a jig, if she could stand up on her own, that was. He wanted Conrad to get to the point and then get out.

'Why was he here?'

'Long story.'

'You in business with him?'

Conrad might be on sick leave but right now, Noah felt as though he was being properly interrogated by police. He set Eva down on the floor when she pushed away from him because she wanted to move around. 'What are you talking about?'

'I asked whether you're in business with Paul.' He waved the brown folder again. 'He's been of interest for a while and when I saw that green car... well, detectives are never off the job, put it that way. It's a case I'd like to solve.'

'I've only recently met Paul and I can't stand the guy. I'd love nothing more than to see the back of him.'

'In that case, it sounds like you might need my help.'

'Since when would you offer to help me?'

Conrad sat down on the sofa uninvited. 'The way I see it, we could help each other. If you're associating with a criminal and you're associating with Maya, then it becomes my business.' He waved the brown folder again. 'You want to know what's in here.' It was a statement, not a question. 'Trust me. In this folder is something you will find very useful in your little court battle, or it could save you having one in the first place. It'll save you stress, money.'

'How do you know about my court battle?'

'Relax, Maya hasn't been blabbing. I assume you've confided in Maya.' When Noah didn't deny it, he sneered, 'Thought as much. I'm a police officer, nose to the ground and all that, and putting two and two together. It's a skill.'

'You've been spying on me, on us?'

Conrad's jaw tightened at Noah's reference to 'us'. 'I'm a detective, comes with the territory.'

'You're an off-duty detective.' And he hadn't even denied that he'd been watching them.

'I'm good at my job. They don't make just anyone a detective.'

'I'm pretty sure your job remit doesn't extend to keeping tabs on your ex-wife's whereabouts.'

'I'd watch the attitude if I were you. Or life could get very difficult.' He cast a glance at Eva.

'Is that a threat?'

'I uphold the law; I don't break it.'

Sure.

Conrad jumped when Eva shrieked. It was a happy shriek, as if to get their attention, and Noah usually discouraged it, but seeing how much it irked Conrad, he let her carry on intermittently during their conversation.

Conrad held the folder out to Noah yet again. 'I'm trying to help you with this information.'

This time, Noah took the bait. He reached out to take it.

Conrad snatched it right back as if they were playing a game for two-year-olds. He held the folder against his chest. 'Let me tell you the way this is going to work.'

Noah saw red. 'All right. Get out. I've had about as much as I can take of people coming in here laying down rules and ultimatums.'

Conrad called his bluff. 'Fine, lose your daughter for all I care.' He headed for the door.

Noah couldn't help it. He followed after him. 'You say this man is a criminal.'

Conrad turned, winning this part of his little game. 'So now you're interested?' He waved the folder again. 'The man is under investigation and this information I happen to have proves it. And it's your way out of the whole mess.'

'All right, what do I have to do?'

Conrad came back inside, a smirk on his face. 'I knew you'd see sense.'

28

Maya pulled the helicopter out onto the helipad and didn't miss Noah watching her surreptitiously from inside the hangar.

Something else was going on with him now because all of a sudden, he was pushing her away rather than confiding in her. She'd tried to talk to him earlier and he'd barely been able to look her in the eye; he left the room when she went in, he kept conversation to a bare minimum, only talked about work.

They had a job soon after the start of shift, and it was one of the worst. Three motorcyclists racing on a strip of country road and one of them lost control, taking the others out with him. Two of them were dead on scene and the third died in the helicopter on the way to the trauma centre.

Bess was in the locker room when Maya went in. 'That was one hell of a morning.'

'Sometimes this job is the worst. Nothing prepares you for days like the one we've just had.'

'Those poor families.' Bess pinched the skin at the top of her nose to stem her tears.

The two victims who died first were twin brothers and right

now, Maya imagined the police telling the family, the devastation, the heartbreak that they'd never ever get over.

Every time they had a loss, it brought back the day her mother died. She hadn't only lost her mum that day; she'd lost her dad too because things had never been the same with him again. And she hadn't seen him since the day she'd attempted to ask for a bit of help at his house.

Maya got her things together and caught up with Noah in reception but he looked much like a frightened rabbit, freezing before he opened the door. They often walked out together but not today; today, he hung back as though he didn't want to come near her.

'Today was a bad day,' she said to him in an attempt to get him talking.

'Yeah, you don't need to tell me.'

'You heading out?'

'In a moment,' he mumbled. 'I've left something in my locker.'

Avoiding time alone with her, more like. 'Right, well, I'll see you tomorrow then,' she called to his retreating back.

'I'll watch out for him.' Nadia was working behind the reception desk but missed nothing. 'He'll be okay, Maya.'

'See you later.' She didn't understand why he'd changed his attitude towards her and, to be honest, she didn't have the energy to try to figure him out.

Instead, she put thoughts of Noah out of her mind and smiled as she emerged into bright summer sunshine. She closed her eyes briefly to the warmth of it on her back but the feeling of letting go of the stress of the day was short-lived when she heard Conrad's voice from the end of the parking bays. She was caught out more now he didn't arrive by motorbike, which had always made it far easier to detect when he was around because she could hear it roaring down the street.

'You look like you've had a bad day,' was the first thing he said.

'Code for Maya, you look like shit?' She noticed a taxi hovering nearby.

'Didn't say that, did I?'

As much as this man was a pain in her arse, she hated being rude. 'Sorry, it's been a tough shift. Three fatalities. Look, I need to go, wash off the day.'

'Stop by, have a glass of wine, relax.' He held up his hands. 'No funny business, I promise. I want to cook for you, thank you for everything you did for me. My arm's still in a cast but I can do enough.'

'Conrad, I—'

'If not tonight then Friday night. We need to talk about Isaac, sort out what's happening at Christmas.'

'I thought you'd already decided.' And so had Isaac, which left a dark cloud hovering over her as to what to do.

'There's always room for negotiation, you know that, Maya.'

To Conrad, negotiation meant the other party or parties backing down and seeing it his way. Negotiation meant different things to each of them, a bit like the word *divorce*.

Conrad's gaze snapped up and when Maya turned to see where he was looking, it was at Noah emerging from the building. 'He looks like he's had a shit day too.'

Maya didn't miss the look Noah and Conrad exchanged, as if something might be bubbling between them, but she knew better than to prod and ask either of them right now.

Conrad turned his attention back to her. 'You two always seem chatty every time you're together.'

She bristled. 'You've only seen us once outside the pharmacy.'

He deflected by asking, 'Are you and he involved?' His demeanour had the hard edge she was all too familiar with and it stayed until Noah began to reverse out of his parking space.

'Not really any of your business, is it?'

'Maya, Maya, why so defensive?' He had that tone she hated, the tone that meant he was in for a round of mind games.

'I'm not defensive. And I do need to go.'

'All right, calm down.'

Who in the history of the world had ever successfully managed to calm down when they were instructed to? If anything, the phrase made a situation worse.

'I'll see you soon, Maya.' And the way he said it left her in no doubt what he was thinking. He was thinking that if she didn't stay on his right side then all it would take was one move on his part and her position as a well-respected member of the Whistlestop River Air Ambulance team and loveable girl in this town would be ruined.

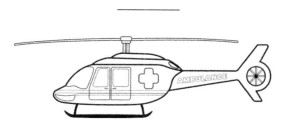

29

As the crew arrived for the start of their late shift the following day, even Bess noticed that Noah wasn't his usual self around Maya.

'Mate, what did you do?' Bess whispered in her ear as they left the locker room. 'I'm intrigued.'

'Well, as far as I know, nothing.' And it rankled her. She'd thought they were friends at least, perhaps something more, but it was as though he'd withdrawn from any temptation. She tried to tell herself it was because he had so much on his mind but she was done being a sucker when it came to men and their neurosis. Was that unfair? Maybe, but she'd been burned before, she wasn't about to let it happen again.

Maya did a ground run for the helicopter. She started the engines and the rotors and all the systems on board and tested everything thoroughly. In the meantime, Bess and Noah were ensuring the medical equipment and drugs were as they should be.

After the crew briefing, during which Noah still wouldn't look her in the eye, Maya went to find Frank to tee up the date the helicopter would have its full service and maintenance inspection by the company he worked for. Frank did a lot of it – Hilda was subject to maintenance and checks after a certain number of flying hours or calendar days but every few months, she got the full works from the team.

But Maya didn't find Frank in the kitchen where she'd expected him to be talking with Nadia as before. Instead, he was in the hangar talking to a tall man with grey hair. And as she got closer, she realised who the man was.

'Here she is...' Frank nodded in her direction. 'I'll leave you to it.'

'Dad, what are you doing here?' She hooked the clipboard with her checklist back in its rightful place, having done all the checks on Hilda that she needed to do.

'I know you're busy...'

'I'm at work, so yes, that's generally how it goes.' She suddenly thought why he might have turned up. 'Is Julie okay?'

'Julie's fine.' He shifted awkwardly. Dressed in a suit and likely having come from a meeting in the office near Bridport, he looked out of place here where they all wore heavy-duty uniforms, not a tie in sight.

'Then what can I do for you?'

He hesitated. 'I hate that we're like this. We struggle to even have a civil conversation.'

'Dad—'

'I know, I know...' He held up the hand that wasn't in his pocket. 'Now's not the time to get into it.'

Bess came into the hangar and spotted Nigel and gave him a chirpy hello, but didn't hang around. She knew the score.

'Dad, if you need me for something, you're going to have to spit it out before we get a call.'

'You busy today?'

With a sigh, she explained, 'Always.'

And when the phone rang yet again, there was no hanging about. Time to get to the next job.

'Dad, I have to go.' She didn't have time to wait for an answer but she was aware of him standing back in the hangar with Frank while she and the rest of the crew got their helmets and she went to start up the helicopter. She didn't look back; she let her thoughts become quieter with every chop of the blades through the air.

The job was straightforward, at least medically. Maya landed Hilda on the beach, which had its challenges, including what the tide was doing and the onlookers who took ages to move out of the way. The patient was airlifted quickly to the nearest trauma centre and they were back at the airbase inside the hour.

She was still smiling, still buzzing, when they got back. At least she was until she took off her helmet to feel the breeze through her hair, headed back to the hangar and saw her dad still inside next to Frank, this time with a mug of tea.

'Didn't expect you to still be here.' She set her helmet on the shelf.

Frank scarpered with a toolbox, claiming he had a few things to see to now he could get his hands on Hilda.

'Hilda?' Nigel looked shocked as though Frank was about to take said toolbox and deal with the woman in his life.

Maya grinned. 'Hilda is the helicopter, named after one of our biggest supporters over the years.'

'Well, that's a relief.'

She looked at him once more before she led the way into the building and through reception. He obviously wanted to get something off his chest and she didn't want the rest of the crew hearing it.

'I'll be outside,' she told Nadia. They could sit on the low wall out front and with another five minutes left on shift, she'd easily hear the shrill ring of the phone as it echoed all around the base from various points if a job came in.

'Could you hang around an extra twenty minutes or so?' Nadia pulled a face by way of apology. 'Vik is running late.'

'Sure thing.'

Outside, her dad sat down next to her on the low wall. 'Who's Vik?'

'He's the pilot on the other team. He's usually on time, as am I, but if either of us is running late, we cover the other one.'

When it seemed all they were here for was the fresh air and sunshine, she prompted, 'What did you want to talk to me about, Dad?'

He leant his forearms along his thighs, hands clasped together. 'I wanted to apologise for my behaviour when you came to me to ask for a favour the other day. For your friend. Noah, wasn't it?'

'That's right, and I'm sure you've got your reasons.'

'I have, but that doesn't excuse me biting your head off. I seem to do a lot of that and don't seem able to stop it.'

That was something they had in common, as though they'd fallen into a different kind of normal than they should have. It certainly wasn't the same for Julie and Nigel.

'There's a reason I immediately saw it from the other guy's perspective rather than Noah's.' Nigel cleared his throat. 'I think I need to explain why.'

'Did Julie put you up to this?'

He seemed genuinely surprised. 'Julie? Your sister has no idea I'm here and no idea of what I'm about to tell you. I'll have to explain it to her too, but I think I need you to hear it first.'

She had no idea what he was about to come out with and he took his time to find the words.

'Things haven't been right with us since your mother died,' he began. 'Or more importantly, since what happened after.'

'What do you mean?'

He had his fingers interlaced, something he did when he was thinking, his thumbs rubbing against each other more and more with rising stress. It was his tell. She'd noticed it when she was a young girl, but these days they rarely had exchanges long enough or deep enough for her to spot it.

'Your grandparents took you and Julie down to Cornwall after Anya died.'

'I remember.' And she remembered the rest too. 'I loved it down there.'

'Do you remember the day I picked you up?'

'How could I forget?'

'I was angry. Distraught, even. And the reason... the reason why is because your grandparents had issued me with a notice of intent to go for custody.' He took in Maya's shock, the way she looked at him, sharing this for the first time. 'They'd had supporting documents drawn up; they were serious. In their eyes, I was unfit to be a parent on my own without Anya.'

Maya almost didn't register Vik's arrival and him waving over to indicate that her shift as pilot was over.

'But you're our dad,' she said. 'I don't understand.'

'Neither did I. Oh, I knew they were hurting. I knew they could see what a state I was in. They were right to be concerned about that. They were even right to take you down to Cornwall at first and I was very happy for them to do so. Parenting is hard and I'd lost the love of my life. I tried to be there for you and your sister, but I couldn't wade through the tide of emotion I faced, not without some help from the doctor.' He loosened his tie.

'Medication, you mean?'

'Yes, medication. With your sister so young and you not old enough to be managing on your own without a parent, I couldn't be sleeping all hours of the day in my grief, taking pills that knocked me sideways. I knew I had to get myself in order, so I let them take you to Cornwall. I thought I'd get myself together and then have you back with me and we'd try to work out how we were going to go on without your mum.'

'And Granny and Gramps weren't prepared to let you do that?'

He paused, thinking of the best way to reply to the girl who'd worshipped her grandparents. 'I think your grandparents sent that letter because hanging onto you two girls was a way to save themselves from drowning in grief after losing their only daughter. They didn't see that they were trying to take something from me; in many ways, they thought they were helping us all. They told me it's what Anya would've wanted. All I saw was a legal battle I didn't want or need and two young girls being dragged through it at their hands.'

Maya found it hard to believe her grandparents could ever do such a thing.

She also knew her dad wasn't a liar.

'Is that why I was never allowed to go and stay with them over the summer again?'

'I panicked. I thought that if you went to them again, they'd find a way of keeping you there, that you'd never come back to me. Instead, you resented me for not letting you go. And then they died and you were so angry.'

Tears welled in her eyes. 'I wasn't angry, Dad. I was heartbroken.'

He couldn't look at her. He knew her attachment to her grandparents, what it had done to her to not have them in her life the way they'd been before.

'I know you blamed me for your heartbreak, your pain. And you were right to.' His voice came out smaller than ever before. 'I should've handled it better.'

'No...' Her voice caught. 'I shouldn't have blamed you, not so harshly, at least.' It had taken her a long time to say it, even though she'd known deep down that she was taking it out on someone who didn't deserve it. Somehow it had been easier to do that, to have somebody to be angry at. 'Granny and Gramps dying was never your fault. I think Granny died of a broken heart and when she went, I bet Gramps didn't want to hang on any longer.'

'I can understand that. Losing Anya was so painful, on some days I couldn't bear it.' He gulped. 'But I should've let you spend more time with your grandparents and then perhaps you and I might have stood a chance at a better relationship.'

She sniffed, fished in her pocket for a tissue but found nothing. Instead, she saw her dad pull out a packet of tissues from his jacket pocket and pass it to her.

'Thanks.' She wiped her eyes. 'Was their intent to fight for custody the reason why they were allowed to visit us but not the other way round?'

He nodded. 'They dropped the custody idea but the trust was lost by then. I was always happy to have them spend time with you but after being scared they'd take you both away, I was always looking over my shoulder. And they never apologised. I thought they owed me that.'

'I think they did too.'

The look he gave her suggested his appreciation.

'You didn't tell me any of this. Why, Dad? When things were always so strained between us, it would've helped me to understand.'

'I never wanted you to hold it against them and when they died and you were so devastated, I couldn't do it to you.' He swallowed hard. She knew that sign too. It meant he was nervous; he wanted this to go well. 'When they visited, I'd hear them talking to you about the house in Cornwall; they'd talk about your bedroom there, they'd say things about the town and you loved it all. You used to ask about the new ice-cream place that had opened up; I heard you say you wanted to go there and I felt so selfish.'

'Dad, I—'

'I don't blame you for any of it. You were a little girl, you'd lost your mother; how could I begrudge any bit of happiness to come your way?' His voice caught and it took him a couple of minutes before he continued.

'I was terrified that one day, Maya, you'd pack a suitcase and want to go to them and yes, I could've stopped you as you were only young and I had custody, but...' He laughed. 'Firstly, when has anyone ever been able to stop you doing what you want?'

She smiled kindly. 'That's a very good point.'

'Secondly, if I'd stopped you then you would've resented me even more. And so the only thing I knew to do was hang around when they were there, make sure they didn't fill your head with promises. But I could see that you wanted them as much as they wanted you and... well, some days that almost broke me in two.'

Her eyes filled with tears; she hated that he'd felt that way, that she'd never known. 'It wasn't that I wanted them instead of you. But when I was in Cornwall at their house, I felt really close to Mum, as though she was there with me. Granny talked about her all the time – sometimes you didn't, you'd change the subject or cut the conversation short – but Granny was forever telling stories of Mum in that house, the things she'd done as a little girl, what she got up to as a teenager. All of it made me feel like I hadn't totally lost my mother, that a part of her was still around.'

Nigel pinched the bridge of his nose. 'It was my way of coping, talking about her less and less so I didn't have to remember that I'd once had it so perfect, that I hadn't wanted for anything at all in life. I'm very sorry that I took that from you: the ability to keep her memory alive at the family home.'

Maya felt the sun on her back, the warmth and comfort of it.

'We needed very different things when Mum died.'

The shrill ring of the airbase phone alerted the air ambulance crew on duty to a job, cutting into the fresh air and quiet that had settled between Maya and her dad.

'I didn't know how to reach you. I'm glad you and Julie stayed close, though; it meant you settled not too far away, it meant I might have a chance with you again someday.'

'You and Julie have such a good relationship.'

'It was easier with your sister because she was so much younger when we lost your mother. She didn't have the same emotions as you because her memories weren't there. And the more you pushed me away, the closer Julie and I became.'

'I never resented your closeness, you know.'

'Because you didn't want it?'

She gulped. 'I'm not saying this to hurt you. But no. I didn't. Not then.'

He seemed to understand; he wasn't surprised either.

'I can't believe Granny and Gramps did that to you,' she said.

'No, sometimes I can't either. But they never really approved of me, at least not at first. They thought your mother could do... if not better, different, more suitable.'

She heard the helicopter behind the airbase start up, the blue team about to head out on a call. 'They always spoke well of you, Dad. I never picked up on any disapproval from them when we were in Cornwall or when they came to our house.'

'Anya and I would laugh about it, at the comments they made to her about me. By the time we started a family, I think they'd got used to the idea of us, or at least that's what I thought until they tried to take my daughters.'

'What sort of comments did they make?'

'They were more hints than specifics, like talking about her high-school boyfriend and the surf school he'd opened up – the subtext there was that they wanted her to move back to the village and take surfing lessons and fall in love with someone far more suitable than a lawyer who wore suits every day. They'd talk about how she'd once wanted to be a baker and open up her own bakery and wasn't it splendid that the old bakery near their house was still around for the locals. Then they said that the owners were approaching retirement and that the bakery would make someone a tidy little business one day.' He said the last bit in a Cornish accent and sounded so much like her granny or at least someone from Cornwall that Maya began to laugh.

As the red and yellow helicopter rose into the air and passed overhead towards the west, her dad watched it go. 'It's hard to imagine you up there doing that.'

'I love it.'

'I know you do.'

As the helicopter disappeared into the distance, Maya thought more about her grandparents and the way they felt about Nigel. 'Granny and Gramps only had one child, they lived their whole lives in Cornwall and for Mum to up and leave for anywhere else, it must've been difficult to see her go. It was a loss of sorts. I understand it. I feel it with Isaac.'

He swallowed. 'And I felt it with you.'

'When I moved out?'

'And well before. After your grandparents died, you grew more and more distant and I felt the loss every day, every time you looked at me like I'd taken away your whole world.'

'You told me once that you were disappointed in me.'

His gaze snapped up. 'I don't think I've ever said that.'

'I remember. You were disappointed I didn't want to try other careers.'

'Oh, Maya, you were so capable, I wanted you to have choices. I was never, ever disappointed in you and the woman you were growing up to be. I'm sorry if I ever made you feel that way.' He waited a beat. 'You know, the way you looked at me never passed. All the hurt from losing your mother, your grandparents, our relationship, it was all still there until the night you left and continued ever since. And it became easier for me to be angry with you, rude even, than try to get you back when I didn't think you'd ever want that.'

Maya's bottom lip trembled. 'The night I left home was horrible.'

'I'll never forget it either.'

'We argued,' she said. 'The way I spoke to you was awful. I'm sorry.'

'We both said things that night; it went round and round in my head for months afterwards, how I could've handled it differently.'

'Me too.'

His voice faltered. 'I could feel you slipping away long before that night. It had been happening ever since you lost your mother. I could never replace her and then you lost your grandparents and I couldn't bring them back either. I so desperately wanted to have you in a job that kept your two feet on the ground, not up in the air where there's danger, where there's risk.'

He got up from the wall they were sitting on, faced away from her and walked a few paces away and she knew he was crying when he said, 'I couldn't lose you, not my Maya.'

'Dad...'

'The thought of something happening to you or to Julie kept me awake night after night. And it was worse when you began your training, when I knew you were up in the air. My worries escalated all the more when you got your first job. I wanted so desperately to tell you how proud I was that you'd followed your dreams, but my fears wouldn't allow it. They consumed me. I couldn't lose another one of my family.'

He turned to face her. 'You want to know the crazy thing? I protected you from my worry of risk and death by not saying a word about it to you and what did you go and do? Not only did you become a pilot; you got a job with the air ambulance, where you see injuries, accidents, loss of life or close calls every single day.'

His turmoil turned to fondness. 'You were obsessed with helicopters from such a young age. Do you remember how we painted the model helicopter and you got so annoyed that I wasn't as careful with my paint as you were? You insisted you did most of it.'

She laughed. 'I remember. And I still have that helicopter.'

'Yeah?'

'Of course. It brings back happy memories.'

'Despite my painting skills or lack thereof,' he smiled. 'I should've known I was never going to be able to persuade you to do anything else with your life. Your darling mother was always about supporting your dreams and never taking them away. I could hear her voice in my head the whole time, "Our Maya," she'd say, "our Maya with her dreams and passions, she'll keep us on our toes." Julie was little, we had no idea what her passions would be, but you were so set on the idea of becoming a pilot.'

He took a deep breath. 'Another reason I didn't tell you I feared the risk involved with becoming a pilot was because I didn't want to reference dying. I thought my girls have lost their mother, their grandparents, I couldn't make you fear stepping out of the front door in case something might happen. I couldn't let my own fears become yours, no matter how much I wanted to sometimes.'

She let his revelations settle.

Eventually, with thoughts of her mother never far from her mind when she was in her father's company, she said, 'You and Mum were good parents and you had a great marriage.'

'That we did,' he smiled.

'I always aspired to that someday, you know – shame I never

had it with Conrad. I started talking to Julie about you as she got a little older. I'd tell her things about you both so she could build a picture in her mind of how our parents were.'

He looked across at her. 'I'd hear you both sometimes. Some days, I enjoyed listening; other days, I'd close the door and detach myself because it was so painful to not have Anya around any longer. I wanted so much for her to see the beautiful young women you were turning out to be even from that really young age. I hated that she missed so much.'

'Me too, Dad. Me too.' She smiled. 'I remember you'd come home from work and Mum would always rush to the door and give you an enormous hug and make you a nightcap if you'd come home really late. I can still remember the look on your face, every time you came home; you were where you were meant to be. You know, I think Julie will be like Mum as a mother.'

'Your sister is much like Anya. Anya never wanted to work outside the home once she had her babies. She wanted to be at home with you both, do everything with you. She lost interest in having a career for herself and it worked for us. You, on the other hand, are more like me than I think you'd ever admit.'

'In what way?'

'Your passion, your drive, your determination. It served me well in my career and while we don't do the same thing, I think it's probably what helps you in yours.'

She told him about the job they'd been called out to the other day when she'd had to land on a roundabout, a risky landing but the only option to get close to the accident location. Her faith that it would work and her calm determination stopped the entire crew from freaking out; it led to a safe landing and take-off, getting the patient the prompt help they needed.

'I'm in awe, Maya. My girl, flying a helicopter, landing on a roundabout with traffic everywhere.' He shook his head as if to let the image settle into his psyche as a proud smile emerged.

Maya moved back to talking about her mother. She felt she needed to. 'After Mum died, you never looked the same when you came home from work.'

Nigel's mood shifted as well. 'No, I don't suppose I did.'

'You looked frazzled whenever you came through the door, you didn't smile as much, you didn't even read stories to me the way you once had. You read but we didn't do the funny voices; you were so strung out. And then I ended up reading for myself anyway so I lost that part of what we had.'

He looked at her. The gap between them was there, but now it was as though a delicate thread had formed, connecting them, like the tentative start of a spider's web that had the potential to get stronger. At least that's what she hoped.

'I missed story time too, Maya. But after your mother died, there was an underlying exhaustion with me that took a long time to overcome. And there was the guilt.'

'Guilt?'

'I blamed myself for a long time that I didn't insist your mum go to the doctor, that I'd missed the signs because I was too busy with my work.'

'I blamed myself too.'

'But you were a kid.' He seemed shocked at her admission. 'It was up to me.'

Maya remembered her mother, so strong, always putting the rest of them first. 'She never would've stood for the sympathy, you know. Neither of us could've made her go and get checked even if we'd tried.'

'I still blamed myself. It took a long time for me to see it was an accident, what happened.'

'It was.'

'It still hits me some days and I wonder whether my depression will return.'

'Is that likely?'

'I've no idea. I hope not. I think talking to you now might help.'

'I never realised you felt that way, you know. I saw you as strong, unbreakable.'

'I kept it well hidden.'

'I wish you hadn't.'

'Me too now, believe me.' He hesitated before he said, 'You say you wanted a good marriage with Conrad and didn't get it.' Their conversation kept getting broken as other things crept in. There was so much to say to each other after all this time.

'I don't think talking about Conrad and me will achieve anything right now, Dad.'

'It still worries me.'

'We're divorced.'

'I know but you and he are very much still in each other's lives.' He waited a beat to give her a chance to deny it, but of course she couldn't. 'Do you want to get back together?'

'Definitely not.'

'Were you ever happy with him?'

She sighed. 'For a while, yes. But it took me years to really know myself, to find my way.' She spotted Noah leaving the airbase, head down, not looking her way.

'Dad, can we carry on talking about Conrad another time? There's a lot I have to say and I will, I promise. But right now, I need something else.' To move forwards, they needed to carry this on, to talk more, to allow each other the time to explain and understand.

But first, she had to ask a favour. A big one. And she was going to have to break Noah's confidence to do it.

She only hoped she and her dad were in a good enough place for her dad to hear her out properly.

30

Ever since Conrad's visit, Noah had been trying to get his head around what Maya's ex-husband had said to him. He hadn't let him see what was inside the sodding brown file. Conrad had treated it much like a ball in the playground where he was the bully holding it out of reach of anyone smaller than he was.

What Conrad had done was made it be known that he was never going to give Noah the ammunition to get rid of Paul if Noah didn't agree to stay away from Maya.

Noah had tossed and turned all night. Not seeing Maya again unless it was in a professional capacity wasn't what he wanted at all, but what choice did he have? He'd been unfriendly, unapproachable at work and it had hurt him to be that way with Maya when all he wanted to do was confide in her, warn her that Conrad was never going to let her go. But how could he? He had to put Eva first. She was his priority now. He owed it to her and to Cassie to do everything in his power to build a life for the little girl who'd already lost so much. And if this went to court then Paul might still win. It was a risk Noah was unwilling to take.

When he woke up, Noah could only focus on one thing – raising the money to pay off that lowlife, Paul. He could do it, just about. And so he drafted an ad for his car. The car he loved. A shiny, black Volkswagen that should sell for around half of what Paul was asking for. He'd add in what he had in his current account and the small amount in his savings and there was the potential for another thousand he could withdraw on his credit card if he said sod the extortionate interest charges.

Panic gripped Noah that this might not be the end of it. What if Paul was to come back for more money after this? Money Noah didn't have.

A knock at the door sent him into a panic. He peeked out from behind the curtain.

It wasn't Paul. And it wasn't Conrad. It was Maya.

He thought about ignoring her, but he knew she'd seen him leave the airbase and his car was parked outside. The car he wouldn't have for much longer.

He opened the door and forced a smile onto his face. 'Maya, what can I do for you?'

She got straight to the point. 'Have I done something to offend you?'

'No. Whatever makes you think that?'

God, he was a rubbish liar.

And she wasn't buying it. She was a clever woman, her intelligence all part of one heck of a package.

She delivered her next words with a distance he hated. 'I've had enough games with the men in my life to last for the rest of my days; I don't need any more. I'll say what I have to say and then I'll leave you alone.'

'Maya—'

'I've asked my dad for some help, legal wise. He's willing to talk to you about your legal stance, at no charge, as a favour to me.'

'But you don't speak to your dad.'

'That's all you got from what I just said?' She huffed and began to walk away, calling over her shoulder, 'Take it or leave it.'

He checked the street for signs of Conrad or Paul lurking and before he could think too much about it, he ran after her, catching her before she reached the gate at the end of the path. 'Please, come inside and I promise I'll explain everything.'

She looked at him as if trying to work out whether he was worth it.

'Please, Maya.' He couldn't leave it like this.

She relented and after they went back into the cottage, Noah closed the door, locked it and ushered Maya into the lounge. He'd figured out the best way to let light in when the curtains were closed was to fling open the door to the hallway, the door to Eva's room and his and the one to the kitchen so the light could come from that direction. Of course the curtains weren't closed when Geraldine was here – he'd encouraged Geraldine to spend as much time out of the house with Eva as she liked, for fear that Paul would show up, but so far he hadn't. Perhaps Paul knew that if the curtains were open, he'd have no luck hassling Noah.

When he noticed Maya looking around, presumably for Eva, he said, 'We won't be interrupted for now; Eva is with Geraldine at a soft play centre. They'll be gone at least another hour by the sounds of things. She texted me to say they were having a great time.'

The smile he loved was back momentarily. 'Those places are hell.'

'I can imagine.' He peeked out of the curtains to check the street for any signs of company again.

'You're worried Paul will turn up.'

'Yes.' He let the curtain drop back in place. 'But not just Paul, there's your ex to think about too.'

'Conrad? I'm not afraid of him.'

'Me neither, as it happens, but there's something you should know.' He gestured for her to sit down on the armchair and he took the sofa. 'Conrad came here to see me.'

Maya's brow furrowed.

He explained their conversation, that Paul was apparently involved in some criminal activity, that Conrad's first suspicion was that Noah was too. And then he revealed the brown folder, that Conrad said he had information that could end this nightmare for him.

'How does he know it's a nightmare for you?' Maya wanted to know. 'I promise I never said a word to him.'

'He'd have his ways given his job.'

'What was in the file?'

'I've absolutely no idea, but he enjoyed taunting me with it.'

'Sounds about right.'

'He also came here about you.'

'Me?'

'He knows we've seen each other out of work, at least that's what he hinted at; he didn't give specifics.'

'He's been spying on us?'

'He was so cocky, he didn't even bother to deny it, claimed it was the way he thinks as a detective.' He took a deep breath. 'You should also know that he is willing to show me the folder... on one condition.' He hated saying this out loud, the reason he'd been aloof when Maya tried to talk to him, why he'd backed off all of a sudden. 'He wants me to stay away from you. He told me that you're his wife regardless of a dumb piece of paper, and that I need to back off. Then he'll give me what I need as long as he has my word.'

'Son of a—'

'Pretty low, eh. And Maya, I hated agreeing to it. But this is Eva's future I'm in charge of. I'm barely able to scrape together the cash Paul's demanding, which means less money set aside for Eva and whatever comes our way. I want her to have every opportunity. This information Conrad has a hold of could stop me having to pay out a huge sum of cash, wiping out my savings, maxing out my credit card because I've got no other money left anywhere.'

Wide brown eyes looked at him, sensing his turmoil and his pain. 'Then you need to know what's in it.'

'But that's only possible if I stay away from you. I'm not sure what he'll do if I agree and then go back on my word after I know what's in the folder.'

'He's a man who likes to play games. He's done it with me long enough.' She came and sat down beside him on the sofa, the in-control and take-no-shit Maya he'd begun to fall for. 'We can't let him do this to you. To us.'

'Us?' It was something he thought he wanted when he first met her but the wanting back then didn't have the depth it had now. Now he knew her, she was so much more than a beautiful woman. She was kind, intelligent, good with people and when you were in her company, she saw you exactly as you were. He felt at ease by her side.

He took out his phone. 'I thought it was Paul at the door when Conrad showed up so I'd already set my phone to record, hoping he dropped himself in it...' He didn't ask whether she wanted to hear the conversation; he set it to play. He'd wanted to explain every-thing in his own words first but this clarified any doubts of the threatening tones that had come his way.

She was sitting so close, it was all he could do to stop reaching out and putting a hand around the back of her neck to gently pull her closer, take comfort with this woman if only for a moment, let her take comfort in him for the way her ex-husband thought he could behave towards her and anyone she wanted to bring into her life.

The recording came to its conclusion at the same time as Geral-dine came bustling through the door with Eva. It was time for him to switch from Noah, a single entity, to Noah the father figure, something he'd never seen coming but something he very much wanted now. He wanted all of it, all the good times and the tougher challenges as a parent. He'd take the sleepless nights, the temper tantrums, the soft play centres that he suspected would be bedlam. He'd do it all if he could keep Eva.

Eva reached out to him and he took her into his arms. 'You had a good time?' He was looking at Eva but his question was really for Geraldine, who deserved a medal for braving a soft play centre.

'We most certainly did,' Geraldine told him. 'But I think my ears will be ringing for a few days. The noise in that place.' She spotted he had company.

Noah introduced Maya and he didn't miss the twinkle in Geraldine's eye.

'I've got it from here, Geraldine,' he assured the most loyal and brilliant nanny, in his opinion, anyone could ask for.

'Don't I even get a cuppa before I leave?'

'I apologise, of course you do. But I'm aware that sometimes I might take advantage; you never leave on time, you're always doing long hours and extra jobs around here.'

'And you know me, Noah. If I didn't want to do it, I wouldn't.' She gave Eva a kiss. 'I'm teasing you, anyway; I have to get going, I don't need a cuppa. I've got ballroom-dancing class tonight.'

'Where do you get your energy?' Noah saw her to the door.

'At my age, you've got to get your fun where you can.' She gave Eva another smile and touched her cheek. 'This one should sleep for a good couple of hours; she's been in the ball pit, squealing and enjoying herself. I fed her before we left and I've changed her nappy. You should get a bit of time to yourselves.'

'You're too good to us, Geraldine. But thank you.' He didn't miss the sneaky nod towards the house either, which meant she was referring to Noah and Maya having some alone time rather than

Noah and Eva. He'd love nothing more, just a shame they had to talk about his life threatening to implode before his very eyes.

Back inside, Maya was happy to give Eva a cuddle when Eva reached for her. 'Noah, I think I have an idea of how I might be able to help.'

'I'm all ears but I think I should get this one down before she passes the point of no return.'

'Good idea.'

He led the way through to Eva's bedroom and drew the curtains, made sure everything was ready to settle her down for a nap. 'I might have to cuddle her in the rocking chair for a bit,' he said.

'Can I do it?'

He hated Paul being anywhere near Eva but when it came to Maya, he would love nothing more. 'Go for it. I'll be in the lounge.'

She came through less than twenty minutes later. 'She's out for the count.' She sat down on the sofa. 'So we have time for me to tell you my idea.'

'You've already done so much; getting your dad's offer of help is more than I could've ever hoped for.'

'Good. But I can do more.'

She settled back to tell him exactly what she had in mind.

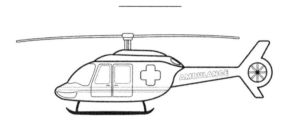

31

Maya wore the lilac dress Conrad had bought her for her birthday one year, and when she turned up at his door that Friday night, he let out a low whistle.

'I'm behind on my laundry,' she fibbed, 'so this was pretty much all I had left given how warm it is today.'

'You get no arguments from me.'

He stood to the side to let her pass. Or more likely so he could leer after her as she walked along the hallway. The way he watched her rankled, it always did, but she had to put up with it tonight and think of the end goal. The laundry was more than up to date at home, but Maya knew the effect the dress would have on Conrad. As long as he didn't see through it as a ploy to get him onside then step one of her plan would be in place.

'Something smells good.' She hoped some pleasantries would help him relax into the evening, revel in the fact he'd got her here for an intimate dinner for two.

'Mediterranean chicken with garlic and herbs.' His chest puffed with pride.

'How did you manage the cooking?'

'I cheated. Got the chicken pre-marinated, ordered in an online supermarket delivery. I've used new potatoes which didn't require peeling and the vegetable tray was pre-prepared too. But all fresh. And...' He opened the fridge and took out a bottle of Chablis. 'I've got your favourite wine.'

It wasn't her favourite, but tonight it would be. 'Wow, it's all wonderful. I'm impressed. Can't have been easy to do one-armed.'

'I'll be glad to get rid of this cast.'

'I'm sure you will be.'

The invite to dinner had come via a text message as she pulled up outside Noah's place, before she knew Conrad had been badgering him. In the text, Conrad said he was going to speak with Isaac and that he wanted to see Maya and talk about their son, so he reiterated the previous offer to make her dinner as a thank you for everything she'd done to help him out.

Maya had ignored the text, shoved her phone in her bag, but then when she was with Noah and she knew what Conrad was up to, she'd come up with an idea.

And now she was here. But to stop Conrad sussing that something was off, she had to act normal, which meant not being overly accepting of everything her ex-husband said and did tonight.

'Did you get hold of Isaac?' she asked.

'Not yet.'

'Conrad...'

'I thought we'd FaceTime while we wait for the dinner to be ready.' He checked the timer on the oven. 'We've got ten minutes.' He'd managed to undo the screw top on the wine by putting the bottle between his legs and poured her a glass, which he handed to her before she could argue.

'Ten minutes isn't long.' She had to grumble, because that's what she'd usually do when he allocated such a small amount of time to their son. But actually it worked out well. It meant she wouldn't have to keep up her pretence for so long if they got on with this and the evening progressed.

'It's long enough, Maya.' And at least a frostiness laced his tone. It would be the way he'd usually react to such a comment from her.

They made the call on Maya's phone – Conrad knew that was the safest bet for Isaac to answer.

'Hey, Mum.' He was smiling but that changed when Conrad came into view. 'Hey, Dad,' he added a lot more sombrely. 'What's going on?'

'We wanted to talk to you,' she beamed.

'How's the exams going, son?' Conrad asked, closer to Maya than she would've liked. His breath fell across her shoulder and down her chest.

'They finished ages ago,' Isaac deadpanned.

'How's the job?' Maya asked. Was Conrad so out of touch with his son's life that he'd forgotten term finished and now he was working?

'It's good thanks, Mum.'

Maya moved the conversation on to talk about the Christmas and New Year trip, or more like they all argued about it. Conrad wasn't backing down, neither was Isaac and Maya knew it was impossible for her to get time off and be away from Whistlestop River.

Isaac ended the debate with, 'I'm nineteen years old; I think that's old enough to make my own decisions.' He didn't say it in anger, he didn't direct it only at Conrad. But he did say it with an air of finality, tiredness at having the same argument weighing his words down even though he wanted to make his point.

Maya knew exactly what Conrad's reply would be too and he

didn't disappoint. 'Son, me and your mother are funding this little escapade—'

'University is not an escapade,' Isaac butted in. 'It's study. It's my future.'

Maya could've applauded her son; it was the sternest voice he'd ever used talking to his dad who thought university a waste of time, a waste of money, that Isaac and the rest of the people at university should join the real world and get a job.

'Let's talk when you're home,' said Maya.

'See you soon,' he said in reply. And then he came closer to the camera as he leaned forward to end the call.

'Why did he have to end it so quickly?' Conrad spat. 'He's a bit soft if he can't deal with a little confrontation. No son of mine is going to be soft.'

Isaac was soft but in a good way. He was kind, empathetic, just two of the things his father very much wasn't. 'You and Isaac need to sort out your differences. You wanted me here because you were going to talk to him, which I assumed meant you were going to be reasonable.' She'd known he wouldn't be but again, she had to stay in character as herself.

'I was reasonable! And it's not like I'm asking him to take a holiday in a concentration camp. He should be bloody thankful. A lot of kids would be.'

'Most kids his age do what they please at nineteen.'

'Maybe that's the problem.'

She couldn't let tonight go sideways; there was too much riding on it. 'I'm glad he cut the call short because I'm really, really hungry.'

'Better sort the dinner then.' But she could tell he was glad of the reprieve from more differences of opinion about their son.

In the kitchen, Conrad checked the timer for how long was left before everything was ready and, true to form – and because he hated wine – he plucked a small glass from the cupboard and set it down next to the bottle of vodka.

'Here, let me,' she offered before he could attempt to open it.

Conrad got the Coke while Maya poured a measure of the spirit, slightly more than he'd usually have but not enough to alert him, and she topped it up with the Coke. If she played this well tonight, she could get him relaxed and the more he relaxed, the more he'd drink which usually had the benefit of sending him to sleep. It had frustrated her when they were first married, but in later years, she'd come to appreciate the peace and quiet.

Maya took the vegetables from the oven rather than have him try one-handed and put them into a serving dish. 'We can help ourselves.'

'Bit posh but okay,' he sniggered.

She set the vegetables on the mats in the centre of the table in the dining room and while he couldn't see her, she poured the rest of her wine into the flowerpot on the sideboard with an apology to the plant for not giving it the nutrients it needed.

'Let me get you a top-up,' he said as soon as she went back to the kitchen and he assumed she'd drunk it all. 'Knew it was your favourite.'

Another thing about Conrad was that he liked to have company when he was having a drink. He'd never liked it when she only had one glass and then stopped. He thought it was dull and it left him in a bad mood, which she really didn't want tonight.

'I'll do it,' she told him, 'you spoon out the chicken.'

She pulled the wine from the fridge and poured a glass full, but while he took one plate at a time through to the other room, she poured half the wine away and topped the glass up with water. Conrad came back for the second plate and when he disappeared with that one, she topped up his glass with a little more vodka.

He winced at his first sip at the table. But it was a taste he liked.

He'd just think she was rubbish at judging quantities and sure enough, he focused on filling his face with his food.

'This is damn good,' he said as he started eating, mouth full, fork ready to shovel in more. Eyes down at the plate, nothing wrong with his appetite.

Maya, on the other hand, felt nauseous at whether her idea was even going to stand a chance. But she forced out the words, 'It's all lovely, thank you.'

'I'll get this again.' He was eating as though his food might disappear if he didn't get it down his neck quicksmart. 'What do you think, Maya? Good, isn't it?'

She murmured agreement. 'Perhaps you could make it for Isaac when he's home. You could talk about his course, find out what it's really about.'

'Yeah.' Which really meant no. Conrad was selfish, he liked it to all be about him, and having Maya here would be all he could focus on now. She expected he was thinking of ways to help her relax, hence the wine, and get her into bed if she let her guard down.

By the time dinner and a dessert of tiramisu was over and Maya had got Conrad several top-ups of his drink, she could tell he was beginning to head towards the sleepy state she needed.

In the lounge, he flopped onto the sofa.

'I'm not sure how long I can stay,' she said, hoping he wasn't so sleepy he didn't mind whether she left or not. 'Why don't I clear up the kitchen for you?'

'No way.' He patted the sofa. 'Sit down, you're a guest.'

The last thing she wanted was to sit with him and have him start mauling her if she was in easy reach.

'You've only got the use of one arm. I'll clear up then I'll come sit down.'

He swigged the last of his drink.

She didn't ask if he wanted another, just took the glass, refilled it and brought it back before she went out to clear the kitchen.

By the time the dishwasher began its cycle, Conrad was fast asleep in front of the television.

And now it was time to sneak upstairs to do what needed to be done.

When Noah had mentioned the brown folder Conrad had waved at him as his little bargaining chip, Maya hadn't taken long to think back to the similar folders she'd spotted at Conrad's previously when he told her he was doing paperwork. The folders were nowhere to be seen now but her first port of call was the study upstairs, the most likely place for their relocation.

She cursed when she opened the door and saw the desk with a whole stack of brown folders like the one Noah had described, none of them labelled, at least not with wording that meant anything to her. She supposed it would have been too much to ask for one to have 'Evidence Noah needs' emblazoned on the front.

She went through one folder, a second, a third, a fourth. She was about to go through a fifth when she spotted a brown file wedged up on the bookshelf next to a few years' worth of the *Guinness Book of Records*. He'd always liked those for some reason.

She pulled it down. It had to be this one, separate from the others, there to grab when he got what he wanted and he felt Noah had stayed away long enough for Maya to lose any interest in him, or for Conrad to worm his way back into her life. The man was seriously deluded.

She knew she'd found what she was looking for when she opened the file and skimmed the information and the photographs. The man profiled in these reports had to be the infamous Paul.

She swiftly took pictures on her phone of each document, including photographs and witness statements. She took in some of the unbelievable information she was reading along the way, her heart thumping at the enormity of it all. She was aware she could be committing a crime here but Noah, and more importantly Eva, was what mattered. And Conrad was well and truly on the wrong side of the law taunting Noah with this in the first place.

She slotted the file back where she'd found it and made her way down the stairs, but in the dark, she hadn't seen Conrad waiting at the bottom.

'What the hell are you doing up there?'

'Bathroom,' she stammered.

'I didn't hear the toilet flush,' he slurred, leaning casually against the front door, obstructing her exit.

'I was checking my make-up.'

'There's a mirror down here.'

'Didn't want to put the light on and wake you.'

'Why are you checking your make-up? I've seen you without it plenty of times.'

He was quick even though he'd been drinking. He was a good detective, took no shit from anyone and knew how to drill for answers. He'd done it to her enough times during their marriage.

'I had an eyelash in my eye, thought I'd smudged my mascara. I didn't want to be pulled over on my way home and completely embarrassed.' She smiled, falsely. 'Any chance of a cup of tea?'

He contemplated her story and either he believed her or she'd soon be in for another round of questions. Whatever way, she had to get out of here.

'You and your tea,' he moaned but nevertheless didn't stop her when she headed into the kitchen. It was the same pattern when they'd been together; she'd have a glass of wine or two and then want a tea and he hated it because it meant he'd be drinking alone.

She put the kettle on, offered him one which he refused, and did her best to steady her hands. They were shaking at the close call but she had to hold it together a bit longer.

The next half an hour was the most painful of all as she waited for him to drift off again, but sure enough, he did, and she didn't even alert him that she was leaving.

She walked out of the door and didn't look back.

And hopefully she had everything Noah needed.

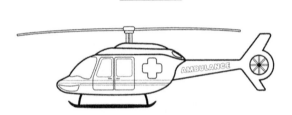

32

Noah arrived at the Whistlestop River airfield with a sleepy Eva in his arms. The posters for the upcoming open day in less than forty-eight hours were in situ and the crews were all ready with what they needed to do. Noah wished he could embrace it more, but right now it was way down on his list of priorities. Maya was supposed to come to his place, but she'd texted him to tell him to meet here instead.

'Why didn't you come to mine?' In reception, he pulled a small teddy bear from his pocket and handed it to Eva, hoping it would keep her calm. It didn't always work but tonight, she was sleepy enough and it was relatively quiet with the crew on shift out back.

'Here is better; Conrad is less likely to come here than your place or mine if he twigs what I was looking for.' She pulled her phone from her back pocket. 'I think I've got what you need.'

He settled Eva on his lap in the seating area at the end of the reception and took the phone to scroll through, one-handed, to see what Maya had found.

'Tell me it's the right information,' she rambled as his thumb nudged the screen to take in picture after picture. 'The guy in some of the photographs looked like the man you described, the aliases Conrad gave you match the names in this file.'

Noah looked sideways at Maya. 'It's him. No mistaking it. It's Paul in these pictures.'

He felt her hand briefly touch his; he heard her offer of a cup of tea and her suggestion he keep scrolling through the information she'd photographed while she went to the kitchen. 'There's a lot to digest,' she said.

When she brought the mugs through to the reception, she must've seen the look on his face, his eyes welled up, the angst trying to burst out of him at the situation he was in.

Maya, deflated, slumped down next to him. 'Shit, it's no use to you, is it?'

He blinked away tears, took the mug from her outstretched hand and set it on the table beside him, pushing it well out of the way of Eva before turning back. 'Maya, it's 100 per cent useful to me. I need to read it all again, properly. But I think Conrad was right, I wanted this information, and thanks to you, I have it.'

For a moment, they just looked at each other, not saying a word, understanding passing between them as Eva settled against him.

They read through the information on her phone together, taking it all in. Their heads were so close, Noah got the occasional brush of her hair against his face and if it wasn't for the total shit-show he was still facing, he'd reach up and run his fingers through it, bring her mouth to his and kiss her for what she'd done for him.

Paul, or whoever he really was, had been of interest to the police for a long time. What he was trying to do to Noah, or what he'd wanted to do to Cassie, he'd done to other women. He'd pick some-one, get to know them, they'd start a relationship and the woman would fall pregnant. Then he'd disappear out of their lives after the baby was born and he'd make sure he was so awful to them that they'd be glad to see the back of him. He'd always make sure that his name was on the birth certificate, that way he'd have rights, and then he'd come back into their lives when the baby was a few months old. It was the same pattern every time, the demands for money or the threat of court. It was all there in the reports, the evidence, photographs, statements from other women.

It appeared that Paul would try to find a weakness with the women – the first had been a drug addict prior to meeting him and he'd threatened to tell her new employer, her family, basically ruin her life unless she paid him the sum he'd asked for. The second had had multiple affairs in a previous marriage so he threatened to paint her as an unfit mother. One woman had served a couple of months in prison in her twenties and he held that over her. Cassie's only skeleton in her closet as far as Noah knew was an eating disorder she'd fought long and hard to get over, and that wouldn't be enough to use against her. Maybe he'd simply run out of women with pasts and got cocky going for someone who had nothing to hide and hoped they'd be too scared of losing their child that they'd pay up regardless.

It looked like one of the women Paul had picked had hired a private detective to find him when he went AWOL, and the private detective had discovered he was in another relationship with a different woman who also had a child. From one of the reports, it seemed one woman had confronted the other and together, they'd worked out what he was up to. Somehow, another couple of women were found along the way. Noah had no idea how and right now he didn't care. He was going to fight on behalf of Cassie; this man had to be held accountable for what he'd tried to do to her and to him, for the trauma to all concerned.

He kissed the top of Eva's head, comforted by the baby-soft feel of her hair, the smell he'd grown accustomed to every time he picked her up, the mix of baby shampoo and laundry powder and just... Eva. She felt like home and this man, this stranger despite the blood ties, had tried to take it away from them.

He felt a huge weight settle on his shoulders, either tension or relief; he had no idea how he felt right now. 'Cassie had a heart of gold, you know.'

'Tell me about her,' Maya said softly.

'She was a pain in the arse a lot of the time.' He started to smile.

'That's kind of par for the course with siblings. Julie and I have had our moments along the way.'

'Cassie was always so bossy, especially when we were little kids. She wanted to play games to her specification, although she was creative and had a pretty good handle on what would be fun without pushing it too far. She once designed an assault course in the back garden, using anything she could find in the garage. It was impressive.'

'Sounds dangerous – and I remember some of Isaac's assault courses; had to put a stop to a few of them before he broke his neck.'

'We had a good garden for it. We used the trees, piles of leaves to jump into, ropes, the swing. We'd time each other to see who was the fastest. I always won.' His voice caught. 'She hated that, and yet she'd presented me with the cardboard medal she'd made and even managed a congratulations.'

'Sounds like she was a lot of fun.'

'God, I miss her.' But holding Eva, a part of Cassie, kept a part of his sister close every day. 'Thank you, Maya. For being here. For what you've done for me. I don't know how to thank you. I'll be forever grateful.'

She held his gaze for a moment but then turned away and

focused her attention on Eva. 'You should get this one home to bed. And you should do whatever you need to with the evidence you now have.'

'If I go to the police, you might get in trouble for looking at confidential information. I don't want that.'

'Don't you worry about me. And I won't be in trouble if you don't let on that you have it.' She'd sent him each of the photos on his own phone. 'You could just say something is off with this guy who's asking you for money. Tell your story. Ears should prick up. If Conrad knew about this guy, his colleagues will do too.'

He contemplated his next move but right now, the only option was to get Eva, who was starting to wriggle around, home and to bed and then he could do some proper thinking.

A car's headlights swung around outside, illuminating the entire reception, and when they didn't pass by, Maya got up. Both of them heard the man's voice yelling her name before they saw who it belonged to.

'Maya...' Noah went to her side, Eva in his arms. 'What happened at the house?'

'I almost got caught.' Maya looked as though this was the last thing she needed to deal with. 'I should've known I wouldn't get away with going upstairs. He probably woke up, found me gone and put two and two together about what I'd been doing.'

Her dark hair, loose, the beautiful dress, he'd only just started to take it all in with everything going on. She'd gone out on a limb to help him and now what?

'I thought he'd go to your place,' she said, 'and he probably has already. But now he's here.'

They looked out at the taxi, which had reversed a good fifty metres away, probably at Conrad's instruction, and at Conrad, who swayed next to the low wall out front.

'I'll go out,' said Maya. 'Don't you worry about me. I'll steer him out of the way so you have a clear path to your car for you and Eva. You have all the information you need now, no looking back.' She pressed a kiss to Eva's temple. 'Kids come first, and this one deserves the world.'

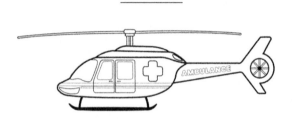

33

Maya's heart pounded when she emerged to confront Conrad outside the Whistlestop River Air Ambulance base.

'You read the file, didn't you?' he yelled at her.

'What file?' She may as well play dumb; it would buy more time. She led him away from the building and he was too inebriated to work out what she was doing.

'You know exactly what I'm talking about.'

'You're going to have to spell it out to me, I'm afraid.' And take long enough doing so that Noah and Eva could get to their car and go.

'Stop bullshitting, Maya.'

'I'm not.' She looked at the taxi to make sure Conrad was facing away from the airbase when she saw Noah and Eva stay close to the building and weave their way around to the parking bays. Stalling for time, she said, 'You must be paying a fortune in taxi fares. Why didn't you call me?'

'You'd only lie.'

'I think you need to go home, sober up.' Emboldened by the adrenaline coursing through her veins and the sight behind Conrad of Noah pulling out of the car park, she told him, 'We'll talk about this another time.'

'Oh, no, we won't.' He cupped his hands around his mouth and called up to the skies, 'Whistlestop River, Maya has been a very, very naughty girl!' He looked at her to gauge her reaction. 'Want me to continue?'

'Stop that right now,' came a voice beside them. Noah. He'd pulled up alongside and got out of the car.

'You again,' Conrad sneered. 'You're a right duo, aren't you?' He pointed to Noah then Maya and back again. 'I see what you're doing here.'

'And what might that be, Conrad?' Maya was so tired of this man.

'You're ganging up against me.'

'We're not in the playground, mate.' Noah intervened, coming closer, one eye on Maya, the other on the car.

'Don't *mate* me,' Conrad bit back. 'Piss off.'

'You're paranoid,' Maya told him. 'The only person against you is yourself. You're your own worst enemy. And you've been blackmailing me for long enough.'

'What, so now you're going to tell everyone your little secret? You'll tell everyone in there...' He jabbed a finger towards the air ambulance base. 'You'll tell them what you did. Little Maya, so innocent... or not, as it happens.'

Noah's voice, low and with a degree of toughness, warned, 'Leave her alone.'

'Don't threaten me.'

Conrad stepped so close to Maya, she could smell the foul scent of alcohol on his breath. 'You two think you're detectives but you should leave it up to the professionals so you don't mess this up.' He pulled up slightly taller, hands on hips. 'You're impeding an investigation, you know.'

Maya had to do something to salvage this. 'I'm betting your work doesn't think that's the sort of paperwork you're in possession of right now.'

She could tell by his reaction, the way his eyes lost more of their threat, that she was spot on. So she continued. 'And as for letting a member of the public get hold of confidential information? Well, that's a no-no. That could get you in a lot of trouble.'

Conrad took a moment to digest what she was saying. 'Well played, Maya. But it'll be my word against yours. I can't help who breaks into my house and goes rummaging—'

'That's where you're wrong.' Noah stepped closer to Maya's side. 'The day you came to my house and tried to blackmail me, offering me the information in that file in exchange for me leaving Maya alone, I recorded it all.'

'Bullshit.'

Noah shrugged, took out his phone, found the appropriate segment and played it out loud for Conrad to hear.

'That's enough,' Conrad snapped halfway through the recorded exchange. Evidently, he didn't want to hear it again either. 'What's he gonna do with the information?' Conrad directed the question to Maya.

But Noah stepped in again. 'I haven't contacted the police yet. We are the only people who've heard the recording.'

'You going to send it to them?' Conrad was doing his best to look as though he was in control, but he was rattled and it gave Maya a modicum of pleasure to watch him squirm.

'Not sure,' Noah shrugged.

Conrad's left eyebrow went up slightly more on the right side, a sign his interest was piqued. 'Why not?'

'I tell you what…' Noah stood a lot taller than his opponent, who staggered again thanks to the vodka and little time to sober up.

'I won't go to the police as long as whatever hold you have over Maya, you let it go.'

Conrad roared with laughter. 'Piss off! You don't get to tell me what to do!'

'Okay then.' And Noah turned and stepped back towards his car. He'd left the door open so he could hear Eva from a couple of metres away where they stood. 'I'll go home and make the call, let the police know about our little conversation. I'll sort everything out for myself and you'll be dealing with the consequences.' He climbed into the car and started up the engine.

Before he could drive away, Conrad stepped in front of the vehicle and slammed his hands onto the bonnet.

Noah wound down his window and warned, 'Get out of my way.'

But Conrad stood his ground.

Noah got out of the car and met him face on. 'I said out of my way.'

Conrad held up a hand and whined, 'Hold on a minute.'

'Why should I?'

'Because...' he said as though they were both stupid. 'Because as I've told you both, this isn't a game for amateur detectives. It's police business.'

'And whatever you're shooting your mouth off about when it comes to Maya is *her* business.'

Conrad's jaw clenched.

'Am I right?' Noah demanded.

'All right. Maya's business will stay Maya's business. You have my word on that.' When Noah looked doubtful, he went on. 'I swear. This is my career on the line. If anyone finds out about our conversation, I can kiss my job goodbye.' He looked at Maya. 'I'm not going to jeopardise that.'

'He's right,' said Maya. 'He wouldn't.'

Conrad addressed Noah, the events of tonight at least making him seem half sober. 'When are you meeting with Paul?'

'Two days' time, when I'm handing over the money.'

'Then I'll be at your place tomorrow morning, 9 a.m. sharp.' He headed for the awaiting taxi. 'We'll discuss it then,' he called back. Petty, having the last word and being the one to walk away.

But that was Conrad all over.

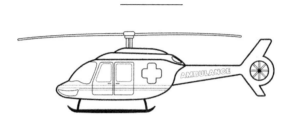

34

Noah and Maya hadn't hung around at the airbase last night, both stunned by what they now knew, by Conrad showing up, by what might happen from this point on. Noah had wanted to get Eva home and to bed and Maya had wanted to go back to her place to try to get some rest and hopefully a good night's sleep before coming to work today.

On shift, Maya was desperate to ask Noah how it had gone with Conrad this morning but when he arrived, she was busy preparing the helicopter, he had his own tasks to do and then they were out on two jobs in quick succession before they had a briefing and a training session. Following that, they were straight out on another job.

The third job of the day involved a beach landing, something Maya ordinarily loved. It was a thrill to land on the sand, given its challenges and its beauty rolled into one. They always got a good audience, mesmerised by the helicopter, keen to have a front seat at the action, and she got a buzz at some of the shocked faces when a female pilot stepped out of the aircraft. But today, Maya hadn't been able to enjoy any of that. Apart from concentrating on the flight itself and keeping everyone safe, her mind flitted to thinking about Noah and Eva, about Conrad and what he had planned for Noah as she waited for the crew to return to the aircraft. Her head spun thinking about whether Conrad was going to stitch Noah up somehow. Or was he really fearful enough for his own career that he wouldn't?

After the job, the crew returned to the airbase. Maya refuelled the helicopter and as soon as she had a chance, she got Noah alone in the kitchen and closed the door.

Noah recapped about Conrad showing up at his place that morning, no sign of the alcohol-fuelled man last night.

'He was professional, I'll give him that.' Noah made them both a cup of coffee once he'd given her the details.

'He loves his job; it means a lot to him.' It was also all he had right now without Maya and if he didn't work a bit harder to get to know his son, accept him for who he was and let him make his own decisions, he'd be even more alone. Perhaps that was what he was happy with. All his focus going into work. It was what she'd seen during their marriage; it wouldn't surprise her if that was all he strived for from now on. Maybe he'd have a woman on the side, an arrangement, no commitment, but that woman would never ever be her. Never again.

'The case has been baffling several officers countrywide for a while,' said Noah.

'Conrad will be glowing inside knowing he'll be the one to bring it to a close. And he won't stitch you up on this – his career means too much to him.'

'Let's hope you're right.'

The plan was for Paul to come to the house as arranged. Noah had been accumulating the cash already given he'd raided his own bank accounts and as he hadn't had time to sell his car, he'd taken out the maximum possible on his credit card. It would cost him in interest, he told her, but he had no choice. He'd also been mortified to have to ask someone else for a loan – Geraldine. But she loved him like a son, any fool could see that, and Maya hadn't been surprised to hear she'd lent him the money without any questions, trusting his instincts and judgements with whatever was going on. Noah had put all the money into a bag, which he was to hand over to Paul.

'I just hope Paul doesn't bolt.' He ran a hand across a stubbly, strong jaw as he spoke to Maya. 'I'd lose all my money and Geraldine's and I'd always be looking over my shoulder thinking he might come back for more.' He abandoned his coffee, turned and rested his hands on the worktop looking out at the rear of the airbase, across the fields beyond. 'Conrad says they'll be able to take action once the transaction is done. All I need to do is keep my focus on Paul, not be looking left and right out the door to see where the police are.'

'I wish I could be there for you, Noah. I know I can't, but I'll be thinking of you.' The way he looked at her had Maya wondering whether he thought about her as much as she thought about him, not only because of the current situation, but because he might be open to starting something more than friendship. 'Do you need me to take Eva for you?'

'Geraldine assumed I would be heading for the open day, so she's offered to take Eva to a children's farm out Salisbury way.'

'Sounds like a good plan.' She joined him next to the window to indulge him in the small talk he likely needed to keep his cool before all of this blew up. 'I took Isaac when he was only a few months old; it's probably the same place. I think the outing was more for my benefit, though, out in the fresh air, something different. Conrad thought it was a waste of time, of course, given Isaac was only ten months, but Isaac smiled so much that day, he laughed at the cows, was mesmerised by the sheep and the goats, loved that we were walking so close to donkeys and pigs that up until then he'd only seen in pictures in books. I went back a lot after that day. I expect Eva will be sold.'

Noah smiled briefly but his expression soon grew dark again. 'I only hope that in twelve hours' time, this nightmare will be over.'

She covered his hand with her own. 'I hope so too.'

'I don't want Paul to ever do this to anyone else ever again.'

'You're a good man, Noah.' She paused, took her hand away when she said, 'Thank you for what you did.'

He didn't register immediately but then found space in his head to recollect the threat Conrad had made outside the airbase. 'For calling Conrad out on the hold he has over you? I haven't known you that long, Maya, but I think I'm right when I say it's about bloody time.'

'Yes, it really is.'

And she was about to change that forever.

She only hoped Noah and everyone else in Whistlestop River would still want to know her once they knew the truth.

35

Noah helped Geraldine put Eva's seat into her car for the trip to the children's farm but all the while, he was paranoid that Paul would spring up, way too early, and he couldn't even look up and down the street. He had no idea when Conrad and any other officers involved would be nearby. They could even be here right now.

He closed the front door behind him after Geraldine and Eva left. One hour to go.

When Conrad had shown up to see him, Noah had expected him to be a total dick, to be laying down the rules and talking to Noah as if he was stupid, an irritation. But he hadn't. Maya was right; the guy had done this before, was good at his job and he'd want a good outcome too. He still had his arm in a cast but Noah had no doubt he'd be taking part as best he could in all of this so he would be the one in control and to gain credit.

Conrad had filled Noah in on some of the other women who'd been duped by Paul or whatever name he went by when he was with them. The guy had covered his tracks to a certain extent, but had begun to get sloppy.

'He never returns to an area more than once,' Conrad had told him. 'So he isn't often recognised. His hair changes in length, facial hair added or taken away, but he slipped up as a lot of criminals do as time goes on. We got word he was around this area and unfortunately for him, he picked a target who resides in the same town as I live in.' He said it as though it was him and him only who'd cast a net and captured his prey.

Noah let him have his moment of pride, of boasting or whatever it was. Because even though he couldn't stand this guy and the way he was to Maya, if Conrad could get Paul out of his life and, more importantly, Eva's, then that was enough for him.

'What should I say to him when he turns up at the door?' Noah asked.

Conrad looked at him like it was the most ridiculous question in the world. 'You say nothing.'

'Nothing? Seriously. I don't think that will work.'

'This isn't a television cop show in which you're an extra; there are no acting roles here, this is proper police work.' He adjusted his belt, tugged at his shirt to straighten it up. 'Tell him you have the money, hand it over, leave the rest to the professionals.'

As the time crept on, Noah imagined the officers taking their positions outside, wherever they might be, on foot or in vehicles.

The remaining minutes felt like the longest minutes of Noah's life.

At last, when 2 p.m. came around and there was a knock at the door, he rose from his position on the sofa, hands clammy, heart pounding. He took a deep breath. This was it.

There were no pleasantries when he opened the door.

'Got it?' Paul demanded. Overconfident, superior, a horrid excuse for a man.

From behind the door, Noah picked up the bag for life, scrunched over at the top, and handed it to Paul.

Paul looked inside, had a quick flick through some of the cash. 'Assume it's all there.'

Noah wanted to keep him talking for a minute, be sure Conrad and his team had a chance to get into position, get ready – he wasn't even sure that was what they were doing, perhaps he really was channelling TV shows for his thought process, but this had to work. There was twenty thousand pounds in that bag, twenty thousand he and Eva could use to live their lives.

'Count it if you like.' Noah nodded to the bag.

'I will, and I'll be back if it's not all there. You mark my words.' He turned on his heel.

Noah called after him. 'And this is it, you'll piss off out of our lives?'

Paul turned and gave a mock salute and Noah, as he'd been instructed, closed the door. And when he leaned against it, his legs folded beneath him until he sunk to the floor.

He was starting to think Conrad had set him up to fail when he heard nothing.

But then, a commotion, voices, shouting out in the street.

Was the nightmare really over?

36

Maya was a bundle of nerves. The summer breeze lifted strands of her hair out of place and she hooked them behind her ear again. Ever the professional, she wore pressed trousers, a crisp, ironed, navy-blue shirt with their logo, The Skylarks written beneath the silhouetted bird in flight, across the back.

Things were well underway at the airfield for the Whistlestop River Air Ambulance. Most of the town were here – the pub's owners, the man who ran the pharmacy, a few faces from the town hall, families she recognised from the neighbouring streets to her own. There was no opportunity to sneak off and try to call Noah. She had no idea how things had gone for him with Conrad and Paul. She'd been checking her phone whenever she could to find out and the fact she hadn't heard a thing had to be a good sign, surely? Or was it the other way round, with no word an indication that things hadn't gone to plan?

Maya had already done a talk to the general public today about Hilda, their trusty helicopter. The real Hilda was sitting out on the helipad, ready to go. With both crews here, they were all participating in the open day with the blue team on standby to go out should they get a job. Inside the hangar was another helicopter, one Frank and the team he worked with had brought here so that visitors to the open day would be able to climb inside, have a good look around and ask questions of Maya or Vik, whoever was on their helicopter stint at the time.

The airbase was filled with people from the town and its surrounds. They always got a good turn-out here, especially when the sun was shining. It was a great fundraiser and they'd had generous donations so far to support the work that they did.

Patrick, an amateur cyclist who had defied the odds and not only survived but got back on his bike following horrific, life-threatening injuries, stood up on the makeshift stage and addressed the crowds, onlookers whisper-quiet while he recounted what had happened to him.

He finished by saying, 'If it wasn't for The Skylarks then I might not be here today. So please, do give generously so the crews of the Whistlestop River Air Ambulance can keep saving lives.'

Some of the members of the Whistlestop River fire station had come along today too and, following Patrick's speech, Maya noticed that Bess had her eye on firefighter Gio.

'You're watching me,' said Bess when she passed by Maya with a tub filled with cold bottles of water to distribute to the crowds.

'Gio's nice,' Maya smiled, taking her head back to the day at hand. Well, the best she could anyway. Gio was over six foot tall with dark hair, a muscular build and very curious green eyes, at least when it came to Bess.

'He is,' smiled Bess as she held the tub and a group of kids descended to quench their thirst. 'But we're just good friends.' She waited until they were alone. 'I've never mixed work with pleasure, don't intend to start now.'

'Can't ignore that spark, though,' Maya teased.

Bess wasted no time batting back, 'Yeah? Talking from personal experience?'

Maya was rescued from having to answer anything about the insinuation she might well have a spark with Noah when a couple of young girls came over to ask her all about being a pilot. They wanted to know if they had to be cleverer than boys to be able to do it.

It was soon time for Maya and Bess to run the demonstration of what happened when a job came in, from the phone ringing to grabbing the helmets and their gear and heading out to start up Hilda. Kate and Bess had done a demonstration of resuscitation, a few of the crew had acted out a scenario of a drowning rescue, and those events were on repeat to some extent throughout the day depending on crowds evolving over the four-hour period.

But those parts of the day were manageable. It was waiting to hear from Noah that was stressful, what had her struggling to focus. And it was knowing what she was going to do as soon as she had her closest teammates with her that had Maya's palms clammy, her heart beating harder, worry lines etched on her forehead.

Maya only wanted to have to tell the whole truth once. Well, three times. Late last night, she'd called her sister Julie and told her everything, sobbing at some points, confessing everything and taking the comfort in Julie's voice. All Julie had been concerned with was that Maya had kept this all to herself for so long and that Conrad had been making her life difficult with his threats to blow it wide open.

The conversation with Julie prepared Maya for calling Isaac afterwards. She'd wanted Isaac to hear the story from her and telling Julie everything first meant she had got some of the emotion out of her story; she could give him the facts without making her son too worried that his mum was in a terrible place because of this secret. Isaac, her darling Isaac, had responded the way she'd always hoped he would. He understood she hadn't been in a very good place in her life, that she hadn't purposely committed any crime, and most of all, it made sense to him now why she stayed in Conrad's life so much.

'Mum, he's no right to do this to you.' His jaw was clenched, something she knew happened when he was angry. The expression lost nothing over FaceTime. She'd first seen it when Isaac was a little boy and a kid had knocked over his snowman on purpose because it was the best one on the street. It was a look that said he was furious and contemplating his next move. 'I'm done with him, Mum. It's not for you to sort out. Dad is old enough to look after himself, talk to me however he wants and if we don't get on then that's between us now. You've tried your hardest; I think it's time you stopped.'

She sighed, closed her eyes. And then he brought up her own dad.

'I know things with you and Grandad aren't great. Grandad knows it too. But the difference between him and Dad is that Grandad still loves and respects you.'

She was beginning to believe that for herself since they'd started to communicate.

'I never said anything before because Grandad didn't want me to. But he knew he had to sort it out for himself – that's another difference. Dad expects everyone else to do the work except him. Grandad isn't like that. He knows he made wrong decisions along the way and I can tell he has a lot of regret.'

'We've talked, recently.' And she'd smiled when she told her son that, as she explained what happened after her mother died, what her grandparents tried to do. 'We're getting there,' she said.

'Good for you, Mum. Grandad is a good man.'

'He is. And I'm glad you and he have always been in contact.'

But Isaac hadn't wanted to focus on his grandad at that point. 'I see Dad trying to get one up on you by having time with me like this plan to go to Ireland. I'm assuming you're not fighting it because of him threatening to tell the whole town the truth about you?'

'I'm sorry, Isaac.'

'Why are you sorry? You're not the one blackmailing someone they supposedly loved once upon a time and the person they have a child with.'

Maya snapped out of her reverie at the open day. She showed an elderly lady the way to the bathrooms, answered some questions from a family about the helicopter itself and why it was called Hilda. And after Nadia did another talk about some of the upcoming fundraising activities they had or ways the general public could hold their own to support the charity, she knew she'd go crazy if she put it off any longer.

She had to tell someone the truth. Conrad's job was on the line if Noah shared that recording, which meant her secret was safe. But Maya had had enough of her past hanging over her indefinitely.

She saw her opportunity when Nadia, mother hen of The Skylarks, headed to the kitchen with Bess, and Frank looked like he was on his way to join them. With the other crew perfectly capable of handling things outside, she slipped into the airbase building too.

'Tea?' Bess offered her when Maya joined the three of them in the kitchen.

Nadia sat on one of the chairs opposite Frank, who'd grabbed a pork pie from the fridge, and closed her eyes. 'I'm just closing my eyes for five minutes; wake me after that time, would you?'

Bess laughed but not when she saw Maya's face. 'What's going on?'

Frank was alert to trouble and popped the last of his pork pie into his mouth. Nadia opened her eyes and Maya only hoped the lot of them would understand what she was about to tell them. She never dreamed she'd do it today, but everything was coming to a head and perhaps a conversation that couldn't last too long given the event today was better. Like ripping off a plaster, it would be quick, over with just like that.

She pushed the door closed. 'I need to tell you all something and if I don't do it now, I'll lose my nerve.'

'Go on, love,' Frank urged. She wondered whether that same concern would show on his face when he heard what she had to say.

'You guys have known me for years, ever since I moved to Whistlestop River. I've lived in the area for over two decades and I love this town. It's a part of me. I'd do anything for Whistlestop River and its people, for The Skylarks.' She felt the hard ridge of the sink as she leant against it.

'We know you would,' said Bess to a chorus of agreement from the others.

'Then here goes,' said Maya. But if she was ousted, she wasn't sure how she would be able to pick up the pieces. She'd worked hard to earn a place in the town, respect, friendships and ties, and to lose them would break her heart.

All she could do now was start at the very beginning, the first day she'd ever come to Whistlestop River. She wouldn't say all of the details out loud, just the basics, the dreaded bullet points to explain.

But it didn't mean the details of what had happened all those years ago weren't still in her head.

37

When Maya finished school, she soon became restless. She had part-time jobs but nothing that engaged her fully. She lacked focus, she was lost. All she knew was that she still wanted to fly helicopters as much as she had as a little girl and without much of a relationship with her father, she was going to fund her training herself. But getting all that money together took time, patience.

The summer Maya turned twenty-one, she was bored and desperate for change. Temporary work had dried up and she spent more time out with old school friends. One evening, she got left in the pub with a girl she barely knew, a girl called Liz who seemed a whole lot of fun. Liz seemed dangerous. Like nobody Maya had ever been friends with before, like someone her father would totally disapprove of. Perhaps that was part of the appeal. The pair of them carried on drinking, they had a ball, a real laugh. They played the slot machines, they danced in a park, laughed their way down the slide, swung high on the swings, used the seesaw until it turned them both green.

They left the park, stopped at one more bar and then kept on walking until they ended up in Whistlestop River. Maya had never been to the town before; she'd always headed further afield in search of more excitement than her home county.

That night, Maya was ready to jump in a taxi home by the time they reached Whistlestop River. She wanted her bed badly but her father's house wasn't really home any more. It was a place with walls, somewhere to lay her head but with very little warmth apart from her sister's love.

'We need to amp this night up,' Liz declared as they lay on a grass bank not far from the town's main street, before Maya had a chance to mention the taxi.

Maya groaned. 'I need to go home.' She was beginning to feel the aftereffects of the alcohol rather than the buzzy high that came initially.

Liz leapt up from the bank and pulled Maya's hand to haul her to her feet. 'We need more booze.'

Maya thought about disagreeing but perhaps another drink enjoyed beside the river might send her to sleep right here in the fresh air, with nature and its sounds all around them. She'd never been scared of the dark, or of creepy crawlies; she wouldn't mind one bit sleeping outside for the night.

And so she agreed and they headed off – so she thought – to the shops to find one that was open for them to buy a bottle of whatever took their fancy.

When Liz stopped at the back of the Whistlestop River pub and bent down, Maya assumed she was tying her shoelace but it didn't take long to realise she wasn't when Liz stood up clutching a handful of gravel.

'What are you doing?'

Liz threw some to the upper windows of the pub. 'Let's make the owners think they've got a ghost.'

Maya had a bad feeling about this. 'We should go.'

But Liz already had another handful and she'd scooped some up for Maya too.

Maya didn't throw hers but Liz did. And then Liz began making animal noises – Maya had no idea what they were meant to be; she assumed owls. All she knew was that she didn't like this, particularly when Liz got frustrated that her plan wasn't working. She wanted to scare the owners and grew impatient when it seemed she couldn't.

'All we'll do is give them a fright,' Liz told Maya, who by now was begging her to leave it alone. 'We'll leg it as soon as we see the upstairs lights go on.'

After another ten minutes of getting no reaction at all, Liz went in for the kill. She picked up a much bigger stone and lobbed it at the window. And not just any window. Her aim was at the fancy stained-glass picture window. It was ornate, most likely it had been there since the pub was established hundreds of years ago.

In that instance, Maya felt sober enough to see the seriousness of what they were doing here, or what Liz was doing as the stone left her hand and hit her target head on. The window was smashed to smithereens.

A light went on, Liz grabbed Maya's hand and before Maya could take in the enormity of what had just happened, they were running away. Liz's laughter echoed in the moonlight. Maya's fear pumped through her veins. And when they reached the little wooden boat moored beside the sign that indicated it belonged to the pub, both girls leapt in and set off down the river.

Maya rowed for her life; Liz was too weak to help, she was laughing so hard. Maya stopped about a hundred metres away when she could no longer hear voices, when she was so spent, she couldn't carry on rowing, no matter how much she wanted to.

They tied the boat up and Maya thought that was it, but the drama was far from over.

Liz ran off towards a shed and Maya wondered whether she wanted to take shelter inside. But she quickly came back and had in her hand a can of something.

Before Maya could even question it, Liz poured whatever was in the can into the boat, pulled a lighter out from her pocket and threw the flame onto the boat.

The whole thing went up.

Maya had never been so scared in her life. 'What did you just do!' she roared.

But she moved quick enough when she heard a male voice yell that he was police, that they should stop right there.

They didn't. They ran. Like cowards. Away from the scene.

Two days later, Maya had the biggest row she'd ever had with her dad. She hadn't left the house since the night outside the pub, petrified the police would come to arrest her. She'd caught a glimpse of the local paper reporting the incident when she went to get a drink from the kitchen and she felt so much guilt, it almost swallowed her up.

'Did you fill in another UCAS form?' her father asked her as she tried to escape back up to her room and leave the newspaper article behind.

She turned halfway to the top of the stairs to face her father. 'What?'

'Don't *what* me, Maya. You heard what I said.'

'I did, but I've told you, university right now isn't in my plan.'

'This again...' He turned to go.

Maya could've easily headed upstairs and closed her door on her father but something made her chase after him into his study.

'You know what I want to do, Dad. I want to be a helicopter pilot.'

His jaw twinged. 'So you say.'

'You don't think I can do it?'

'It's a lot of study, a lot of money, and you might not even like it after all that so—'

'Said every single person at university! Who knows that they'll love their field of study?' She was yelling at him now, something he wasn't impressed with but seemed too shocked to address. 'Helicopters will be my life, Dad. Get that into your thick head!'

She'd gone too far.

She knew she had.

And she couldn't retreat fast enough to escape the bellow that followed.

'I am still your father; you do not talk to me like this in *my* house. Under *my* roof. If your mother was here—'

'Yeah, well she's not, is she! Neither are my grandparents; you took them from me too!'

When she ran up to the top of the stairs, his voice followed, something about showing respect, she didn't much care. All she knew was that she had to get out of here. And this time, for good.

She pulled a big rucksack from the wardrobe, the suitcase from under the bed and threw as many of her things in as she could.

'Maya...' Her door had opened so quietly she hadn't heard her sister Julie come in. 'What are you doing?' But Julie knew what this was; that's why her eyes filled with tears.

Maya sat down on the bed and held out her arms to her sister and they sat there together, sobbing, hugging, Maya doing her best to explain that she wasn't walking away from Julie, only the man they called their dad, the man who hadn't understood her in a very long time.

Maya left that night. She had no idea where she was going, she just knew she had to go. It was pouring with rain, she got on the bus that went from 100 metres past the driveway to the family home and sat on it until the driver announced it was the last stop.

Whistlestop River. The town she'd been in before. She stepped off that bus, saw the sign and almost tried to clamber back on again and beg the driver to take her anywhere but here. The place where she'd behaved so abominably.

But the driver had already driven away and she was stranded at the side of the road in the town that didn't deserve her.

She walked away from the sign, around the back streets until properties spread out, landscapes came into view in the fading light. She found a bus shelter and decided to wait to see if another bus came at this time of night. The skies grew dark, the temperature fell enough that she dug out the blanket she'd put in her suitcase.

She huddled beneath it, clutched it tighter and tighter as the darkness surrounded her. Nobody else came to the bus stop, nobody bothered her; it was deserted. Maybe it wasn't even an operational bus stop at all.

Whatever it was, she fell asleep in it.

Maya woke up to the sound of a distant car horn and realised it was gone midnight. Her body was stiff, she was hungry, she shivered. She knew she had to move. She hadn't brought much money with her, she had no food, but how could she go home?

Maya wasn't sure how long she kept walking. Going around another bend, her rucksack on her back, dragging the suitcase behind her, she saw a sign: The Whistlestop River airfield.

She drew closer to the airfield and when she reached a metal barrier, she threw her suitcase over, then her rucksack, and then climbed over herself. She hoped they didn't have guard dogs here and almost turned back but as her heart thumped and no beast came barrelling towards her, she put one foot in front of the other to head for the building a couple of hundred metres away.

She reached the ground adjacent to the airbase building. It was the middle of the night now and she watched as someone dragged the helicopter from its helipad back into the hangar. She felt a sense of calm, a sense of peace. She didn't care about being cold and hungry in this moment; she was watching something she envied and longed to be a part of.

She stayed in the shadows. She thought the air ambulances operated 24/7 but she must have got that wrong because the hangar door was closed by whoever was in there.

She left her suitcase and rucksack in the bush at the very edge of the field and ran closer to the airbase building, hid behind a car. Crew members emerged one by one.

She heard a couple of them yell goodnight and as soon as another car left and she couldn't see anyone else, but the lights were still on inside the building, she ran to the door. It was open. She crept inside as quietly as she could. A few weeks earlier, she'd read in the newspaper that the airbase was fundraising for a new hi-tech CCTV system, which hopefully meant their security wasn't great now. She'd worn a hoodie tonight for warmth and pulled up the hood just in case, making her harder to recognise if someone did catch her at it.

She slinked up the stairs at the side, into a room that had a couple of really small beds. She heard nobody and after ten minutes had passed, gradually all blocks of lights around her disappeared, one by one, until she was in total darkness. She heard the big door at the front close and the sound of it being locked but she waited another twenty minutes, until she knew the coast was clear.

She wasn't going to do anything bad. She didn't want to damage anything or steal, but she needed warmth, shelter, food. That was it, then she'd leave.

She went down the stairs on her bottom in the dark but there was enough moonlight filtering in that she could find her way through reception and to the kitchen. She found cheese in the fridge, some bread in one cupboard, chocolate in another. It had taken the edge off. She could go now, no harm done.

Maya made her way from the kitchen and into reception but

with the door locked from the outside, it was hopeless. She was stuck. She looked around for a spare key but couldn't find one and the drawers in the desk section were locked.

She went back up the stairs, searched in the kitchen but found no sign of a key there either. She was trapped.

She took a big knife and a smaller one back down to the reception. She managed to force the top drawer, then the second, where she found a cash box.

She looked at it. Was she a thief?

She wasn't, but she had to survive.

Before her conscience could talk her out of it, she forced open the box, took all the cash from inside, the notes, the coins, every last bit. She swore she'd pay it all back when she could: when she got herself sorted.

She forced open the third drawer and it was in there she found a keyring with two keys on it. One of them had to be the right one, surely.

But neither of them were.

She tried one of the keys in a door at the far end of the reception, a side entrance, but no luck there either.

And then her head went to the hangar and its huge doors to let the aircraft be brought in and pulled outside.

One of the keys fitted the internal door. She let herself in, the smell of engine oil letting her know how close she was to the helicopter. She tried the other key in the padlock used to secure the hangar doors and it worked. She had it off in seconds but froze – was it alarmed? The main building obviously wasn't, she'd been walking around inside and there hadn't been a sound, but perhaps they'd saved it for the external doors.

Only one way to find out.

She yanked open the door at one side, putting all her weight behind it. She'd planned to make enough of a gap to squeeze through, but no alarm sounded.

Relief washed through her.

All she had to do was run, grab her bag and suitcase and disappear. Nobody had to know she'd been here.

But as she turned to close the hangar door again, she caught sight of the helicopter.

There it was in all its glory. The lights weren't on but she could still make out the bright yellow of its body and tail in the moonlight that filtered inside, its main rotor blade, all the parts she'd been able to name since she was a little girl.

She was drawn back over to it as if it was a magnet. She ran her fingers along the pilot's door, imagined what it would be like to open it and get inside, to take off. She looked out at the night sky, stars not visible with the rain tonight, but she could imagine being up there, being free from everything else, being herself, Maya the pilot, not Maya the girl who'd lost her mum, her grandparents, her dad, pretty much.

She tried the door to the helicopter and unsurprisingly it was locked. She circled the aircraft, tried the other door, in awe of this beast she dreamed of flying one day. She couldn't ignore the passion; it was like a fire inside of her, it would never be extinguished.

It was a split-second decision. She didn't process it; one minute, she saw the crowbar on the tool bench in the corner and the next thing she knew, she was using it to try to get inside. She had to sit in that pilot's seat, even if it was only once. She wanted to feel the helicopter beneath her, view the control panels and equipment in the cockpit.

She tried over and over again, the paint coming off, the damage plain to see, but she couldn't stop until she got in.

She felt a surge of adrenaline, excitement, when finally the door gave in and opened.

She climbed into the pilot seat and put the crowbar down on the other seat next to her. Being inside a helicopter, right here up front where the action took place, was something she dreamed about.

But she wanted more. She leapt out, went over to the hangar doors and pulled them both all the way open so that she could feel as though this were real.

She didn't know how long she sat there pretending she was a pilot, that she could leave her troubles behind and take to the skies, but it was warm, comforting, the rain hammering the hangar and helipad beyond. In here, inside this aircraft, she was someone else.

When she grew tired of pretending, she leaned back in her seat and closed her eyes. She'd take a minute, only a minute.

But she shouldn't have done that.

The next thing she knew, she was waking to a rapping on the pilot side window.

Shit.

And now someone was opening the door, exposing her.

'Well, well, well, what have we here?' The man locked her in his gaze.

She froze, she daren't say a word. How could she?

It was fight or flight. She leapt to the other seat, lifting the crowbar out of her way, expecting to open the door from inside, jump down and run off into the night. But the man had climbed in himself and she turned to defend herself, the crowbar in her hand.

Smash.

The crowbar didn't defend her but it did smash into the flight instruments on the dashboard and she didn't need to look closely to know her split-second reaction had caused damage.

He took the crowbar from her and when he backed out of the

aircraft, she followed after him. She couldn't do much else. He'd be too quick for her if she tried to get out the other side, she should've known that.

The rain continued to pour beyond the open hangar doors, a rumble of thunder sounded, a flash of lightning reminded her that a storm had closed in.

Her legs went weak; she slumped to the floor.

'Let me help you,' said the man and she looked up at him with red-rimmed eyes. 'Come with me.' He took something from his pocket and showed it to her. A warrant card. 'I'm a police officer. You can trust me. I'll make sure you don't get in trouble.'

And in that moment, she'd really believed him.

38

Nadia was at her side the minute she finished telling them the whole story, or at least most of it. Maya's mind briefly went through the options – was she going to be yelled at? Told to go away and never come back?

But it was neither. Nadia enveloped her in a hug which went on and on and she only broke it off so Frank could do the same.

'Now, now,' Frank murmured into her hair, 'it sounds like an ordeal for you, a terrible accident, that's all.'

'I remember hearing about it,' Nadia recalled suddenly. 'There was a lot of damage.'

'There was,' said Maya. It wasn't only the door and damage to the interior of the helicopter. Leaving the hangar door open like that on the night of a big storm had caused untold amounts of damage to the hangar and more to the aircraft. The newspapers had reported it, the headlines sensationalising the accident and the weather damage that soon became an act of vandalism, at least in the eyes of the press and the entire town. The helicopter was costly to repair, the crew hadn't been able to go out in the helicopter until it was all fixed and rechecked for safety. Lives were lost because of her recklessness.

'Oh, Maya.' Frank put a hand on her shoulder. 'You didn't do all of that damage.' Because he remembered it too, the personal accounts from crew members who were devastated, past patients saved by the air ambulance who condemned such an act by a despicable individual or group of lowlifes.

'But it happened because of me. People died and it was my fault.'

'What? That's not true,' said Nadia.

'It is,' Maya sobbed.

'It wasn't your fault,' Nadia reminded her firmly.

Maya was so ashamed, distraught at her part in such a terrible thing. She'd read about the events of that night in the newspaper, how the rescue teams weren't there in time to save the young boy who'd fallen into the river and his father who'd jumped in after him.

'Maya,' Nadia persisted. 'Listen to me. Nobody could've saved that father and son. The son died instantly after a blow to the head, the dad reached his body but couldn't bring him back to shore, the current was too strong. He drowned. He was gone soon after the emergency call came through. The newspapers detailed the whole story. The helicopter wouldn't have made any difference, do you hear me?'

Maya locked eyes with Frank, then Nadia. 'Really?'

'Yes, really.' Frank shook his head. 'The media like to sensationalise and headlines about vandals tends to sell papers.'

Maya put her head in her hands, a sense of relief flooding through her insides, although it wouldn't change the fact that a father and son had died that night. And that was a tragedy no matter whether her actions had played a part or not. But all this time, she'd thought it was her. She'd thought that if only she hadn't broken into the helicopter that night then that little boy and his dad would be alive right now. The shame had been almost too much to bear at times, it had eaten away at her, she'd never forgiven herself and she'd made it her life's mission to get to every emergency call she could, to save as many lives as humanly possible, even if it meant flying when conditions were risky.

Nadia rubbed Maya's shoulders. 'Why tell us now?' She had one eye out of the window. They all had to get back to the open day soon, carry on as if nothing was out of the ordinary.

'It was time.' She didn't need to say the rest, that the man who helped her that night was Conrad, that he'd held this over her for years. At least not yet, anyway.

'I never forgot about any of the things I did back then,' she said. 'But knowing the helicopter wouldn't have changed the outcome is a comfort in some ways.' Maya wiped her eyes with the tissue Nadia passed her. 'I never forgot the broken window at the pub, the boat, the way the landlord and landlady felt victimised and left as a result.'

'They didn't leave because of that,' said Frank. 'Petra and Steve left the pub and the town due to stress all right, but their stress was because their son was ill and they wanted to move to be closer to him. They didn't make that well known; their son had mental health issues and they were private people when it came to family. As far as I know, they're still happy and living in the West Country where they run a beautiful little old pub.'

'You kept that all to yourself, Maya,' Nadia said, as though it pained her personally. 'That must've been incredibly hard. But it wasn't you who broke the window or set fire to the boat, and the damage here was all an accident. You didn't mean harm; there were extenuating circumstances.'

'You're making excuses for me,' Maya smiled. 'It's kind of you. And I want you both to know that I paid back all the cash I stole and then some by way of anonymous donations as soon as I got sorted.'

Frank put a hand on her arm and gave it a squeeze. 'You have a good heart, don't ever doubt that.'

When one of the blue crew members rapped on the window for Nadia, she gave Maya one last hug and left her to it.

'Was it you who made the anonymous donation for the window repair at the pub?' Frank asked.

'No, I was going to, but it was already done before I got the chance.' She shrugged. 'I've no idea by who.' She watched Frank. He was building up to say something else, she could tell. 'Frank, just say it.'

He nodded at her ability to read him like a book. 'I have a feeling Conrad knew all about the trouble you got into back then. It was likely him who didn't fill you in on the details that would've told you the lives lost weren't down to the helicopter being unavailable. And… I wouldn't mind betting he's held that night over you ever since.'

One look gave him the answer and he wrapped her in his arms yet again, muttering a few choice words about her ex-husband. 'I'm glad you told us. And I'm glad he no longer has that hold.'

'Me too, Frank, me too.'

She pulled away and was about to excuse herself to get back to the open day when she saw a peculiar look pass across Frank's face as his gaze passed over her head.

'What is it?' She turned to see for herself.

He said quietly, 'The side window is open.'

There was a small window at the side of the kitchen which opened onto an internal hallway. Maya didn't see the significance but when she stood on tiptoes to see what Frank had, she did.

Her dad was sitting on one of the chairs right outside the kitchen.

Which meant he'd heard it all.

39

When Maya opened the kitchen door and came face to face with her dad sitting on the chair against the wall in the corridor on the other side, they looked at each other, and neither of them moved. It was Nadia coming back along the corridor taking charge who shunted them into the kitchen, told Maya that Vik could handle the helicopter questions, that they should take some time. Frank must have filled her in on the open-window situation.

Maya went back into the kitchen first, heard her dad come in afterwards, turned at the sound of him pulling the internal window closed. He pulled out a chair from beneath the table and sat down.

Maya went over and sat next to him.

'That was the night, wasn't it?' he said with no preamble.

'The night I walked out, yes.'

'The worst night of my life except for the night your mum died.' He looked directly at her.

Maya wished she'd waited to tell Frank and Nadia, maybe told her dad first. But whatever way she'd done it, it would've been painful.

'I'm making tea.' She didn't ask whether he wanted any. She had to do something. She couldn't sit here waiting for the reckoning that had to be coming, the judgement at the things she'd done wrong and wished she could erase.

She set the mugs down in front of them both at the table. Her dad didn't reach for the sugar to add to his drink. When had that changed? There was so much she didn't know about him. And perhaps she never would if he walked away again now after the things she'd admitted.

But she still had to tell him the rest.

'There's more to that night, other than what I shared with Nadia and Frank,' she said, checking the internal window was closed, even though she'd seen him do it.

It took her a good minute to form her first words, her explanation. 'The man who'd chased after us when the window was smashed, the boat torched—'

'Was Conrad,' he finished for her. 'It doesn't surprise me. And I suppose he was the one who found you here too?'

She nodded.

'Was he here officially?'

She shook her head. 'He said he'd seen me with another girl near the pub, that he'd given chase but we got away. He spotted me again the night I left home, saw me at the edge of the airfield.' She explained the whole night to him, every detail, leaving nothing out.

'I was in a state, Dad. When he said he'd help me get away, I believed him and so I ran with him. I tried to close the hangar doors but when we saw headlights from another car, he told me to just run. And so I did. We picked up my things and I didn't look back.'

And having someone on her side that night, someone who seemed to want to help her and appeared to see her as the Maya she really was, had meant everything.

'Conrad listened to me that night. We talked for hours. And then he got me a place to stay, I was safe. He didn't hassle me. I was warm, I was looked after, I wasn't hungry. And that's all I could deal with at first. He slowly helped me get on my feet. I got a temporary job at a supermarket so I could pay back the money Conrad had lent me to get me started and so I could fund my board at a bed and breakfast he'd found for me, which was at a reduced rate thanks to him.

'Shortly afterwards, I started dating Conrad. We went for dinner, then it was a movie, then it was happening more and more and gradually we got closer and closer. We got engaged. I thought I'd found my happy. We got married, I moved in with him.'

'He swept you off your feet,' said Nigel. 'He was like a knight in shining armour.'

'He was.' Except instead of a knight come to save her, he'd turned into a man who wanted to keep her no matter what, who wanted her to be so afraid of him ruining her life as she knew it that she stayed with him.

'We'd not been married long when I began to see another side to him. He kept mentioning the night with Liz, and the night he found me here. He told me what was in the newspapers about the pub incident, that local gossip was that the same vandals had broken into the airbase and damaged the helicopter, taken money, left the hangar doors open so that there was storm and water damage to the inside. Word was that they'd done it for kicks, Conrad told me that. It was horrible listening to it recounted so many times, but I honestly believed he was protecting me, that he still wanted to keep me safe.

'Over time, especially after he'd had a couple of drinks, I started to realise he might be taunting me with it, but I wasn't sure. He'd talk about both incidents, especially the one at the airbase, he'd monetise the damage, talk about how locals had held fundraisers to get the Whistlestop River Air Ambulance back to being fully operational with a helicopter as well as cars.'

'He was blackmailing you.' Nigel's grip tightened on the mug of tea he hadn't even touched.

Maya nodded. 'He was subtle with it, really subtle. At first, he'd only say that had it not been for him then I would be in serious trouble. He'd leave it at that, it wasn't a threat, but the more he reminded me of it, the more I realised that was exactly what it was. He had some knowledge, a power, he had a hold over me.'

'Not really the recipe for a happy marriage.' Her dad's words were laced with sympathy and something else... fury. 'How did I not see it for myself?'

'I didn't see it, so I never would've expected anyone else to.'

'That man...'

'I know. But I'll never regret Isaac. Naively, I thought perhaps having a child together might make our marriage stronger, drive Conrad to be a better man. But it didn't. Conrad found fault with everything; he used any opportunity he could find to moan at me. And it went on and on. Isaac was learning piano and we got him a keyboard for his birthday but all Conrad would do was complain that it was too loud. Isaac loved school and Conrad couldn't relate to it. He might have liked some of his teachers when he was at school but as for the establishment, he was done with that as soon as he was old enough to get out. He joined the police, said education after school was a waste of time, so you can imagine what it's been like with Isaac going on to further study and now university.

'When Isaac was almost ten, Conrad began to bring up both incidents more often. I was progressing with my training, on my way to a career, a part of life that wouldn't include him. And I think he was insecure. He knew I wasn't happy in the marriage and I think he realised that I'd see my unhappiness even more when I carved out time for myself away from our relationship and out in the real world. He wanted to make me uneasy, fearful. He didn't want to lose me. The irony was that he forgot marriage meant he was supposed to stop sleeping around.'

'He cheated on you?'

'Multiple times. And I always knew. He's a good police officer – you'd think he'd know more about covering his tracks, but he never did. I used to think he wanted out of the marriage as well, but during a blazing row one night when the word divorce was mentioned, he said that if I ever left him then the whole town would know the details of what I'd done at the pub, at the airbase. He told me people were more likely to believe him than me. And even though that wouldn't necessarily be the case, I couldn't take the risk because he said that if I was prosecuted for what I'd done, I'd lose Isaac. I couldn't bear the thought of losing my son. And so I stayed.'

'But you pursued your career.'

'I did. But he didn't support it. He saw, and referred to it, as *Maya's little hobby* when I first started studying. He never saw it as real, not until I got my first job flying helicopters for tourists once I'd completed all my training, the theory and the practice, and Isaac started high school. Even then, he thought I'd lose interest and go back to being a stay-at-home wife soon enough. But I didn't. The more I flew, the more I wanted to keep doing it and I was determined to go all the way, become a HEMS pilot. He hated it when I joined The Skylarks. I expected him to threaten to tell them what I did if I joined the crew, but he didn't. Perhaps he realised it was local for him, he'd be able to keep a partial eye on me if I was there.'

Nigel took such a deep breath his shoulders rose. He did it when he was thinking deeply. And now the way he was looking at her reminded her so much of the times as a little girl when he'd run to her side and protected her.

'That man, what he did to you.' His own eyes filled with tears. 'You were trapped in a marriage and couldn't get out.'

Maya thought about the time another kid had pushed her off the seesaw in the playground and she'd fallen to the ground. Her dad had come running and given the young boy a piece of his mind. Conrad would want to watch his back in the street from now on if he was to bump into Nigel because the look on Nigel's face was similar to that day. And it made Maya feel safe. She'd forgotten her dad ever had the ability to make her feel that way.

'My biggest worry with the secret became Isaac finding out what his mother had done. I never wanted that. But it also became about my reputation in Whistlestop River as I settled into the town more and more. I didn't want to be judged and lose the respect of people I'd come to know, to admire. I was scared I'd lose my job.'

Her dad pushed away his cup of tea. 'I wish I'd been there for you more.'

'You were there, Dad. But you and I didn't understand each other.'

'We didn't. And that's my fault.'

'No, Dad. It's both of our faults. It's circumstance, it's life, and events all rolled into one.'

'I'm glad I know everything now.'

'Me too.'

A knock at the window from the outside made them both jump.

Maya had been in their little bubble in here, the open day carrying on around them.

She went over to the window and waved down at the little boy who must have jumped up to make the knock. He pointed at the helicopter and Maya gave him a thumbs up.

'I'd better get outside, Dad.'

He stood, brought both mugs over to the sink and looked at the crowds beyond the windows, the crew buzzing about. 'I came here today to see the work you do. I wanted to understand you more.' He turned to face her. 'I couldn't be more proud. Of the woman you are, your honesty, the mother you've become, the sister, the daughter you have always been. And for all of this here, doing so much good in a town that should feel lucky to have you.'

'You're proud of me?' She said it as though trying it on for size.

'Very much so.'

And for the first time in forever, he opened up his arms. And Maya didn't need telling twice. She stepped into a hug from her dad after all these years.

40

Noah found a place to park at the airfield, although it was a challenge with both crews here today plus visitors.

He scooped Eva into his arms. 'Come on, you.'

Eva's soft hair tickled his chin as she snuggled up against him, tired after her trip to the children's farm where, according to Geraldine, she'd cried when a goat came too close and laughed at the noise of the chickens. Noah had told Geraldine everything. He'd had to; it was obvious something had gone on. But it had allowed him to tell her why he'd needed the money he borrowed. It also helped her understand his absolute need to take Eva with him now rather than leave her with anyone else.

This little girl had landed in his life out of nowhere; he'd become an overnight dad with no warning. But despite all the dramas, he wouldn't have it any other way. He couldn't imagine his life now without Eva in it. His house would be quiet, his home empty, and his heart the same.

'Shall we find Maya?' he whispered as he went around the back of the airbase to where the open day was in full swing. He zoned in on the helicopter in the hangar, the place she was most likely to be and, sure enough, there she was talking to a group of half a dozen boys who were firing questions left, right and centre about aviation and in particular helicopters.

Maya spotted him and he could tell she was doing her best to get away, but he was quite happy to watch her for a while. Outside the hangar, he pulled Eva's sunhat from his back pocket and put it on her head, hoping it would stay put.

Noah enjoyed the feel of sunshine on his face, the feel of a really good country summer. Mind you, even if the weather changed and brought with it high winds and rain, he wouldn't care because Paul was well and truly out of their lives.

Maya extricated herself at long last and, before anyone else could grab her attention, she came striding over.

His smile said it all.

Maya wrapped her arms around him and Eva, taking them both by surprise. 'It's over?'

'It's over,' he said into her hair. He didn't want to let her go.

When she pulled back, she checked, 'He's not coming back?'

Noah recapped the events of the morning. The commotion he'd heard outside after he'd handed over the money to Paul had indeed been Conrad and his colleagues confronting him and taking him away for questioning. The money had been returned to Noah already and before Conrad left his place earlier, Noah had told him to leave Maya alone.

And Conrad said nothing. He didn't like it. But what could he do? Noah had that recording and if Conrad did anything to upset Maya then it would find its way to his superiors.

'Conrad won't be bothering you again either,' Noah told Maya now. All he wanted to do was hold her in his arms, protect her and keep her safe.

Maya shook her head when he told her the details. 'I should be annoyed he feels he can interfere in my life at all, but I'm not. I no longer care. I'm just relieved you have Eva, the police have Paul and hopefully he'll get his comeuppance, and having you say that to Conrad...'

Noah didn't break his stare with this woman, this amazing, strong, clever and beautiful pilot he wanted to get to know more. And now it was as though the barriers that had been there previously had lifted away and both of them could step forwards.

Nadia came over to remind Maya she had another talk to do about the helicopter starting in ten minutes but, before she went on her way, she hugged Maya tight.

'What was all that about?' Noah asked when she left them to it.

'I'm going to blurt something out now and then I have to get to work, but please, can we talk about it later?'

Puzzled, he nodded. 'Go for it.'

'I want to blurt this out because I don't want you hearing it from anyone else.'

'Maya, just say what you need to...' He used one hand to stop Eva's fingers from poking him in the eye. She'd gone from sleepy to alert and interested again.

And so Maya went for it. She told him what happened all those years ago, before she left her father's home, the trouble she got into, the man who had come along to rescue her. And when she finished, she looked at the ground, ashamed, and embarrassed, when she shouldn't be feeling either of those things.

Noah reached down and took her hand, squeezed it. He planted a gentle kiss on her temple. Conrad wouldn't bother her again, so he tried to quash down the anger he felt at what the man had held over her for so long, making her question herself, fearing for her reputation, her job.

'Maya, we all do things when we're young,' he whispered into her hair. 'Most of us at some point have been pulled into situations we don't like and we don't always know how to get out of them.' He didn't let go of her hand. 'You wait until you hear some of my stories. They'd make this beautiful hair of yours curl some more.'

'Noah, I—'

'Go... over to the helicopter, people are waiting and need you. I'll be here. I'm not going anywhere.'

And he wasn't. He'd found his place here in Whistlestop River, a home at the old signal box cottage with Eva. A little family. And now Maya, a woman he hoped would very much be a part of all of that.

* * *

Maya's mind was partly on the helicopter: talking to a gaggle of teenage boys, telling them what all the controls did, regaling them with tales of some of the trickiest places she'd ever had to land – they'd lapped up that part of the talk, the riskier the better. Doubts crept in that they wouldn't be sensible enough for the job no matter how much they said they wanted it, but she also knew that part of being a pilot was having an absolute passion for the job, the knowledge that every flight came with risks, that it was your reactions and skill in any given situation that mattered.

She looked over in Noah's direction more than once. He'd been watching her at first, his smile suggested he'd accepted what she told him, but then he'd wandered off into the crowds and now she was done, she couldn't see him anywhere.

The open day was coming to a close. The crews had been lucky. Apart from a call right before the start of the event and a second job which was so close by that they'd sent the rapid response vehicle out with the blue team at the helm, they'd been reasonably quiet. But it felt like one of the longest shifts she'd ever had with the emotion wrapped up in the day.

The crowds began to thin and finally Maya spotted Noah at the other side of the airfield. He was talking to someone, his back to her, but Eva gave her a grin as she approached and it warmed Maya's heart right through.

She didn't think her heart could swell any more until Noah turned and revealed who he was talking to.

'Isaac!' She threw herself at her son, wrapping her arms around him, her feet leaving the ground momentarily. 'You're here, you're not due home for another week!'

'Thought I'd surprise you, Mum. And it's almost your birthday, I couldn't miss that.'

She squeezed even tighter. 'Having you home is the best present I could ask for.' She finally let go of him. 'I swear you look more grown up every time I see you.'

He groaned.

Noah bounced Eva on his hip. 'Is this what I have to look forward to with this one?'

'Yep,' smiled Maya. 'I'll tell you now that it's a bumpy road, parenthood. But you'll love it.'

Geraldine appeared next and wasted no time scooping Eva into her arms. 'Hello, little one.'

'Haven't you had enough of her yet?' Noah laughed.

'Never. And I thought you two might need some time.'

Isaac looked from Maya to Noah and back again and blushed a little when he realised what was going on. He'd always done that, he hated it, but Maya didn't. Because no matter how much he grew up, it told her that her little boy was still in there somewhere.

'And who is this?' Geraldine asked, addressing Eva as though she could answer who the strapping young adult male was.

Maya introduced Geraldine to Isaac.

Geraldine grinned. 'Ah, so I've just put my foot in it, I assume.'

Isaac began to laugh. 'Not at all. Mum's love life is her business.

And I can see my grandad, so I'll go say hi. He's helping the crew pack everything away.'

Maya spun round. Sure enough, Nigel was talking to the Whistlestop River Freewheelers, helping them put away their banners and fold up the table. She felt her breath catch. Her dad. Here. Her dad. Proud. Getting involved in the job he'd never seemed to be interested in.

Isaac went over to his grandad and Geraldine took charge of Eva.

Noah stepped closer. 'So, your love life, eh?'

'I can't believe he said that.'

'I can.' She didn't have to look up into his eyes to know his focus was fully on her when he said, 'Alone at last.'

'Apart from a few dozen or so people...' She finally looked up into those eyes that sent flutters of nerves and excitement cascading through her.

He reached for her hand and his fingers slotted between hers. 'I heard you that night, you know.'

'What night?'

'The night I told you about Justine and the phone call. We were at mine and you went to check on Eva.'

She remembered. He'd heard her?

When she looked down at the ground, he put his opposite hand beneath her chin and tilted it upwards. 'So you think I'm kind and wonderful?' He was smiling.

'Yeah, yeah, okay, no need to go on about it.'

'Do you still think I'm those things?'

'I do.'

'I'm glad. If you're up for it, I think we need to go on a date, find out a lot more about each other.'

'That sounds like a plan.'

'Is tonight too soon?'

She gulped. 'Tonight is perfect. But I feel I should warn you that I'm so tired, I might not be able to keep my eyes open.'

'Then how about a date on the back porch at my place? It's not the most exciting venue but there'll be beer...' He put his hands on either side of her face. '...there'll be nachos...' His lips were tantalisingly close to hers. 'We could watch the sun go down over the river. And we could say goodbye to the bench?'

Confused, she waited for him to say more.

'I've got a porch swing on order, especially for you.'

Her eyes closed as her words came out on a whisper. 'It all sounds perfect.'

And no matter how many people were about to bear witness to the start of something for Maya and Noah, he kissed her as though it were only the two of them out here.

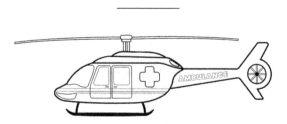

41

It had been six weeks since the Whistlestop River Air Ambulance open day. Noah had started the process of applying to adopt Eva so he would officially become her father. He knew, having found out that Paul had been charged and a couple more women had come out of the woodwork, that the guy would never get close to Eva again, but he still wanted the finality, the completion of a circle that he knew would be exactly what his sister had wanted.

A few weeks ago, Eva, now fifteen months, had taken her first steps and Noah's excitement had been off the scale for his little girl, who'd spent every day since trying out her new party trick. He'd put cushions in the lounge and had moved any tables well out of the way so she could practise without getting injured. He'd also gone out and bought a bumper pack of child safety catches, locks, corner protectors to stop her hurting herself on the edge of tables, something to stop her opening the toilet and putting her head inside. She was suddenly into everything. It was both exciting and terrifying. But with Geraldine there to give him advice and Maya too, it was a case of bring it on. All of it.

Noah was sweeping up inside the hangar at the base when a

call came in. He and Bess collected all the equipment and made their way through the reception, heading out to the rapid response vehicle given the call was so close and easily accessible by road. Maya gave Noah a little smile as she went to grab the door. They'd been careful to keep it professional at all times at work, as had the rest of the team, but some days it was hard not to reach for her, to pull her into his arms and lose himself in a woman he'd thought was way out of his reach. Cassie would've loved her.

'I'll see you tonight,' he said softly before sneaking a quick peck on her cheek that nobody else clocked.

Maya blushed. He was still getting used to Maya being coy when it came to his affections. It wasn't the part of her personality he knew so well – she was the capable, in-control pilot at work. But he liked it. He liked everything about her.

Bess grinned when he got into the car. 'Saw that,' she said.

So he hadn't got away with it after all.

'Just drive, woman.'

Bess laughed; she loved to tease him. And he didn't mind it either. Yesterday, she said he was like a cartoon character with hearts in his eyes, and as he drove away from the base, he couldn't deny it. Perhaps she was right.

 * * *

With Bess and Noah out in the rapid response vehicle all shift and the helicopter back in situ and ready for the off, Maya had something special planned. She'd cleared it with the powers that be, she'd made a donation to cover any financial costs and when her dad arrived in reception to what he assumed was a cup of tea and catch up with his eldest daughter, she felt mischievous but excited. She'd kept her life separate from his for far too long and him coming to the open day had shown that he wanted to change that as much as she did.

Her dad kissed her on the cheek and she led him through reception. 'I'm still getting used to this place,' he said. 'I'm still getting used to my daughter, the pilot.'

She beamed. Over the last few weeks, they'd had lunches together and they'd talked, really talked, about life when her mum was alive, about her life since, about Julie and their grandparents and about Isaac. She'd even been taking a bit of advice from her dad about Conrad. He'd suggested she took a step back and let Isaac and Conrad sort things out themselves; he told her that if anyone had pushed him to try more with Maya, he wasn't sure it would've helped. He'd had to get to that point himself; it was part of what was making it work between the both of them now.

Maya had no idea whether it would work with Conrad and Isaac. Right now, they were as they'd been before, at a stalemate over this Christmas and New Year request. But Conrad no longer had a hold over Maya, so her dad was right; the rest was down to them.

'Mr Anderson.' It was Nadia. She'd come into the room now with a clipboard and papers plus a pen, which she handed to Maya's dad.

'Oh, please, it's Nigel.'

'Very well,' Nadia smiled pleasantly. 'Nigel. Here are the forms I told you about. No pressure, remember.' She gave him a smile, another one for Maya and left them alone.

'What's going on, Dad?'

'I thought my company might hold a fundraiser for this place.' He looked up from the forms he'd already begun to peruse. 'Unless I'd be stepping on your toes. If it's too much—'

'Dad, no. It's not. It's amazing.' She didn't know how to possibly express her gratitude, the feeling that he finally saw her, here, a part of this. 'But... leave the forms for now. Please.'

Confused, he set them onto the nearby table.

And Maya went out of the room for a second but returned with a helmet. 'Put this on.'

'Excuse me?'

'Put it on, Dad. I want to show you what I do, properly.'

'You mean...'

She nodded. She couldn't keep the childlike grin from her face. 'We're going up in Hilda. We're all clear to do so.' She grabbed her own helmet and led the way.

Nadia and Frank gave them a knowing wave as they went out to the helipad and climbed into the helicopter.

It felt surreal doing this. Finally, she was showing her dad what she'd wanted him to see and experience for so long. She was showing him what she did here as a member of The Skylarks.

The blades chopped through the air. The noise of the aircraft would have drowned out their voices were it not for the microphones on their helmets.

'Hold tight,' she laughed and then clocked his face. 'I'm kidding. You're safe with me, Dad.'

She let out a 'woohoo!' as they soared above the Dorset landscape, the people and the houses and cars on the ground getting smaller and smaller. It was a fresh start for Maya, a new beginning, with her dad finally being able to see this part of her and her life.

Her dad asked question after question, his chest swelled with pride as his daughter flew them over the Whistlestop River, its winding ribbon-like presence beneath them as they returned to the airbase thirty minutes later.

After she set the helicopter down on the helipad, she waved over at Noah, who emerged from the hangar.

'I like him,' Nigel shouted over the noise of the blades, which had not yet come to a standstill.

Maya looked across at her dad, unable to wipe the smile off her face.

'Me too, Dad. Me too.'

ACKNOWLEDGEMENTS

As always, my heartfelt thanks to the entire team at Boldwood Books. With particular thanks to Rachel Faulkner-Willcocks my editor extraordinaire, whose advice and expertise has again guided me through the tough task of writing another book.

A big, big thank you to Lauren Dyson, critical care paramedic with the Dorset Air Ambulance. Lauren has been fantastic answering my many questions about what it's like to be a part of an air ambulance crew. Thanks to Lauren (and I admit, watching a fair few episodes of Cornwall 999) I have a good understanding of what it's like in the helicopter, what the crew faces out on a job, and what happens back at base after another mission.

During my research, I have only had a glimpse of the vast, life-saving job that the crews of the UK's air ambulances do but I hope I have managed to bring realism to this first book in my brand-new series.

Finally, to you, my reader! Without your support, I couldn't do this job I absolutely love. I'm so excited to bring you another book and I hope you enjoy your journey with The Skylarks.

Helen x

ABOUT THE AUTHOR

Helen Rolfe is the author of many bestselling contemporary women's fiction titles, set in different locations from the Cotswolds to New York. She lives in Hertfordshire with her husband and children.

Sign up to Helen Rolfe's mailing list for news, competitions and updates on future books.

Visit Helen's website: www.helenjrolfe.com

Follow Helen on social media here:

facebook.com/helenjrolfewriter

x.com/hjrolfe

instagram.com/helen_j_rolfe

ALSO BY HELEN ROLFE

Heritage Cove Series

Coming Home to Heritage Cove

Christmas at the Little Waffle Shack

Winter at Mistletoe Gate Farm

Summer at the Twist and Turn Bakery

Finding Happiness at Heritage View

Christmas Nights at the Star and Lantern

New York Ever After Series

Snowflakes and Mistletoe at the Inglenook Inn

Christmas at the Little Knitting Box

Wedding Bells on Madison Avenue

Christmas Miracles at the Little Log Cabin

Moonlight and Mistletoe at the Christmas Wedding

Christmas Promises at the Garland Street Markets

Family Secrets at the Inglenook Inn

Little Woodville Cottage Series

Christmas at Snowdrop Cottage

Summer at Forget-Me-Not Cottage

Standalones

The Year That Changed Us

Come Fly With Me

LOVE IN EVERY CHAPTER

WHERE ALL YOUR ROMANCE
DREAMS COME TRUE!

THE HOME OF BESTSELLING
ROMANCE AND WOMEN'S
FICTION

 WARNING:
MAY CONTAIN SPICE

SIGN UP TO OUR
NEWSLETTER

https://bit.ly/Lovenotesnews

Boldwood

Boldwood Books is an award-winning fiction publishing company seeking out the best stories from around the world.

Find out more at www.boldwoodbooks.com

Join our reader community for brilliant books, competitions and offers!

Follow us
@BoldwoodBooks
@TheBoldBookClub

Sign up to our weekly
deals newsletter

https://bit.ly/BoldwoodBNewsletter

Printed in Great Britain
by Amazon